The Use of Myriad *Arts*

This is a work of fiction. Names, places, characters and incidents are either the product of the author's imagination or are used fictitiously. Any resemblance to actual people, living or dead, business establishments, events or locales is entirely coincidental.

Published by Winterbourne Publishing, Western Australia.

ISBN: 978-1-7637115-1-8 (ebook) / 978-1-7637115-2-5 (print).

The Use of Myriad *Arts*

Wendy Palmer

1

IT WAS THE SUMMER OF THE Great Stink, Parliament greatly regretted its riverside location, and Genevieve McAvey was attending a hanging.

She had come to Newgate to support her cousin, the widowed Lucinda Llewellyn, who in her turn was there to avidly watch the man who'd murdered her husband swing.

The former Bishop Varley was sentenced to hang not for that murder, but for the murder of orphans. Since Lulu and her twin, Alexander Locke, had orchestrated the whole affair – uncovered the evidence, winkled Varley out of his hiding place, used bribes and other points of pressure to ensure a fair judge, that was to say, a judge fairer to their desired outcome than to the Church's – she was grimly satisfied with the outcome.

Genevieve spotted the twins' distinctive bare heads, towering height, and broad shoulders at the entrance to the Magpie and Stump. They'd secured a prime viewing location upstairs, away from the heaving crowd she was currently forcing her way through with the magnificent bearing of a ship under full sail, ignoring the second glances her obvious situation engendered.

The sweat and stale perfume of the unwashed mass of people, the ordure squelching under her boots, the noxious smoke from the surrounding buildings: the once trying smells of London were a distinct relief from the fetid smell from the Thames, decried as a deadly sewer by Dickens. That stink would smother the city as the day warmed into yet another sweltering nightmare.

'It's sickening how disgustingly happy that little shit makes you,' Lulu was saying as Genevieve approached her cousins, ignoring the stares directed at all three of them.

'Supportive as ever, my darling baby sister,' Alex said amiably, looking off across the mob.

'I haven't strangled him in his sleep, how's that for supportive?'

'It'll serve.' Alex turned and smiled at Genevieve. He could read intentions, a talent that fell just shy of an Art, and must have sensed hers, as familiar to him as Lulu's, and wholly centred on obtaining a seat as soon as possible. 'Hello, my dear. You're looking blooming.'

Genevieve narrowed her eyes at her sandy-haired, mellow-eyed cousin. What she was, in fact, was nine months gone with child, and dressed head to toe in black crepe over bombazine because she was gone with widowhood about as long. She felt many things in the unnatural and ungodly heat and stink of London this summer – blooming was not one of them.

'Are you indulging yourself, Alex?' she asked as he took her arm to help her up the stairs to their rented room with a superlative, and no doubt superlatively expensive, view of the scaffold. Tall, broad, strong, he was as affable as ever, a calm, comforting presence at her side. 'Lulu hasn't mentioned that in her letters.'

Alex replied in the affirmative, but in that tone that meant he was not encouraging further questions, which surprised her. She knew he preferred men and had never given him any indication that she condemned him for it, mostly because she didn't.

'How are your people?' he asked lightly, squiring her to her chair, so she was diverted into telling him that Miss Delacorte, Mr Oliver and Mr Fletcher were all quite well, thank you.

'And did you two pass a pleasant birthday last month?' she enquired in return.

'Exceedingly,' Alex said, sitting beside her. 'I received the best possible gift.'

He spoke with a smugness that either had to do with his current indulgence, or with his long overdue reconciliation with their elder brother, Sir Kingsford. On the one hand, it was a secretive sort of smugness, which lent itself to the former explanation, but on the other, she had sent her birthday congratulations via Sir Kingsford's country estate.

Once, the twins would have spent the day with her. She was, suddenly, too young again, trapped in her second Season, resenting the twins for their freedom, pitying them for their grief, and happy for them as they began to find their way – and yet, simultaneously in all this selfish tumult, managing to feel sorry for herself because she could not be a part of it.

A breakfast had been laid out, though none of them touched it. Food tended to turn Genevieve's stomach this far along.

Lulu, never one for dull social niceties such as enquiring after the health and wellbeing of old friends, sat and pulled from her ever-present club bag an epitome of her secret vice, magazines and instructional manuals aimed at ladies. She'd consulted these heavily as a confused adolescent trying to replicate the pinnacle of womanhood, but these days found them a source of both comfort and amusement.

This one was called *The Arts of Beauty, or Secrets of a Lady's Toilet.* Because Lulu knew how much such books annoyed Genevieve, she made a show of reading from it with attentive regard, before giving up the game by snorting and quoting out loud, '*Two heaving hills of snow*, is it?'

They all chortled, like the utter children they were. 'Oh dear,' Genevieve said. 'Do tell.'

'A countess recounts her methods for keeping the bosoms in order,' Lulu reported sagely.

'Unruly things.'

They laughed again. Despite her odd melancholy, it was a blessed relief to sink into frivolity with the twins again at last. Lulu had been lost in deadly rage since her husband's murder, Alex dragged along for the duration. Genevieve had not been able to support her as well as she had in their tumultuous adolescence.

Then Genevieve's own grief had consumed her as Lulu began to emerge from hers. It had been the twins' turn to fail to offer adequate support; they had gone coy and mysterious, and Alex had all but vanished.

But she didn't want her thoughts mired in darkness and recriminations today, no matter the setting.

'Have you seen the latest fashion plates, Lulu?' she asked, gamely reaching for lightness. 'Crinoline cages? Excessive this season, aren't they?'

'I don't know how I'm supposed to kick someone in the head wearing those,' said Lulu.

'Easier than in pounds of petticoats, surely.'

'Easiest in these.' Lulu kicked up an exemplary ankle, showing off her rather fancy Turkish trousers.

She regularly wore such pantaloons or bloomers in aid of her professional needs: she was technically an enquiry agent, along with Alex, though they mostly took contracts for bounties, mostly for rogue Artisans. Alex had had a recent flirtation working directly for the Agency for the Benefit of Registered Artisans, but had not stuck with it. They'd been a team in the professional sense for as long as the McAveys, and that had been coming up towards fifteen years.

A wave of dizziness took Genevieve. She lost her thought, and found it again, rubbing absently at her stomach, the silken crepe smooth under her hand. 'They make me feel *ancient*, these girls and their fashions.'

'Have you seen the ruffles this season?'

'Oh, God, the *ruffles*.'

Alex, thoroughly left out of this particular discussion as the two women literally talked past him, sighed extravagantly.

'Oh, as if you have a leg to stand on, waistcoat monkey,' Lulu said, rounding on him in mock outrage.

Her smile snapped off. The death-bell at St Sepulchre's had begun its slow and sonorous peal, tolling out the last moments of the condemned man's life.

Lulu's breathing seemed to stop. She rose to her feet as Varley was brought out the little yard door to the looming gallows. He was dirty and small against the mass of humanity jeering and shouting at him, hair grey, beard besmeared and knotted, back bent, hands tied before him. His lips were moving continuously; he was praying, Genevieve thought. He didn't look like a murderer. His feet stumbled across the uneven and dirty ground as two prison guards helpfully dragged him to the scaffold.

Lulu stood right at the window, as patiently intent as a lonely child awaiting the arrival of her favourite country cousins. If Genevieve hadn't come, she suspected Lulu would have bulled her way past the policemen at the barrier to stand directly under the beam.

But maybe not, for Alex had come, and he did not do well in crowds, and Lulu, for all her brusqueness, adored her brother. Lulu reached behind her, not looking around. Alex took Lulu's outstretched hand, their fingers interlocking.

Genevieve took his other hand, and felt him give her a comforting squeeze. It was not as if she wanted to watch a man dangle by the neck until he was dead, no matter what he had done, and especially when he looked like a frightened and pitiful half-naked old man.

Lulu thrust her chin towards the executioner, a bulky man standing by the trapdoor. 'Slipped Jack Ketch a sovereign to botch it with a short rope, make it really slow,' she told them, voice low. 'His assistants are keeping his friends back, if he had any left and they wanted to hang off his legs to hurry it along.'

'Oh, good,' Alex said, with a shake of the head. 'We're in for a show, then.'

'Fuck off, Lexi, I worked months for this moment.'

'I know, Lulu,' he said gently. He kissed the back of her hand. 'You go right ahead and enjoy every fucking second, baby sister.' He leaned for a better view, glancing around the excited throngs and murmuring something that sounded like, 'You too, sweetheart.'

His sister stared through the window, gaze fixed on the whey-faced and shaking excommunicate as the hangman tugged the merciful hood over his head. 'I know it's not a civilised desire,' she said. 'There's a reason I didn't invite Kings or Miss Knight to attend.'

'Would Sir Kingsford have come?' The eldest Locke cousin, half-brother to the twins, was notoriously reclusive, and gave his opinion on London frankly in his frequent letters to Genevieve.

'He'd have come if I'd asked it,' Lulu said.

Alex squeezed Genevieve's hand again, pointedly. She started and then said, 'I could set him on fire, if you truly want him in paroxysms of agony?'

Genevieve was a weapons Artisan, and her Art was fire. Not that she usually directed it at people. Not even utterly reprehensible people who had murdered orphans and unassuming archaeologists.

Lulu snorted, seeing right through her. 'Thanks, Gin,' she said. 'I'll bear it in mind.'

On the scaffold, the hangman tightened the noose. Genevieve could hear the howls and cheers of the crowd even through the closed window. The old man about to face divine judgement for his earthly crimes raised his bound hands and clutched them to his throat.

Lulu took out a ring, set with rubies. 'Journey safe to hell, Varley.' She kissed the ring. 'I love you, Peter. This is for you.'

'He would've hated it,' Alex remarked to the air.

'Shut up, Alexander, he knew who he married.' She seethed silently before spitting out, 'Fine. I love you, Peter, and this is for me and the kitten.'

She pointed right at Varley as the executioner pulled back the bolt and the trapdoor dropped. She stood, motionless and fixated, through every moment of Varley's slow, thrashing, choking, tormented demise. Genevieve turned her gaze from the scaffold, Alex's hand on her shoulder. She saw, above the jam-packed mass of joyously seething humanity, a very still figure, standing on the ledge of a barred window let into the thick wall of the prison, quietly watching the death throes.

Genevieve's attention snagged there. Such was the popularity of hangings, and this dispatch of a despised churchman in particular, that there were seats on the rooftops all round, but surely no mundane human could have reached that lonely vantage point. It had to be an Artisan, using his or her Art in quite the macabre way to obtain a safe, unobstructed, and priceless view.

And the figure, now squeamishly directing his gaze down to his feet with a frown, looked very much like a man Genevieve knew to be dead. Or at least, had been informed was dead, by the duplicitous pair sitting next to her.

Just as they had informed her that her own husband was dead, which she had recent reason to also doubt.

The hanged man gave one last twitch and was still, dark-coated men moving in to cut the rope. Lulu raised her gaze and looked through the clear glass directly at the Artisan who looked like Christopher Whitebrickleyhurst. They nodded to each other, once.

As a suspicion began to bloom in Genevieve's mind as to the identity of the little shit making Alex disgustingly happy, Lulu stepped back from the window and looked at the other Lockes.

'Well, then,' she said. 'Shall we go for ice-cream?'

2

THEY SENSIBLY SHUNNED THE PENNY-LICKS and made their way towards one of the new ice-cream parlours, walking, slowly but gratefully, further from the river. The day was already heating up in this long and unreasonably hot summer, which meant the putrid smell, ever lingering in the air, was already rising to its sickening heights as well, and the flies were rising in its wake.

Genevieve held a perfumed handkerchief to her face and let the stalwart Alex, the unyielding Lulu, and her own bulk clear them passage through the ebbing throng on the shaded side of the narrow street. Even if the crowd and the heat and the nose-burning, lung-clogging smell hadn't made their pace glacial, her waddle would have done so. It was unusual for one simultaneously in full mourning and so heavily pregnant – she was, at the very most, two weeks away – to walk the streets. She received startled looks, and Alex, taken for her husband, received more than a few righteous glares, to first his bemusement and then his and Lulu's amusement.

At least she was not having pamphlets for fallen women urgently thrust in her face by people with kind, innocent faces or sour, tight faces in roughly equal proportion. Female Artisans, running so hot that they were nominally exempt from dictates about the layers, the endless, *endless* layers, of clothing required to stay fashionable, respectable or warm – even in this torrid weather – or all three, were mistaken for unfortunates on a regular basis.

Artisans were rare enough that so-called Artistry Dress was not always recognised as a choice, or, more often, mistaken as an excuse – loose fit, loose morals, as the snide little saying went. Some Artisan women cleaved to more conventional fashions, suffering through the inconvenience and discomfit to avoid leering propositions and those endless pamphlets.

Genevieve, of the impervious Locke family, did not bother herself: these days, even properly attired women, Artisan or no, might be mistaken for unfortunates. Frankly, some of those so-called unfortunates earned enough to dress a great deal better than many of the women who had their wages from long hours in the factories, and Genevieve could guess which of the two employment options might be more attractive during this awful summer, if you did not have the leisure to lie about indoors with a fan or the means to leave the city entirely.

Collapsing into a chair inside the tiled ice-cream parlour, she blotted her flushed face. The tin containers of ice-cream were kept on ice and Alex had won them a table close enough that the chill air permeated their way. The parlour was too busy to be truly cool, but it was a relief to be out of the sun, out of the wretched stink – a waft came in every time the door opened, but perfume and burning incense helped keep it at bay – and off her feet. If she couldn't decamp out of stinking London, this would do.

'You should get out of the city before it's too late, Gin,' Alex told her.

Genevieve considered him, narrow-eyed again. That had been far too close to her idle ruminations for a man with a mere talent for sensing intentions, over which he had so little control that he struggled among crowds.

Yet they were in the heart of the biggest city in the world, in an enclosed space made excessively popular by novelty, and Alex still looked as relaxed as if they'd been gathered around their own table at the Locke townhouse. He'd even loosened up enough to wear the slightly rumpled look of a man returning from a good night at a music hall or the increasingly rundown Vauxhall. Grooming himself unto pristine heights was, previously, his technique for regulating himself under the bombardment of too many minds, particularly since he and Lulu had come home from the Crimea.

Somewhat before then, to be scrupulously accurate.

'You're doing your dissection look,' he said, a common complaint from the twins growing up – she could manage quite the icy stare with her pale blue eyes.

'Are you not overwhelmed, Lexi?' she asked him.

'I have better control now. I can—' He made a small gesture near his temple. '—dial it away out of focus. Like on a stereoscopic viewer.'

'Oh. Enough to try the Artisan test?'

The Agency had formalised the registration process, but the official Artisan test had become established well past the time when her Art and the twins' talents had come on. She wasn't sure if he'd eventually taken the test and failed or if he'd never tried, preferring the secret advantage – and immunity to Agency rules – to the benefits of open Artisan status. Ambivalent, he'd always desired circumspection; even among Genevieve's closest friends, only Oliver knew about his talent.

'I don't do so well on tests,' he said. 'I also don't run hot and I don't walk around hungry all the time and I'm not overly bothered by iron *or* silver, it's not an Art, it's a talent, let's leave it at that.'

'Artisans get much more freedom,' she pointed out.

Alex smiled. 'I'm the feckless younger brother of a wealthy and erratically indulgent baronet, how much more freedom do you think I need?'

Genevieve had to ruefully allow that Alex was in the enviable position of not requiring the protection of the Agency, and therefore not requiring submission to its strict regulation of the uses of Art either. This fact alone might account for the dearth of Artisans to be found among titled men. Perhaps it was not that they barely existed, but that they did not want to be known to exist.

He grimaced, taking her silence as pointed. He conceded, 'Except from the erratic baronet himself, I suppose.'

Lulu glanced up from perusing the menu. 'I'm getting the parmesan flavour.'

'You'll make Gin ill,' Alex chided, immediately flipping his and Genevieve's relative positions on the mildly-annoyed-by-interfering-cousin scale.

'If she can survive the smell of actual shit, she can survive the smell of old cheese,' Lulu said savagely, before waving one of the harried waiters down. Once he'd taken their order, Lulu – having asked for Chinese orange – resumed. 'Yes, you should get out of the city, Gin.'

Alex nodded. 'Kingsford's doors are always open to you.'

The waiter set a glass bowl in front of Genevieve. The scoops, vanilla, since she truly could not stomach stronger flavours in her condition, were already melting.

Lulu, poking at her own melting confection with a long-handled spoon, added, 'He'll tolerate the others.' She took a spoonful and made a considering face. 'Even Fletcher.'

'Especially Fletcher,' Alex said. Fletcher was very proper, or tried hard to be. Kingsford liked that. He tasted his chocolate. 'This is melting too fast.'

'If only Reuben were here,' Genevieve said. 'He could freeze the bowls.'

She saw it: the flare of some emotion – guilt? – from Alex, never good at dissembling, and Lulu's quelling glare his way.

Lulu had stayed with Genevieve for a time, when she'd first been widowed. But Lulu was as abrasive as her brother was soothing, and she hadn't liked Reuben, or they hadn't liked each other, and his death hadn't changed that. She'd eventually left Genevieve to the ministrations of dear sweet Miss Cecelia Delacorte, which was certainly the better arrangement.

It didn't account for the strange coyness of both twins. Lulu was unusually distant and Alex, by far the poorer liar, completely absent on the excuse of strangely bureaucratic errands, chasing down old birth records and other mundanities. Sir Kingsford had written, often, dutifully, and dryly, but he did not leave the estate and she wasn't so close to him: he was older, and hard to get close to, regardless.

At least she couldn't blame Alex for leaving the letter-writing to his brother. He had trouble with the written word that he blamed on stupidity and Genevieve thought was to do with never having guidance controlling his talent-maybe-Art. Perhaps, that, too, had resolved with this better control that he had learnt from *someone*. Perhaps he could have written, and hadn't. Lulu definitely could have written, and hadn't.

The twins had disappointed her, to be honest, her beloved cousins had let her down in her crisis, when, some fifteen years ago, she and her parents, the older Locke patriarch and his portraitist wife, had held firm through theirs: Lulu's exile from the family home, their father's sudden death before reconciliation, their grief and their emerging talents and Alex's clashes with Kingsford, odd and cold and ill-equipped for the guardianship of struggling adolescents.

She swallowed hard on bitterness and pushed her bowl away. Her stomach was bilious. How anyone could put anything in their mouths, with the stink so solid it lingered long on the tongue, was beyond her.

Alex glanced about at the other patrons casually. The parlour was newly opened, and thus very fresh and clean. But he was not admiring their setting.

He was making sure Christopher Whitebrickleyhurst, also known as Kit Whitely, was staying out of sight.

Kit Whitely, door Artisan. The Artisan who could unlock anything. The cold-eyed Artisan who'd looked an angry Reuben McAvey in the eye and hadn't turned a hair. The crafty Artisan who was somehow impervious to the iron that should have stopped him cold. The Artisan with such tight control of an unusual Art that he might have served as guide for a man struggling with a wilful talent. The Artisan who was dead, at last report.

The Artisan who could unlock *anything*.

She and the others had, glancingly but bruisingly, encountered Whitely late the previous year, when the solidity of the baby she now bore like a flagship had been but a tidal whisper more intuited than known, and Reuben had been by her side, more ill-humoured than she had ever known him but still her beloved partner in life and in work.

Whitely had been dressed like a servant in the castoffs of an overfond master; she'd later gathered he was wearing clothes borrowed from Kingsford. Wildly drunk and dusty with the debris of mountain tunnels, he'd run rings around them, filched the antique knife Reuben had set them after from under their very noses, and scurried for shelter, flagrantly, behind the twins.

He'd then turned up shortly after Reuben had vanished, alone and lost, draped in white like a sacrificial lamb, off-kilter in a way that threw his former blank self-possession into sharp relief. By then, Genevieve and the others, Cecelia, Oliver and Fletcher, had been chained up in a cell, after being taken like naifs in their respective sleeps by agents of the same establishment from which they'd intended to liberate the contested knife – before cold and clever Whitely got there first.

Whitely, who could open locks with a thought, had left them in chains: truly, an absolute little shit.

Genevieve still had no clear idea of the sequence of events in Gallentry, that remote English-heavy outpost in an ancient Welsh valley, established as a sect, a tax dodge, or both, by a now-powerful charitable religious order. Lulu and Alex had said they were hunting Whitely for a bounty, but were remarkably vague on the details.

Any lingering curiosity went out of her head when Lulu, with her psychometric talent, touched Reuben's wedding band and told Genevieve, as kindly but directly as only another widow could, that she had no sense of Reuben from it and that therefore he must be dead.

After that devastating blow, Genevieve had not had the wherewithal to mark when the Agency disseminated news of Christopher Whitebrickleyhurst's death, standard practice for any registered Artisan within their tiny, scattered community. Cecelia had been as genuinely upset as she'd been over Reuben, that was how it had finally come to Genevieve's attention.

And yet, there Kit Whitely had stood, on the window ledge high above the scaffold, still dressed like a valued servant, still indifferent to the smudges that must be collecting on his dark coat where he brushed against the grimy red bricks, still wearing his hair too long and snarled into wild curls, still holding himself apart to dispassionately watch chaos unfold.

Well. Alex had given her the perfect opening sally, really.

'We were thinking of leaving for the rest of the summer,' she concurred, 'not that I particularly intended to inflict childbirth on Kings. But then yesterday, we received a very odd parcel at our workroom. A bit more than a parcel, really.'

It was a thrice-damned mystery box, whose iron-and-silver lock could not be touched by any Artisan – except the one leaning so insouciantly in his high vantage above the execution – or picked by a regular thief or cut open or melted, whose corners could not be pried apart by telekinesis or crowbar, and whose painted wood could not be broken open by axe or set on fire or even so much as scorched to allow mundane tools to knock through the char.

And Alex had an Artisan in his pocket who could open it.

And he wouldn't bloody admit it. He listened to her description of the locked box and the various attempts to open it, politely, neutrally, interested. He did not volunteer any assistance whatsoever, no matter that she plainly said it needed an Artisan who could manage locks, no matter that she did not bother to hide her intentions as to who that Artisan would be.

Lulu didn't even manage the veneer of polite interest, scraping the melted orange cream from her bowl without a single indication she was even listening. However, once Genevieve fell into nonplussed silence, she said, 'Any markings? Luggage label?'

'No. It came with a letter, though. Unsigned, before you ask.'

Lulu held her hand out. Her talent was tracking; it made no difference to her if the letter was unsigned, she would know the direction of the writer, and, vaguely, their distance from her. It was not a true Art, which would have given her an exact location, and possibly an entire life history and travel path as well, but it served.

She usually only touched objects whose known owner had some definite attachment to the item, be that enduring personal attachment or temporary physical trace, soon to fade. Genevieve wasn't sure if she would glean a sense of the identity of this correspondent. She might; she knew him, after all.

And so did Genevieve. He'd made no attempt to disguise his hand.

From her reticule, she retrieved the letter, anonymous, superficial, gifting the box to them for their services to Agency, Crown and country. Lulu had barely touched it before she'd dropped it to the table and sent Alex a significant look.

Ah. She knew.

Genevieve opened her mouth to demand the location of the letter-writer, and blinked, and closed her mouth.

Alex squinted at the dashed lines of ink, wincing. He'd either guessed, from his twin's demeanour, the truth and did not want to read it, or he still did not manage the written word well, for all his relaxed demeanour and newfound control.

'Just the form of address will do it,' she said crisply, shaking off an odd sense of having forgotten a salient question.

He held it at arm's length – he'd forgotten his spectacles, or was too vain to fish them from a pocket – and read the first two words aloud. 'Dearest Vivi.' He stopped. 'McAvey called you that.'

'Yes. Only him.'

'And the hand is his?'

'An exceptional forgery, if not.'

Alex folded the letter and gave it back. He was wearing the blank expression Genevieve thought of as his Locke face, when he was being the impassive enquiry agent and bounty hunter, competent collector of rogue Artisans.

'What do you think?' he asked her.

'I don't know what I think,' she said frankly. 'All I know is that we've had this mysterious box the size of a closet delivered directly to an address only a few people would think to use, with a letter addressed to me by a sobriquet only a few people know of, and the logic diagram of those two things narrows the possible culprits down to hardly anyone at all.'

'Gin,' Alex said, sounding genuinely puzzled, 'are you asking us if we sent you a strange box?'

'Lexi,' she said, 'I'm asking you and Lulu if you lied when you told me Reuben was dead.'

The twins exchanged a glance.

'Ah,' she said, pressing her hand to her stomach. 'And that's why the pair of you abandoned me, widowed and in this fragile condition.' She was half-joking, and very much half *not.*

Alex swallowed heavily before he admitted, 'Widowhood seemed the lesser of two evils.'

'You well know the other reason I would have felt nothing when I touched his wedding ring.' Lulu sounded very flat; she watched Genevieve without blinking.

Genevieve did indeed know why, but she had spent all last night and this morning refusing to let herself realise the full ramifications. She had to face it now: if Lulu felt nothing in touching a personal item, and the owner still lived, there was indeed only one possible reason.

'He had no attachment to it.'

She wasn't widowed. She was abandoned.

Genevieve looked down at her interlaced hands. Her fingers, swollen like the rest of her, were too large for her delicate wedding ring now. She was wearing Reuben's. She touched the plain gold band with her right index finger, tracing the cool smoothness.

Lulu nodded. 'He had no attachment to his wedding ring, that he deliberately left behind when he took you all to Gallentry to steal a knife he said you were meant to protect and that he fully intended to steal for himself.'

'Which he *did* steal for himself, at some cost to others,' Alex added.

'And who the fuck knows why?' Lulu's husky voice was luckily drowned out by the noise in the rest of the parlour.

Genevieve wished she was wearing gloves; she did, sometimes, even though Artisans didn't have to, because the city was a sooty, grimy place. She sometimes covered a new dress with a shawl and her pale gold hair with a bonnet for the same reason.

It had been too hot this summer. If she'd had gloves on, she told herself, they could keep the fire threatening to leak from her hands contained. She stroked the gold under her finger.

'I'm sorry, Gin,' Alex said. 'We thought it better if you didn't have to wonder. We were trying to… We wanted to make the wound not as bad as it might be.'

She nodded, still mute, eyes burning. Flames were flickering on the edges of her vision. She wondered if it was the pregnancy that had taken a layer off her self-control. For all that her Art was fire, she was like ice inside, and she put the hurt into the ice. She felt herself freeze up, as if her beloved husband, ice Artisan, had laid hands on her.

She lifted her chin and gave her cousins a cold, accusatory stare.

From her set expression, Lulu was still implacably sure they'd done the right thing; it was left, therefore, to the softer twin to be placatory. 'We didn't think through what it would mean. It was very difficult, to have to avoid you. I know you've got Oliver and Cecelia—'

'And Fletcher.'

'If you must,' he said, with the ghost of his easy smile. '—but I do know your family wasn't there for you like we should have been, because we chose to lie instead.'

‘*I* chose it,’ Lulu said. ‘It’s bad, Gin, not knowing. That’s a shadow you can’t walk out from under, like you can from a widowing.’

Lulu had lost her own husband, and had known it on the instant, thanks to wearing his ring, but she’d never found his body, and she hadn’t known exactly what had happened without a good deal of bloody-minded piecing together of scant clues. The hanged man, Varley, had killed Peter Llewellyn over an ancient copper knife – the same knife Whitely had stolen but the twins were now reliably informing her Reuben had ultimately appropriated.

Varley had been an unacknowledged telepath Artisan, who saw the Art in others and called it blight. He’d been using the knife to attempt to cut the Art – in his mind, the devil, an old-fashioned, witchy, sort of judgement – from orphaned Artisan children, murdering the poor innocents in the process. Genevieve had not a whit of an idea why Reuben might want a knife that supposedly drank Art. She wasn’t even convinced it truly did that; it had been Varley’s notion, and Varley had been mad.

‘Bad for the baby, too,’ Alex added to her long silence.

Genevieve’s fingers spread wide over her rounded stomach. ‘And what are we to do now?’ she murmured, talking partly to herself and partly to the little stranger nestled in her womb.

From the corner of her eye, she caught familiar movement and knew the twins were exchanging glances again, those silent and yet eminently speaking mutual looks of theirs.

‘Two words for you, Gin,’ Alex said heartily.

‘Divorce. Court.’ Over Genevieve’s gasp, Lulu went on, ‘Though, really, it’s seven words.’

‘The downfall of civilisation as we know it?’ Alex looked down at his fingers. ‘Damnation, that’s eight.’

Lulu tsked. ‘The Court for Divorce and Matrimonial Causes.’

‘She’d have to prove adultery as well as the desertion. Or bestiality. Shouldn’t be difficult to manufacture some evidence.’

‘You two!’ Genevieve said, torn between offended horror and black laughter, as they had certainly known she would be. ‘Good Lord, did you look up the rules?’

‘Yes,’ they chorused, and, ‘Before the new Act achieved Royal assent, even,’ Alex said – which was a full two months before Reuben had gone missing, actually, *and* while the twins had been distracted with their vendetta against Varley. That spoke an ocean-worth of volumes as to the twins’ opinion of her husband. Not that they’d ever bothered to hide it overly much, nor he his of them.

Genevieve experienced a strange dislocation, a waver in her head: it was true that the twins and Reuben had despised each other, but just as true that they'd engaged in the slow and painful politics of introducing him, red-headed younger son of a clerk, very modest middle-class, to her peerage-hunting father. They'd liked him well enough then. She could not pinpoint when they had stopped liking him.

She cleared her throat. 'You're both so very tactless. I'm a grieving widow, for Christ's sake.'

'You're officially a deserted wife,' Lulu corrected. 'You can take the weeds off, at least.'

'You want tact and soft comfort, I suggest you turn to your Seaman William Oliver Bennet, Gin,' Alex chimed in.

Genevieve ignored that. 'I should be throwing my bowlful in your faces, you lying pair of rats.'

She didn't manage much heat; she'd put it all in the ice, in case she lost control of it. A weapons Artisan could not lose control. A pyrokinetic Artisan, in this long, dry, foul summer, could burn the city to the ground with the merest spark of a thought.

'You should.' Alex leaned back, thoughtful. 'You used to have the same hot temper as the rest of the Lockes.' The two women looked at him sceptically and he smiled. 'Ask Sir Kingsford if I don't have a temper too, *ladies*, it's just not as quick as yours, or yours, Gin.'

'Hence, fireballs,' said Lulu with a nod at her cousin, 'when your Art came on.'

She closed her eyes, feeling again the moment her Art had bloomed. It was the season, the Season, her second, because the younger Locke brother, Reginald, had earned the bestowal of an old but heirless baronetcy through service to the Crown, and so the elder, Theodore, in friendly competition, wanted a title for his daughter, who was wealthy and beautiful enough to dangle as irresistible bait for a peer. *That*, at least, was nothing either of the unconventional Locke twins could ever match. Her father never said so aloud.

And so, the elaborate dresses, hot and constricting and never quite exactly the latest thing because she never had quite the right dressmaker at the right time. The morning calls, which were never in the morning but were reliably awkward, so many cards left, to so little avail.

Her mother had apologised for both: of the artistic bent, she embraced the nascent Artistic Dress, leaving her flailing when it came to helping Genevieve with all the minute nuances of fashionable undress, half dress and full dress and the graduations in formality of each category. What she had *failed* to embrace, having similarly failed to anticipate her husband's ambition, had been the friendship of the mamas of the Ton, which meant her attempts to arrange morning visits and engineer "chance" meetings with potential suitors had also failed.

'This is not your fault, Ginnie,' Antoinette Locke had told her daughter. 'Never think so.'

'Do try to smile more, though,' Theodore had helpfully added.

Thus, then, endless etiquette books, poring over them exactly as Lulu had pored over similar fare the previous summer. They were always a little too out-of-date, a little too contradictory, to not trick her into betraying herself as the arriviste that the real upper-class girls, daughters of old money and old nobility, labelled her.

The ballrooms, overheated and overcrowded.

The whispers, from other young women, behind their hands, sharp eyes dissecting every misstep she made.

The looks, from men who had already decided all she was good for.

Controlling her temper, the hot, quick Locke temper, pretending she was ice, pretending she was ice, pretending she was ice, and, deep within, her anger and humiliation and resentment was burning, and burning, and burning.

Then the Lockes had attended a private ball held by a viscount, Lord Marlough, with an earl for a father and an eligible, complacent, braying son. Her father endured late nights at his club until he garnered the offhand invitation his wife could not win directly from Lady Marlough. The viscountess must have seethed to have to add Mr and Mrs Locke and their uppity daughter to her guest list.

'Their boy's practically your age,' her father had said. The Honourable George Marlough was over ten years her senior, older even than Kingsford. 'And one day, he'll be an earl.'

She'd crossed the ballroom unescorted and walked out alone into the manicured garden of the stately home, clutching her stomach, convinced she was about to vomit, convinced she would die for the fever burning through her, and convinced she'd be glad of it.

Hence, fireballs.

Her eyes snapped open. She'd clenched her fingers so hard on the edge of the table that her knuckles were aching, like her mother had complained of after holding her paintbrushes too long in the winter chill.

'Why aren't you raging at us?' Alex asked her gently.

'*Because* fireballs,' Genevieve said.

Neither twin managed to look even slightly nervous. Instead, they once again exchanged a look. Alex said, 'Gin, do you understand why we didn't like McAvey, even before he pulled this shit on you?'

Genevieve had another of those wavering moments: she remembered sitting on the upper staircase, hand in hand with Reuben, eavesdropping on her parents in her father's study. The twins sat behind them, Alex holding her free hand, Lulu with her own hand on her shoulder, listening in solidarity as her father shouted at her mother that he had not worked so hard and paid for so many fucking ball dresses and riding habits and walking dresses and hats and fans and pearls and hothouse flowers for his only daughter to marry a— Here, she could not quite hear, in her mind, what he had said, but it had not been flattering.

She'd started to shake off all those comforting, supporting hands to stand and go into the fight, and Reuben had murmured into her ear, 'Can't fight fire with fire this time, Gin.'

And the twins had laughed their low complicit chuckle at the inadvertent joke, because she was a fire-wielding weapons Artisan by then and the adage was simply too apt. They had liked Reuben once, hadn't they?

Lulu snorted. 'Aside from his constant sly digs at us for being perverts?'

'I hated that he did that,' Genevieve said. 'I—' She stopped.

'That,' Alex said. 'Exactly, that. Gin, you always spoke your mind—'

'Loudly, at great length.'

'—and then you married him, and you didn't anymore. Suddenly you were just…quiet. A quiet little mouse. He diminished you.'

'That's nonsense!' Genevieve exclaimed. 'I had a temper when I was young, but I grew out of it, and I happened to be married to Reuben as that happened, because we married young.'

Lulu slapped the table, making their scalloped glass bowls jump and the spoons rattle musically. 'That is *bollocks* because—'

3

GENEVIEVE BLINKED AND GLANCED AROUND. Lulu had been saying something, hadn't she, in her forthright way – they'd been about to argue, perhaps, though she couldn't recall why – and now Lulu was standing up, taking her leave.

She was wearing the same puzzled frown as Genevieve, but it quickly cleared. 'I'm off to collect Miss Knight before we miss the train home.' She looked straight at Alex. 'I don't like goodbyes.'

'All right, baby sister,' Alex said, standing as well. 'I know.'

'Stay safe, Lexi,' Lulu said, nodded to Genevieve, and turned to walk out. Then she spun about and pulled Alex into a fierce hug. 'Tell that little shit I will hunt him down and eviscerate him if he lets anything happen to you.' She pulled Genevieve to her feet, too, and into her arms. 'Tell Mrs Murphy the same.'

'I will do no such thing!' Genevieve said. 'She's too good at midwifery to need threatening, in any case.'

'Better be,' Lulu said. 'Have Miss Delacorte write me the news, I'll be back forthwith to hold the baby and whatnot.'

'Bring Miss Knight next time.'

'Delighted,' Lulu said, somewhat more vaguely than was her wont.

She barged her way out, followed more slowly by Alex, his arm looped companionably through Genevieve's. Both heat and stink hit like a blow to the face as they stepped out, and she was glad for his solid support, even more so since she was still muzzy from that strange lapse of attention.

Those lapses seemed to be happening more often. She blamed the baby – the ever-present weight and worry and exhaustion and terrifying hope of carrying it – if she thought about it long enough to blame anything at all.

‘See you home?’ Alex asked amiably, though it wasn’t really a question; when Genevieve said, ‘Oh, just walk me to the ’bus,’ he smiled and flagged a hackney.

On a different day, a different summer, a different life, she would have been both content to and capable of walking all the way, crossing the expanse of Hyde Park for a rare taste of greenery in the crowded, dirty city, and that would have been a much nicer taste than that which currently lingered thickly in the stale hot air. As it was, she had to hide a sigh when the traffic was so bad, and her, and her bladder’s, discomfit in the jolting stop-start of the growler so great, that disembarking early became the better option.

Alex still solicitously holding her elbow, they strolled through the ornate gates to Holland Park, meandering to stay in the shade, through structured gardens and past deep ponds and the picturesquely round and conical-roofed icehouse belonging to the kitchens of old Holland House.

Eventually, Genevieve ventured, ‘Kingsford wrote that you’re going travelling, Alex?’

He made a noncommittal noise. ‘Japan. We’re taking the train to Southampton tomorrow morning.’

‘No wonder Lulu’s worried about you. You don’t even speak the language.’

‘That’ll be fine, I’ll talk loudly and slowly,’ Alex said with one of his affable smiles.

‘The English way,’ she said, amused even though she very much did not want to be.

He snorted. ‘I’ve arranged through the consulate for a guide to meet us in Shanghai and escort us from there.’

‘Is that a safe port? I do believe relations are currently quite poor between us and China.’

‘Looked like a second opium war was brewing for a while there, didn’t it? We can always divert if the diplomats don’t get the new treaties signed while we’re en route.’ He smiled, slyly. ‘What a blessing for international relations that Artisans are strictly forbidden from any involvement.’

‘What a blessing for your career that they yet again overlooked regulating people with mere talents.’

‘Don’t know what you’re talking about,’ Alex said. ‘The peninsula’s merely a lovely place for a sojourn.’

‘Tell that to the remnants of the Light Brigade.’

‘They’ve buggered off to Australia.’

She raised her eyebrows, icy, and he tipped his head, ruefully acknowledging the silent and yet still acerbic rebuff. The war and its aftermath, the many amputees left destitute by their service to their country, was nothing to jest about. But the twins would not have been involved with the soldiers, except recreationally. Reading between the lines of the newspaper reports raving about miracles, Genevieve suspected they'd been assigned to deal with an illicit snowstorm Artisan, just in time to prevent the loss of a convey of ships carrying winter supplies.

Coincidentally, legend had it that it was an Artisan of a similar weather ilk but more amenable disposition aboard a certain Scottish ship in 1589. The Danish ships of Princess Anne had already been turned back by sundry contrarious winds, labelled as witchcraft. King James's ships, during his grandly dramatic crossing to fetch his bride himself, were supposedly protected by an Artisan sailor revealing his true nature to save his king from further demonic pacts.

In a frankly unbelievable turn of events, the sailor's show of fealty was not itself damned as witchcraft; if the king had decided so, Scotland might have fallen prey to the full hysteria of the continental witch trials. There had already been some instances of persecution, though not, it had to be said, of actual Artisans, not often anyway. Instead, the king had decreed a debt to Artistry.

Genevieve, like much of the small Artisan community, had reasonable doubts about this story. It would have taken a whole swath of weather Artisans working together to either incite or combat an unnatural storm, or even to soothe a natural one, and there was nothing in the near-mythical accounts to suggest there had been.

To be scrupulously fair and open-eyed regarding this wholly mysterious and wholly fortunate chapter, it would have taken a single *compulsion* Artisan aboard the royal ship to skew King James's judgement towards the benevolent.

Regardless, the incident brought the aegis of first the Scottish Crown and then the English Crown forever over Britain's Artisans, with even higher honours and rights accorded after the foiling of the Gunpowder Plot a few years into the Jacobean reign. It had made their shores a haven for Artisans fleeing the witch hunts of Europe and the colonies, a boon during a contentious century of wars, uprisings and rebellions.

No wonder so many continental governments rushed to sign Artisan-banning treaties; by then, the British Empire sheltered the vast majority of Artisans willing to be publicly acknowledged as such. As demonstrated by the unofficial governmental secondment of the Locke twins to the Crimea, that did not mean that nations did not quietly put into play the more subtle Artisans in the theatres of war, diplomacy and trade, nor that nations did not deploy the equivalent of Agency enforcers, or private agents with talents and practice, to just as quietly remove them from the board.

Genevieve had no real idea how the political situation in relation to Artisans stood on the far side of the world, however, even if she'd wager that the mutual deterrent of illicit Artistry had been the one thing preventing open hostilities from breaking out between Britain and China once more.

Suddenly suspicious this trip was cover for more government work, she frowned at her cousin again, now with some real worry rather than disapproval.

Alex coughed, which might have been a sound of chagrin or of amusement; knowing him, it was both. 'Making *safe* and *private* travel arrangements is half the reason I'm in London.'

That diverted her. 'And the other half.'

'Yes. Varley's hanging.' He glanced away, as if he could still see his sister, striding off down the street. 'It wasn't enough, but nothing was ever going to be enough. She's more at peace now.'

Genevieve was pleased to discover his diversion had not worked on her for too long. 'But she's not going with you.'

That was evident from Lulu's demonstrative farewell, the height of emotion for her, even if she hadn't outright said she was due to take a train home, which was, bizarre only if one ignored the existence of one Miss Edith Mary Rose Knight, currently a renovation project in an isolated Somerset village.

Alex shrugged. Genevieve nodded. 'Who are you travelling with, Alex?'

He still didn't answer, no doubt trying to find a form of words that didn't involve lying to his cousin yet again.

'Kit Whitely,' she said for him.

He linked his fingers together, looking down at his large, capable hands, her elbow captured in his. That was enough of an answer; Alex was not good at dissembling, at least not with the people he loved. He was very good at it when he was being Locke, but he found even that harder without Lulu. Really, the twins had made a rare tactical error with Lulu's abrupt departure.

'Is there something I can help you with, Ginnie?' he asked, the childhood nickname slipping out, perhaps unconsciously, perhaps deliberately.

The redirection was blatant this time: *leave the lad alone.* She sighed; very advanced pregnancy lent itself to sighs of the heaviest sort. 'I want the box opened, Alex. And you already know how you can help with that.'

'Gin. If that man's sent you a *coffin* after disappearing all those months ago, Jesus fucking Christ, *don't open it.*'

'You know we have to.'

'I know no such thing,' her cousin said. 'Bloody Artisans.'

'What does that mean?' she said, pulling her arm free so she could set her hands firmly on her hips.

'Nothing,' he said, all innocence, before saying, 'You're like cats, the lot of you. You never leave well enough alone. It's exactly how Lulu and I catch you.'

Genevieve huffed, again amused despite herself. The twins might have been effective enough to be safely utilised against foreign Artisans without causing diplomatic incidents, they might have been competent enough to take the others of her team, at least individually, but she could launch fireballs. Besides, her people working together would never be taken by a mundane team, even the formidable Locke twins.

Though the team wasn't what it had been. She could launch fireballs, and that's all she could do, and surely she should be able to do more with her Art than that adolescent game. Cecelia frowned these days, when she tried to take or create memories. She said she felt like her Art lingered at the bottom of a deep well, that she had to dive for it. Fletcher could once have influenced a veritable crowd with his compulsion Art without having to lay hands on them, and now found himself practising his touch-based control.

And Oliver, well, Oliver was, politely, a medley Artisan, with no primary Art and a variety of secondary Arts, and he was currently exercising his telekinesis Art as if he hadn't had – years? A decade? Longer? – to have practised that and much more besides.

Her amusement faded. They had too many mysteries to solve. 'I want your door Artisan to open the box for us.'

'Christopher Whitebrickleyhurst is dead,' Alex said flatly, face blank.

'And Kit Whitely is not,' Genevieve said sternly. '*Alex.*' It was alarming to watch her beloved cousin draw himself behind his Locke persona so he could keep lying to her. 'I saw him.'

Alex shook his head, not in denial but in refusal.

'I have the right to offer him the commission, cousin,' she said. 'You bloody owe me that, for lying to me about Reuben.'

Alex kept right on shaking his head. 'I owe you something, but he doesn't.'

'He can say no,' she said. 'I mean, he probably will, the little shit, so why not let me ask him?'

'He'll say yes.' Alex had abstracted his gaze, eyeing off the doorways of the outbuildings they were passing as if he expected an ambush. 'He'll bitch and moan and make you work for it because he does like to be a bit of a shit, but he'll say yes because, as remarkable as it may be, the lad also likes to be helpful. Very much so.'

'Then who are you to stop him being so? He's a grown man, he doesn't need a nursemaid. The very opposite, I should think, having met him.'

'Sure, he likes to be in control. I like to let him think he is.' He glanced quickly over his shoulder, at the rose garden they were passing, at the arched bower there, covered in blooms wilting in the heat. He turned back, tsking to himself. 'You know what I don't like? Letting him help you open a sealed coffin most likely sent by McAvey, who, whatever he's got planned for you, also has it in for the obvious choice to open it. Yeah, all right, I'll be going along with that profoundly blatant trap.'

'Reuben didn't have it in for Kit Whitely.'

Alex got a look on his face which reminded her she knew very little of what had happened in Gallentry, when she and her cousins had treated each other almost as strangers and thought that was normal, and Reuben had been vicious and that had seemed normal too.

It was this frustrating ignorance that made her abruptly furious in a way she hadn't acknowledged before. It tingled hot through her fingers and into her palms.

She iced herself over again: temper was bad for the baby, and she'd nursed the mite along this far, after her incompetent womb had proved itself apt to prematurely part with its contents, as the mealy-mouthed doctors so charitably characterised her recurrent miscarriages.

Instead of snarling at Alex, therefore, she said, 'It's not like you to have your head turned by a pretty face, Alexander.'

'Then let's assume there's more to him than that, Genevieve,' Alex said mildly.

He took her arm again; they walked on, Genevieve trying not to fume, stroking her swollen side to remind herself why matronly calm was so important.

They passed out of the park and reached her home, where she paused to look up at the façade. A new and luxurious detached townhouse, in a new street by the park, it was painted a wickerwork shade that did not do much to disguise the growing soot smuts, set off by large white-framed bay windows and a glossy black front door with a brass mail slot for the penny post.

She experienced one of those foggy moments of disorientation, the familiar and the strange overlaid like one of Alex's out-of-focus stereoscope images.

This was not the small apartment they'd rented immediately after their wedding, both her father and her new husband proud and stubborn about refusing to allow the flow of funds from one to the other to make the early years of the marriage slightly fiscally easier. It was not the snug townhouse they'd leased once their success had warranted better accommodations.

It was not the flat-fronted and terraced Georgian home she'd grown up in, by Belgrave Square, which her father, nouveau riche and newlywed, had purchased off the development scheme back when the window tax had still been in effect. That had passed from her father to Sir Kingsford, his nephew, though Genevieve had inherited much of the contents. Kings had little use for the Locke townhouse himself, but Alex and Lulu still stayed there during their London sojourns.

She did not know why she had not inherited all of it: her father had not been the type to be contemptuous of daughters. It would have fallen to Reuben, certainly – it was commonly said that Artisan women had all the freedoms of men, yet that signified nothing against the venerable institution of marriage and its concomitant laws – but her father had reconciled himself to the affront of the mésalliance, eventually. He'd even grown to like her husband, eventually, if at first only as a worthy opponent across the chessboard. It would not have been a reason to cut them out of inheriting at least the copyhold, if not the freehold; if he had been so very concerned, he could have settled it all upon her under the doctrine of separate estate via a trustee.

Instead, Sir Kingsford had it. Perhaps *he* was her trustee. He'd have been the most likely choice, under such an arrangement, but she did not know.

She did not know when she and Reuben had relocated to Holland Park. She did remember giving up the lease on their longtime marital home, and moving into the Belgravia townhouse, to ease her mother's widowhood, in the nebulous period between the death of one parent and then the other.

She did not know when her father had died.

She did not know when her mother had died.

She did not know—

Alex pushed the gate open, and stood square in the gateway, idly swinging the gate back and forth. 'I'll come back and help you,' he said quietly. 'Let me get Whitely away, and then I'll come help you spring the trap, all right? If you won't leave well enough alone.'

Genevieve blinked at him. He'd mistaken her long musing silence for anger. Still, she could use it.

'Very well,' she said coolly, and offered him her hand for a studiedly limp farewell, which both plainly upset him and plainly did not turn his resolve a single iota: he would help but he would not offer up the one person who could *actually* help.

So then Genevieve went inside and told the others they'd be kidnapping Kit Whitely.

4

'AND IT BETTER BE TONIGHT,' she added. 'They'll be away on the train early tomorrow.'

The others were rearranging the furniture in the spare back bedroom on the second floor, or at least Oliver, with his physical strength and uncertain telekinesis Art, was doing so while Fletcher fussily directed him, in consultation with a book of crisp pages and plentiful ink illustrations. Cecelia, short and curvy, watched with folded arms and a fond smile.

Genevieve had followed the noise upwards, and immediately launched into the plan, before being diverted. 'What…are you doing?' She looked at the new bed doubtfully. 'Are you finally deigning to join us, Fletcher?'

It was a spacious and modern six-bedroom house. The main bedroom on the first floor had lain empty since October, and Genevieve had the adjoining room, connected by a pair of dressing rooms; a small modern bathroom and Reuben's locked study occupied the rest of the floor. This floor held the nursery, still sparse but at least ready with the large cot; and the front chamber Cecelia had occupied since widowhood had fallen upon her dearest friend; and the rear chamber Oliver took when the basement of his lodging house catastrophically flooded with the contents of the neighbour's cesspit; and this intended guest chamber, which instead was, or had been, neglected storage for drape-covered furniture, worn rolled-up rugs, and paintings, a collection she *did* inherit from her parents.

'That would not be appropriate, Genevieve,' Fletcher said, mouth downturned.

He wouldn't call her Gin; he found the little joke in respect to a drink once called Mother's Ruin beyond the pale. It was a miracle he even addressed her by her given name, even though she'd known him for as long as she'd known the others.

Behind him, Cecelia rolled her pretty eyes and gave Oliver a nudge, friendly and comforting. He was a big man of northern complexion, bald by dint of regular shaving, tattooed, nose flattened from breakage, phlegmatic of constitution but open of feature; his features wore an embarrassed grimace right now. He'd taken his room here under protestation, and wouldn't have done so if Cecelia hadn't already been in her new role as respectable lady's companion, and if Genevieve hadn't made a not entirely insincere plea for a male presence in the house. Even then he'd made diffident noises about taking a servant's room on the lower ground floor by the kitchen, or up in the garret under the eaves, or even out in the carriage house at the back of the garden where the coachman would live if the McAveys didn't patronise the local livery stables instead.

Genevieve gave him a reassuring smile, and turned back to Fletcher. 'So what are you doing, then?'

'This is your accouchement chamber, for your time of trial,' Fletcher said, holding up the book with one hand – she only had time to read part of the main title, *Rules for Wives*, and none of the extensive subtitle – while he waved his other hand in a flourish about the room.

They'd cleared almost all the detritus, most likely out to the storeroom over the workroom or up to the attic – poor Oliver – and the room now gleamed from a scrub-down – poor Bridget, their overworked maid-of-all-work, and probably Cecelia too, since she found it unnatural to sit idle while others worked – its rug beaten, its brushed curtains pulled back to let in dappled sunlight through a thin muslin shade soaked in chloride of lime, its chemical scent comfortingly sharp. Genevieve could glimpse the shadows cast by the young oak tree that shaded the window.

Fletcher talked her through the new room, displaying pages of the book as his inviolable reference.

A light birthing bed, with plenty of room for doctor and nurse to move about. A firm mattress, so she would not sink low. An extra blanket, on the right and at the foot – for she must lie upon her left side, on the right and at the foot. A layer of mackintosh. Some extra layers of blankets, and a thin summer counterpane to throw over her, once she had dutifully lain down – upon her left side, on the right and at the foot. A cushion, to protect her feet when she pushed hard against the bedposts in her extremity, and did she notice, Fletcher enquired, that the bed had no footboard? For those got in the way and would not let her plant her feet as firmly as she might like.

The room itself, quietly isolated from the noise – what noise? – of the rest of the household, and ventilated – pointing at the window, as if anyone would dare open a window this summer – and cool. A chair, for the friend chosen to attend her – here, no expectant look towards Cecelia, since she was unmarried and thus unsuitable.

A jug and basin and carbolic soap. Another basin, because she might vomit. And castor oil. And sewing thread and scissors. And lard. And – *Oh, good Lord,* thought Genevieve, *he's going to tell me there's a vaginal syringe.* He didn't, but indicated that, in the chest of drawers, lay the receiving blanket and – he looked unsure – other linens and napkins and towels, and a bed-gown and chemise—

'I fetched those for you,' Cecelia said quickly, doing her best, with her expression, to communicate that poor earnest Fletcher was trying his own best.

'The book,' he said, 'the book seemed to assume people know what belongs in here, so there were not as many specifics as would have been actually helpful.'

That was probably, Genevieve thought, because the author of the book had never actually had to prepare a lying-in room himself. Fletcher would have done better to consult the women Genevieve had already contracted to attend her: Mrs Murphy, a pain Artisan who had turned her Art to midwifery, and her partner Miss Adler, a healing Artisan.

She could not be paid to allow a doctor at her bedside when Artisans existed who could take the pain away and heal the injurious strain even as it occurred.

Not a second time, anyway.

Still, it seemed quite thorough, and the poor dear man had his heart firmly in the right place, if only because he was convinced that the right place was the only proper place for it to be, and also that *someone* had to be the master of the house if Reuben was gone and Oliver was too circumspect.

'Thank you, Fletcher, this was very thoughtful of you,' she said, mostly so he would stop talking.

He gave a shy, uncertain smile and an awkward bow. 'You should have the nurse here soon,' he added in a rush. 'She's meant to be here at least a week before…'

'Your plan,' Oliver prompted as Genevieve sat gingerly on the special birthing bed, wondering if Fletcher understood that these existed to keep the birth of the innocent child separate from the relations in the marital bed that had conceived it. He'd have dissolved into an embarrassed fluster, surely, if he'd known it.

Sitting had been a mistake. A heavy flood of exhaustion swept over her. 'We are taking Kit Whitely from the Locke townhouse.'

'Oliver and I to fetch Whitely out of his bed? Should be simple.' Fletcher twiddled his fingers, by way of indicating he'd compel the door Artisan to come along quietly, with barefaced disregard for the illicitness of such an act.

'Locke.' Oliver, never a man given to idle words, took refuge in monosyllables when his thoughts were going too fast, or when he was feeling under strain, or both.

He'd been almost nothing *but* monosyllables, those last few months with Reuben.

'They'll have Alexander to deal with,' Cecelia translated. 'What do you plan to do about that, Gin?'

Fletcher frowned. 'We simply have to not wake him up, and his bedroom will be far from a guest chamber, surely.'

'Fletcher, you dear man,' Cecelia said. 'Their bedrooms will be side by side, if they're not sharing a bed.'

Their upright friend looked blank. It was not unusual for men to share beds in tight lodgings, but the Locke townhouse could by no possible stretch of the definition be called tight lodgings. It obviously hadn't occurred to Fletcher that Alex and Whitely had another reason to share.

So he just stared in puzzled silence until Cecelia added, 'You'll most likely have to prise Mr Whitely from Alex's arms.'

It still took another long moment before Fletcher realised what Cecelia was trying to tell him. Then he gaped. 'That's. That's improper. And illegal!'

Genevieve looked at him, a frown of her own forming. The Locke twins had been raised by wolves – indulgent mother, eccentric father. They might have had some access to higher society, given their father's wealth and influence and new minor title, but they'd cast themselves out before ever joining it. Lulu hid nothing about her true self, and Alex, after failing Lulu in his teen years, determinedly refused to be secretive or defensive either. Reuben had liked to openly make little jokes, his constant sly digs, about Alex's preferences and about Lulu.

And Kit Whitely, drunk, had in no way been subtle in his own leanings when they'd all met him last year. He might as well have hit Fletcher over the head with it.

'I thought…' Fletcher was well and truly tangled now. 'I don't know what I thought. I suppose I thought Reuben was merely being provocative. Locke's a very big man to be a margery. I suppose he does like those fancy waistcoats. And he goes about cleanshaven.'

He rubbed absently at his own sideburns, which did not approach the magnificence of the mutton chops sported by older men, being more patches of fuzz decorating the side of his narrow, thin-lipped face. Genevieve caught Cecelia and the cleanshaven-all-over Oliver exchanging looks of complicit amusement. They were both from the masses of the labouring class, Cecelia consigned to a matchmaking factory before her Art had unexpectedly blossomed, Oliver a mariner in the merchant navy like his father and many brothers, quietly employing his own emerging medley of Arts as he worked first the trade routes, and then, once his Art-driven size made shipboard life too cramped, the docks.

That made them more worldly and infinitely less judgemental than Fletcher, rigidly proper as only the sheltered son of a prosperous middling-class doctor could be, aping the forms of his betters without acknowledging the hypocrisy behind the thin façade of propriety.

Genevieve herself had been an endowed heiress intended for a titled man, even after her rather dramatic Art came on. But she'd grown up with the Locke twins, one who had turned out to be, in Fletcher's word, a margery, the other a woman. Her cousins had not set out to corrupt her, but they did not shy from telling her their truths when she asked, which, naturally, she did…and eagerly read the sensational novels they slipped to her, the less salubrious of which – full of pulsating and flocculating – she definitely made sure to peruse in private, and to tuck out of sight between-times.

Consequently, her eyes were opened to noticing all sorts of things. She knew brown-skinned Cecelia with the foreign family name – and Genevieve had received enough sly snideness about her own French-sounding given name to know Cecelia must have suffered worse – had had little enough to hope for except a husband who did not drink away quite every penny or fling his fists about too strenuously, until her Art had gifted her the independent means to eschew marriage…yet she did not feel the need to eschew the occasional discreet liaison.

She knew Oliver, erstwhile Seaman William Oliver Bennet, would almost certainly be familiar with men bedding men in more than theory only, given a navy-adjacent life. And for all she thought she knew, perhaps he was familiar with bedding *Alex* in more than theory only, given that Alex had been the one to introduce Oliver to her, and given that Alex, bucking against his brother's cold authority, had had only one reason to be frequenting dockside taverns.

Not to say that Oliver would *ever* have taken advantage of Alex then, when Alex had been very young and still grieving. But they had been in each other's ambit for many years since, and Alex never missed a chance to wield his robust charms at his old friend.

Her stomach gave a flutter, akin to the first quickening of the baby but very different to its sturdy kicks lately.

'That's not right,' Oliver said in his low rumble, confounding her. Then, having had time to order his thoughts while Fletcher finished his aghast spluttering, he went on, 'Gin, Alex said no. I went along when Reuben ordered wrong things. I wish I hadn't.' He shook his head once, firm. 'I won't go along with this, not even for you.'

He coughed, reddening. Genevieve lifted her chin, too set on her course for niceties. 'Then don't come along. Stay here with Cecelia. Fletcher and I will manage.'

Oliver made a frustrated gesture with one clenched hand. He was in shirtsleeves and waistcoat, coat discarded, as remained acceptable among Artisans of mixed sex even in the queen's strict reign. His cuff, too loose, rode up, and she glimpsed the colourful floral tattoos that she knew spread from his hand to decorate his entire forearm, a souvenir of his years asea. He had an inked octopus gathering astronomical symbols into its tentacles on his other arm. She'd often seen it, whenever he rolled back his sleeves for Artisan work.

'Gin,' Cecelia said insistently into the teeth of her sudden abstraction, 'you don't know how angry Alex will be if you do this.'

'The only man I've ever met with less anger in him than Alex is Oliver,' Genevieve said, and it was her turn to blush at the warm look Oliver gave her for the compliment. It was true enough. 'My cousin will forgive me anything.'

And he owes *me.*

'Still,' her friend insisted. 'He's in love now, isn't he?'

Genevieve paused. 'Is he?' she said, wrinkling her nose. Kit Whitely, that sly little shit, was hardly deserving of it. 'Surely it's infatuation, at the outermost?'

'He protected Whitely at your expense,' Oliver said quietly. 'He is unquestionably deeply in love. There could be no lesser reason for him to not leap to help you. He will be furious if we take Whitely from him.'

'But he'll forgive me eventually,' Genevieve maintained. She'd asked permission; since she hadn't received it, she'd ask forgiveness instead, and she'd bloody well get it. Eventually.

Oliver grimaced, eloquent with it.

She was tired to the bone, and achy as if falling ill with ague, except that

Artisans enjoyed notoriously vigorous health. She still had to tell the others the truth about the letter that had accompanied the box, that the writer was anonymous but not unidentifiable, which they'd have known if she'd let any of them read that smug salutation – *Dearest Vivi* – for themselves. She had to admit that Reuben was alive, that she was a deliberately deserted wife. She had to have Oliver break open the locked door of Reuben's study.

Kit Whitely would've been helpful there, too, she supposed, now that she was resigned to looking at the books of accounts, easy to ignore in her months of grieving, reliably upright Fletcher delegated to meet with Reuben's – her – man of business and manage the household funds until she recovered enough to take the reins. She supposed they'd also be searching for clues to his treachery, his intentions with that knife or what might be inside that locked box haunting the workroom.

She wanted, suddenly but fervently, to strip off her widow's clothes, the dark colours and sombre fabrics she had worn all these months. None of her regular wardrobe was suitable now, with her womb great with child, but all her black gowns were wrong: she was not a widow. She desired, as sharp as a craving for sweet pudding, the crimson silk walking dress she'd seen gracing another enceinte wife, the merest half-decade younger than her. She could send to her dressmaker, and have it delivered in the morning, thus delivering herself out of the mourning.

It wouldn't, of course. She had still lost her husband, whom she loved deeply, and lost was the right word. She'd misplaced him without even knowing how. Her grief was ripped apart and stuffed anew by her confusion and anger and shame, none of which she could let free.

Besides that… Her thoughts faltered. Would she not still be in mourning, half-mourning at the very least, for one or both of her parents? When, exactly, had she lost them? Her natural sorrow there felt faded, overcast, as if it had been a long time ago, but when?

Her face must have been showing her misery and bewilderment. Oliver touched her hand briefly. 'How are you faring, Gin?'

'The book says you might need a purgative to clear your bowels,' Fletcher told her officiously, pointing at the castor oil.

'Thank you, Mr Fletcher,' Genevieve said grimly, while Cecelia gave her a merrily complicit look and hurried him out of the room.

That left Oliver, now putting his coat on by the doorway instead of hovering solicitously by her side: he couldn't, or wouldn't, linger in a small room alone with her, no matter how much licence Artisans were accorded.

There had been a time she had felt herself insulted by such priggishness – she was an *Artisan*, not a woman – but that was long past.

'I'm sorry your excursion did not go so well,' he said, and then gave his crooked little smile at his own folly: she had, after all, gone, unescorted, to attend a public execution, and to watch her cousin gloat about it. Fletcher had been appalled, Cecelia too, if more quietly. 'You're usually happier after a visit with the twins.'

Genevieve managed a small smile of her own. She wanted to tell him the truth: *Lulu lied to me, and Reuben is alive. He left me, he stole that weird knife, he sent the box, which Alex thinks must be a trap. I've inveigled my cousin into abandoning his lover to help me and I refuse to feel guilty about it one whit, nor about taking his lover anyway.*

It was simply too humiliating, and too shameful – what Reuben had done to her, and what she was doing to Alex. Oliver would be understanding about the former, and, worse, understanding about the latter as well – even as he gently leveraged the remorse she wouldn't allow herself to feel to persuade her to renege on her plan.

She narrowed her eyes in anticipatory annoyance at that thought, suspicious of his sympathy. Oliver looked away, adjusting his coat. His shirt collar was open; if he'd started his day with any sort of neck-tie, he'd stripped it off as the heat of the day became unbearable to his Artisan body.

Genevieve could see the flick of a tattoo, long and thin, curling from the nape of his neck, licking a collarbone. It had the sinuous curves of a snake, but she knew it was the tail of a much larger tattoo, one wrought in glossy scarlet and gold and grass-green. Like his more visible tattoos, the ones across his hands and forearms, the Art-coloured dragon was a memento of his earlier life shipboard.

She started. How did she know Oliver had a bright Oriental dragon tattooed on his chest? It might be tolerable for an Artisan to refuse warm flannels and strip off his coat in front of a lady Artisan, and even roll back his sleeves to bare his forearms, but never more than that. Yes, they'd worked together for a decade and a half, and yes, Artisans had more latitude than most. But he'd never taken his shirt off in front of her and Cecelia, and he surely never would.

Reuben must have mentioned it some time, that was all, probably in that mocking way he assumed was amusing, and probably to try to shock the wife he insisted on pretending was delicate even though he knew she'd grown up with the feral Locke twins.

He surely hadn't described it in any detail, however. So how did she know about the gorgeous wealth of colour, glowingly, silkily rich, sheer Artistry, and the intricate strokes delineating the scales of those sinuous loops? How did she know the dragon's head lay on Oliver's muscular left breast and its narrow forked tongue encircled his nipple?

Why did she feel like she'd lightly kissed that sleek head, a habitual fond gesture as she rolled sleepily from a shared bed? Why did she feel like her tongue had traced the path of the dragon's tongue, during times with an entirely different feeling than fond habit?

How – *how* – did she know his nipple was pierced? She could feel it stiffening under the administrations of her mouth as she tongued and sucked the small gold hoop, feel the rumbling response through his chest where she was pressed naked against him.

How did she know the dragon's tail caressed Oliver's nape and ran the entire length of his spine and seemed to writhe when he arched his back in…in *pleasure*?

Genevieve had been raised a lady, the daughter of a wealthy gentleman who'd planned for titled grandchildren. She'd followed polite society's precepts as far as she could, even as she'd watched her cousins throw those precepts to the wind, even as she'd chafed at the dreary humiliation of her Season, even as her Art had bloomed and her mother had spoken wistfully of the larger world that was open to her now. She'd only known the touch of her husband. She'd never so much as allowed a kiss to be stolen from her.

And right now she could taste Oliver's mouth under hers. More than that, she could taste his skin, his—

'Gin?' Oliver reached out a hand and she flinched, staring at him with wide eyes.

He raised his hands to her then, placating, watching her. He was confused, she saw, confused and perhaps a little hurt.

His hurt feelings were confirmed when he went oblique. 'The baby?'

'I'm fine.' She was being fairly monosyllabic herself. 'I'm fine, Mr Oliver.'

A shocked expression crossed Oliver's broad features. They hadn't been formal with each other for *years*. She'd thought of him as Oliver from the evening they'd first met. She didn't think she'd *called* him anything but Oliver a single time following the first occasion they'd tackled a rogue Artisan together.

But, holy God, she could feel him rocking under her, tight muscles, boundless strength, thick body solid against the arch of her own as she cried out – she had to put as much distance between them as she could while she tried desperately to force the thoughts of things *that had never happened* from her mind.

'Mrs McAvey,' Oliver said without inflection.

He offered a stiff nod and walked out, ducking his head, hunching his big shoulders like he did when he was trying not to scare people with his thuggish bulk.

'Sorry,' she said helplessly, but he'd already gone.

5

VANQUISHED BY EXHAUSTION AT LAST, GENEVIEVE lay on her side, on her left no less, and closed her eyes, hand rubbing over her stomach, feeling the tautness of the skin beneath the fabric, trying to push away that strange, impossible memory, Oliver arched under her, head thrown back, neck bared to the graze of her teeth, that dragon gleaming on his chest.

It was not, God help her, the first time she'd had such appalling thoughts about one of her oldest friends. That first time, though, had purely been Reuben's fault.

Reuben had been, the last few months before he'd absconded, jealous of Oliver. It had taken her some time to understand that, to notice behaviour she could only pray Oliver had not noticed for himself. A faint hope: he noticed patterns.

The previous summer, she and her husband had sunk into a fallow period in the marriage. It was, perhaps, the inevitable consequence of her womb's failures.

Last year, with child again, and full of unreasonable certainty, she'd been determined to do everything right. No dancing with her husband, and certainly no marital relations. No joining him and the others in their Agency enforcement contracts. A careful rein on the Locke temper and the Art flames, and so much resting she was almost driven to the silly fashion magazines Lulu liked so much, except she'd been too busy consulting other instructional manuals.

Her single-minded resolve worked. Overseen by the most modern of doctors, she finally carried a child to term.

She suffered a stillbirth.

He never opened his eyes or took a breath, a little slip of life blown from the world before he'd ever had a chance to properly enter it, taken away while she was still groggy from the chloroform.

She was grieving and guilty, full of self-blame and an overriding sense of confused failure, unable to understand what she had done wrong – much, in fact, how she felt now, with the similar careless loss of a husband, except far sharper.

Worse, what was already a hard blow in itself brought into stark relief memories of their first devastating loss, their little girl, born in the second year of their marriage, and lost to them after three days, carried away in her sleep for no reason anyone could explicate except that God had wanted His angel back.

Cecelia had had to drag Fletcher from the black-draped parlour after he'd dared that platitude, and at least he did not trot it out again for their stillborn son.

The twins did their best, but that was near the culmination of Lulu's obsessive hunt for the man who'd murdered Peter, after she'd dulled the worst of her grief with government work in the Crimea. She was fixated, Alex distracted. It was, Genevieve understood now, the prelude to their failure to be there for her again this year.

It did no good to tell her that procreation was something many Artisans struggled with, for all the rude good health their own bodies enjoyed. All those handbooks, written by real doctors to help her keep her baby safe – she'd read and reread them through the pregnancy and turned back to them now to understand what had gone wrong. They all said – they *all* said – it was the mother's fault. She was not absolved of that responsibility by dint of being an Artisan mother.

Even as she rested and healed, readying herself to return to working side by side with her husband, they had turned from each other. A frost had grown, creeping ever thicker from her guilt and grief, his self-contained sadness.

And then came the tap-tap at the bedroom door, straight after her birthday early last August. She had not bothered to mark it, but, amid the usual notes from her cousins and friends, her husband had left for her a small gift, followed swiftly by that polite little knock.

The first time Reuben came into her bed after those weeks of estrangement, it was like he'd never touched her before. He was passionate, and attentive, and almost possessive in the way he claimed her mouth, stroked her skin, nuzzled her breasts, dug fingers into her hips. He'd spent quickly, before she had time to warm up, but she was so ridiculously grateful he'd tapped on the door, that the man she'd loved since almost the moment she'd set eyes on him had chosen to turn back to her, that she could have clutched his shoulders and wept.

With that blessed resumption of marital relations came, too, almost a second blooming, all through the last of the summer, Reuben's regular knock, sometimes as soon as they retired for the night, sometimes after he'd come in late smelling of brandy, sometimes even during the day when Bridget and Cook were out on errands or busy with chores downstairs.

It was different than before. They were changed by their grief, and that obviously extended to the bedroom. She hated to have to admit it, even in her own head, for it was nothing she could ever say aloud, but Reuben had become like a callow youth, thrusting away on top of her, gasping 'Are you there?' into her hair when she was nowhere close, spending regardless. He'd sometimes been rougher, more insistent, than she was used to, and yet, after the initial burst of eagerness, almost indifferent, always doling out the same few perfunctory kisses and strokes before performing the procreative act to the exact moral specifications of the time: she always on her back, he always atop, pleasure almost frowned upon as too enflaming. The one time she had offered to use her mouth, hoping for a return of their usual reciprocation and variation, he had appeared utterly disgusted with her.

Yet he was so sulky if she turned him away that it became easier to comply, as a good wife should do anyway. And didn't she welcome the chance to try for another child? She was getting older. Her chances of fulfilling the wifely production of a healthy heir were at the lowest of ebbs. And so, she dutifully accepted him, and went back to those early torrid memories in her own head when she began to find the tap-tap too onerous and her spirits too dismal.

One afternoon, they were alone in the house, their tiny household staff visiting the costermongers, and the others departed after a morning training in their big workroom in the converted carriage house. She'd been reading *Wonderful Adventures of Mrs Seacole in Many Lands* in the parlour when Reuben had unexpectedly drawn her up the stairs and into his bedroom, eagerly pushing up her skirts, unbuttoning himself, murmuring exhortations against her neck between biting kisses, pushing her not onto the bed but against the wall.

It had been surprising, and alarming, and thrilling, the way relations had been between them in the early years, when he had seen and satisfied an unrecognised need in her for something more than the quiet passivity and absence of desire expected of a respectable wife.

Possibly, he'd said back then, *out of sheer relief for the narrow escape from a gilt cage – not, mind you, that I'm* at all *complaining, love.*

She remembered frantic times like this. She remembered visiting Mrs Murphy and, drawing on an upper-class hauteur she hadn't had to use for a while, coolly enquiring if marital relations were safe to continue despite the baby she was carrying, their first. Thanks to Mrs Murphy's calmly amused reassurance, she'd pounced on her husband the moment he returned home, catching him before he'd even properly undressed and washed from his labours that day: straddling him on the chair he'd been sitting in, her skirts and petticoat pulled up, her open drawers coming in exceedingly handy, his shirt stripped off and his own drawers peeled open, her fingers tangled tight into the side-laces of his body belt, his fingers leaving smudged marks on her thighs as she rode him hard enough to jolt the chair across the floor and almost tip them. She'd climaxed almost immediately; he'd barely held on to his self-control long enough.

The memory of that, and other times like that, was enough to make her acquiesce readily to his urgency now, feeling naughty and daring and gratifyingly desirable, body responding accordingly, thighs slick. Reuben's hands were hard on her hips as he thrust into her, rattling the door beside them, grunting and panting and then half-shouting in her ear as he spent, self-control no longer equal to waiting on her pleasure.

He buttoned up and hurried to his study. Genevieve heard his over-loud greeting and realised Oliver hadn't left with the other two at all, that Reuben had summoned him for some meeting there, that he'd been sitting in the very next room with the door ajar, patiently waiting while she and Reuben had loudly carnal relations.

Face burning, she could only hope he hadn't heard the rhythmic noises, rattle and thump and gasp, from the bedroom, or, if he had, he had misunderstood. Oliver could be stubborn about failing to understand what others wanted him to understand, and she could find no way to doubt that Reuben *had* wanted him to understand.

The way Reuben linked an arm proprietorially around her waist, or nuzzled his nose under her ear, at the oddest times came clear. It was whenever she was working closely with Oliver on Artisan business.

Reuben tried to pull her up to the bedroom again, the next week, and she put a stop to it; she could barely look Oliver in the eye as it was. Reuben sulked, terribly, and then, days later, found her upstairs in the storeroom in the carriage house, moving aside dustsheets.

He came to her confidently, cuddling up to kiss her neck, stroking his hands over her waist, and she turned into it, grateful she was forgiven for ruining his game, as strange and cruel as it was.

'I thought you were at work downstairs, darling,' he said. 'Why are you up here? Lost something?'

'I'm looking for my mother's paintings.'

He checked, and looked at her closely. 'Vivi, you sold those.'

'I didn't,' she said. 'Not these ones.'

The paintings she was fruitlessly seeking had been Antoinette Locke's own private collection, never intended for any eyes but her family's. She'd made endless quick and vibrant portraits of the twins, after Lulu had revealed her true self, and when their talents had been coming on, and there'd been plenty of Genevieve herself, of course, some capturing her at the height of her cool beauty during her Seasons, but most a sort of record of her developing Artistry, conveyed in a series of sketches and paintings.

And Mother had traced the course of her courtship, too, and the early years of their marriage. She could see that she might let Reuben force her to put them into storage, but never to consign them to the ownership of strangers.

'You did. We have less room on the walls here, and none of your mother's things suit this house anyway.'

He looked about pointedly; the storeroom held the pieces of inherited furniture she'd had brought over, leaving the dark and heavy Georgian pieces for Kingsford, who would like them if he took even a single moment to consider them. She'd taken the brightly upholstered chairs, exuberantly clashing, from the family's back parlour, and some of the honey-coloured tables from the drawing room, and a matching sideboard and cabinet, her grandmother's, and a curve-backed divan, a Regency Grecian couch which her mother had had reupholstered, and the garishly painted wooden folding chairs for the garden, all favourites of her mother's, and therefore of hers.

She and Reuben had argued, and the furniture, like the paintings and the rest of the contents of her mother's studio, old paints and easels and stretched canvases and her stool, had been consigned to the carriage house storeroom.

She opened her mouth to insist she hadn't sold those private paintings – she *wouldn't* – and closed it again. Arguing with Reuben was fruitless.

She'd asked him to send a note if he was going to be home late, and he came home later than he ever had and then, when she challenged him the next morning, produced the note he'd indeed sent. It had slipped off the entrance hall table, where Bridget had set it. Where, actually, *Genevieve* must have set it, after reading it, because Bridget was a dutiful and diligent servant and would not have failed to pass the message on. Or did she wish to summon the girl and dress her down over a mistake she had not been the one to make?

Or that old argument about the furniture, the accusation that she was clinging to her upper-class roots in a way that disrespected her middle-class husband; why else would she want to sully their very new marital home with such outré rubbish? Had she forgotten how much she had claimed to like the modern furniture he had filled the house with, was all that money he'd spent for her wasted because she suddenly preferred battered old chairs which didn't even match the curtains?

That was nothing to their conflict over the way he felt entitled to interrupt her no matter what she was doing. She accepted it, in part, because she had accepted, in part, the role that a wife was expected to fulfil: the dutiful domestic angel, responsible for making the home a haven for her husband and mothering his children and giving him her time and attention.

But another, larger, part of her had seized the freedom that Artistry had gifted her with both hands, and she would take an interruption while she was busy with household management, but when he interrupted her, time and again, as she concentrated over a handful of flames, on the edge of working out how to make a line of fire whip across the floor like a burning snake, and with things so very trivial, yes, she snapped, and then he shouted, and she was put back in the wifely place that not even being an Artisan could free her from. He might then refrain for a day, or perhaps two, and then he was back to interrupting her just as often as he felt like, because he, as her husband, had a right to her attention whenever he wanted it.

That was the way arguments went, with Reuben raising points she somehow couldn't find a way to refute, that always made the cause of the conflict her and never him, that made her doubt her own mind for how forgetful or careless she seemed to have become. Any victory she might win was sour, because of his fiery outrage if he felt she had questioned his authority, or his cold affront if he felt she had belittled him – his sulks, bluntly – and because to think of their marriage as a battleground that needed a victory meant she'd already lost anyway.

And so now, in the storeroom holding the last remnants of her parents' lives, about to argue about her mother's lost paintings, Genevieve stopped herself. She didn't want another dispiriting fight. She didn't want another example of her disturbing forgetfulness, if he proved she had sold them, after all.

She hadn't, but somehow she couldn't be sure she hadn't.

So she smiled, and responded to his next kiss, and never mind that he hadn't apologised for being so unfathomably rude to Oliver, so shabby in his treatment of his own wife.

'No one's here,' he whispered, running a hand over her hip suggestively.

He was already nudging her towards the divan, shrouded under the dustcloth. He tugged at her skirts as he herded her from behind, hard bulge insistent against her back. She resisted; she was terribly and truly shocked. This seemed a quick and furtive act, something a gentleman might do to a paid companion, or a willing barmaid, but not to his wife.

But, at the same time, it was nothing she'd not done already with her husband. She'd not been shocked then, nor seen it as furtive or…or degrading. It had *never* felt like that with him before.

She'd cherished their wedding night, certainly, the care her husband had taken with his new bride, the look on his face when she'd explained that the books suggested he get the deflowering over with as quickly as possible, the gratifications he had revealed to her with his mouth and fingers, the laughter they had shared.

'The sheets are smouldering, Gin,' he'd murmured, and it had taken her a moment to emerge from her haze of spiralling ecstasy and realise he'd meant literally, her Art flowing from her in direct proportion to his slow, sweet ministration of pleasure.

'There's a little less application of the male member than I was led to expect, love,' she'd said, languorous with repeated climax, and he'd smiled and suggested she be patient in that regard.

And indeed, they'd moved on to well and truly applying the male member. They'd fucked on every conceivable surface of their furnished apartment, their first rented home, once the charwoman was gone for the day. He'd had her like this before, in their modest little parlour, curtains firmly shut, the loud squeak and judder of the couch making them both gasp with laughter in between their moans of pleasure. He'd had her over it, too, and they'd lain together and used their mouth on each other at the same time.

And she'd had him: he'd introduced her to the rush of using silk bonds and leather implements to make a big man helpless with a blissful pleasure so intense, it edged to pain. He'd taken her over his lap and lightly spanked her, all his strength held to fine restraint. She'd knelt for him while heat sparked through her palms as she spread them over his broad thighs, right on the edge of scalding him as she took him in her mouth. And there'd been more games like that, more occasions when his strength might have hurt her, and never did, and her fire might have burned him, and never did.

All that had taken trust, mutual and unfaltering. But now Reuben pushed her towards the divan, and she realised that she loved her husband as much as she ever had, but the trust had somehow evaporated since her stillbirth and their undiscussed frost, and the lack of trust transformed something thrilling and erotic into something sordid.

Reuben pulled off the shrouding cloth, sending a cloud of thick dust into the air, and pushed her down onto the divan. He ran hands up and down her body and kissed her deeply, and she reminded herself of how sulky he'd been, and told herself how much more interesting this was, how much better, than when he gave her a few obligatory kisses and then lay atop and rutted, barely bothering to touch her except perhaps a hard squeeze of her breasts. At least this way, she could feel desirable; it was even, almost, a relief to take on a role other than wife for a small space of time.

Then, downstairs, she heard the door that led into the main workroom from the little mews-door vestibule, where a servant might have dozed as he awaited the return of a carriage. She heard familiar heavy footsteps walking about the workroom, where she and Reuben would have been, if she hadn't happened to come upstairs.

She chilled even before Reuben muttered, 'That's Oliver.'

She tried to sit up, expecting Reuben to rise so they could put themselves into order, but he pushed her down. 'I'll be quick. You be quiet.'

'No,' she said, keeping her voice low.

He had one hand under her petticoat, fingers prying, the other fumbling at his trousers. He was speaking abruptly ugly words into her ear. 'He can hear us, Vivi. He knows I'm having you, tumbling you like a whore in a back alley. Do you know how much he'd pay to have his cock inside you like this? Shall we call him in? Shall we let him watch?'

She didn't react for a moment, the blow of those appalling words too great. And more: Reuben had implanted an awful, outrageous, treacherous vision, and yet himself was completely absent from it.

Oliver, just Oliver, was there instead, watching her writhe before him as she pleasured herself under his instructions, dark eyes growing velvety with want. He was leaning over her, big hands spread at her waist, mouth grazing her bare stomach, tasting downwards. His lips and tongue were driving her to abandon, her hips jerking unstoppably under his skilful, relentless attention, her nails skating over his scalp, her spine arching as she demanded more, and she was crying out and *pleading* for more now, begging to feel him, and he was giving her what she wanted, turning her so he could take her over the divan with long, powerful strokes, so hard and deep inside her, gasping syllables with every thrust, *God*, and *yes*, and *Gin, fuck, Gin, my love—*

It pealed deep within, a sonorous truth, mind and body in accord: *Yes. This. Him.*

Reuben moved over her, insistent. It was all wrong: he was the wrong size, the wrong weight, the wrong *face*, and *he had put this travesty into her head on purpose*, solely to be cruel to a good man who was meant to be their friend.

She hit him, a sharp but glancing blow across his face in reflexive horror. He sat up, staring at her. She hadn't hurt him, she thought, simply surprised him. She hadn't even left a mark. He was, for a wonder, chastened rather than outraged. He tidied himself and went down to meet Oliver, who had, again, been summoned to an unnecessary meeting under the most awkward of circumstances, some weak excuse about trying something new with one of his minor Arts.

Genevieve hid in the storage room until Oliver left, and then brushed past her husband without a word, tossing away her besmirched dress and scrubbing herself in the bathroom until her skin was red.

Reuben came to her in the workroom, after a few days of cold silence and once again with no thought to the interruption.

'I went too far,' he said stiffly, a slim explanation meant to stand in for an apology. 'I thought it would be exciting for both of us. I didn't mean to say so much.'

Letting the Art she'd been working dissipate – she'd been trying to raise an empty match tin using a cyclone of flame, a feat she was sure she had managed before yet was struggling with now – Genevieve straightened and looked him in the eye.

She spoke forthrightly for the first time in some time. 'You don't have to be jealous of Oliver.'

His eyes flashed with something cold, but he laughed in her face, espousing mocking denial as if it had not been blatantly obvious that that ugly emotion lay behind the ugly game. 'God, that would be vile. Madame de Villeneuve's Beast, mooning over the fair Beauty.'

It was an odd insult: the Beast had won said Beauty before being revealed as a true prince. Reuben seemed to realise it. He said, 'Or perhaps Aphrodite, chained to hideous old Hephaestus, forced to seek her gratification in the arms of Ares instead.'

He trailed a finger along her clavicle and lower, tracing the line of the gold chain of her necklace. He seemed to believe he'd doled out a compliment rather than grievously insulted the constancy of his wife.

Valiantly steady, Genevieve said, 'I will not have you play these cruel games aimed at our friend and colleague.'

He dropped his hand, and his sly smile. 'It was meant to be a marital aid,' he told her coldly. 'It's excruciatingly dull, you realise, when you lie there like a log.'

She'd walked away, fingers tingling.

Still, the tap-tap had come on her door soon after, and he'd been slower, more attentive, and she had managed to think only of him and keep out any extraneous thoughts, especially regarding how his weight atop her was not nearly substantial enough.

As near as she could count it back, that night was when this baby was conceived, and wasn't all that a fine start to life for the little mite.

Reuben didn't touch her again once she told him she was with child, which she did the very moment her missed monthly courses, sore breasts, and overwhelming fatigue gave her the usual robust early hint. Officially, in the medical and legal realms, she could not be sure till she felt the quickening, but the baby's position in her incompetent womb was too precarious for wait-and-see. She wouldn't risk delaying the precautions of minimising her use of Art and eliminating conjugal activities.

She'd been shamefacedly relieved, and hopeful. She'd thought perhaps the grief of losing their son might be alleviated if she managed to shepherd this next unmet child through to a successful birth, and then her husband might return to the man he'd been before, and she could welcome him back into her bed with pleasure.

She'd thought perhaps he was relieved, too. He must have been especially relieved mere weeks later when he walked away in Gallentry, with knife, sans wife.

The baby, she realised, had been quiet all day. It had not been so quiet since quickening.

She took a breath, hand pressed over her navel. She reminded herself Mrs Murphy had warned her the baby would quieten down, as if conserving strength for what would be an ordeal for it just as much as for her.

It was bizarre how often she let slip to the recesses of her mind their lost child, the miscarriages, the stillbirth, when she had been so, so obsessively careful during her last pregnancy because of that miserable history. She'd never have gone out into the heat and stink and crowds to attend a hanging, of all things. Yet she had thrown this one's life to the pitiless Fates, perhaps due to exactly that, fatalism.

Strange, too, how the others seemed to ignore those past losses, as if mentioning them might bring down doom on the fragile life growing inside her. Surely, when Fletcher had decided to lecture her on the injurious effects of going to Varley's execution – he had, she realised, been consulting that wives' handbook already – he'd have been much more strident about the dangers of frights and shocks and unnecessary exertions if he'd had that last loss in mind.

Fletcher's general overreliance on ubiquitous handbooks and instructional manuals and magazine articles would have been laughable, if he hadn't reminded her so much of Lulu, taking notes from the ridiculous publications aimed at young ladies during the tumultuous summer she'd been exiled from the Locke estate and found refuge with her uncle and aunt and cousin – and the space to learn how to be a woman to her own satisfaction.

Genevieve remembered sitting with her in the garden of the Belgravia house. She was eighteen, and preparing for her upcoming debut. Lulu was fifteen, and angry, and quietly sad, and pouring all of that into intense research into what made a proper woman. Genevieve undertook to poke fun at her and those manuals, but also to help her select make-up and hair-styling and ribbons for her hat with the advice taken directly from the bloody things, her mother painting nearby and calling out her own commentary. Antoinette Locke took a strong stand against stripes.

She remembered hearing the commotion in the house, and looking up to see Alex coming out the back door. He'd arrived with Sir Kingsford, to bring the terrible news: Uncle Reginald, thrown from his horse, dying still estranged from his daughter.

Lulu, never one for public weeping, accepted Alex's embrace and his abject apology for not following her to London in defiance of their father and went with him into the house to pack for home.

And Fletcher reminded Genevieve of herself, too, when she'd fallen hard for Lulu's technique and turned to earnest study of etiquette manuals and conduct books in a desperate attempt to please her father during her dismal second Season. Then, more recently, she'd turned from the expertise of Mrs Murphy, placing her faith in modern medicine and the handbooks for mothers during her last pregnancy, refusing to recognise that they were as flawed as the instructional manuals she'd teased Lulu about.

She hated those books now, with their officious, confident, wrong advice, for their uselessness and for the guilt they'd plastered onto her. Yet she knew, intimately, their appeal for people who were desperately trying to navigate the rules of the rapidly changing world by any means they could. Those conduct manuals were a lifeline for the drowning, and it was too wicked they might just as commonly turn out to be anchors to drag them down.

Genevieve had let her thoughts wander widely, perusing those memories that were still clear to her, from before her marriage, and struggling to focus on later, disjointed memories, lost in fog. She was trying not to let a familiar fear, a lurking and dreary expectation, flood her.

But the baby had still not turned or kicked or pushed a tiny, insistent hand against the wall that hemmed it in.

She waited. She waited. She breathed, and she waited.

The baby kicked.

'Oh, you little bastard,' she said, and fell deeply asleep.

6

Genevieve awoke in the evening, disorientated by the dimmer light amid the lingering prickly warmth and by the unfamiliar room she'd napped in, if sleeping like the dead for the entire afternoon could still be called napping. At least the long sleep had banished the heavy, dragging feeling in her limbs, if not the ever-present pressure on her bladder. Her head did not feel much better. She would bathe it with cool water and vinegar, but later.

After a visit to the bathroom, she looked for the others. They weren't in the house, so she walked down the narrow garden to the carriage house and let herself in. The big downstairs area meant to hold the carriage and stalls was instead a single spacious room, for practice, and for experimentation, though only Oliver did that. Cecelia and Fletcher were relatively clear on the capabilities of their Arts, focussing instead on improving their execution.

It was here that the box had been delivered, specifically addressed to her, care of Holland Park Mews. The big carriage door was barred, and the smaller vestibule door kept locked; the others each had a key, but it went otherwise unused. The knock of the carter had been a complete surprise; she'd almost sent him around to the area stairs, before he'd handed over the letter.

She intended to go straight to Oliver and apologise properly, but the tall rosewood box claimed her attention as soon as she came in. She stood before it, arms folded and resting on the rise of her stomach. It was an exaggeration to say it loomed in the centre of the room, but Alex's designation – coffin – was stuck in her head now and she couldn't convince herself anymore it was simply a strangely narrow single-door armoire. It was covered in florid curlicues and embossed points that seemed designed to snare the gaze, but more than that, Artistry wreathed it, thick and intricate. Their communal efforts to open it had left it scratched, scorched, and dented, but otherwise sound and whole.

She stared at the lock with thwarted intent; she'd already tried to melt it, to no avail. It was iron and silver, and otherwise reinforced by odd warding Art.

When she turned from contemplating their failed efforts, she found Oliver quietly at her elbow. 'Oh, you gave me a start.'

'You were thinking.' He meant he'd been content to wait, loath to disturb her.

'Oliver.' She took both his hands in hers and squeezed, and watched his slow, crooked smile creep over his broad face. She would have said more, but he shook his head: apology understood and accepted.

Cecelia and Fletcher were at work in the back corner. Fletcher sat in a chair, one of the old folding garden ones. Cecelia rested the tips of her ungloved fingers on his bare hand, which he had set on his own opposite shoulder. That was their compromise, since Fletcher wouldn't hear of Cecelia, an unmarried and unrelated woman, touching the skin of his face or neck, or even his hand upon a clothed knee. They were both staring at the plain whitewashed wall in front of them. It was blank, but then an image shimmered into life there, flickering and rippling, and then steadying as Cecelia slowly breathed out.

The image was moving. It was a memory, Fletcher's memory. It caught a dark-haired young woman seated in the middle of other guests on the other side of a formal dining table, in the moment that she glanced across and smiled at him.

'That's Miss Landrau,' Fletcher said, as the image stuttered and started over. Shy glance. Smile.

'Is this a significant memory, or a recent memory? Or both?'

'Recent,' Fletcher said. 'That's at dinner last night.'

'She seems to like you,' Cecelia said warmly.

'Mother says it's time I think about getting married,' Fletcher said. 'What she *seems*, is suitable.'

Cecelia laughed. 'Ever the romantic.'

'It's not about romance and all that fleeting…' He couldn't bring himself to say "passion", which Genevieve found both amusing and vaguely familiar. He cleared his throat pompously. 'It's about finding a suitable helpmeet to make of our home a domestic sanctuary through the application of feminine virtue. That is the role, the very *raison d'être*, of a wife.'

It sounded like he was quoting something near-verbatim. Genevieve wondered if men had a *Rules for Husbands* manual, or if he'd absorbed this high standard when reading the *Rules for Wives*; those types of books had no end of strictures regarding the woman's role in the family home.

'Well, all right,' Cecelia said, 'but you are allowed to *like* the future Mrs Fletcher, you know.'

They both watched the image flicker, Fletcher's memory caught on that one moment in the candlelight, the shy glance, the smile. 'I…do, I think.'

His friend gave his hand a delighted little tap, but knew better than to say anything more.

Genevieve coughed lightly for their attention. 'I need to tell you all something.' She was rubbing her stomach again; she stopped. 'Lulu was mistaken. Reuben is alive. He stole that antique knife we were meant to be bringing under Agency oversight, and he chose to leave.'

Cecelia looked suitably surprised and horrified, but the men exchanged an infuriatingly knowing look over her head.

'This,' Genevieve said sternly, twitching her index finger between them. 'What is this?'

Fletcher shifted uncomfortably, his topper suddenly in his hands so he could turn it round and round. 'I've been consulting with Mr Hartley, Reuben's man of business, you know—'

'*My* man of business.'

'I've been acting on your behalf,' he assured her. 'And, well. Your accounts – Reuben took all the ready money he could lay hands on, in the days before we departed for Gallentry. And that. That didn't make any sort of sense.'

'And now it does.' Genevieve stared past her friends at the wall, wishing she could make her own mind as blank.

But she was awake now, or awakening, and she had to face facts. If Reuben had planned his departure, and she supposed he had, for he'd left his wedding ring behind and disposed of the key to his study, then naturally he would have gone to the bank and taken all their ready money.

Fletcher had been manfully quiet on the matter of household funds, but they would be running low. Thanks to the foresight of both her father and her husband, she'd have investment dividends. That was something to be grateful to Lulu for, actually, because without her cousin flatly perjuring herself with sworn testimony of Mr McAvey's death, it would have taken two years before Genevieve could apply to be officially deemed deserted, or widowed *in absentia.*

In the meantime, however, the others must have been subsidising her while she couldn't contribute to the team, mind a black well of sorrow, body exhausted by its interesting and growing condition. They'd supported the household from their savings, and from the regular contracts from the Agency and other employers. Cecelia and Fletcher professionally attended inquests and sessions of the Central Criminal Court when there were no Agency contracts to be had, and that would have been the piecework they were left with, without the firepower of the two weapons Artisans, one absconded, one wrecked. Oliver would be back to regularly helping his brothers at the docks.

She thought, in shame, of how she had desired to send out for new silk dresses she would no longer need within the fortnight.

'How very ignorant of me,' she said quietly. 'Now I have been made aware, please do present the debts incurred on my behalf.'

Here Cecelia, who had been standing silent and frowning, clasped her hands. 'We are friends,' she said, low. 'And if you will not accept our help on those grounds, accept it in exchange for our part of the fair rent of reposing ourselves here.'

'There is not rent between friends,' Genevieve said, unwillingly offended by this blatant contravention of the etiquette of housing guests. Her father would have been appalled, though perhaps no more than by her living arrangement itself, bunking with a wharf rat and a factory girl in a pretty house by the park.

'There are not debts, either,' Cecelia said, and Genevieve suffered herself to be embraced even as she inwardly vowed she would have receipts from Fletcher for all three of her stalwart companions.

Oliver pressed a hand to her shoulder in either silent agreement with Cecelia, or silent commiseration with Genevieve; his wry smile gave her no real clue, and he had the rare ability to gently take her side against her own opinion.

Fletcher hovered stiffly, managing to be both wistful and disapproving. For a man who'd undertaken the voluntary Artisan test to earn an official Agency hallmark, he did struggle to either abide or adopt the freedoms it granted.

'We should,' Genevieve said, upon release, 'search his study.'

Fletcher briefly wore his most censorious look. A man's study was his private domain after all, a sacrosanct space behind a locked door. He managed to swallow it quickly, ducking his head and putting a hand in his carefully smoothed hair, accidentally releasing a few insistently wayward locks.

But they intended to invade another sacrosanct space tonight, and Genevieve needed to keep herself busy, to ensure her tired and swollen body didn't persuade her into lying down again so it could drag her back into a deep sleep the others might paternalistically decline to wake her from. She needed it, she knew, but she needed the box opened more.

And perhaps, God help her, perhaps within the walls of the study, they would find the reason Reuben had abandoned her, and perhaps it would even be a good enough reason to justify why she still loved him.

'It might exonerate him,' she said aloud, to pacify Fletcher.

They thus trooped back to the house, through the garden where the first stars were coming out. The temperature was finally cooling towards bearable, and the smell was not quite so oppressive. They intercepted Bridget with the first of the dinner trays prepared by Cook before she departed. It held a large portion of lamb and pea pie, the grey and gelatinous slab turning Genevieve's stomach.

She redirected her overworked maid to the dining room, which would at least save her from multiple traipses across to the carriage house, and led the others up to the locked door of her husband's study. She did not have the patience to be subtle: she put her hand over the lock, feeling the sting of the iron even as she burnt out the wood all around it, the varnish acrid in the air as it heated and dissolved.

It was laughable, really, that Reuben had locked it and apparently expected that single precaution to be enough. But it had been, hadn't it, for months, and even now she hesitated to step over the threshold into his private space.

It struck her properly then. He had betrayed her, and left her, and left their child, and she still loved him, and still respected him and his privacy, far more than he had ever respected her.

She spread a hand over her stomach, and reminded herself, through the duration of one slow breath in and out, that they might find evidence to absolve her husband in here. She stepped in. The others followed.

The room was pungent with the fresh smoke from her assault on the lock, underlain by the malodour that must have slowly seeped in from the summer stench through the imperfectly sealed front window. A thick layer of dust coated all the surfaces.

Fletcher made the desk his business, so Cecelia and Oliver spread out to the bookcases and shelves. They'd amassed a fairly substantial library, mostly around thaumological researches and histories, earlier editions of which Genevieve remembered consulting extensively in the aftermath of the surprise arrival of her Art. There was also a complete set of the journal proceedings since the Agency had come into being, some collections of natural histories, and a few of the more worthy fiction tomes. The rest of the shelves, and much of the desk, held accounts and ledgers.

Cecelia, sniffling a little as the dust began to rise from their shuffling and riffling, pulled down what looked like a simple commonplace book such as Genevieve's mother's more conventional acquaintances might have kept to note quotations and recipes, ideas and mementos. Mrs Jameson's had been published a few years before. This one had been crammed, unheeded, between staid ledgers, otherwise it probably would have been relegated to the shelves in the drawing room, or even disposed of, as Reuben had done with so much of the older paraphernalia of their lives when they'd made the move from Belgravia.

But instead of being full of commonplaces, the book contained yellowed clippings from London newspapers. Genevieve looked over Cecelia's shoulder as she paged through it, softly exclaiming as she came across their oldest, long-forgotten cases. But Cecelia wasn't letting herself become too enthralled, and quickly set it aside to continue her search.

Genevieve flipped back through the pages herself, to confirm something that had caught her eye during Cecelia's breakneck perusal. Ah, it was as she had thought: she had been Mrs Locke in these breathlessly fawning articles about the early exploits of the Myriad. It had been a professional name, like Mrs Murphy, although she'd been married by then.

She frowned. She *had* been married by then, hadn't she? Or had they still been courting during their first few commissions? She couldn't quite remember. It had been a brand new '44 when she, Reuben and her cousins had sat on the stairs and shamelessly eavesdropped on her parents' argument as to whether she'd be permitted her choice of husband. The Society, the precursor and progenitor of the Agency, had begun facilitating employment for Artisans later that month. She might have been affianced for their first legitimate commission, then. Her mother would have started clipping the articles then, a minor hobby Antoinette may or may not have persevered with.

Genevieve wasn't sure when she'd stopped using Mrs Locke as her professional name, but in the very last article about the so-called Myriad before Reuben had vanished and her world had fallen apart, she'd been Mrs McAvey.

It had been in the scant few weeks between her full recovery from childbirth last June and conceiving again in early autumn. They'd gone after a flagrant fraud, an Artisan able to produce illusory stigmata at will, garnering such a crowd of fanatically devoted followers that the Agency had felt obliged to send in a team used to more directly destructive Artistry. Reuben had sneered over the triviality of it, though she could recognise now that he had already been distracted; otherwise, he might have made Cecelia renege on the contract acceptance. But even discounting the fanatics, it had turned out the rogue Artisan could do more with illusion than merely make his hands and feet appear to bleed – she shuddered at a sudden feeling of spiders crawling over her skin – so it hadn't been as easy as all that.

The arrest had been controversial, and thus in the papers, because a certain sophistry suggested that if Artistry was a holy gift, rather than a devilish pact, then the stigmata technically couldn't be false. Arresting the Artisan for fraud implied the Agency was contradicting its own firm stance that Art wasn't witchcraft, at least according to the broadsheets that loved to rake the coals. They'd positively salivated as the debate ramped up again when the allegations about Bishop Varley came out a few months later.

Genevieve wondered why she'd abandoned her professional name and used her actual married name. Perhaps – she touched her stomach, stroking it like a pet – it had been the only thing she could think of to appease her stubbornly incompetent womb.

Oliver had taken down a bound book, the prettily gilt spine one of many, but attracting his attention regardless. She wasn't close enough to read the title, but her glimpse of the distinctive gilt wreath centred on the front of the plain binding told her it was her copy of *A Christmas Carol*, published earlier in the same winter as her affiancing.

She'd forgotten she possessed a first edition of the perennially popular ghost story, and for some reason, that lapse, of all the memory lapses she constantly struggled with, struck her hard. She caught herself running a hand over her stomach again.

Oliver opened the book, frowning. Genevieve recognised the familiar bright illustration on the frontispiece, and the red and blue lettering on the title page, before he turned back to an inscription written across the yellow endpaper in faded black ink. Almost as soon as he'd glanced at it, Oliver snapped the book shut again, frown now magnified enormously. Staring straight ahead, he slipped the book into his coat, as stealthy as a pickpocket – a buzzman, if the twins' favoured Gothic stories were to be believed.

Before Genevieve could query this odd behaviour – it was indisputably *her* book, long lost amid others of similar bindings, and she wanted it – Fletcher called out from the desk.

'I've found something. Not convinced it's relevant. But it does…does answer a question or two.'

He'd uncovered a swath of paperwork tracing the sale of the Belgravia house to Sir Kingsford Locke. A few impersonal letters were included, transactional missives between Reuben and her cousin.

Her father had left the house to her, after all. Or he'd left it and other effects to her mother, with the usual stipulations to ensure that both Antoinette and Genevieve would be taken care of, and then Genevieve had inherited upon her mother's death, which had been…which had been fairly recent, had it not? Last summer, before or perhaps after the stillbirth, quite suddenly. She'd lost her baby, her mother, her childhood home and her husband all in the space of a few months. No wonder her mind felt so vague and hazy much of the time, not even considering her condition.

Either way, the inheritance had evidently gone to her husband under coverture, of which Cecelia's current cause had much to say, and neither parent had thought to stipulate it for Genevieve's sole and separate use in their wills.

Or perhaps one or both had. Her signature was on these contracts and deeds of sale, alongside Reuben's. A couple of loose letters were tucked into the pages, addressed to her from Kingsford, which she had no memory of reading. The briefest perusal indicated he was querying whether she truly agreed to the sale. The final missive ended with the promise that he would return the property to her, and only her, upon her merest word.

He had paid out though, substantially. Some of those funds must have gone to buying the Holland Park house, and its modern outfitting, but a good proportion of it was unaccounted for, according to Fletcher, or at least the reports he had from Mr Hartley.

Fletcher brightened and dived into a snowdrift of papers in a drawer. He pulled out an invoice, the name of the premises writ large within ornate bordering at the top: A.F. Gatwick, purveyor of clockworks. Addressed to Reuben and dated last summer, the invoice was marked overdue, and then stamped and signed off as paid. The crabbed black writing did not itemise, but totalled an eyewatering amount, more than the most fashionable and luxurious carriage and most highly-bred team of horses might have cost.

'Look at the dates,' he said. 'He paid it off as soon as the sale of the house was finalised.'

'Is this a cover for gambling?' It was the single vice Genevieve could think of that might have drained their finances so dramatically, in both rapidity and extent, without leaving much of a physical trace on Reuben or the household itself.

Oliver firmly shook his head.

'One would not typically receive a polite reminder in the post if months overdue on a gambling obligation of this size,' Fletcher explained with elusive tact.

Cecelia had come to look it over, too. She tapped the address at the top of the invoice. 'That's near the apothecary,' she said.

That was Mrs Murphy's and Miss Adler's shop. The midwifery kept Mrs Murphy busy enough, but Miss Adler's proprietorship was both profitable in its own right and supplied her partner in medicinals for the women under her care.

'Artisan district,' Oliver rumbled. 'Explains the cost.'

Genevieve nodded decisively, relieved to have a direction. 'We must visit—'

7

THEY WERE OUT IN THE CARRIAGE house.

They must have eaten, or at least Genevieve's stomach now had the bilious feeling she suffered every time she ate, rather than the hollow feeling that sapped her when she refused to eat. One of the others, probably Cecelia, had gathered the meal remnant and brought it over on a single tray to sit on a side table in case of recurrent hunger after the exertion of Art. This told Genevieve she might not have eaten enough to satisfy her ever-fussing friends, and she should brace herself for some gentle nagging.

For now, they settled to practising. Cecelia took Fletcher's chair, but Fletcher didn't lay fingers to her hand. He stood a few feet away, trying to enforce coercion Art upon her without touching or speaking, a very advanced skill.

After long moments of intense frowning, he asked, 'Anything?'

'I'm craving pineapple,' Cecelia said helpfully. 'Is that you?'

He sighed and moved closer, staring at her so intently that Cecelia started giggling and had to be severely told to sit quietly so he could concentrate, which made her giggle more.

Oliver was practising his telekinesis Art. He used it commonly enough when aiding his brothers dockside, but that was a simple, limited application, a metaphysical tool for lifting the bulkiest, heaviest crates, like a body belt to protect his back was a physical tool. Right now, he was trying something far more delicate: mentally moving his paper-knife from the house, bringing it across the garden to his hand here in their workroom. It was small and light; the difficulty of the challenge was in calling it to him, through two cracked-ajar windows, without line of sight on it. He stared in the direction of the house as if he could see through walls.

Genevieve sat in the other corner, a few buckets of water positioned about her. She let fire bloom between her hands. She could toss this fireball like an arrow across the room and hit any target. Yet she couldn't help but think that that had been the first thing she could do with her Art when it manifested, an adolescently enthusiastic strike. She remembered Kit Whitely, taunting Reuben for only being able to produce ice spears with his ice Art.

Indeed, her Art was not fireballs, it was fire, setting the air itself on fire, and what had she been doing for all her years with Oliver and the others if mere fireballs were still all she could do? As disloyal as it felt to admit it, Reuben had coasted on his natural ability, but she had worked to develop hers, hadn't she?

Even as the question occurred to her, a sort of ripple or pulse or cloud or – a sensation, anyway, hard to capture in words if only because she could not focus on it – swallowed her. It was that foggy feeling again, but this time she could almost see it descending upon her like a personal pea-souper. As thick as it was, she could almost resist it. She could fight it—

Oliver scrambled towards the side table as the paper-knife came flying through the narrow window high above it. He missed his catch, and it bounced across the floor, the dull double-chime jolting Genevieve back to herself. She smiled at Oliver in congratulations and turned back to the fire cupped in her hands without thinking any more about it.

Thinking about what?

She murmured, 'That we used to be formidable.'

'You still are,' said Oliver, making her start.

She looked up. It was very late: the high windows showed full dark outside, the sole time of true ease in the heat and stink of this highest of summers. One of the others, probably Oliver, had lit the lamps. The tray with leftover food was now picked clean; the others had evidently taken refreshment as their practice had taken energy.

As sometimes happened, she'd been in her Artisan reverie for some time. That was why Reuben had had to interrupt her so often. She had been wrong, as usual, to snap at him.

Oliver was behind her, floating his paper-knife over his spread palm, slowly rotating it, a small motion she knew took immense control of his blunt telekinesis Art. The thin, flat steel blade was set into a corkscrewing handle of marine ivory, the pale coils as fat and organically muscular as the octopus tentacles tattooed on his forearm. It was one of his favourite possessions.

It must have been a gift from someone who knew his skin intimately.

She shook her head, chasing away the intrusive thought and the strange twisting feeling that trailed along with it.

Oliver smiled at her, wry, looking almost caught out. But he finished his thought without letting the paper-knife drop from its Art-powered hover. 'You've always been.'

Genevieve was not foolish: she didn't need the twins' teasing – *I suggest you turn to your Seaman William Oliver Bennet, Gin* – to know Oliver held her in warm regard. She held him in much the same. And perhaps, in a different world, a wealthy heiress and a self-described wharf rat might have been tempted to make more of their mutual regard. In their world, however, it was miraculous enough they'd managed to cling to their friendship across what was not a social divide but a great echoing social chasm. The bridge had been Artistry, and even that had not made for a robust connection without some stubbornness on both their parts.

And while she was not above allowing herself to briefly bask in his admiration, she was also somewhere in the hinterland between wifedom and widowhood, and still deeply loved her missing husband despite herself. Oliver would always be her friend; he would never be more than that. Reuben had not needed to be jealous. Even if she *had* met Oliver first—

Her thoughts led into the smothering fog. Something in her mind twisted and tried to find a different path. A welter of scents assailed her: the spiciness of cinnamon and cloves, the subtle aroma of hot tea, the faint malodour of kitchen drains. She felt the touch of a warm hand. She heard a voice in her head, her own voice, saying, in arrogantly assured tones, 'You *are* an Artisan. We can help each other.'

It was a memory, piercing through the muddle in her head like the abrupt lift of morning mist to reveal the soaring blue of a spring sky. She had taken Oliver's hand, she had said—

Oliver spun on his heel.

His hands were raised, face setting into the stony expression that meant he was rapidly accessing Art. Genevieve turned the same way – or, really, ponderously rotated on her planetary axis – own hands coming up with flames already rising high from her palms, as clear a warning as the rattle on a snake in the Americas.

Kit Whitely stood by the door to the little vestibule that in turn opened to the mews, one hand raised in surrender, the other splayed against the wood of the doorframe. His cool green eyes met hers. He had the sort of face that promised heaven; his eyes were wicked.

As unruffled as he had been when she'd threatened him with fire under Reuben's command, he said, 'Quite the response. Is that healthful for your condition?'

'*Do not*,' Genevieve snarled, and swallowed.

She had threatened to burn this young man alive. Oliver was right. They had done wrong things under Reuben's command. They had been unthinkingly obedient. She didn't understand it.

She clapped her hands together, quenching the flames, and matched his cool tones. 'Do not presume to tell me what is or is not healthful for my *condition*.'

He slouched to one hip. 'Somewhere in the middle on the Locke temper scale, it seems. How lucky for all of us that Miss Lucinda's precipitating catalyser did not give her flames.'

Genevieve raised her eyebrows at his phrasing. It used the formal, if redundant, Agency terminology for the traumatic event theorised to trigger Artistry within a narrow window of opportunity, to wit, adolescence. The shocking details of the Varley Affair, where the bishop had indiscriminately beaten orphan children, force-blooming Art in those possessing the latent potential for it, added grim evidence to the case.

Whitely had caught her silent surprise. 'I read,' he said, a touch testily. 'They did manage to inflict *some* literacy on us.'

'Startled me,' Oliver grumbled, reverting to the taciturn, as he often did around strangers. He jerked his chin indicatively as he added the succinct, 'Wards.'

Genevieve followed his gaze to the door, frowning. That was right; one of Oliver's litter of lesser Arts was the ability to create minor embedded Artworks of the warding variety. Both vestibule doors, out to the mews and into the workroom, had not only been locked, but also warded, set to warn Oliver of encroaching Artistry. How had she forgotten that? It was one of the first Arts he'd admitted to, back when he was resisting the very notion that he could be an Artisan at all.

'I went around those,' Whitely said, in the same vague way he had explained his ability to ignore the constraints of iron back in the Gallentry cell all those months ago. 'Might have broken them, actually.'

Cecelia hadn't even started to react; she didn't have weapons Art and she didn't have a fighter's instincts, not physically anyway. Now she came hurrying over and took Whitely's still upraised hand to shake. 'Mr Whitely! I'm so very glad you're not dead.'

'I am, also,' he said politely.

'But what happened here?' Cecelia asked, looking down at their joined hands in surprise.

He withdrew his fingers from hers and put the hand behind his back, nodded to Genevieve, smiled at Oliver, eyed off Fletcher. Smiled again at Oliver, a less polite smile. 'I've come about the box.'

Genevieve tilted her head. 'Does Alex know you're here?'

'I am here because I'm aware I left you chained up in a dungeon for longer than I had to,' Whitely said. 'And I'm also aware you could have told Alex that, and didn't. And also because he loves you and will regret not helping you more, after a time. And *also* because if I help you before then, we might stand a chance of making it away on our steamer.'

That had been a long-winded way of avoiding a short and simple answer. 'He doesn't know you're here.'

Whitely didn't reply.

'Did he tell you about my request, then?'

She didn't think he would have, given how certain he'd been that Whitely would want to help and how adamant he'd been that he not. Whitely gave a simple shake of his head to confirm it.

'How did you find me?'

'I followed you home,' he said, which neatly answered the next question as well, how he'd known about the box at all.

He must have been nearby, using his highly specific teleport Art for eavesdropping. Unconscionably rude. But he hadn't overheard the entire conversation, because he was merely suspicious that Alex might change his travel plans to help his cousin, rather than indignant that he'd already promised to. The park, then.

'But how?' she demanded. 'We were walking through the gardens, far from any door. One of us would have seen you.'

'The rose bower.'

She remembered the glance Alex had given the arched trellis with its trained tumbles of stalks and leaves and wilting flowers as he'd said something Whitely might have considered provoking. *I like to let him think he is*, indeed.

'That was hardly a door.'

He presented her with a small and decidedly smug bow of acknowledgement. 'My Art begs to differ.'

'So I suppose you just walked in through our locked and warded doors here?' Fletcher demanded, disgruntled.

'Do you not understand the nature of a door Artisan…' Whitely lowered his eyes for a moment and then finished, 'Mr John Fletcher?'

Fletcher folded his arms. 'I've never even heard of a door Artisan.'

'Teleportation and telekinesis,' Whitely told him. 'Hooked to doors.'

'Thresholds,' Oliver announced.

Whitely stilled, before he smiled his angelic smile. 'You know how I love a thinker, Mr—' Again came the pause. 'William Oliver Bennet. But not Mr Bennet?'

'Mr Oliver, for Artisan business.'

'How do you know our proper names?' Fletcher remained determined to be difficult. 'We've never been introduced to the likes of you.'

'I *read*,' Whitely repeated, this time more than a touch annoyed. Genevieve was not the only one puzzled by this answer. He looked from blank face to blank face. 'The Myriad? You're in the papers? Not lately, admittedly. Not since igniting that furore over the stigmata last year.'

Again, a spring day gleamed through fog. She had an awareness, ever-growing, that glorious sunlight would soon break through, but for now it was still a glimmer, shrouded.

They were the Myriad. They had been in the papers. They had joined together, Artisans tended to be solitary, but they'd had a point to prove to the Society charged with forming the Agency at an increment of inches per year, and they'd—

They'd stopped a thief, and deterred a fraudulent medium, and chased an earthworker Artisan first out of London and then entirely out of the country. His forte had been threatening to shake the gentry's homes down unless paid not to. He'd fled their attentions, spitefully quaking Guernsey hard enough to rattle windows back in Devon on his way to France, a reversal of the continental exodus of the seventeenth century.

Then the newspapers got wind and an *Illustrated London News* reporter came calling. He'd been fixated on Genevieve, the heiress with the pyrokinetic Art, and she'd tried to direct attention to the others.

She'd said, 'We have myriad Arts, all working together.'

He'd said, 'Oh, the Myriad, I like that,' and Genevieve had avoided newsmen ever since.

It had been a preposterous name, and had stuck. And she and Oliver and Cecelia and Fletcher had stuck too, taking enforcement contracts first from the Society and then, at last, the Agency, to quell the use of illicit Art in London and further afield, particularly when the rogue Artisan had Art beyond the skill or range of Agency enforcers. They were eventually in direct competition with the Lockes, though the twins tended to the sorts of contracts that anonymous government men wanted carefully swept under rugs, while the Myriad performed the fancy flourishes feted atop scarlet-hued carpets. Reuben had liked it that way. He'd liked the name, too.

She'd had her own professional name, the way Oliver, rightly Mr Bennet, was Mr Oliver, for Artisan business. She remembered that now. She'd been Mrs Locke.

She started. She *knew* that. They'd found a book, like a commonplace book, and it had been filled—

'You don't have Locke's blessing to be here?' Fletcher asked, sounding disapproving.

Whitely turned that cool look on him. 'Do I require his blessing to be here?'

'I don't know how things work with…' Fletcher swept a hand in the air to encompass what he wasn't saying. 'I mean, if you play the part of the wife, you need his blessing, surely.'

Whitely suddenly looked more devilish than saintly. 'Why am I the wife?'

Fletcher flailed and then said, 'Because you're the pretty one?'

'Well,' Whitely said, after a delicate pause in which Genevieve valiantly fought the urge to laugh, and Cecelia lost the battle and covered her mouth to hide it. 'I put Mr Locke to bed some time ago and he doesn't wake up once he's out, isn't that right, Mr Oliver?'

He looked at Oliver in innocent enquiry. Oliver folded his arms, reluctantly beginning to smile; he blushed, too. Whitely started looking less innocent and more interested. At least he was distracted from eyeing off poor blundering Fletcher like he was somehow going to use his harmless little Art to turn him inside out.

The door Artisan was barely hiding his own smile as he finished, 'He will never even know I came here.'

'Don't much like going behind his back,' Oliver said seriously, and Cecelia made a noise of agreement.

There was no pleasing some people; the kidnapping was off the bloody table now, after all. But then their objection to taking Whitely had never been about *Whitely's* feelings on the matter.

'I don't much like him going behind mine,' Whitely pointed out.

'I didn't much like him and Lulu telling me my husband's dead when he's not,' Genevieve snapped.

She would not be made to feel guilty for using Whitely as he wished to be used – Alex had betrayed her first, and she wasn't the one who had snuck from his bed to deliberately act against his wishes.

'Since it is axiomatic that your husband is set on villainy,' Whitely said, 'they made the best decision they could under the circumstances.'

The enveloping fog did not just deaden Genevieve's mind; it took the edge off her feelings as well. She knew she felt too little anger, too little alarm about what Reuben might be planning. Nonetheless, she did not think it could be villainy. She was only mildly curious about what it could be, then, and only if the question was placed directly in front of her, bills and invoices and accounts stacked up high enough to be glimpsed through the fog. As soon as she looked away, it was gone.

But she did feel anger to have the Locke twins defended for their part in the matter. And she did want the box opened. So Alex could go whistle, for all she cared for him at this very moment. Except—

'I don't like you,' she informed Whitely bluntly. 'You are cold and sly and I think you are using my cousin and abusing his good nature.'

Whitely favoured her with a long, cool, stare. 'As forthright as the rest of the Lockes,' he said eventually. 'You want me to justify myself, I suppose?'

Taken aback by his lack of overt reaction to her challenge, she could think of nothing else to do but nod, at which he said, 'Justify yourself first, then, *Mrs Reuben McAvey*.'

Cecelia gasped, Fletcher said, 'I say!' and Oliver shook his head. But Genevieve felt no shock, no insult. Instead, she reached for justification for the man she had chosen to marry, and found none except a love that seemed more blind by the minute.

Whatever her expression was, it seemed to settle Whitely's hackles. He coughed lightly and fiddled with his sleeves, head dipping briefly in something that might have been an apology if she'd squinted at it.

'If it's any consolation, I'm also bewildered as to why the soft-hearted idiot deigns to care for me.' His attention snagged. 'That's rather beautiful.'

He drifted past her, past the others, attention fixed on the box, focus narrowed in on the tracery of Artistry festooning it, imperceptible to mundane eyes.

'Oh, beautiful,' he murmured again.

His hand hovered over the lock and then he took a turn about the box without touching it, admiring it very much in the nature of one artist respectfully admiring another's artistry, the mundane but no less transformative sort.

'Can you not open it?' Genevieve demanded.

'Not yet, no.' He was wearing a tiny smile. 'Which is interesting in and of itself. I can open anything.'

'Obviously not,' Fletcher scoffed.

Whitely paused in his stroll. Watching Fletcher, he slowly removed his coat and started to roll up his sleeves.

'And,' Fletcher said, obviously feeling advantaged, 'you should be wearing cufflinks with that shirt. And a good deal more clothing in general. Must you walk around half-naked?'

Whitely looked down at himself. Light coat, no waistcoat, no neck-cloth, no gloves, no hat, and a shirt thin enough to hint at the absence of underlayers. He was, indeed, half-naked by any decent standard, and underdressed even for an Artisan, really. If Genevieve's knowledge of male Artistry Dress could be extrapolated from her husband to men in general, he should at least wear the undershirt meant to preserve his outer clothing from bodily soil. She supposed he gave no thought to Alex's laundering bill.

Fletcher, of course, was dressed entirely as was proper for a man of his social standing, according to the books and plates he consulted; he was so appropriate, it was almost inappropriate for an Artisan. He had to walk around feeling overheated all the time. No wonder he was on the edge of out-of-sorts so often.

'I run hot,' Whitely said, looking back up from examining his state of undress. He dropped his coat on the floor. 'Artisans run hot. We're allowed to dress for our work, like the pit lasses can wear trousers and the farmers can wear smocks and fisherwomen can hike their skirts up and show their legs and be damned to what people who don't have to work for a living say about it.'

Fletcher folded his arms and scowled at the smaller man. 'I'm just as much an Artisan as you and I still manage to be decent.'

Whitely lowered his lashes and murmured, 'Perhaps I have more Art than you.'

'What!' Fletcher yelped. 'There's no correlation between how powerful you are and how hot you run.'

'Isn't there?' Whitely eyed off the decimated tray on the side table. 'I'm hungry, is there more food?'

This was not a change of subject. Artisans ran hot, and they ran hungry. Whitely with his angelic mien was now implying he had so much more Art than Fletcher that he not only had to dress much lighter but that he had to eat more too.

Cecelia was smothering a smile again. She found Whitely and his unmitigated cheek charming; she'd found him charming when they'd met him drunk and wild last year and she quite obviously found him no less so sober and provoking.

'There's scones in the kitchen, Mr Whitely,' she told him.

'No more Mr Kit, Miss Delacorte?' he asked her.

'I know your proper name now, Mr Whitely.'

'But you can call me Kit, Miss Delacorte.'

Cecelia was openly smiling back at the door Artisan in unfeigned delight now, until she abruptly sobered. Genevieve assumed this was because she had caught Fletcher's disapproving eye, but her friend suddenly approached Whitely.

'I must extend my deepest apologies for trying to use my memory Art on you, back in Gallentry.' It was almost a blurt; it must have been troubling her, behind the usual light manner she used to forcibly railroad her opponents into underestimating her.

'It wasn't your Art that concerned me,' he said, and there was a concentrated pause while all of them resolutely did not look at the Artisan who could have burned him alive with a single thought. Even Whitely mustered the courtesy to not look her way.

'I am also sorry for using coercion on you,' Fletcher said ungraciously. 'It was borderline illicit Art, and I must thank you for not reporting me.' His face screwed up, but he managed a muttered, 'Much obliged, Mr Whitely.'

'I do not inform on behalf of the *Agency*,' Whitely told him, with such delicate distaste that Genevieve was inexorably reminded that their ideals during the formation of the Agency had not entirely come to fruition, particularly as it related to this young man. 'Anyway, *your* Art is no danger to me, no matter your bad habits.'

Fletcher drew up on his dignity. 'What do you mean?'

His huffy indignation was tempered with a real anxiety he would never think appropriate to openly express. Genevieve was not the only one who'd noticed that their Arts had diminished.

'It won't work on me anymore.' Whitely held out an opened hand, palm bent to flex his wrist, skin laid bare and taut. 'Have a try, you'll see.'

The fraught, if not pregnant, pause this time centred on that hand, extended in a way that was intended to be provocative and yet was somehow vulnerable. Genevieve finally saw what Cecelia had already seen – his littlest finger was a mere nub, excised. She was sure he'd had all his fingers when they'd first met him last year. His shaky state during his brief incursion into the dungeon cell flashed through her mind. She'd been fairly shaky herself; if he'd lost a finger by then, she'd not noticed the lack.

Whitely's impertinently challenging expression twisted when he noticed the direction of their rapt gazes. He put the hand behind his back, silenced.

'Shall I fetch you some scones, Mr Whitely?' Cecelia enquired, stepping bravely into the breach.

A smile flickered back into place. 'Mr Fletcher can fetch them.'

'What!' cried Fletcher again. 'But—'

Genevieve turned sharply, or as sharply as an exceedingly gravid woman could. She was still tall and imposing, perhaps even more so than usual, and had moreover her so-called dissection look, with which she lacerated Fletcher before he could lay out which sex, and which class of that sex, he considered appropriate to be delegated to the kitchen.

He did not dare finish his sentence nor even look towards Cecelia. He muttered ungraciously to himself and, collecting the tray, went out the garden door.

'Now he's gone,' Whitely said, suddenly sounding much brisker. 'Is there anything else I need to know regarding this box you want me to open?'

Genevieve glared at him now. 'Are you implying Fletcher might have something to do with it?'

Fletcher had been with the team almost from the start. She'd met him soon after— She stopped. The thought slipped and resumed. She'd met him even before she and Reuben had formed the association the newsmen called the Myriad. He was surely trustworthy.

'He was especial friends with Reuben McAvey, was he not?'

'I'm sure he thought so,' Cecelia said. 'But it turns out none of us were especial friends with Reuben, were we?' She met Genevieve's eyes, frowning.

'I suppose not,' Whitely said, after a silence just lengthy enough to imply he was wondering why they'd all so slavishly followed the man then.

Genevieve said, 'Fletcher knows no more about it than any of us do.'

Whitely nodded. He walked once more around the box. 'I can step from this side of the door to the other side of the door, but I'm not sure it's a good idea to go inside blind.'

'It's a bad idea.'

They turned at the new voice. Alex stood in the vestibule doorway. But not really Alex. He was being Locke, wearing his professional face, pistol pointed to the ground, calm and alert. His gaze was flickering to the tops of their heads, reading their intentions.

Ironically enough, if he'd had Artisan status, it would have been illegal for him to deliberately read their minds, except on Agency business, but his mere talent went entirely unregulated in that regard. It wasn't the *only* loophole the Society had failed to stitch closed as it created the Agency, but it was the largest.

As he eyed them, calm, competent and armed, Genevieve was reminded that he and his twin had spent a good deal of time now bringing in rogue Artisans, for private bounties, for the Agency, for the army, for the government.

Oliver evidently remembered the same. 'Here voluntarily.'

'Oh, I know,' Alex said. 'There's not a force on God's green earth that can hold the man if he's where he doesn't want to be.'

That had a bit of a bite to it. Whitely took a step closer to the box, expressionless. He rested his palm lightly on the wood, the same way he'd casually had a hand on the doorway Alex now stood in.

Cecelia was moving forwards, reacting as fast as Oliver had when Whitely had startled them all and it might have been a physical fight. This was a quieter conflict. Cecelia rose to the challenge with skills honed through the long years it had taken her faction to negotiate fair rules for Agency governance while being shouted at by older, richer, privileged men.

'Goodness,' she burst out giddily. 'Mr Locke! I haven't seen you in a terribly long time.'

'Good evening, Miss Delacorte,' Alex said. He put his pistol away and offered up a genuine smile.

'Your waistcoat!'

He ran a finger along his waistcoat. Now Cecelia had pointed it out, Genevieve noticed he was dressed elegantly and with some care, far more pristine than he'd been among the crowds. She knew he would not have taken his time dressing if he'd woken and found his lover gone. He'd've dressed in haste and then spent the trip over here grooming himself to keep his worry under control.

He gave no sign of concern now, however. 'It's a new dye,' he told Cecelia, giving the material a tweak. 'Synthetic.'

'It's so *bright*, I love it!'

'Cecelia, my dear, you can have an entire crinoline made in this colour, with gold braiding to boot. It would suit you down to the ground.'

He'd been paying more attention to the fashion plates in Lulu's magazines than he'd pretended. 'Mauveine measles,' Genevieve said with some asperity. 'Ladies, we're about business.'

Alex grinned and waved her off.

'I must visit the haberdashery,' Cecelia said, somewhat mechanically.

She wouldn't, not straight away. She'd visit the girls who worked the new dye factories first and make sure their lungs were still clear enough to breathe and their skin still clear of rashes. She'd spent her entire life at the forefront of causes. Her latest, now the Agency was firmly established, was a Ladies Committee for suffrage, but her very first had been campaigning for better conditions for factory girls. She'd been a matchgirl before her Art bloomed; some of her sisters were in the textile factories.

Alex's smile turned rueful. 'Write, and let me know, won't you?'

He resettled his coat. Only now did he turn to Whitely. Genevieve expected him to make at least some gesture of fondness towards the man, whom he had, after all, lied to her face to protect, but he merely looked him over, neutral again, Locke the bounty hunter.

'Take your hand off the box. You are not crossing that threshold.'

Whitely obeyed, so instantly, ostentatiously compliant that it went right through to suspicious. 'I am frankly astonished you woke up.'

Alex strolled towards him. 'Bed got cold. You unlock it already?'

Whitely tapped the side of his head and gave Alex an angelically sweet look that twitched along Genevieve's nerves. 'Read my intentions and find out.'

This earned, for unfathomable reasons, a quickly smothered smile. 'I know better than that, Mr Whitely.'

He didn't seem bothered that Whitely had given away to Cecelia the talent he'd long wanted kept quiet. It belatedly occurred to Genevieve that Alex had only ever wanted to be sure *Reuben* didn't know about it.

'If we're going to argue, can we do it in private?' Whitely asked.

'Keep trying it on,' Alex said, by which Genevieve guessed that if he let Whitely get him alone, the door Artisan would have him literally wrapped around him as fast and as tight as he had him metaphorically wrapped around his little finger, and that that was almost certainly the intention Alex would have experienced if he'd been foolish enough to accept the invitation to read it.

'At least sit down,' Whitely said. 'It's not fair you get to loom over me.'

Alex swept another look about the room, ignoring the occupants in favour of seeking out threat. He eyed off the box, and then took Whitely's hand and drew him further away, to the chairs pushed against the wall next to the table. He sat, and held Whitely's hand, and looked up at him. He opened his mouth to say something.

'I do not interfere with your commissions,' Whitely said. 'What makes you think you have the right to interfere with mine?'

'A commission, is it?'

Now Alex wasn't ignoring his cousin: he was looking at Genevieve in a way that made her very glad Whitely had shown up before she'd tried to take him forcibly. Alex would perhaps not have forgiven her as readily as she had assumed he would.

She was glad she could honestly say, 'He approached us, Lexi.'

'A debt is being paid,' said Whitely agreeably.

'You could have discussed it with me before vanishing in the night, hours before we're supposed to take the train.'

Whitely made a rather theatrically thoughtful face. 'How was I meant to discuss something you were keeping secret from me?'

'Ooh,' said Cecelia, before putting her hand over her mouth.

Alex had briefly shut his eyes. He hadn't been expecting the challenge, obviously. 'How did you know about it?' he asked Whitely.

'You know how. Like to let me think I am, hmm?'

'Eavesdropping, how exceedingly disrespectful of you.'

'Shall we talk about disrespect, Mr Locke? Shall we *discuss* it?'

Alex went still. His eyes flickered. 'Let's not.'

'Let's not?' enquired Whitely with icy courtesy. 'Because, *actually*, you be as angry as you want to be with me, Alex, since I'm really quite angry with you.'

This flatly unfriendly statement made Alex smile again. 'Good. We can have the argument in private now, if you like.'

'You already lost the argument, baby,' Whitely said.

Alex looked at the ceiling, still smiling. 'We've barely started the argument, sweetheart.'

'And yet you've still lost.'

Alex's light grip on Whitely shifted; he was no longer containing the man, but holding his hand. 'Kit, I will not have you risk yourself—'

'You have no right to stop me.' Whitely had flipped back to speaking in that cold and level voice. 'This is my decision, it is my *choice*, Alex.'

Alex let him go and slapped the top of the table, very much like his sister. He shot a look around at the silently watching Myriad contingent, and lowered his voice, though not quite enough. 'You don't have to earn me, sweetheart.'

Whitely made a small noise and said, 'That's not what this is.'

'Isn't it? I won't let you walk into this, Kit, I love you—'

Whitely scoffed in sudden, savagely furious, mockery.

'Mr Whitely!' cried Cecelia, sounding appalled.

Genevieve, shocked herself, started forwards, fairly sure she was about to slap the man for this affront against her cousin. But Alex caught her eye and shook his head. He was half-laughing, but he was also trying to school his features into a stern raised-eyebrows kind of look.

Whitely blinked a few times and bit his lip. 'Sorry, Alex,' he said. 'That is actually very sweet.'

'Oh, is it?' Alex said, his mockery far gentler. 'Is it, really? Is it actually very sweet? Could it be that I love you and will not stand by and watch you walk into what is so obviously a trap meant for you that it might as well have *Kit Whitely* written on it in bright bloody gaslit letters?'

'It's still my choice, Alex.'

Alex took a deep breath. He drew Whitely to his feet and turned him to face the box. Whitely immediately leaned against him, head on his chest, even as he obediently examined the box. Alex rolled his eyes in a way that made it clear this was a typical tactic; he also dropped a kiss onto Whitely's curls in a way that made it clear it was a tactic that typically worked. And Whitely relaxed against him in a way that made it clear it was a tactic that typically worked on him, too.

'That is a trap,' Alex said, pointing at the box with one hand while looping the other arm casually across Whitely's chest to tuck him even closer. 'That is a trap *designed* to make you want to walk into it, sweetheart.'

'Oh, hardly.' Whitely's hand had come up to rest on Alex's arm, fingertips crooked against the good wool of his sleeve. That missing finger was an accusation that Genevieve could not quite hear.

'Kit,' Alex said, shaking his head. 'It's a box only you can open. It's a favour you can do for someone dear to me. It's an interesting technical challenge. It's a new trick for your Art to learn. It's a way to show off. It is absolutely everything you love. It is *designed* to tempt you, and only you, in an alarmingly specific way.'

'Not *absolutely* everything I love,' Whitely murmured, eyelashes lowered.

'You already unlocked it, didn't you?' Alex asked with a sigh.

Whitely paused before saying, 'I have not.'

'You're going to.'

'Yes.'

'Yeah, all right.' Alex drew his pistol out again. He nodded to Genevieve and Oliver, silently telling them to prepare themselves, and waved Cecelia back. 'If you insist on it, you can do it from over here.'

'I, in fact, cannot,' said Whitely. 'There's an—'

The lights seemed to extinguish, or Genevieve felt as if she were ducking her head underwater in a warm bath, or there came the roaring sound of a stormy ocean. Then it all cleared away and she was shaking her head, as were the others.

Except Whitely, who had freed himself from Alex's light embrace and was standing with his hands on his hips, looking both irritated and amused.

'I'm going to try again,' he said. 'Pay attention. Try to fight it. I can't be the only Artisan capable of this. On the box, there is—'

And the world faded out, as dim and waterlogged as the thickest of fogs. Genevieve's head broke the surface again.

'Balls to the lot of you, try harder!' Whitely said. 'Oliver. You've got wards. You must be able to do this. Go around it, can't you?' Oliver shook his head, frowning. 'Focus. Look at the box. It has embedded—'

A sharp jangling noise snapped Genevieve back into awareness. She glanced around and saw that, again, she and Cecelia and Alex were blinking or shaking their heads. Whitely had his hand around Oliver's wrist; Oliver was looking confused as to how he'd arrived at the box. Whitely must have towed him there while he'd been lost. Bits of dull brass, the cogs and springs of clockwork, lay scattered at their feet.

'Thank you, Mr Oliver,' Whitely said.

'For what?'

'Try to remember. You'll need it.'

'What?'

'To go around it,' Whitely said, ever so helpfully.

'You are a wee bit infuriating,' Oliver informed him, which, really, they were all thinking.

'Mr Oliver has a stern voice,' Whitely said with extravagant delight. 'Alexander, did you know Oliver has a stern voice?' Oliver blushed properly this time. Whitely feigned a gasp. 'You *did*, didn't you? Is it Will Oliver now?'

'Yes, I did know he has a stern voice,' Alex said. 'Because sometimes when you're being a right little shit, *Mr Whitely*, you need someone older and wiser to tell you you're being a right little shit.'

'That seemed unnecessarily pointed.' Whitely edged right up against Oliver as if for protection.

Alex both fought off one of the smiles Whitely kept provoking, and glared a little. 'Get away from him,' he said, using his own stern voice.

It was not entirely clear exactly which of the two men he was addressing, but Whitely immediately sidled sideways, all wide innocent eyes and tiny smile. 'I'm not trying to be difficult. If I was capable of adequately explaining it, I would.'

Oliver said, 'Try.'

This was blunt to the point of rudeness, though Genevieve knew it was purely frustration cutting his eloquence to shreds. It took Whitely a moment to recognise he had been given an invitation rather than an order.

Slowly, he said, 'You helped me remove an embedded Art from the box. Like the one on—'

He stopped, eyes blank, as stonily frozen as if he'd met the eye of a Gorgon. After a stark second, he blinked. He looked confused. Then he looked deeply offended.

For some reason, he scowled at Genevieve. 'It's like that, is it?'

'If there was an embedded Art, how did you overcome it?' Cecelia asked.

He was still staring at Genevieve. 'I went around it,' he said slowly, testing each word. 'Oliver helped me break its source.'

He indicated the clockwork bits strewn about. Oliver shook his head in denial, or plain bemusement, which mirrored Genevieve's feelings completely.

'He has a secondary Art,' Alex said. 'It lets him fight off outside influences.'

'I do not, I just have a very disciplined mind,' Whitely said. He was frowning intensely.

'I call it his contrary Art,' Alex added. 'Go ahead, argue. Prove me right.'

Whitely shot him a look, then turned to Oliver. 'Not that having secondary Arts is a bad thing, Mr Oliver,' he said sweetly. 'In fact, it's really quite an attractive thing.'

'Stop it,' murmured Alex. 'What you're saying is that rather than this probably being a trap for you, it is one hundred percent *absolutely* a trap for you. So I think we're backing away slowly without unlocking it now, sweetheart.'

'I already unlocked it, baby,' Whitely said, and he glanced at the box.

The door swung silently open.

Out oozed mud, the pungently fetid smell reminiscent of the rankness that had choked the city this summer. It came in a slow, thick wave that spread across the floor with very much the consistency of melting chocolate ice-cream. Genevieve felt her gorge rise at the sight and smell. Whitely and Oliver backed away from the creeping encroachment until its momentum petered out.

Stillness returned to the room.

'Well. That was anticlimactic.' Whitely prodded the mud with the very toe of his boot.

The mud reared up like a sentient creature and swallowed him whole.

8

IT SUCKED BACK INTO THE BOX with an obscene slurp. Even as Alex and Oliver lunged in an instinctive attempt to drag Whitely out, the door slammed shut.

'I have never felt more like saying I told you so,' Alex said, palms laid to the wood. 'Oliver, help me tip this over. Cecelia, fetch me an axe.'

'Already tried axes,' Oliver said. He tugged fruitlessly on the door; it was locked again.

'Get me a fucking axe *right fucking now*.'

That was a sign of how upset he was. He happily swore in front of his sister and Genevieve; he never swore in front of Cecelia, even though she heard worse than Alex's language all the time, in her Artisan work and among her own family.

Cecelia dashed to where they'd left the tools they'd tried on their mystery package earlier. Oliver, brows raised, went to the other side of the tall box and the two men carefully lowered it until it lay on its back, the wood on the bottom now exposed.

Alex took the silently proffered axe from Cecelia, hefting it much more easily than her.

'Most Artisans think in straight lines.' He sounded different than usual; this was Locke the bounty hunter in full flight, casually testing the weight of a very sharp axe as he stared at the box in calm evaluation. 'Every problem's a nail to a hammer, as they say. Tried to go through the door even after it was obvious it was warded against Art. None of you thought to try the top or the bottom of the box and I'm wagering the Artisan who embedded that warding Art didn't think of it either.'

He hoisted the axe and cracked it through the bottom of the box with one controlled blow. He began to wriggle the blade of the axe, breaking the hole open wider, and Genevieve came beside him and turned the wood to ash with a precise application of flame.

Nodding to her in professional appreciation, Alex knelt and reached into the box, up to his shoulder. He grunted in triumph and pulled hard, dragging Kit Whitely out by an ankle.

Whitely had his eyes squeezed shut. Strangely, there wasn't a trace of mud on him, and none oozed out behind him. He lay still for long enough that all four of them were leaning over him in concern and had to jerk out of his way when he suddenly lurched to a sitting position. He took a fast look at all their faces and grabbed hold of Alex, very tightly.

'Alex,' he whimpered.

'That's unexpected,' Alex said, stroking his hair. 'Where are you hurt?'

'I'm fine,' Whitely whispered, muffled into his chest. 'I got a fright. Sorry, Alex. You were right.'

Alex's face was briefly a picture of befuddlement, but then he shrugged and pulled the smaller man to his feet. He picked up Whitely's discarded coat, gently helped him into it and buttoned it up slowly, no doubt calming himself down. Then he looked around at the rest of them.

'Good evening to you all,' he said. His arm was around Whitely. 'Genevieve, if you need anything else, don't call on us.'

But even as he said the words, he was raising his eyebrows to her, a pointed message reminding her of his promise, that he'd get Whitely away and come back.

As he walked a silently compliant Whitely towards the vestibule door, Fletcher came through the garden door, burdened with a new tray, laden with a plate of piled-up scones, a little bowl of jam and one of cream, and a large teapot and cups and saucers.

'Scones and tea,' Fletcher said, sounding wounded to discover they were leaving already. Notwithstanding, he carried over the tray to them to proffer his bounty.

'Scant sleep and train tickets,' Alex countered. 'Thanks anyway, Fletcher.'

Whitely took a scone as Alex put a hand in the small of his back and guided him out the door.

'It'll be dry without the jam and cream,' Fletcher shouted after them. Looking put-out, he set the tray down. 'What did I miss?'

'Everything,' Oliver said.

'What took so long?' Genevieve asked.

'I couldn't find the plates,' he said. 'And then I thought the scones were a bit stale, so they'd definitely need at least some cream.' He looked sadly at the door where Whitely had walked off with a deficient scone. 'And then I couldn't find the thing, the tool, to whip the cream. And then I thought tea would be nice and I had to build the fire back up in the stove. And then I couldn't find the tea – really, they do not organise things logically in that kitchen. And then I thought the tray needed a little something else since we had guests, so I had to find a little vase and a flower to put in it. But, nonetheless, here it is and would any of you care to partake?'

Cecelia and Oliver were standing either side of Genevieve. Without turning her head to look at them, she was certain she was not the only one staring at Fletcher open-mouthed.

'My goodness,' Cecelia whispered reverently. 'We should always send Fletcher to the kitchen.'

He looked both mortified and pleased. 'I like things to be done properly.'

He picked up the teapot and began to pour, and then his hand shook, enough that steaming liquid spilled all over one of the saucers. He put the pot down and mutely pointed at the box.

Kit Whitely was standing next to it.

He was very still and had his hands demurely linked together, eyes lowered. Aside from his coatless state, wild hair, and a few smudges on his trousers, he was very much the picture of a devoted servant awaiting his master's command.

'My goodness,' Cecelia said again.

She immediately started towards the interloper, and Oliver reached out one large hand and rested it on her shoulder, halting her before she could walk herself into danger.

'Shapeshifter,' he rumbled.

Some Artisans could duplicate themselves and send their copies through walls to spy or reconnoitre, but those copies were translucent, wavering, fleeting. Others could talk to versions of themselves in other worlds, or at least they said they could. But in this situation, where the copy was solid and visible and perfect, it had to be a shapeshifter, one of the rarest Artisans in an already rare tapestry.

Reuben had sent them a shapeshifter in a box. It had drawn in and copied Kit Whitely, of all people. She couldn't understand why, except her cousin had said Reuben had it in for Whitely and she supposed now that he must do.

'When I was crossing through the mirrors.' The Whitely copy's voice was low and flat. 'I kept feeling like I might get trapped in one.' It was looking at them now, eyes clear and guileless. 'I feel like that now.'

'I suppose you would,' Fletcher said. He carefully poured another cup. 'Would you care for tea?'

'Is Alex safe?' the shapeshifter asked.

'Yes,' Genevieve said. 'He left with… Well, he left with you. The person you copied.'

Its fathomless gaze came to her, and it blinked slowly. It said, 'What did you say?' dreamily.

'Alex left with Kit Whitely.'

'I'm Kit Whitely,' it said, sounding more alert.

Cecelia spoke gently, as if to a frightened child. 'You must be new at this. You just think you are. It wears off, or so I've heard.'

A frown dislodged the eerily smooth expression. 'I beg your pardon. I don't understand.'

'You're a shapeshifter,' Fletcher said. 'When Whitely moves far enough away, you'll remember that.'

'I'm not the shapeshifter,' the shapeshifter said. It looked down at its clasped hands and pulled them apart with an aborted curse before shoving them into its disarrayed curls. 'I'm not the sodding shapeshifter! Oh, God, Alex!'

His face was wild, and then he went blank, as blank as he'd been when Reuben had instructed Genevieve to set him on fire and she had moved to obey without a single question in her mind. That was how he dealt with fear, she understood then, by hiding it completely.

She felt the tidal rise of Art in him, powered by a panic that was not at all visible. The door of the box whipped open so hard, it cracked off and fell to the floor. The corners of the room started to creak, and the seam of the ceiling gave an answering groan.

Anything was a threshold to Whitely's Art, it seemed, when Alex was under threat. He was going to open *everything* that had so much as a line in it that indicated it could be torn apart.

Fletcher ran over to lay hands on him, shouting, 'Control yourself!' with a good strong dose of coercion in it.

Whitely turned on him a look that said he was utterly in control of himself and everybody was bloody well about to know about it. He'd been entirely correct: the coercion Art hadn't touched him.

The ceiling gave another shimmer, puffing plaster dust. Genevieve stared up at it. Oliver, wincing, wrapped his arms about Whitely, bringing to bear one of his minor Arts, the smothering of another Artisan's Art, related to his warding ability.

For a moment it seemed to work, and then Whitely gave a shake of his head and must have volleyed back with his contrary Art. The whole room shuddered. It felt exactly like the localised earthquakes the rogue earthworker Artisan had been causing back in '43. The door out to the vestibule flung open and slammed shut again, cracking the plaster.

Genevieve realised Whitely was going to bring the carriage house down. What a terrible way to learn he really did love her cousin.

Shapeshifter

THE AIR IN THE MEWS WAS still warm despite the late hour, and smelled like the shapeshifter's mouth tasted.

It still ate the scone, which was indeed dry.

As it got further from this one, the one it had copied, this one's memories, way of thinking, way of moving, all that made him him, softened, faded, became an echo. It made it hard to continue in this one's shape inside, and it left a void that was not yet filling with its real self.

At least the outside was easy. That took hardly any Art at all.

'Are you sure you're all right, Kit?' asked the big one. The shapeshifter had known his name a moment ago. He pulled it to a stop. 'You're only like this when you're very scared or in a lot of pain.'

He took the shapeshifter's face in his hands and raised it so he could look into its eyes. The mews was narrow and very dark. He had to peer closely.

This one loves the big one immensely, the shapeshifter thought.

Also, neither this one nor the shapeshifter liked questions, and this one had a definite method for dissuading those.

The shapeshifter went up onto tiptoes and brushed its mouth against the big one's mouth. It hoped the big one couldn't taste mud. It reminded itself not to make itself taller. It had to stay at this one's height.

The big one stepped back with a shake of his head. 'Yeah, all right, where exactly are you hurt?'

He lifted the shapeshifter's hands and examined them, presumably looking for the injury he was worried about. He turned them over and stared at them, back and front, before saying, 'Damn, I forgot to give Gin a message.'

Holding the shapeshifter's hand in his, he led it back down the mews towards the carriage house. The shapeshifter remained oblivious until they got close enough to the source of his current shape. Memories and personality seeped back into it – into *him*, this one thought of himself as a him – and he understood that, without giving away a single hint with tone of voice or change in demeanour, Alexander Locke knew he wasn't truly Kit Whitely.

The shapeshifter also understood how he'd gone wrong. This time when he put his mouth on Alexander Locke's mouth, it was greedy and needy and generous and he practically pushed the big man against the wall with the force of it. Alexander Locke made a satisfying noise before managing to disentangle himself, far too swiftly for the shapeshifter's liking.

'This one loves you,' the shapeshifter told him.

'That's nice,' Alexander Locke said easily, leading the way into the little vestibule. He cut him a glance before saying, 'Maybe this one could not sneak off to take unnecessary risks, if he loves me so much.'

'You give this one everything and this one gives you nothing back. He wanted to give you something back.'

Alexander Locke halted. 'I fucking knew it,' he muttered.

'He had nothing, and he was used to nothing, and he was happy with nothing. And then he had something, and he got used to something and he was happy with something. And then you came, and you gave him everything and now he wonders if he will still be happy with something when you take everything away.'

'Why does this one think I'll do that?' Alexander Locke had his free hand on the door back into the main room, but he paused with a thumb to the latch. 'This one knows I love him, right? Whether he's useful to me or not?'

'This one knows he means something to you. But you are his everything. That's too much.'

'Thank you,' Alexander Locke said slowly. 'I should keep you on retainer. Now you just have to tell me you didn't hurt this one.'

The entire building shook.

In the wake of that shudder, the shapeshifter lifted his brows and said, 'I might have.'

In the moment of taking Kit Whitely into the box, the shapeshifter had slammed his head into the wood, knocking him woozy. He had the strong sense that he had been meant to keep going in that vein until Kit Whitely was terminally worse than woozy, that that was something he was fated to do, that he had to do, that he had no choice but to do.

But by then he had been solidly in the shape of his victim, and so he'd gone around that compulsion as a matter of pride.

This was not the sort of thing Kit Whitely knew how to explain to others, so the shapeshifter merely added, 'I think I was ordered to kill him.'

Alexander Locke's mild smile dropped on the instant. The door flapped open under his hand and slammed shut again right in his face.

Alexander Locke kicked it out of his way with a startling application of force.

9

THE VESTIBULE DOOR SLAMMED BACK OPEN with dramatic force and Alex was standing there, Kit Whitely peeking out at them from behind him.

It was as if the entire room exhaled. The tension washed out of Alex the moment he saw his lover safe and well. Whitely's Art snapped off, and he went limp in Oliver's hold. The last puffs of dust from his assault on the ceiling silently drifted, as grey and gritty as the worst of the city's dirtied snow. The walls and doors settled into what might very well be a new configuration in their frames.

Oliver didn't let Whitely go, though. Genevieve didn't want Whitely and his double to come close together, either. It felt dangerous, and that felt irrational, and she still didn't want it.

'But this one is not nearly as compliant as he pretends to be,' said the shapeshifter, tucking himself under Alex's arm to survey the room with blithe unconcern.

Putting a spread palm to his chest, Alex said 'Fuck,' on a long exhale, and then, 'Contrary Art.' He squeezed the shapeshifter with something that looked like gratitude.

'I can't copy Art,' the shapeshifter told him.

'I know, sweetheart, I know.'

'*Mr Locke*.' That was pure acid from Whitely.

The shapeshifter mimicked the narrowed-eyed expression Whitely was wearing. 'This is how this one looks when he is jealous. This is how I look when I am jealous, too.'

Alex removed his arm from around the shapeshifter's shoulders, pulling a face. 'Sorry. He's rather convincing, Kit.'

Whitely elbowed Oliver, who assumed the attitude of forbearance he adopted whenever his youngest brothers or nephews decided they could wrestle him. But Alex gave him a frown and a pointed flick of his index finger. Whitely, dutifully released, stepped away and tugged huffily at his shirt, as offended as a cat escaping the enthusiasm of a toddler.

Cecelia said, 'How did you know he wasn't Mr Whitely?'

'I don't kiss right,' the shapeshifter explained mournfully.

'Oh, the treachery,' Alex said, mild in the face of an outraged choke from Whitely. He lifted the shapeshifter's wrists. 'Finger missing from the wrong hand. He didn't copy you, Kit, he mirrored you.'

Whitely went a sallow ashy colour and sat down like his knees had melted into water, huddling into himself. He'd been frightened of being trapped in a mirror, Genevieve remembered.

'Kit?' Alex started forwards, both surprised and concerned. 'Go stand with Genevieve, lad,' he said over his shoulder as the shapeshifter tried to stay with him, catching hold of his sleeve.

'No!' the shapeshifter said, bypassing the sleeve to grab tight onto his arm. 'No, no, no.'

Genevieve looked as warily at the shapeshifter as he was now looking at her. It had not escaped her that Alex also didn't want the two versions of Whitely near each other.

'You do attract the strays, don't you, Locke?' remarked Fletcher.

'Oliver, would you take him, please?' Alex sounded a little desperate.

But Oliver was already kneeling next to Whitely, Cecelia beside him. 'You're not actually caught in the mirror, Kit,' she was saying. 'It is truly just a shapeshifter.'

Oliver pulled Whitely's arms down so he could look him in the eye. 'Not a mirror, Mr Whitely. Look. Cufflinks.'

Whitely's breathing slowed. He lifted his head and looked to where the shapeshifter was clinging on to Alex with both hands. The coat had pulled back to reveal cufflinks, which bore the same star as a pair of Reuben's, but in shades of pale old-bone yellow; it made them look like the ghost version of the real gold-and-enamelled-blue pair.

Both Whitely and the shapeshifter looked at the cufflinks and then looked down at Whitely's own loosely turned back sleeves.

Their expressions were identical. It would have been more unnerving if Genevieve hadn't grown up with a matched pair who quite often exchanged a look that might convince the gullible they could read each other's minds.

'Oh, indeed,' she said, enlightened. 'Fletcher told you you should be wearing cufflinks and that must have still been on your mind when the shapeshifter took you into the box. He picked up on it without realising you're not actually wearing any.'

Whitely stood up, ignoring the attempt at a helping hand from Oliver and Cecelia. He made an imperious fending-off, shaking-off motion at them and eased away, shoulders set in a stiff line, face set in determined composure.

'That's my coat he's wearing,' he said in a remote sort of way.

'You have plenty of coats now, Kit,' Alex said. 'The lad can keep it.'

'And where, precisely, were his hands when you noticed them, Mr Locke?' Whitely enquired while refusing to look at him.

'Sweetheart, I can't come to you until someone takes him off me,' Alex told him. 'He's probably under a compulsion to kill you, and I won't rely on his ability to keep fighting it off. He's not you, after all.'

'That's better,' Whitely said repressively. 'You sounded like you'd forgotten that.'

'For some reason I didn't pick you as the jealous sort,' Alex said, 'and yet now I can't understand why on earth I didn't.'

Whitely folded his arms. 'Fine, take the taller, prettier, nicer version of me to Japan, then.'

'He's exactly the sa— Oh, you will not provoke me.'

'We'll see,' Whitely murmured.

Alex, chuckling, started to peel the shapeshifter's fingers off his arm. 'Come on, sweetheart, go to Oliver.'

The shapeshifter clutched tighter, the fabric of his coat creasing under his fingers. 'No, Alex, please, I want to stay with you.'

'You like Oliver. He'll take care of you, won't you, Oliver?'

'Thanks,' Oliver said dryly. He nodded to the shapeshifter. 'I will.'

Alex extricated himself, the shapeshifter apparently transfixed by his smile long enough for him to win free. He retreated over to Whitely as Oliver crossed to the shapeshifter, as delicate as a hostage exchange from one of the twins' ridiculous Gothic novels.

The shapeshifter looked sulkily up at Oliver, plainly not pleased with the swap. 'This one is either promiscuous or he likes tall men.'

'Ooh!' said Cecelia, and 'Well, that seems petty,' said Fletcher.

'Is this my personality?' Whitely asked. 'How do you tolerate me, Alex?'

'With a great deal of pleasure, sweetheart.' Alex swept him into a fierce embrace. 'Jesus, Kit.' Whitely wriggled away, scowling. Alex laughed. 'I should have known he wasn't you the moment he admitted I was right.'

'Hah!' Whitely leaned around Alex to demand, 'Take my face off.'

'I don't have my own face, though,' the shapeshifter explained.

'Yes, you do.' Whitely straightened and his eyes brightened; he was suddenly looking at the shapeshifter with sharp curiosity instead of suspicion. 'Are you very young?'

'I don't know. Are *you* very young?'

'You're not me. How do you take a shape? Do you only mimic people?'

'Any living thing. I take the shape of people I've touched.' The shapeshifter blurred, making Genevieve blink. It felt like trying to make out the face of someone through a strong heat shimmer, or someone deep, deep underwater. When she looked again, he'd shifted into Alex. 'I've touched this one.'

'Oh my God, how does *anyone* tolerate me?'

'*Treachery*,' repeated Alex, grinning. He'd shed the last of his concern the moment Whitely had started taking an academic interest. 'If I didn't grow up with a twin, that'd be disconcerting.'

The shapeshifter reverted into Whitely in another shimmer. He looked weary, a hint of shadow about his wide green eyes. Genevieve suspected he was too tired to try to assimilate another shape when Whitely's form was already familiar, like shunning new heels in favour of worn-out but comfortable slippers. But, as if Whitely's question had corrupted his mental reckoning, he looked younger than Whitely now, a good deal younger.

Oliver, beside the shapeshifter, had raised his head like he was a hound scenting the wind.

'Takes some Art to change shape,' he said. 'Not much to maintain a shape.'

'But some,' Whitely said.

'Some.'

'So just—' He opened his hand. '—release the Art and you'll change back to your actual self.'

The shapeshifter clutched his belly. His knees began to buckle and he doubled over, edges blurring. 'No,' he said, 'No, no, no. I am made of mud, I am made of mud, I am made of mud.'

Oliver lunged; so did Alex, catching the shapeshifter before he could tumble all the way to the ground. Whitely sighed. To Genevieve's surprise, she found herself exchanging an exasperated shake of the head with him. The soft-hearted people in the room appeared to have forgotten that the shapeshifter was very much a Trojan soldier, smuggled within the gift horse. Who knew what his intentions were.

Well. Alex did. He sat beside the collapsed shapeshifter to let him lean on his shoulder as the strange spell began to pass. To Whitely, he said, 'He was upset and he looks like you, what did you expect me to do?'

'Don't get any bright ideas, Alex,' Whitely replied. 'You can barely manage one of me.'

Alex reached out a languid, yet still fast, hand and yanked Whitely down to his knees. He put the arm that wasn't cradling the shapeshifter around his shoulders. He said, very softly in his ear, 'You're everything to me, too, my little hedgehog.'

Whitely stiffened before rounding on the shapeshifter. 'You have no discretion!'

'How am I managing you now?' Alex asked him pleasantly, and Genevieve snorted and walked away to give them privacy, following the others over to the box. Out of the corner of her eye, she saw Whitely, wearing an offended expression and a tiny smile, squirm free.

She created a small lick of flame in her hand, and held it high within the interior of the box. Her flame flickeringly illuminated bare wood, bearing a few scratches but otherwise unmarked.

'No mud,' Oliver murmured.

'Not even the smell of it,' Cecelia added.

Fletcher squinched up his long nose in disgust. 'Could he actually be made from the stuff that oozed out of the box, then?'

Genevieve heard the shapeshifter give a whimper. 'It doesn't work like that,' she said. 'They're rare, but they're Artisans like the rest of us. Reuben did not create a human out of mud, for God's sake.'

She looked around. Whitely was coming back from the tea tray, a scone in each hand. He'd cut each one open and piled in jam and cream.

'You're not a golem,' he told the shapeshifter, holding out one of the scones. 'You are not made of mud.'

The shapeshifter brightened considerably and sat up to take the offering. 'Thank you,' he said. 'We didn't have scones in the workhouse.'

'You're not from a workhouse,' Whitely said irritably. 'Those are my memories, not yours.'

'But it feels true.' He crammed half the scone into his mouth and chewed enthusiastically.

'You eat like someone from a workhouse,' Whitely conceded.

'Magdalen?' the shapeshifter mumbled about crumbs.

'I would think not.'

'You should stay away from him, Kit.' Alex rose. The shapeshifter curled his free hand around his calf, under his trouser leg, happily munching on the rest of the scone. Alex ignored it. 'In case the compulsion takes control.'

'He doesn't hit hard enough to hurt me.' Whitely absently touched the curls on the side of his head as he took a bite of his own scone.

As if in silent contrition, the shapeshifter removed his hand from Alex's leg. Alex rewarded him with a casually fond pat on the head but also took the opportunity to move closer to Whitely.

'I think you're very young and very new,' Whitely told the shapeshifter. 'It's not safe for someone as young as you to spend too much time in other forms.'

Alex cleared his throat. 'When you say *young*—'

'Art comes on around the age of sixteen,' Whitely told him while still staring at the shapeshifter in that disconcertingly assessing way, the look Genevieve had mistaken for calculating and now realised was simply aristocratically self-possessed. 'But that's an average. I think he's quite substantially younger than that. Feel good about kissing him now?'

'I didn't feel good about *him* kissing *me* in the first place. If he's that young, wouldn't he remember your orphanage, not a workhouse?'

Whitely turned his impassive, thoughtful gaze on Alex. He gave a single nod.

'I was never in an orphanage.'

The shapeshifter spoke with a certainty that sounded both solid as steel and, given his professed lack of memories other than Whitely's, entirely unwarranted, but Whitely merely gave another thoughtful nod.

The others were crowding around now. Cecelia handed the shapeshifter a cup of tea and another scone. He sat cross-legged on the ground, alternating sips with bites, keeping his eyes down.

'His own memories are coming back.' Whitely knelt before the shapeshifter, bending to catch his downcast gaze. 'I need you to try now to release this form.'

The shapeshifter's hands began to tremble. Fletcher swooped over and rescued the cup and saucer before he could drop it to smash to smithereens on the scuffed wooden floor.

'Careful, it's heirloom,' Fletcher said prudishly, before frowning and looking at the teacups, which certainly were not heirloom. 'Did we…sell off the good tableware, Genevieve?'

'Fine,' Kit said, Alexander's hand resting on his head. 'Keep my sodding face like you're keeping my sodding coat.'

'There is no need whatsoever to swear at the child,' Genevieve found herself saying.

Whitely closed his mouth and examined her.

'That's her dissection look,' Alex said complacently. 'Step carefully, Mr Whitely.'

Whitely, tipping his head, turned to the shapeshifter to speak in more conciliatory tones. 'Your own shape will return when you're ready. You are not made of mud. You were only hiding there. What happens if I take those cufflinks away with me?'

The shapeshifter looked down at his shirt, a replica of Whitely's, part of the form he was wearing. He held up an arm, the better to consider the ivory-coloured cufflinks. 'I think. I think I will come back to myself missing a finger in truth,' he said, but with the lilt of a question to it.

'Probable,' Oliver said.

'Keep it in mind. It's not any living thing, it's any *organic* thing, but don't be complacent. Wear real clothes so you don't have to worry about losing buttons. Do you know your name?' Whitely looked at him with his head on one side. 'I think you know your name now.'

The shapeshifter thought about this question even longer. The more he thought about it, the younger he looked, a subtle shift of bones under the skin of the face he wore, a narrowing of the shoulders, a loosening in his posture. He might now be the chastened younger brother of the man kneeling before him. If a true reflection, he was even younger than Whitely had guessed.

'I think,' he said at last. 'Massimo Miraculi?'

Whitely blinked and then said, 'Someone has a sense of humour.' He pressed the shapeshifter's hand. 'These do-gooders will insist on taking you to the Agency to register. It's voluntary, you don't have to.'

'It is in his best interests to do so,' Fletcher said pompously.

'The Agency does provide an awful lot of protection to registered Artisans,' Cecelia said.

Neither of them quite had Whitely's full story. Neither, to be fair, did Genevieve, except the twins had abruptly become interested in advocating for reform of Agency procedure, an oddity she'd barely noted in the freshness of her mourning; they'd recruited Oliver and his good name, when she'd been too mired to help. She suspected Whitely would vehemently disagree with Cecelia regarding the Agency's lauded protections.

Alex calmly said, 'It has its moments, but it is getting closer to its founding ideals.'

‘Self-governance,’ Oliver said.

‘And it’s always been Artisan-run,’ agreed Alex.

Whitely made an impatient gesture. ‘Fine. But do *not* tell the Agency you can shift into anything you want. Tell them you can change into a cat, and only that.’

‘I like you,’ the shapeshifter told him.

‘Fine.’

‘I like everyone, I think.’

‘That must be your personality coming back, because I definitely don’t.’

‘You like very many people,’ Massimo told him. ‘You just don’t want to admit it because it makes you feel vulnerable.’

Alex snorted and Whitely rolled his eyes. ‘Discretion, learn it, my God.’

‘Were you truly this adorably earnest at this age, Kit?’ Cecelia asked him.

Alex’s fingers tightened in his lover’s curls. Genevieve had the strong sense that if Whitely had ever been in any way adorable or earnest, it had been in self-defence. An orphanage, a workhouse. There were enough hints there.

Smiling like an angel, Whitely rose. ‘Yes, Miss Cecelia, I was.’

Alex tucked him under his arm, expression distant. Genevieve supposed he had his talent’s dial turned up high, reaching for intentions as far away as he could. He spoke quietly. ‘Look. Your best path now is to track down the Artisan who made the embedded Art.’ He jerked a thumb towards the scattered bits of metal on the floor near the box.

‘That’s a Locke twin speciality,’ she said.

‘I’d highly recommend you call on Lucinda’s area of expertise, yes. But that was an out-and-out murder attempt on Kit, either to remove him before he can open something McAvey doesn’t want opened, or purely for a special sort of fuck-you revenge. I’m getting my lad on that bloody train down to Southampton and well out of England before he tries a direct attack.’

When Genevieve frowned and opened her mouth, he held up Whitely’s hand, exactly as he’d held up Massimo’s, to show off the missing finger. ‘*Frostbite*, Gin, I’m not fucking around when I say McAvey has it in for him.’

‘He can look after himself,’ she said indignantly. ‘He was going to bring the bloody roof down on us when he thought you were in danger.’

‘Not on purpose,’ Whitely interjected. He jerked his wrist free.

‘Yeah, he’s a marvel,’ Alex said flatly. ‘You know what else he is? Not immune to a fucking ice spear through the heart. I’m not taking chances with him, and I’m not hearing arguments, Mr Whitely.’

'I would not dream of offering any, Mr Locke,' Whitely said in demure tones.

'Once I've seen his ship make it safely out of port, I'll come back and help you, as promised.'

'Excellent,' Genevieve said on an exhale. 'Thank you, Lexi.'

'What?' Whitely did not like having his suspicions confirmed; he dropped any pretence of demureness. 'Alex, you will do no such thing. He doesn't like you either!'

'Kit—'

'You know you can't make me go. What are you going to do, lock me in the cabin? Try it.'

'I *can* make you go, though, can't I?' Alex leaned in, bringing all his personable confidence to bear against Whitely's mutinous expression. 'Please, sweetheart. I'm asking you to stay safe. You'll do that for me, won't you?'

'That is very manipulative, Alex.'

'You'd know,' Alex said, caustic but smiling.

Whitely shot a look at Genevieve before letting Alex take his hand and draw him towards the door. There was something of resentment in that glance, and resignation. But she also saw what Alex had foretold she would see: a startling willingness to help, because she was Alex's cousin, because he wanted to make amends, because he liked to be helpful but didn't know how to offer help freely.

And she had let Reuben use her to threaten to burn this young man alive.

'Wait.' Genevieve looked between her cousin and his lover. 'No… No, I don't think so, actually.'

'I'm escorting him out of the country first,' Alex said patiently. 'That's the best offer you're getting. Lulu will help you track the clockwork while you're waiting for me to get back. Then we'll tackle it together.'

And, since he always had been very good at reconciling himself to difficult jobs, he added, 'The Locke scions working together at last.'

The offer pulled at her heart. She remembered daydreaming with Lulu in the garden of her parents' home, making plans for her new Art and Lulu's new talent. Alex had still been hiding the blooming of his troublesome mindreading talent from almost everyone; Lulu had folded him into their plans, regardless. It had never come to fruition, she and the twins following their diverging paths.

Temptation lodged under her ribs in an almost palpable lump, though, upon reflection, Genevieve decided it was heartburn from the insistent press of the baby. 'We don't need your help, Alex.'

'I concur,' Whitely said immediately.

Genevieve ignored him. 'We can protect ourselves against whatever Reuben thinks he's doing, and we can track him down, too, if that's what we decide to do.'

Alex smiled at her and then, very deliberately, met Oliver's eyes. Genevieve, knowing both men too well, read there the silent message, both grave and entreating. *I am trusting you to take care of Ginnie,* that look said. *Because I want to but I cannot bear to risk Kit Whitely, who does not hesitate to risk himself.* Oliver dipped his chin.

'Stop that, both of you,' she ordered.

Whitely said, 'If you would allow me. Think about timing. Why has McAvey come back at this juncture? Varley, the original owner of the knife he claimed for himself, finally swung a few days ago. But also…' He pointed to the bulge Genevieve was sporting. 'Can't be long now until your… situation…resolves itself?'

She folded her arms, affronted by the rudeness of the gesture *and* the circumspection of the words. 'Just damn well say—' The meaning hit her. 'You think he wants the baby?'

Her hands suddenly locked about her rounded belly, fingers making a useless shield.

Fletcher said, 'He took a knife that cuts the Art out of Artisans. There's no Art in babies.' In his fussy way, he was trying to be reassuring, and Genevieve glanced his way gratefully.

But Whitely shook his head. He'd still been letting Alex hold his hand; now his own grasp tightened, squeezing Alex's larger hand tightly as he spoke with some difficulty. 'I touched it. It… I don't know what it does. I know it told Varley—'

'It's some old knife,' Fletcher scoffed, 'it doesn't—'

'It's a knife, and it wants to be used,' Whitely said. 'Varley wanted to save orphans from themselves, and the knife told him to cut. When I touched it, it told me it would make me safe.'

'That's not so bad,' Cecelia tried.

'It's a *knife*,' Whitely repeated, face pinched and bleak.

Alex put his arm around him, a solid comfort Genevieve could have used right then, the sort of comfort her husband would once have given her unstintingly.

'Everything's a nail to a hammer,' Alex said, as he had said before, but now it rang with such dire portent that he snorted and looked disgusted with himself.

'The question is,' Whitely said, looking at them in turn, 'what does McAvey want?'

After a surprised silence, the others all answered at once. 'Respect,' Fletcher said, as Cecelia said, 'Standing,' and Oliver rumbled, 'Power,' under both of them.

Genevieve had found no simple words to encompass her husband's ambitions, but her fingers were clutched about her stomach again, tight, trying to cradle a child that did not even exist yet. She looked up to meet Whitely's sombre, knowing gaze.

Carefully, she said, 'I don't disagree with you, Mr Whitely, when you claim the knife gifts the wielder what he most wants, in its own fashion. But the rumours swirling about last year suggested it would cut out Art. And I think…I think that's exactly why he wanted it.'

'Oh, remember at the Society meetings?' Cecelia said. 'He advocated that Artisans should be ranked and sorted according to their Art.'

'Ironically, that would have put Gin at the top and me at the bottom, and McAvey somewhere in the middle, exactly as we already stood socially,' Oliver remarked.

'He always did underestimate your medley, Oliver,' Genevieve told him.

Fletcher was nodding. 'That's right, he thought his Art should earn him greater respect than he felt the other Artisans accorded him.' With a disapproving glance at Whitely, he added, 'We all know it's behaviour that accords respect.'

Whitely folded his arms and tried to look cross, but managed only provokingly amused, wickedly so once Alex gave him a companionably complicit nudge.

'Oliver is right, Reuben wants power so he can get everything else he thinks he deserves,' Genevieve said. 'Regardless of what the knife *can* do, when he laid hands on it, he knew what he *wanted* it to do, which is what it is *rumoured* to do: cut the Art from Artisans. But he will additionally want it to feed the Art to him, instead of destroying it like Varley wanted.'

'Every one of Varley's victims died,' Whitely said, all trace of humour gone. Every one of Varley's victims had been orphaned children, as Whitely had been.

'Not to be grim…' Cecelia said slowly.

'If Varley had been trying to *harvest* the Art rather than destroy it…' Fletcher went on.

'The children would still have died, but it does not follow that the Art would have,' Oliver finished.

Alex said, 'So McAvey might very well get his heart's desire, then. He might have spent the last eight months perfecting the technique, in fact.'

'Not for the baby,' Whitely said, 'because there's no Art to be found in children, until it blooms or is made to bloom.' He had gone very stiff and cold-eyed, and Alex tucked him even closer, but he didn't seem to notice. He looked seriously at Genevieve. 'But perhaps for while a powerful pyrotechnic Artisan is maximally hampered by the *physicality* of the baby. Still willing to let Alex go?'

As tense as he was, he was poised and apparently prepared to accept the answer he didn't want to hear. Prepared to be helpful, to people who had not treated him at all well.

Genevieve forced her hands back by her sides. 'I can take care of myself just as well as you can,' she told him. 'And I'm certainly better equipped than you to take care of those I love.'

Again, she experienced a moment of fellow feeling with him, as he granted her the tiniest nod of respectful acknowledgement. She found the others gathered about her, a silent message, supportive from Oliver and Cecelia, slightly reproachful from Fletcher.

'And I have the Myriad here to help me,' Genevieve politely added, not without an internal wince at the tweeness of the name. 'So off you go, you two.'

She suffered Alex to kiss her cheek. 'Post those clockwork bits to Lulu,' he instructed. 'She can discern their direction well enough from Lovelly. Safer all round than bringing her back to London. Don't tell her I said that.'

If Reuben had disliked Alex and Whitely, he'd despised Lulu to a bigoted degree. Genevieve had no intention of risking her at all...and no intention of telling her so.

Alex exchanged one last meaningful look with Oliver and finished with a ruffle of Massimo's hair. 'You all have fun with your troublemaker,' he said. 'I'm taking my troublemaker to Japan.'

'He's taking his pretty wife on a honeymoon, Fletcher.' Whitely winked at Fletcher, who looked appropriately appalled.

'Fuck off if you think you're the wife here, Whitely,' Alex said cheerily, and tugged him out the door.

10

GENEVIEVE AND THE OTHERS WERE THUS left with a young and rather disconsolate shapeshifter Artisan of unknown provenance, excepting the highly salient fact he had been delivered by an absconded husband acting towards some nefarious purpose outside their ken but possibly to do with a highly unpleasant *harvest.*

It was late, and Genevieve was exhausted, so the most pressing matter was to find the young Artisan a bed where he could be watched, which immediately eliminated the spare rooms in the downstairs, attic and carriage house respectively. But Fletcher had taken over the last spare room upstairs with his old-fashioned birthing bed arrangement.

'We should throw him from the house,' Fletcher said.

This was difficult to gainsay: Massimo Miraculi had been, and likely still was, a trap. Kit Whitely had slithered from its jaws, but they could not know if it was still set for them.

Or, indeed, if it had been successfully sprung, since Cecelia was already shaking her head and taking Massimo's hand to further her counterpoint, which was that she was too soft by half and would not see an urchin tossed into the street at this ungodly hour, nor any hour.

Oliver, also kind-hearted but given to thinking both more deeply and further ahead than the rest of them, considered the matter as he put the wards back on the doors Whitely had come through. When done, he came quietly to stand by Cecelia. Genevieve had to take the scant comfort that Alex had read nothing at all of wicked intentions in their unexpected guest; he would have said, if he had.

'He could sleep on the birthing bed,' she suggested. Its chamber was by Oliver's, and he could set wards about the doors to wake himself up if the boy did not stay put.

Fletcher inhaled, with more than a little judgement to the theatrical sound.

'Nursery?' Cecelia suggested judiciously. 'Let's make up a nest of cushions and blankets, that'll be nice, won't it?'

Massimo responded to her jollying with a slow blink. He looked, if it were possible, even more exhausted than Genevieve felt, the walking embodiment of dead on his feet. They'd taken it in turns to ask him questions while Oliver had set the wards, but managed to obtain little sense from him. More would have to wait till morning.

'He may sleep in my room,' Oliver said now.

Genevieve tipped her head in a silent concern that he shook his head at. Once again, she reminded herself that Alex had not uncovered any poor intentions in the boy, and that Oliver could set wards to protect himself, and was full of common sense to boot.

'Is that…' Fletcher looked deeply uncomfortable. 'Is that appropriate?'

Oliver studied him. Fletcher devolved into stammered statements by which it became apparent that Kit Whitely had strongly implied, nay, suggested, perhaps even openly averred, that Oliver engaged in unsavoury activities, that was to say illicit relations, with men, specifically Mr Alexander Locke, and Oliver had not defended himself against the accusation.

'And I am very sorry to say it!' Fletcher finished, once he'd finally managed to circumspectly allude to it. He made a face and muttered, likely louder than he'd meant to, 'And you're both such big men, how would you have even fit together on a bed?'

Genevieve watched Oliver give way to his slow and crooked smile. He generally projected the semblance of a sombre man. He also had a rather idiosyncratic, almost puckish, sense of humour, when provoked.

He said, 'Ample space on the floor,' and departed with Massimo before Fletcher could quite discover which prong of their two-pronged conversation the riposte belonged to.

Fletcher took his leave then. Even if he could have been persuaded to stay, the sole suitable free bed was situated by Genevieve's room, and he could not have been pressed into that with one of those strange prods the guards in Gallentry had possessed.

Cecelia accompanied Genevieve to help her ready herself for bed, a nicer arrangement than ringing young Bridget up at this time of night. She cleaved to the modern conveniences of a front-opening corset and lazy lacing, *very* lazy now, the corset worn solely for the breast and back support it provided. But the minor nightly rigmarole of undressing body and hair remained a far more pleasant undertaking with assistance in such an advanced state.

In the first years of their friendship, intimacy thrust upon them by the nature of the Artisan work they pursued together, such assistance, more necessary then, had made Genevieve feel both uncomfortable and exceptionally ungrateful, because Cecelia herself acted with such unstinting grace.

Genevieve had been, back then, neither fish nor fowl, raised by nouveau riche parents to be an aristocrat's wife, the mother to earls, and yet dividing her free time among the cheerily subversive twins and the agitating labouring faction of the nascent Agency. In a society where every station was firmly delineated in a hundred subtle ways, she had flailed when Artistry granted her a taste of the freedom she'd desperately craved.

There were no helpful etiquette books explaining how a colleague from a different social class could stand in a servant's role without crossing unspoken lines tangled suspiciously between taking advantage and incurring obligation. Genevieve could not help but think allowing the service was either an insult or a debt, and Cecelia knew it, and knew therefore that Genevieve was involuntarily denigrating the gift even as she accepted it.

It had taken Cecelia's pointed, kindly honesty to break it open. 'Goodness, Gin, stop thinking!' she'd exclaimed, wielding a hairbrush in their shared quarters as they'd sojourned overnight to chase the earthquake Artisan out of England. 'I loved doing this for my sisters when they were little. Let me enjoy myself without your father's artificial sensibilities getting in my way.'

Now Genevieve smiled at Cecelia in the mirror as her friend's nimble fingers drew the pins from her hair and freed the pale locks to tumble about her face, which looked a little puffy, and more than a little wan. Involuntarily, she recalled the chiding of Lulu's ladies' magazines: restraint, cheerful temper, and a sunny smile led unfailingly to a good complexion.

She grimaced. At least her hair was suitably thick and lustrous to make amends for her recent lack on that front, and it was why cold cream had been invented, after all.

Despite the late hour, Cecelia looked as fresh-faced as ever. She'd been young when they'd met, they'd *all* been young, yet Cecelia had already been a veteran of strikes and workers' rallies, habitually dressing like a staid matron as counterweight to her youthful mien. These days, she had the pleasure of seeming some years younger than her true age, with enough ready money to indulge the fashions she'd ignored back then…as long as they didn't hurt the factory workers.

It struck Genevieve, as she watched her friend through the medium of the mirror, that she and Cecelia called each other by their given names. It was not so very uncommon among Artisans, but she could not, in the moment, recall the circumstances which had led to her and Cecelia extending the mutual courtesy past the disparity of their classes. It was dispiriting that the fog that swirled about her memories was affecting one of her oldest friendships.

Cecelia smoothed a hand over her hair, following the path of the tortoiseshell comb in her other hand. 'All right, Gin?'

'Cecelia, how did we meet all those years ago?'

Even Cecelia, memory Artisan, had to think about it before she finally said, uncertainly, 'At the Society. When all we Artisans were arguing over whether we needed an advocacy agency or not, and if we did, what sort of agency it should be. We— Oh, yes, we all met there, and you met Reuben there, too.'

'Did I?' Genevieve said. Then, 'Yes. But later. After I met you and…'

'You… Reuben put out a call for Artisans to join him. Because we needed something like the Agency but it didn't look like the Agency was ever going to happen, so we, so *Reuben*, sorry, decided to take matters into his own hands. And not many Artisans like the idea of working together, but I did.' She gave a laugh, still unsure. 'He wasn't all that impressed by memory Art, nor by me, but I think… Didn't you persuade him?'

'Did I?' Genevieve frowned. 'I must have, I suppose. Because I liked you.'

'I am very likeable,' Cecelia said, with a cheerful little bob.

Genevieve patted her friend's wrist and relaxed into her ministrations, the long strokes of, first, combs, and then the harder brush, down the full extravagant length of her hair.

'It's nice that Fletcher will marry,' Cecelia said after a few moments.

'It will be good for him,' Genevieve agreed.

They looked at each other in the mirror again. Cecelia was wearing a small but cheeky smile. It would not be fair to say that she and Fletcher had argued over this point; fairer to say that he subscribed to the widespread view that marriage was a general good for society, while Cecelia cleaved to the more radical notion that it was a specific good for some members of society, a subsection that did not necessarily include women.

It had shocked Fletcher, to discover that Cecelia intended to never marry.

'But you must want children,' he'd said.

'I can obtain one readily enough if I do,' she'd said, and giggled at the look on his face. 'Mr John Fletcher! Is this your business, sir?'

Fletcher had obligingly agreed that it was not. Genevieve greatly admired how Cecelia could protect herself while sounding so friendly about it, though she well knew the tactic originated in a certain level of vulnerability. Genevieve, with wealth and status behind her, could stand on her dignity with straightforward frosty disdain, an uncomplicated weapon conveniently amplified by her icy blue eyes.

'It's nice, also, that Alex has found someone who suits him so well.' Cecelia said it simply, without allowing it to turn into a question, but she also watched Genevieve's face to gauge her reaction.

'I will concede Whitely makes him happy.' *Disgustingly happy.* Genevieve fidgeted with some of the bottles and jars on her dressing table, disordering them. 'And their…marriage…appears to be working. It was enlightening to see them argue and yet remain civil about it. That's not possible in the usual sort of marriage.'

Cecelia quickly looked down, sweeping up scattered pins to drop into their jar.

'Oh.' Genevieve suppressed the urge to bite her lip. 'I suppose it *is* possible to argue and remain civil in the usual sort of marriage. But not in *my* marriage.'

It hadn't been possible to tease each other, either. It hadn't been possible to trust each other without reservation. All of that had gone, with the stillbirth. She'd never guessed she'd have cause to be jealous of *Whitely*.

Cecelia sighed. 'I would say I don't wish to speak ill of the dead…'

'But he's not dead,' Genevieve finished for her.

'Reuben was not a man who tolerated criticism well.' She shrugged. 'A learned skill, to be sure. But you can *also* be sure it was not a skill he intended on learning to tolerate from his wife.'

Genevieve heard the words trying to emerge from her mouth – *a good wife should never criticise her husband* – and firmly clamped it shut.

'Do you think Whitely is right?' she asked instead. She traced fingers over the material now hanging loosely over her bump. 'Has he reemerged now because the baby is about to come? Is the knife…*telling* him something he wants to hear?'

She felt a deep pang of regret and fear: she never should have let Alex go. If she was the target, so be it, she would defend herself with fire, even against her beloved husband. But no one truly understood what that damnable knife did. Varley had been so incoherent at trial that many commentators entirely discounted his ravings about the ancient dagger he'd uncovered in the mythical King Arthur's realm.

But if Reuben's true aim was, after all, the baby, a child, she remembered with a sickening lurch, he would have total legal rights to… Oh, *God.* She should have clung on to Alex with both hands. She should have demanded attendance from both him and Lulu, the three junior Lockes as closely entwined as they had been in their youth.

'We'll all take care of each other, Gin,' Cecelia said. 'Oliver strengthens his wards every morning, you know. He'll start doing it hourly, if you ask it. Kit waltzed through them. Reuben can't.'

'Shall I never leave the confines of the house, then?' That would, in her current mood, almost be best.

'Is it not called confinement for a reason?' Cecelia countered, but with a merry smile to make it less pert.

Genevieve gave her belly another rub. Cecelia had a point. She had reached the time, in the course of her delicate situation, where she should not be venturing far from the safety of the house, and from the birthing bed Fletcher had so helpfully and yet so very horrifyingly set up.

Thinking of it, she looked up as if she could see through the ceiling. There'd been a few muffled thumps and scrapes earlier, as Oliver settled Massimo onto a pallet in his room. Genevieve trusted Oliver's good sense. Even if the innocent-seeming shapeshifter had hidden bad intentions from Alex, Oliver was kind but never foolish with his kindnesses.

'Let's get through the next few weeks, Gin,' Cecelia said softly. 'Once the baby is here, we can plan our next moves. In the meantime, you'll be perfectly protected in the house.'

Once the baby was here, Reuben could use the courts to take it. Genevieve made herself breathe. She would fight that with every last drop of her wealth and privilege, and flee to Scotland or the Continent if neither law nor public sentiment sided with the abandoned wife. She would fight any less lawful attack with fire.

He wouldn't do that to me, the foggy part of her brain tried to insist.

You know he would, whispered her more sensible self.

Cecelia began to move away. Genevieve caught her hand. 'You never liked him.'

Her friend did her the courtesy of refusing to dissemble. 'I didn't, no. He was unbearable, before he left. And he…'

When she trailed off, Genevieve glanced up to catch her befuddled expression in the mirror. Her rich brown eyes were flat and dark, the usual light dancing in them dimming as shadows swirled. Genevieve, hand over her mouth, watched the fog take over her friend.

She'd thought it just her. She'd thought it symptomatic, of the baby, of grief, of worry. She hadn't known it was real enough to be seen reflected in a mirror. She thought wildly of Whitely, fearing himself trapped on the wrong side of the looking glass. *This* was what would have been waiting for him.

'Of course, I had much good will towards him,' Cecelia said dully. 'He was our friend, and your husband. And we always worked very well together.' She put a slim-fingered hand to her temple, muttering, 'Muddled. But I do remember that. We worked well together. I respected him.'

'Cecelia, something is *wrong*,' Genevieve burst out, and then she felt the fog encasing her, too.

Horror-struck, she met her own gaze in the mirror, and saw the same alien eddy moving behind her eyes. Heat washing through her, she held on to the edge of the dressing table as if to a sliver of raft after wreckage.

She held on, fighting to stay above the water. 'No! No, no—'

11

A LETTER ARRIVED THE NEXT MORNING, at the second delivery. Genevieve perused it over a light breakfast, brought up by Bridget with the mail. She did not want to eat, and Cook had an entire list, comprising some sensible and some superstitious items, she did not want her to eat, and so they came to a happy medium over overcooked porridge and bread soaked in fresh milk, both so bland and soft Genevieve could trick herself into swallowing a little.

Bridget helped her dress and coiffured her hair, without commenting on the scorch marks Genevieve had somehow left on the dressing table, the scent of burnt varnish lingering. Surely aware by now of the ructions in the household, the girl remained dutifully noncommittal as she smoothed Genevieve into her full-mourning attire, which she perhaps no longer needed to wear, but felt a shamefaced reluctance to put aside. She had still lost her husband. She did still mourn him.

Carrying the letter, she went downstairs, leaving Bridget to this stinking summer's daily task of setting bowls of chloride of lime mixed with water near the windows and pouring more down the drains.

Cecelia was, according to Bridget, out applying her Art at the courts. However, Oliver had already returned from helping his brothers with some early lading work in Wapping – he went whenever he was free, in case his little Arts made the difference the day a cable snapped or a stacked load toppled – and washed and eaten. Now he was in the half of the long drawing room that they habitually used, sitting awkwardly in one of the hard-cushioned, straight-backed stuffed chairs precisely arranged by the fire. He was reading a journal, the pages already methodically cut, his tentacle-handled paper-knife lying by.

Their new guest, Massimo Miraculi, sat tucked into another chair nearby, legs curled up, arms wrapped around himself. Genevieve supposed Cecelia had delayed to supervise him while Oliver was out, which he had probably found more pleasant, or at least less quiet.

His dark hair was still in wild curls, his eyes still a striking green, but he looked even less like Whitely this morning, and even younger. He wore fresh clothes, a shirt and trousers simple enough to have come from Oliver's nephews' wardrobes, which perhaps explained why he currently reminded Genevieve of those rambunctious boys, in appearance if not manners.

Despite the *Boy's Own Magazine*, bought from a newsstand or borrowed back from the nephews Oliver bought it for, lying open on his lap, Massimo wasn't reading, but watching Oliver warily. He transferred that wariness to Genevieve as she paused at the threshold, eyeing her with the alert tension of a shy woodland creature about to bolt.

Perhaps he couldn't read. Oliver might not have thought of that, even having gone to both lengths and expense to ensure all his nephews *and* nieces were educated. He wanted better lives for them than his brothers had, commissions if they went to sea, a higher class of work if not.

He was engrossed in the most recent *Proceedings of the Royal Society for Thaumological Research*, funded, published, and distributed under the auspices of the Agency to all registered Artisans whether they liked it or not. Oliver liked it; Genevieve liked his terse summaries. She'd been far too distracted, for far too long, to read it herself. She hadn't even managed to turn the pages of the very first edition of the brand-new *English Woman's Journal* yet, though Oliver and Cecelia had both thoroughly devoured it.

She watched him reading for a moment, turning the letter over and over in her hands. She would impose on him, she decided, to help her move her mother's comfortable furniture out from storage in the carriage house, and they could send the tasteful, modern pieces Reuben had chosen to a consignment agent.

It occurred to her that she could impose on Sir Kingsford as well, and move not her mother's furniture, but the entire household, back to the Locke townhouse, where she'd grown up, where she and her husband had returned to live with her widowed mother, where she'd lost her little boy this time last summer.

She touched her stomach. It felt like inviting disaster, to return to a place haunted by the loss of one baby when she was so soon to welcome a new baby into the world.

Perhaps that was why Reuben had abruptly sold her childhood home, with, she recalled now, her permission. Perhaps it had nothing to do with paying off expensive debts incurred in the Artisan district. Her husband had grieved the loss of their son so very quietly, as was his wont. Perhaps selling the townhouse to Sir Kingsford was his way of being loud for a change.

Still. She glanced around the wallpapered walls of the drawing room and felt not fondness for her new marital home, but distaste, a feeling strengthened by the mingling stuffiness of the stinking summer heat and cloy of the gaslight fumes.

She'd lived here less than a full year, and only a few months with Reuben. There were no good memories here, none at all, and not merely because she could barely hold onto her memories as a rule.

Glancing up to discover her lingering in the doorway, Oliver held up the proceedings journal. 'They finally decided they've accumulated enough evidence to declare that Art runs in families.'

Genevieve dismissed her maudlin mood. 'All those mothers and daughters hanged in the old witch trials wasn't enough to give the hint?' she asked dryly.

If she'd said that to Reuben, or to Fletcher, she'd have risked a long lecture explaining her error. Oliver simply smiled. He knew, or at least trusted, that she understood that the persecution of innocent rural outcasts for witchcraft had only muddied the scientific study of Artistry, as well as being a blight on the nation's history; as to that, it would certainly not be the last blight the nation collectively earned itself, and, thanks to King James, not the worst of them.

It did not help that Art often did seem to arise *de novo*, as for Cecelia – which might have been a real phenomenon or might have been an artefact of not knowing the particulars of her ancestry in the meticulous detail boasted by those with more reason or leisure time to trace it. Fletcher, case in point, had turned up a distant eccentric relation who, in retrospect, must have been an Artisan. There'd be quite a lot of that, sprinkled across the black sheep and exiles and oddities dangling in every family tree.

Within the Locke family, the twins pointed to a great-aunt on their mother's side, since Kingsford, scion from their father's first marriage, didn't have even a whisper of an inclination, let alone a talent. Genevieve's Art made her posit a Locke grandparent instead, but perhaps hers came through her mother's line as well, and the Locke brothers had an inclination of the more mundane sort, towards a certain type of woman.

Meanwhile, Oliver had stories about older relatives on his own mother's side; it was why he used her name for Artisan work. His father hadn't been happy about the eldest Bennet son becoming an Oliver. The incessant teasing from his younger brothers had taken on a nasty edge that only sharpened the more he interfered in their children's educations. Oliver was well used to being an outsider in his own family: like Genevieve, he was neither fish nor fowl, and subject to snide comments and bitter accusations he blandly ignored. It had stood him in good stead when he'd held firm on having the girls of the family educated.

'You'll ruin them for their husbands,' one of his brothers had snorted. 'What's next, teach 'em to play chess?'

'Good idea,' Oliver had said, and did just that.

Genevieve put her hand to her forehead. She had a memory, clear but entirely puzzling, of watching Oliver hunched over a chessboard in lamplight, holding a pale Merrifield queen in one big hand. A tiny girl, five years old at most, solemnly galloped a dark knight across the inlaid squares to assail a tower, and looked up at him with bright expectation.

Both the chess set and the warm lamplight came from the cosy family parlour of the Belgravia house, but she felt no sense of wrongness: Oliver and his niece belonged exactly where they were.

The memory shone gold, and then was gone, lost into the fog, even as something within Genevieve, analogous to her fire Art, flared up to try to burn the encasing white blankness away.

Genevieve returned Oliver's smile and gave a little nod, letting him know he was welcome to tell her about the journal's findings. She liked the way Oliver explained things; he was never tedious about it. Massimo listened as attentively as she did.

The Agency's current conjecture, Oliver said, was that people with mere inclinations unknowingly intermarried to create latent talents and Arts in their offspring, a latency forever unrealised unless the precipitating catalyser triggered it. It owed much to the many theories of evolution under discussion at several other royal societies over the last few years.

Though if Lamarckism had any truth to it, Lulu would have proven it by sheer strength of will in striving to turn her talent into a real Art.

Genevieve did not think mere interbreeding could be the whole simple story. It seemed to her, it had always seemed to her, that the twins had lost their father, and only had talents, and she had had a bad night at a soiree, and ended up with highly-prized weapons Art. She knew Cecelia had had an appalling catalyst for hers – *nothing so unusual for factory girls*, she'd said, so matter-of-factly that it had broken Genevieve's heart – and yet had one of the most peaceable Arts possible. She'd wanted everyone to forget it had happened, so she could get on with campaigning for reforms that would ensure it couldn't so easily happen to other girls.

On the other hand, if the ton weren't outright hiding their Artisan sons, the theory did explain the dearth of Art in the upper classes, who did not often face the level of adversity needed for precipitation. Unless they were a spoiled heiress who wanted to stamp her foot at her father for having to marry a man with a title, Genevieve supposed, or who spent too much time with her cousins to do anything other than chafe at prison bars made from narrow stacks of bullion. It was a nice enough prison, if one had to have a prison – but Art made it so one didn't.

The scientists of the Royal Society for Thaumological Research had not yet come out and openly suggested upper society should start tossing its sons into ponds if it wanted a higher quality of Artisan, but it was likely only a matter of time before some inflammatory tabloid started drawing comparisons with force-blooming orchids through hothousing.

Or, indeed, the exact opposite – Varley had been trying to cut the devil's gift from those poor Artisan orphans, and his trial had stirred up the strident minority who still associated Artistry with witchcraft, the devil's work. They'd be making their opinions known with pamphlets and sermons, as they had after the arrest of the illusion Artisan producing false stigmata.

The newspapers might join in, pundits suggesting Artisans, already poor at procreation, be barred from even trying, so that Artistry died its natural death and the nation could move on unencumbered into a modernity that had no place for what amounted to sorcery with a pretty tablecloth flung over it.

Genevieve stroked her stomach. Artisans were sails in the age of steam, horses in the age of rail, penny stamps in the age of the telegraph—

She found a letter in her hand. She sat to read it, surprised to find the envelope already open. She didn't remember opening it, though she was sure Bridget had delivered it sealed.

Inside the envelope, the letter was wrapped in a short note in Alex's distinctively laborious hand. *He won't let me read it*, it said, *but please know he intends no insult.*

The actual letter was in a surprisingly well-formed clerkish hand. Most of it was uniformly neat and legible but *Oliver, read this* was scrawled at the top in large letters, which was already an exceedingly odd start because the missive itself had been addressed to her, and the salutation was to her, or at least to Lady Genevieve. That was Whitely's mistake; she'd never had any right to be so addressed.

It went on:

I am aware my form of address is incorrect. I am holding off a strong embedded Art for now by thinking of you as someone different to Alex's cousin, but I believe I have earned myself very little time.

I asked Mr Locke when his uncle and aunt had passed over and how is it that Sir Kingsford has the Locke townhouse instead of you, and he couldn't remember anything of it. I asked him why any self-respecting Locke would marry someone like McAvey, and when, and it was as if he could not even remember the questions long enough to answer me.

None of this perturbs him in the slightest.

You have so many questions surrounding you that you – that all of you – refuse to ask, and I think do not even think to ask. I think someone has put a compulsion on you to force you not to think about it. The same thing affects anyone who knows you – they are compelled to not think of you, or to think of only very specific memories of you, memories that might not even be real.

It's worse for anyone close to you. It's worst when you try to fight it.

I think it must be in the necklace you wear.

What necklace? Genevieve thought. She glanced down. She was holding the opened letter. She began to read again.

You will forget this letter. Go back to the beginning and read it again. Give it to the others to read. Not Lulu. Keep Lulu out of London. Mr Oliver's warding Art is the best chance of circumventing it – give it to him. Then read it again for yourself.

Read it again.

Read this again, Ginnie.

Fight it.

Whitely hadn't bothered signing it. Genevieve set it down. After a little time, it caught her eye, and she read it. She set it down, puzzled.

Oliver put aside his journal. 'What's this?' he asked, tapping his name at the top of the letter with a single blunt finger.

'It's from Whitely,' she said. 'It's very strange, it says— I don't know what it says. You have my permission to read it.'

He read it quickly, and then again, slower, and then put it down. He seemed about to say something, and turned back to his journal saying nothing. Massimo had glanced over, but was now absorbed in pushing broken scraps of intricate clockwork around on his lap, spread over the pages of the magazine he wasn't reading.

Genevieve read the letter. 'What necklace?' she said aloud, touching her neck. Her fingers grazed over a fine gold chain.

She put the letter aside then, at a query from Bridget about the weekly menu on Cook's behalf. By the time Cecelia and Fletcher arrived within a few moments of each other, she'd forgotten all about it.

Bridget brought in the tea things and Cecelia poured Genevieve a cup of weak tea. For a hung moment, Genevieve didn't recognise the woman setting the saucer before her. She heard herself saying, with strangled, desperate fury, *Cecelia, something is* wrong.

'Cecelia,' she began, then looked at her friend properly. She normally had such a healthy glow about her, but now seemed dispirited, her eyes dulled. 'Was it a hard morning?'

The court visits could be taxing. Sometimes Cecelia was called on to delve into the memories of the accusers, sometimes the accused, sometimes the witnesses, and show them to the magistrate, or to the police to aid their investigations. Any of those memories might be brutal; they might be familiar. She couldn't flinch.

'Oh, Fletcher was with me,' Cecelia said, tilting a wan smile his way. It was easier when her partner joined her, since he could compel the involved parties to speak truthfully. She then must sink into relevant memories solely if the course of events remained unclear because of genuinely confused testimony.

Fletcher didn't return her smile. He was slowly turning his teacup in its saucer, and didn't look up.

'I'm just tired, Gin.' Cecelia held her own cup in both hands, gloves removed, as if warming her fingers, which seemed unlikely during this endless heatwave. Indeed, she added, 'It's already hot and smelly out there.'

Sweltering and stinking would have been the more accurate description. The *London Standard* had headlined the unbroken string of blistering temperatures, and there was no relief in sight. The river waters were sinking ever lower, exposing mudbanks covered in rot and excrement to steam under the unrelenting sun.

Mournfully, Cecelia said, 'I'm dreading going back out there but I must attend my committee meeting tonight.'

Genevieve was quietly shocked. She had known Cecelia for…

She tsked under her breath and concentrated, imagining flames lighting the way through a thick fog. She had known Cecelia for almost half her life now. She'd seen her throw herself into cause after cause: she'd started with workers' rights, then working class Artisans' rights, and now devoted all her energies to women's rights, mostly around reforming dress, voting, and the entire institute of marriage. Even exposed to stories and memories of the most appalling treatment by husbands and fathers, by police and magistrates, by factory owners and office managers, Genevieve had never seen her despondent. She'd always been energised by the fight, not overwhelmed. But now she seemed drained.

Cecelia made a concerted effort to straighten her spine and square her shoulders. 'I'm hot and tired, but aren't we all,' she said, injecting into her voice her usual cheery tones. 'I'll be right as much-needed rain after a spot of tea.'

'Miss it for once,' Fletcher said irritably. 'It's hardly the Langham Place Circle, after all.'

He immediately quailed; Cecelia had raised her eyebrows, small smile lingering, and though Oliver was seated out of her field of view, Genevieve could guess the look he'd have sent him for that indelicacy. It probably matched her own quelling frown, in intention if not degree.

'Every small gain means something to someone,' Cecelia said stoutly; as usual, the accidental challenge had lifted her spirits instead of dousing them. 'And I won't let the Missus Murphys down, regardless.'

That was their collective name for Mrs Murphy and Miss Adler, since they almost always came as a pair.

'I'd go with you myself, if not for…' Genevieve assayed a general wave towards her stomach, not without a flash of guilt for her unread copy of the first *English Woman's Journal.* She had, she reminded herself, been rather out of the world with grief and gravidness for some time.

Fletcher, by way of graceless apology, said, 'I would at least escort you there, but I must attend Miss Landrau this evening.'

He said this with such despondency that it was his turn to be eyed off by his concerned friends. Cecelia said, 'You seemed quite happy with the prospect only yesterday.'

'Oh.' He fidgeted as if he hadn't been inviting the query. 'I had an unpleasant letter in the first post.'

Genevieve glanced down, her gaze drawn as if by magnets. A letter sat unfolded beside her empty cup. She touched it, both surprised to find it there, and somehow *not.*

'Miss Landrau desired me to know her parents did not wish my suit to continue unless I sundered my association with this house. I am to go to them with reassurances that I have done so.'

She stared at his dismal face with alarm. 'But I'm a… Aren't I a respectable widow?' Was word somehow spreading that she was a disgraced and abandoned wife?

'It's not you, Gin.' Cecelia's tone was paradoxical: annoyance and amusement and resignation, all mixed into her usual lightness. 'It's me.'

'It's both of you,' Fletcher said reassuringly. 'I mean… I address you both by your given names, you see. If we had an Artisan etiquette manu—'

'No!' Cecelia and Genevieve cried together, underpinned by Oliver's low rumble of the same sentiment.

The short, sharp outcry made Massimo jump. He looked around at their faces before returning to playing with the bits of clockwork, arraying them into patterns. If he *were* spying for Reuben, Genevieve mused, he'd have low spirits and bickering to report.

'My goodness, Mr Fletcher.' Cecelia waved a finger, her chiding offset by her smile. 'We may act almost as we like in polite society by announcing we're Artisans. We all agreed amongst ourselves to standards of *legal* behaviour. Do not wish for the standards of our *social* behaviour to be nailed down by some manual-writing ninny!'

'But then I could point to the page that allows me to address my colleagues as we have all consented to be addressed.'

'Point to the thickest of the Agency by-laws, that will serve your argument well enough.' Cecelia hesitated. 'You do intend to argue the point, do you not?'

Fletcher paused, thin lips pursed, expression sour. 'I don't,' he admitted eventually.

'Are you here to tend your farewells to us?' Genevieve asked with some alarm. Fletcher was awkward and prissy; she still considered him a friend. She'd assumed he returned the sentiment, but then, he had just referred to them as his colleagues, as was his unvarying habit.

'I am answering her summons tonight to tend my farewells to *her*,' Fletcher said. 'I shall not be threatened into putting aside my colleagues.' A long pause, before he corrected himself with a wince of discomfit at all these unseemly pangs of emotion. 'My friends.'

Cecelia touched his hand, wordlessly expressing condolences. 'But perhaps she will relent. Perhaps her parents do not understand the contingencies of being an Artisan's wife. As a land-lubber wouldn't know what it is to be a captain's wife, right, Will?'

'Land-lubber.' Oliver was always amused when any of them tried to use nautical slang, though he'd been off the ships long enough that his brothers would have both the grounds and the merciless desire to tease him in his turn.

Cecelia's answering smile was more real this time, and Fletcher at least managed a lacklustre nod of acknowledgement. 'Perhaps.'

Genevieve noticed a letter lying beside her. She read it, then set it down, and stared into space. Eventually her eye was caught by Massimo playing with broken pieces of clockwork, the dull brazen metal catching coppery highlights as the young shapeshifter sorted and stacked the bits.

'Is that the embedded Art from the box?' she asked abruptly.

Her tone had been too sharp. Massimo flinched violently, and then his edges blurred and a black cat was in his place. He leapt off the chair, scattering metal bits in his wake, and fled the room.

Cecelia looked somewhat disapproving, but Genevieve was too riveted on the pieces to feel remorse. 'We should send for—' She remembered Alex, the night before. He hadn't wanted his sister in London. 'We should send these *to* Lulu. She can tell us where they came from.'

'I know where they came from!' Fletcher blurted. He bustled out, and his footsteps sounded loud in the quiet house as he hurried up the stairs.

He was back within moments, holding an invoice, that at first Genevieve did not recognise at all, but then realised was familiar: they'd seen it the evening before, when they'd searched the study.

'I'd almost forgotten about this.' Fletcher sounded baffled as he held it out towards her. 'How unforgivably careless of me.'

Genevieve took it and looked at the letterhead at the top. A clockwork shop, in the Artisan's district. She could see why Fletcher thought it might be related. Except—

'Can't be the box,' Oliver said. He stood, a ponderously inevitable avalanche of muscle and height, immediately making a spacious room smaller. 'Better keep an eye on Massimo.'

'Why can't it be for the Art on that box?' Fletcher demanded.

'It's dated from last summer,' Genevieve said. Oliver nodded as he turned to depart, to track down where a little black cat might be hiding. 'Surely Reuben didn't plan to send us a shapeshifter in a box almost an entire year ago?'

Disappointed, she laid down the invoice, beside a folded letter.

'It is,' Cecelia said, a delicate frown between her eyebrows, 'our only connection to clockwork.' She sounded as if she was pushing out the words, and looked concerned by her own effort.

Genevieve began to gather up the broken cogs and springs. She supposed she would send a few bits to Lulu, and wait to see what her cousin had to say about it.

Even the act of addressing a package suddenly felt like too much effort. She wanted to ring the bell, and instruct Bridget to send a note to Lulu on her behalf, summoning her.

The thought arose unbidden, but firm. *Keep Lulu out of London.*

She looked again at the letter. She knew the handwriting, suddenly. She touched her neck, and found a thin chain.

She thought of Whitely, his *I went around it*, so provokingly vague. Yet she felt herself on the very precipice of grasping exactly what he'd meant. She also had a recollection – had he said something, or written it? – that he thought Oliver was the only one of them capable of circumventing compulsion.

That was enough to trigger a certain level of Locke stubbornness. She was a weapons Artisan. She carried fire within her. She didn't need to go around. She could burn her way *through.*

The address on the invoice was right near Adler's Apothecary. She needed, she decided, to visit her midwife.

12

'I'LL GO WITH YOU,' CECELIA said, managing to not sound exhausted by the prospect of leaving the house again. 'I'll pop Mass over to the Agency for registration while Oliver escorts you.'

'Escorts me?' Genevieve said. 'I'm with child, not five years old.' At their mutinous expressions, she added, 'I attended a *hanging* alone.'

'That was before – before,' Fletcher said.

Before they knew she was abandoned, not widowed. Before they knew the box had been a trap. Before they knew Reuben had a knife which might be *telling* him things.

Before they'd decided a pyrokinetic Artisan couldn't take care of herself. She tightened up at the judgement of it.

'If you don't mind the company,' Oliver said, when he came back down with a human-shaped Massimo. 'I need to see the Missus Murphys regardless. *I* would like the company.'

Which was a much more diplomatic way of phrasing it, and came with his shyly crooked smile, but did not lessen the cloying feeling of their unnecessary, and decidedly unwanted, care.

Nonetheless, Genevieve acquiesced, if with poor grace. Massimo should really be registered, regardless of Whitely's opinion on the matter, and the Agency was around the corner from the Artisan precinct where Miss Adler ran the apothecary she'd inherited from her father.

And that other premises, too, address specified at the head of the mysterious account that she slipped into her reticule while fixing her attention entirely on her annoyance over the interference of the others.

Due to her condition and the ripeness of the air, they called over to the livery stables for the carriage. Oliver charmed it before they embarked, with wards for both detecting errant Art and for smothering its potential effects.

Genevieve noted the carriage as another saleable asset, though it occurred to her it might only be leased. At some point, after her imminent confinement, she would have to sit down with Mr Hartley, or Fletcher, and get a solid grasp of her finances.

Stiggins was at the corner of the precinct, stink and heat notwithstanding. He waved his battered bible as he declaimed into the environs, perking up when he spotted them disembarking.

'Practitioner of the devilish arts!' he cried, pointing, not quite *at* but near Genevieve, tall and striking, very visibly in that interesting condition, very visibly in the *other* condition thanks to the widow's weeds, and tellingly bareheaded. The scant respect may have had to do with Oliver standing, stoic and huge, close by her side. '*All that do these things are an abomination unto the Lord.*'

She put a hand on her hip, staring stonily at the soapbox preacher. He, and others like him, had been much more persistent since Varley's trial; it verged on admirable, given the current unpleasantness of so-called fresh air. He usually started his day in front of the Agency, to inflict his views on the greatest concentration of the city's Artisans, as well as their more mundane clerical co-workers. Once the Agency moved him along, sending out a few enforcers to chivvy and menace, he decamped around to the nearby precinct, with its run of Artisan-owned premises. The customers there were mostly mundane; Stiggins's aim, if he could be truly said to have one, was to remind them they must have no congress with the spawn of the devil.

'Don't quote bible verses at us,' Fletcher told him, slipping easily into a matching self-righteousness. 'Isaiah 44:11. *As to Artisans, they are of men.*' He added an apologetic look towards Cecelia and Genevieve, and slightly modified his next sally. '*And I have filled them with the Spirit of God, in wisdom, in understanding, in knowledge, and in all manner of Artistry.* Exodus 31:2. So knock it off with the witchy nonsense.'

'Oh, Fletcher, don't argue with him!' Cecelia, one elbow linked with Massimo's, tugged at Fletcher with her spare hand, previously employed to hold a scented handkerchief to her nose.

Encouraged, Stiggins bellowed, '*Those Artisans are coming to disrupt the power of nations, tearing them down*! Zechariah 1:21. I know thee by thy countenance, witch!'

This time he did directly point at Cecelia, who laughed and waved her three middle fingers at him. This might seem an innocuous gesture to a bystander, but Genevieve knew it was a cheeky invitation to count her devil's marks – her three teats. She nudged her friend, half shared amusement, half caution.

'Ah, you see!' Stiggins bellowed. 'Accused of the damnable sin of witchcraft, she of the hellish league sheds no tears but merely mocks! *The Lord thy God doth drive them out from before thee*!'

'*He carried all Jerusalem into exile: all the officers and fighting men, and all the skilled workers and* Artisans*—a total of ten thousand.* That's the Second Book of Kings 24:14, we were right there as part of civilisation from the very start! *And* we've been acknowledged by the Crown since King James granted us a royal warrant!' Fletcher shouted back. 'This is bigotry and zealotry of the worst order!'

'The storm the Scottish impostor accredited to salvation by thy devilish ilk was *caused* by thy devilish ilk and your satanic master. The vain fool was bamboozled and betwitted by witches and suckled by their unnatural imps!'

Fletcher gasped. For all his flaws, King James had been the lifesaving patron of English Artisans, and was thus esteemed within the tiny community.

'Mark 4:39, the rebuke of the storm!' he shouted, cut off as Cecelia tugged him away with a shake of her head.

She was perfectly happy to stand before a crowd to orate for systematic change and challenge to institutional authority. If the Church itself had begun to espouse such views, as ever so occasionally one of its various arms or orders was tempted to do – before the Crown had a word – then she'd have been first in line to fight it. But she'd never thought the battle with individual cranks worth it.

Stiggins roared 'Blasphemy!' in their wake as she, Fletcher and Massimo disappeared around the corner towards the Agency, but did not succeed in reengaging his opponent.

They would be some time: Massimo would have to take the Artisan test, which involved producing some reliable indicator of Art and confirming which, of iron and silver, hurt more, or smothered his Art more. It didn't affect everyone to equal degree, of course; there were even some metalworkers who could work each metal, as long as enough other metals, especially copper, were mixed in. And then there was Whitely, who appeared unaffected by silver, and somehow went around iron.

As Genevieve was going around her own wavering constraint: even as she felt the fog descending to turn her from the precinct, she lit a figurative flame against it, firmly reminding herself she was here on legitimate business.

When she and Oliver walked into the apothecary, the fresh herbal scent, with its strong undertones of rosemary and lavender oils, was an immediate relief from the heat and smell outside. So much a relief, in fact, that Genevieve stopped and swayed, eyes closed, body flushing, a tantalising prickle shivering over her of some great revelation a scant whisker out of reach.

A moment later, she was being guided across the shop floor, behind the counter, and through the rear door. The stronger smells of the workshop assailed her. This was where Miss Adler made her salves and pessaries and tonics, the clashing scents arising from various processes of distilling and crushing and chopping and drying all too much, and all too familiar, so strangely familiar.

Her wave of confusion and ill-feeling passed. It *should* be familiar. She'd visited the apothecary regularly since the year she'd first begun to help the committee in charge of first advocating for and then creating the Agency. The year she'd met Cecelia, and Fletcher, and the Missus Murphys. The year she'd met Reuben.

And then it had been winter, Christmas just gone, and she'd visited here, this very workshop, and—

She found herself helped into a soft-cushioned chair. She opened her eyes to discover that the gentle hand that had been stroking her hair during her brief, very brief, hardly worth noticing, dizzy spell had not been Mrs Murphy, but instead Oliver, crouched in silent concern by the chair. She turned her face towards him, brushing her cheek against his bare wrist.

'Is there… Is that mistletoe?' she muttered, hearing her own words with dreamy confusion.

Oliver looked up, breaking into a smile. But there was no mistletoe. He shook his head in a bemusement of his own, dropping his hand, shifting his weight to put distance between them. 'Summer, Gin. Too hot for Christmas.'

Oliver's frown had to be matched by her own. She touched her flushed cheeks. 'I don't— Why—'

The young shop clerk had fetched Mrs Murphy from upstairs, and she bustled in now, closing the door behind her. 'Mrs McAvey, you should not be leaving the house! The reckoning's an estimate, not a guarantee!'

'I'm with child, not *dying*,' Genevieve said with a great deal more irritation than Mrs Murphy strictly deserved, and with dunderheaded failure to remember that the two things went hand-in-glove too often to jest about.

Mrs Murphy still kept her long auburn hair set into a bun at her nape, though it had faded to a sandy shade in the years Genevieve had known her, and was threaded now with grey. Her Irish burr had never faded. She was, supposedly, a pain Artisan, though this was one of those borderline cases: she'd been practising as an Artisan before the test became a requirement, and she was grandfathered – grandmothered – into official registration partly due to her heavy involvement in creating the Agency. She took pain away, yes, but she used what might once have been labelled witchcraft material along with soothing, only-maybe-Art-endowed passes of her competent hands. Miss Adler was definitely an Artisan, Genevieve had seen her healing Art firsthand, and she imbued her salves and tinctures with an embedded echo of it too, but Mrs Murphy may very well have been skating by on a talent, competent care, and a whole raft of traditional herblore. She'd lobbied hard against the test being anything other than voluntary, registration a self-regulated process.

And what of it? What woman wouldn't want to parley a talent, mundane or otherwise, into Artisan status, particularly when, like Mrs Murphy, she had no interest in marriage despite her professional name, and no need for it if she could claim the benefits of Artistry to facilitate a substantial independent income. Midwifery was not the most profitable profession, being so very necessary to the poorest but encroached on by male accoucheurs for a generation or more among wealthier patrons. Only the halo of their Artistry kept the Missus Murphys in demand with paying clients, and even so, they also ran the apothecary, bolstered by both shop clerks and naps.

Genevieve wouldn't want anyone else by her side, come her crisis in the next week or so, but it was a bitterly learned lesson.

They had been there for her first labour, and Mrs Murphy had insisted on Genevieve's husband being present, too, so that his Art could counteract hers, should the pain become too much. That had not, in the end, been the danger; she was not an Artisan who could maintain Artistry through such intense pangs. It was the ever-shortening lulls *between* contractions where fear and exhaustion might have eventually made her lose her hard-won control, if her husband and her friends hadn't been there by her side.

But when she'd faced her second confinement, she'd been, to her regret, swayed by the books lauding the prevailing medical advice; those preachy manuals had, to her mind, successfully taken her this far and so she cleaved to them. It meant a doctor, and no Art-wielding but old-fashioned and unlicensed midwives, and no husband or too-emotional mother or too-innocent unmarried friends allowed. All of it, including her pain, would be managed the modern way.

Mrs Murphy did not hold a grudge. She'd still agreed to be there, as the supposedly married friend. She'd held Genevieve's hand and wiped her brow and reminded her how to breathe, but any further application of skill or experience earned sharp rebuke from the doctor. It must have taken iron will for Mrs Murphy to bite her tongue on all her expertise and bow to Genevieve's wishes to let the doctor lead.

Without her husband to vouch for the containment of her deadly fire Art, and with Mrs Murphy's own efforts compromised, Genevieve had accepted the doctor's ruling for the use of chloroform, falling into a deep twilight that wiped out all awareness of her body's travail.

She'd woken to a tiny form, whisked away before she'd even come to her senses enough to fully comprehend what had happened. Her husband's quiet grief brought the message home.

Genevieve put her hands over her stomach in sudden shame. She had tried to be so perfect last time, and still ended in dismal failure, letting down her poor lost child and her husband both. And yet she had been careless, indifferent to the new potential life in her care, in her grief over Reuben's loss. Mrs Murphy was right: she should not be out here, in the summer stink and crowds, in her imminent condition, not if she wanted even the slightest chance of Mrs Murphy and Miss Adler bringing the baby living into the world.

'I'm sorry to snap at you,' she said to Mrs Murphy. 'I do know I'm on your sufferance this time, when I snubbed you last time. I'm so sorry, Florence.'

'Oh, Genevieve, my dear child,' Mrs Murphy said, patting her knee. 'We would never hold any sort of grudge against a woman trying to make the best decision for her baby as she can.'

'In retrospect, a terrible decision.'

Mrs Murphy's eyes sharpened. 'You do know it wasn't your fault? The queen herself uses doctors and chloroform, darling.'

Genevieve was rendered speechless by this blunt reassurance. Still crouching by the chair as if expecting her to swoon again, Oliver was suddenly watching her with unsettling scrutiny.

'I—' she started. 'It— They say it's the mother's fault.'

'Who says?' Mrs Murphy demanded. 'Did that horrid little man dare tell you that to your face?'

'The advice books,' Oliver growled, face set in a dreadful scowl. 'She was reading them obsessively.'

'They're written by experts,' Genevieve managed weakly. 'They were…meant to be comforting.'

From the expression on her face, Mrs Murphy might have engaged in some creative cursing if her young shop clerk hadn't been hovering, and perhaps if Genevieve's baby had not been nestled right there; she did hold to some older superstitions.

She said, firmly, 'Sometimes the little ones don't live, and there's nothing anyone could have done differently to change that. I apologise if I didn't tell you that clearly enough. The doctor definitely should have taken it upon himself to do so.'

'Why would he?' Oliver said. 'If she knew it wasn't her fault, she might think it his.'

'I should never have used a doctor instead of you, that is where the blame lies, in that choice,' Genevieve said, the words heavy. 'My husband and my mother both tried to warn me, and I—'

Mrs Murphy's hand stilled on hers, fingers coolly wrapping her heated fingers. If she truly had Art, she was flooding Genevieve with it now, soothing emotional pain rather than physical. 'My dear. The outcome would not have been different.'

'The chloroform.'

'No, darling. The outcome would not have been different. Your little boy was simply not going to live. That is the way of it.'

She was suddenly weeping, and couldn't dash the tears away, because Mrs Murphy had hold of one hand, and Oliver had the other.

'I've done terribly by this little one,' she said, voice wavering unsteadily through the steady drip of tears. 'You're right, I should be home in bed.'

'I don't deny that would be my preference,' Mrs Murphy conceded, 'mostly so I don't have to deliver the mite right here on my floor today. But most women don't have that leisure. They go about their lives much as usual and suffer the usual slings and arrows and still manage to produce healthy babies, sometimes mere hours after walking off their factory shift. Sometimes *during* their factory shift.'

She managed to free a hand to wipe her face. 'But not I,' she said, 'and my incompetent womb.'

Mrs Murphy made a rude noise and rose to her feet, putting her hands in the small of her back and arching to stretch out from her crouch. 'Nothing you've done could have much harmed the little one, I'm sure I've at least told you *that* before.'

Genevieve pressed her lips together, maintaining control of her expression by a thread. Mrs Murphy had reassured her, throughout her first pregnancy, that the continuance of marital congress was perfectly fine right up until the very accouchement. She and Miss Adler had both reassured her of other activities that couldn't harm the baby, too, but that was the little nugget that jumped straight to mind at this most inopportune of times.

She was very aware of Oliver by her side, and also that he had begun to blush. He had many younger brothers, and nephews and nieces; he had been around the womanly condition often enough to guess what had made her draw up into faux-aristocratic ice.

There was really nothing like scalding embarrassment to wash away the last of this pointless dwelling and unfounded shame. *Hysteria*, Reuben would have labelled it.

'Yes, all right,' she said briskly. 'And if you would have a moment to…'

She trailed off and raised her eyebrows suggestively, which was enough to have Mrs Murphy send the shop clerk back to her station, and Oliver out to have tea with Miss Adler. The midwife performed the ritual of laying hands on Genevieve's stomach and listening to her heart beat and those other small and more private medical reassurances, before pronouncing her and her baby perfectly healthy and diagnosing a return home to wait out the last days.

'Please do recall how short your first two confinements were,' Mrs Murphy added, as she and Miss Adler farewelled them both. 'It only gets shorter – a woman's body remembers what to do.'

Genevieve hoped it did; her woman's mind certainly did not.

Shapeshifter

MASS TRAILED MISS DELACORTE AND MR Fletcher along the street with his head down to demonstrate how thoroughly small and obedient he was, though he brightened considerably when they passed an eel jelly stand. He tugged Miss Delacorte's sleeve.

He feasted on the resultant treat until they reached the Agency building, an odd combination of medieval guildhall and modern office building. The grim edifice was enough to set the frown back on his face, in a far more sincere fashion than he'd fixed it there for his hosts' benefit, and to put jitters into his stomach.

Miss Delacorte paused before the unassuming front doors. 'You know, it really is voluntary, Massimo,' she told him. 'We should have asked before now. Do you want to register?'

'It is advantageous, in terms of legal and social protections, employment opportunities, and ongoing advocation,' Mr Fletcher said. 'Suspicious if you don't want to, I should say.'

'Fletch!' Miss Delacorte said, quite sharply. '*Voluntary*.'

'It's all right,' Mass said meekly. He balled up the greasy waxed paper and wiped his fingers on his coat. 'We can go inside.'

Inside was a high-ceilinged reception hall, full of marble and mahogany, blandly grand. The experiential remnants of Kit Whitely, flashing deep apathy, compared it to a bank. It was dim, and the air smelled clean, almost searingly cold and fresh in his nostrils after the assault outside. That had to be the work of Artisans.

He looked around with wide eyes. It was a bustle of mundane clerks in drab colours, some enforcers positioned around the walls, uniformly wearing practical black shades, and a few Artisans, men and women, coming and going and dressed as they pleased, which was as disappointingly staid as everyone else. Alexander Locke's waistcoat was an aberration. Most everyone else dressed like Mr Fletcher.

Mass felt a little sad. He liked Alexander Locke's waistcoat. Partly because he had the sense he'd been in a sea of unremitting grey before encountering that expanse of mauve brightness. Partly because, although he had lost all but the vaguest impressions from Kit Whitely's memories, he'd ended up staying near him long enough that he'd managed to hold on to something of him, and of his contrary Art – which wasn't really an Art, or Mass wouldn't have been able to take hold of it in the first place.

Miss Delacorte seemed momentarily confused. 'Oh, that's right. They reorganised to increase the security of the registry. Registration's in a private room now.'

They managed to find this, a small chamber off the hall. The little man behind the giant sloping desk at the centre of the room did not seem overly impressed by the rare emergence of a new shapeshifter Artisan.

He looked over his glasses and below his thick eyebrows at Mass, eyes narrowed. 'Do I know you?'

'I would think not,' Mass said, in exactly Kit Whitely's tones.

'Your older brother, perhaps.' Sighing and tapping ink off his nib, he flipped his imposing ledger to a new page. 'Name?'

'Massimo Miraculi,' Mass said. He was trying to stand behind Mr Fletcher, who was only halfway letting him, to Mass's great annoyance.

'You young ones and your ridiculous pseudonyms,' the clerk muttered. 'You're not going on the stage, you know.'

'Stand tall,' Mr Fletcher whispered, prodding him. 'Posture is important. Speak up.'

'It's my *name*,' Mass said firmly, though he wasn't entirely sure it was. 'Mass, for short.'

'I'm writing you down as Mass Miracle,' the clerk said, then added, 'Hah!' as if he'd worked out the punchline to a joke. 'Birthdate.'

With more confidence than for his name, Mass asserted, 'Twenty-second June, '45. I'll be thirteen on the summer solstice.'

Miss Delacorte made a small sound, and he looked up at her, flinching. She shook her head and smiled, though she still wore a frown between her brows. He didn't like that.

Mr Fletcher said, 'Most Artisans are quite a bit older than this when they bloom and come register.' For all that he had been reassuringly sure that registering was the best course of action, he now also looked concerned. He drummed his fingers on the desk, which made the clerk transfer his put-upon look to him. 'There's precedent. He'd have to be fourteen to sign on for an apprenticeship contract, for example.'

'Once, it would have been as young as eight,' the clerk pointed out. 'Younger, even. Five-year-olds down the mines. They used to allow *horrible* exploitation of workhouse children under the apprenticeship system.'

'You are not being helpful,' Mr Fletcher said crossly.

'*If* you would allow me to finish,' the little man said, successfully outdoing Mr Fletcher in primness, 'there was horrible exploitation *until* the establishment of member unions roughly analogous to some of the base functionality of the Agency.'

'What do you think, Mass?' Miss Delacorte said. 'Do you want to wait until you're older before you make this decision?'

Mass had no idea. All he really knew was that the grown-ups who had kindly taken him in wanted him to join their club, and he wanted them to stop looking concerned. 'No, I'll register.'

The clerk made a pleased clearing of his throat. 'And what can you do, then?'

'Shapeshift,' Mass said. Miss Delacorte had already said that, when she'd presented him at the desk.

He would not be perturbed. 'What sort, son? Animals, objects, part, full?'

Mass opened his mouth to boast: any living thing. As big as an elephant, as small as a flea. A cold finger touched the base of his spine. He needed to please his new grown-ups, but he also remembered Kit Whitely's brusquely well-intentioned warning.

He said, 'Cat.'

The clerk pointed to the vacant space behind his desk, by which Mass guessed he was being invited, or instructed, to give a demonstration. He didn't have all his memories, but he did know about his shapes. The first time he'd tried to shift into an elephant, expanding from his compact size into its enormity – oh, Mass Miracle, he *got* it now – he'd made the mistake of using an illustration. The poor disproportioned creature he'd become took one wobbly step and fell over.

After that, he'd gone, or perhaps been taken, to the zoological gardens to see a wide variety of animals in the flesh: elephants, the hippopotamus, all sorts of cats. He might have made himself a cat the shape of a tiger, big soft paws, unfeasibly large head, long, sleek body, coiled muscular power. It still worked best if he turned into an animal he'd touched, same as people.

So he shifted into a small black cat, a replica of the shy kitchen kitty from the place he'd been before, and sat looking up at the clerk, licking a paw for verisimilitude.

Looking more impressed now than sceptical, the clerk told him to turn back. 'And people too?'

Mass looked quickly at Miss Delacorte and Mr Fletcher, but they'd moved over to the doorway, overtly disinterested in his answers. He shook his head.

He was taken through a security grill for the Artisan test, though the formality hardly seemed necessary. Well past the grill, down a long hallway, sat a telepath Artisan, who found no ill intentions in the forefront of his mind and waved him through.

That was right. All the ill intentions were buried in the very back of his mind, simultaneously held at bay, and yet sheltered by, the secret contrary streak he'd borrowed from Kit Whitely.

13

OUTSIDE THE APOTHECARY, OLIVER TUCKED A packet away, some herbal remedy. Quietly, he said, 'I did not know you blamed yourself.'

Genevieve felt a tremble of the same emotion that had brought her low in the workshop, but out here, with the full stink and heat and jostle of the London heatwave to distract her, she was able to keep it under control. 'It is difficult to find a different culprit, when the little one is under sole consignment.'

'Gin…'

'This way,' she said, marching – well, waddling – further along the street, hand dipping into her reticule to crumple the invoice and strengthen her resolve.

'The carriage is back that way.'

She wanted to return to the carriage. Her swollen calves and aching back wanted that. Her eternal dragging exhaustion wanted that. Her complaining bladder wanted that. The anchor in her mind, that pulled her back into the fog whenever she tried to escape, wanted that most of all.

She rubbed her thumb over the edge of the invoice in her fist, picturing a flaming torch, picturing fireballs leaping from her palms in a frosty garden, picturing a lit match that could not be extinguished. 'I need to—'

She stopped at the brass number screwed into the brickwork by a glossy red door, and looked up at the shopfront. It was, like the rest of the premises along here, tiled along its bottom half with beautiful glazed green tiles. Gatwick's Clockwork was frosted onto the plate glass, in the centre of a stylised cog.

Looking at the name on the glass, and peering past it into the interior, did not trigger any sort of stir in the thick fog that enshrouded most of her memories.

'They're closed.' Oliver turned away, a peculiar wave of relaxation rippling over him, apparent in the sudden release in the set of his broad shoulders.

Genevieve's feet started to follow, but she heard that infuriatingly cool voice in her head: *I go around it*, it said. *Can't you?*

I will go through *it, you little shit,* she informed the voice.

The hand holding the telltale account shot out and pushed on the door, which opened without the usual jingle of a shop bell overhead. She went inside, ignoring both Oliver's admonishing call of her name, and the fog that was making her stumble, making her want to return to the carriage, making her turn—

Oliver, as reluctant as he had been, had followed her without further complaint, and she bumped into him in the doorway as her mind shut down and her body tried to leave. He steadied her with his hands about her shoulders. He looked down at her with his velvety dark gaze hooded.

Mistletoe, she thought, and couldn't explain it.

It enraged her that she couldn't explain it, and she spun on her heel.

The clockwork shop was as far from the apothecary as could be, all gleaming copper and steel mechanisms, bright gaslighting, and the thick tang of metal and machine oil, except that both shops bore the evidence of an organised mind in the neat arrangement of shelves and cabinets. Genevieve did not sense any sort of Artistry amid the cogs and intricate springs of the mechanical workings on display, though mundane artistry abounded.

She started back as a small four-wheeled engine chugged out from under one of the display plinths, barely missing a turned wooden leg. She recognised it as a dribbler, one of the little mechanical locomotives that made for an enchanting, if somewhat dangerous, toy for children. Dribbler engines were fuelled by methylated spirits and powered by steam, leaving the eponymous dribble of water behind them.

Except, this one wasn't quite that. It was clockwork, powered by Art, which made it a good deal less likely to steam right into a wall, tip over, and set the curtains on fire.

Oliver crouched by the toy train, stopping its forward momentum so he could study the mechanism. He looked fascinated.

The thought came unbidden: he would have been the best of fathers.

She felt a pang of sorrow, unnecessarily outsized. Her friend was only a few years older than her. He could, and probably would, still marry. Cecelia's light teasing suggested that his landlady, at the lodging house he'd had to evacuate, had held something of a torch for her quiet, respectful, helpful tenant. If he wished for children, he would surely have them.

But Oliver looked up from the little Art engine with no trace of wistfulness, rather, confusion. 'My nephews have one of these.'

Genevieve raised her eyebrows. The expense, from a place like this, would have been prohibitive. Oliver loved his nieces and nephews. He didn't spoil them with toys meant for upper-class children.

A man was watching them curiously from behind the counter. He was elderly, white-haired and red-cheeked, which gave him the reassuringly jolly look of the Santiclaus type that arrived from America on festive cards. The resemblance was enhanced by his blue coat and the half-moon spectacles perched on the end of his round nose. He wanted but a crown of holly. She presumed, from his age and air of prosperity, that this was Mr Gatwick himself.

Genevieve approached, careful not to allow her enlarged body to accidentally brush any of the mechanisms. Though copper abounded, steel was worked in too, and that was smelted iron. She wasn't sure her body, the proverbial basket for a kid, could take more shocks today, even if the processes that formed steel would make the iron in it merely tingle instead of burn.

'Hello again,' the man said smoothly as they approached.

Again? thought Genevieve. He was glancing between them, so she didn't think the greeting was meant purely for a returning Art-dribbler customer.

But as they came close enough, he did turn his attention entirely to Oliver. 'And how may I be of assistance today, sir?'

'Mr Gatwick? We've come about this invoice,' Genevieve said, laying the slip on the counter and smoothing it out to make the writing more legible.

Gatwick, adjusting his spectacles on his nose, peered at it, and his look became wary. 'Now, here, I warned your friend about it,' he told Oliver. 'It was only ever a temporary effect, at the breadth he wanted. You can't be coming in to complain now. If it's lasted the year, you've had a bargain no matter the price.'

Oliver looked down at where the man was tapping an impatient finger on the invoice. 'What was only a temporary effect?' he rumbled. 'Why did you say "again" when you saw me? Did I buy one of those trains?'

'Which friend?' Genevieve put in. 'Do you mean Mr Reuben McAvey? Did he buy a…box off you recently? Or a lock, for a box?'

He stiffened. Tone cooling from irritated to a bland, distancing professionalism, he said, 'Forgive my error. I will not further discuss my clientele's private business.' He flipped closed a ledger on the counter.

'But the invoice, here,' Oliver said. 'I'm not here to complain about it. Wondering…can the effect be renewed?'

Gatwick's eyes narrowed behind his neat little spectacles. He squinted at Oliver for a long moment, evidently weighing the temptation of custom against the risk of…of who knew what. 'You don't remember coming here before, do you?'

Oliver smiled and said, 'I came here with McAvey, this time last year.' He paused, then ventured, 'We weren't buying any lock back then.'

It was sheer brazen bluff on Oliver's part, but it seemed to work. The clockwork Artisan gave a small nod, more to himself than to Oliver. Shooting another glance at Genevieve, lingering, insultingly evaluative, he said, 'The work can be renewed, yes. For the same price again.'

'I need to see the original specifications,' Oliver said. 'I want to make some changes.'

Genevieve admired Oliver's subterfuge as the man pushed the big ledger aside, and pulled out a smaller, plainer book from under the counter. He flipped through the pages. The riffling was too fast to make out details of clients or commissions, but there were not so many pages before he reached the one he was looking for; his prices reflected, then, the complexity and rarity of the work he did.

She realised the clockwork and clever mechanisms and minor Artistry in the shop comprised only his public business. Unease crawled up her spine, but she brushed the feeling aside when he turned the book towards them both, saying, 'Look here, this was the commission.'

When she leaned forwards to look, she felt his fingers brush her neck. He tugged loose a necklace chain, and murmured, 'Well, now.'

Genevieve tried to pry those impudent bare fingers away. She was too surprised for it to be more than a feeble effort, her Art safely at bay, but Oliver, looking up from the ledger too late, loomed over him, reaching to seize his wrist.

Gatwick made a fist about the large cabochon gem dangling at the end of the chain, smiling like the jolly Christmas figure he resembled at their strangely slow and ineffectual reaction. 'I cannot say I appreciate having my hand forced without proper payment, but needs must, I suppose.'

Art swelled.

*

THE OTHERS ARRIVED back at Holland Park, out of sorts because Genevieve and Oliver had not waited for them, and they'd had to make their own way home through the hot and stinking streets.

'I forgot you were with us,' Genevieve said in bafflement.

Reuben was right, she thought, she made such stupid mistakes. The baby had only made it worse, riddling her brain with silly lapses she couldn't account for. She couldn't even remember the carriage ride home from the apothecary.

'Never mind,' Cecelia said, though plainly baffled herself. 'Mass is all registered now, at least.'

She paused, gloved hands worrying at each other, as Oliver handed Massimo a wrapped box, a small token of congratulations for his newly official Artisan status. Massimo – Mass, it seemed – tore the paper off and opened the box to discover a floor toy very like one of the popular dribblers. He burst out into excited thanks and ran upstairs to play with it.

Once he was gone, Cecelia said, 'You should know, he's about to turn thirteen. He gave his birthdate as the same as Rose's.'

For a blank moment, the name meant nothing to Genevieve. Then she remembered, in disorientating flashes: her little girl, tiny but lusty-loud in her arms, suckling heartily at her breast, blue and still in her blankets. Genevieve had dreamed of an empty cot for months afterwards.

'I think Reuben must have convinced him that's his real birthday, to torment you.'

My husband would never hurt me like that, Genevieve thought, and almost had to pinch herself to remember the brutal truth. She loved him. He, at some point, had stopped loving her. Perhaps it had been the moment he'd touched the copper knife, and it had whispered to him exactly what he wanted to hear, in a way she'd never been quite a good enough wife to do for him.

But a nasty jape centred on their first lost child – it suggested the worm of discontent had started right then, all those years ago. But he'd only begun researching the knife, unknowingly echoing Varley, in the wake of the stillbirth. If she concentrated hard enough, she could rediscover moments, very many shining moments, of joy and pleasure within their marriage, but not since the stillbirth.

Perhaps that was when he had turned from merely not loving his wife, to hating her.

Cecelia gathered her hands into her own, and chafed at fingers gone cold and stiff. 'Gin?'

Genevieve pulled free and mustered a smile. 'I'm fine.'

Fletcher went to attend his appointment with Miss Landrau, Cecelia to her committee meeting. Oliver had intended to go with her, but after a quiet conference which Genevieve was sure was about her, chose to stay.

Genevieve, Oliver and Mass thus spent a quiet evening together in the drawing room, Bridget having helped Genevieve into a demure but comfortable wrapper. She desultorily turned the pages of a newspaper. She'd once been a great reader, and could now barely glance at the page before the print blurred, her head beginning to ache. Oliver rose and turned down the gasoliers, and lit a paraffin lamp instead, its light not as bright as the gas, but cleaner, with less soot and fumes.

She closed her eyes, to listen to Oliver's honeyed growl of a voice as he read to a very withdrawn young shapeshifter. It would have been lovely, almost familial, if Mass hadn't seemed so sad and subdued.

It was odd. He had been happy earlier, hadn't he?

She knew she shouldn't feel sorry for him. As much as they couldn't bring themselves to evict the child, he was Reuben's tool, harmless only under constant vigilance. Yet, it was increasingly difficult to remember that in the teeth of his sweet smile, timid manner, and waiflike face.

For his Art to have taken the form it did… Young Mass must have very much needed to hide, to be overlooked, to fit himself into the space available to him. If he could have been invisible instead, he might have done so, but she'd never heard of any Artistry managing that. Whatever he had gone through didn't bear thinking about, but they would not make it worse for him by making him anything other than welcome.

He pepped up when Bridget delivered a tea tray laden with thick slices of buttered fruit cake, and even more so when Genevieve pushed the plate over to him. She didn't think even the most soulful of puppies could have managed a more adoring look than he gave her then.

She smiled fondly down into her cup, with amusement and sadness mingled, too, because he made her think about Peter Llewellyn, Lulu's mild-mannered husband, and the traditional Welsh stories he used to tell them. She was put in mind of the bwbachs, long-nosed little creatures that asked only for copious fresh food in exchange for nestling benignly within their chosen household.

The tea was herbal, made from the concoction in the packet Oliver had brought home from the apothecary, a blend designed to settle nauseous stomachs and pique appetites. He'd noticed her lack of enthusiasm for food, she supposed. It was both annoying and thoughtful; on balance, the latter. It helped that the subtle flavours of the tisane, ginger and chamomile, were pleasant, and did ease the constant bilious pressure in her belly. She ate the one fruity slice Mass had not demolished.

At last, before the dully ticking clock chimed ten, Genevieve decided to retire early, her exhaustion finally winning over her will.

At the bottom of the stairs, Oliver sent Mass on up to their shared room before turning to her. 'He's twelve,' he said, sombre. 'I will not be offended if you want him moved from my room.'

Genevieve had another of those frozen moments, but at least this one was entirely explanatory: she was astonished at the implication.

Before she could say so, he said, 'The pantry by Bridget's room. I'll ward it so I'll know if he opens the door.' He paused. 'If he passes its threshold.'

That was probably because it had occurred to him that Mass could turn into something very small and scurry out under a warded or locked door; he would be as slippery as Whitely, she supposed, if he took it into his head to be so.

But that little storeroom downstairs was narrow and windowless, musty and chill, unpleasant to linger in, let alone sleep a whole night. It would have to be cleared out, and the pallet dragged all the way down from Oliver's room. Then it would be pitch-black without a lamp, and Genevieve didn't like to think of their young, sweet shapeshifter trapped in the dark.

Anyway, the thought was entirely unnecessary. 'Oliver,' she said. 'By your side is the safest place for any child. He stays with you.'

A shy expression of pleasure crossed his face at her open avowal of trust. He silently offered her his arm.

Her dudgeon was only mild. 'I'm with child, not without legs.'

'You are *very* with child,' he said, arm held patiently crooked.

He made her laugh, as he so often did, and thus relent; she hooked her hand about his elbow and let him escort her up the stairs, and did, perhaps, lean on him near the top. He walked her to her bedroom door and took her hand.

He lifted it to his mouth. He didn't kiss the back of it, which would have been strange but nearly acceptable. Instead, he gently turned it, and kissed the tender skin of her inner wrist, the veins stark blue tracery under her skin.

''Night, Gin,' he said, in a slow and rumbling undertone that shivered right through her, a flash from the pulse at her wrist all the way to an answering pulse at her core.

''Night, Oliver,' she purred, eyes half-lidded, a promise of *later, soon* automatically insinuating itself into her murmur.

She was halfway into her room and he was halfway down the hallway before it struck both of them that that had been firstly, a scandalous exchange, and secondly, an utterly bizarre exchange.

He turned around, face flaming scarlet in the lamplight of the hallway. 'Gin – Mrs McAvey – I can only beg your pardon, I don't know…' He trailed off, before saying, with deep bewilderment, 'I do not understand why I did that.'

Genevieve, for her part, stood looking down at her wrist, where the touch of his mouth lingered on her pulse point. She should have been appalled, but instead found herself surprised by the familiarity of the sensation.

Yes, this, part of her was insisting. *Him.*

Wonderingly, she traced the tingle with the tips of her fingers, feeling the echo of the startling, enlivening bolt of sheer response that had shot through her.

'Artisans are allowed to touch each other,' she managed to say.

'Not like that, they're not,' he said.

Genevieve's breathing stopped. Oliver straightened too, wearing a blank look. She knew he must be grappling with the same confused and maddeningly faint recognition that had taken her. It hung there between them: they had said those words to each other before, after the first time they'd combined their Arts to catch a rogue Artisan, pre-Agency, and she had—and he had—

'Good night, Mr Oliver,' she said, brisk and impersonal.

'Good night, Mrs McAvey,' Oliver said.

They turned from each other, smooth and serene.

14

ANTOINETTE LOCKE SAVED THEM.

The heatwave peaked, but did not break. The headlines shouted of temperature records smashed. Genevieve dutifully kept to the house, falling into the heavy, slow drift of time that accompanied the anticipation of imminent childbirth. The others continued in their usual routines, weighed down by the oppression of the summer and their own, more figurative, burdens: Fletcher's severed connection, Cecelia's never-ending causes, Oliver's exhausting, unappreciated family responsibilities.

Mass quietly settled in amid their morass. As befitted an Artisan whose Artistry took such a chameleon form, he was eager to please, to not cause any trouble that might remind them he'd been inflicted on them by Reuben. His suspicious provenance should have been more prominent than it was, but he seemed so entirely innocent that not only did they very quickly stop asking questions, they forgot they had done so.

He remained absurdly, adoringly, grateful every time Genevieve pushed a plate of cake and cream his way, and, furthering her fond thoughts of Welsh goblins, he took to helping Bridget about the house with good will and surprising competence. Perhaps there was some truth to his vague mention of the Magdalen refuges to Whitely. She'd thought they were solely for women, but she guessed she'd been wrong; perhaps the fallen women's bastard children, of either sex, were raised there, too.

The days were long and growing longer. Tired of the interminable waiting amid the interminable heat and stink, Genevieve eventually went out to the storeroom to take the dustsheets off her mother's furniture. She was determined to set the house up to her liking, especially now they were accommodating their mild-mannered baby Artisan as well.

This dusty room was where Fletcher had had Oliver move the forgotten detritus that had been in the temporary birthing chamber, so it was even more crowded than on the horrible day Reuben had played his disgusting trick on her and Oliver.

She found herself trying to become angry and disturbed again, but the emotion melted like ice in this weather, leaving a shallow impression of fossilised wifely forbearance. She felt twisted about, in a weary kind of way.

She uncovered the divan, remembering Reuben trying to push her down on to it. Remembering the idea he'd put into her head. Oliver watching her, eyes darkening with desire, pupils dilating as he drank in the sight of her need, her hunger for his mouth on her. Leaning over her, ready to gratify her every desire—

'Gin?' Oliver called, and Genevieve started violently and jerked away from the divan as if he'd caught her in a compromising pose. She stumbled, tripping over her own boots as one heel caught the hem of her skirt.

He lunged in from the doorway and caught her, his strong forearms wrapping around her as her stomach, greatly enlarged, pillowed against his torso, the thick muscle of physical labour suddenly apparent through his shirt. Startled, he held on, bracing them both against her gravid weight, and she had to bite her tongue to stop herself from snarling at him to release her at once. It wasn't his fault Reuben's lewd insinuations – lewd actual, unthinkable words – had infected her.

Then Oliver was putting her back on her feet, stepping away, head bowed, hands held up in silent apology; he'd recognised her shock, but ascribed the reason to the same old dreary chains, the strict mores of mundane society, so very hard to shake off, even for Artisans, even after all these years.

She said, 'Thank you, Oliver,' with something of a bite to it, irritated more by the situation than him. 'You were looking for me?'

Oliver looked adorably confused, a man who had come upstairs and forgotten why, as bad as her and her foggy lapses. He gave himself a shake. 'Tea's on.' He looked around. 'Should I bring a tray?'

'No, no, I'll come.' She took a step towards the door, then said, 'After, though, will you come back here with me? I want to bring my mother's things into the house. Do you remember the rear parlour back at the Belgravia house?'

He must do, she thought, unbidden. He'd played chess with his nieces there often enough, and her father, too. That must have been before she was married, when she and Oliver, and the others, had begun to work together, as part of the push to create the Agency.

And Reuben, too, of course.

Confusedly, she finished, 'I want that here.'

Oliver nodded, immediately, if silently, pledging his support to the endeavour, and it would be him taking it on, with his strength and his telekinesis, exactly as it had been him helping Fletcher establish his accouchement chamber. He probably considered that scheme as well-intentioned but misguided as Cecelia did, yet had applied his Art to helping his friend regardless. Genevieve hoped he was not now turning the same placid acceptance on her own misguided venture. Perhaps her mother's comfortable, comforting furniture would seem dingy and out-of-place, as Reuben had insisted it would.

He was right, she thought. The back parlour of her parents' Georgian home had been small, dark and cosy, perfect for quiet family evenings, and thus for the warmth of shabby, treasured pieces like these. The large, long drawing room of this modern house, with its ornate fireplace, high ceilings, built-in cases, polished gasoliers, and glossy piano, would make a mésalliance with her inherited pieces.

If such judgements were perturbing Oliver, he did not show it. He tugged at one of the armchairs, rocking it onto its front legs to test its shape and weight.

Behind it lay a large crate, familiar to Genevieve. Her mother had moved her paintings in wooden boxes like this one, well-wrapped for the travel.

It was probably empty, she thought, even as she wiped the dust off and pried at the lid. Antoinette would never *store* paintings like this.

But it seemed she had. Once Oliver had used a small burst of materials Art, a subset of his telekinesis, to crack the wood around the iron nails holding the lid shut, they discovered that the crate was stacked to the brim with canvases, the regular rectangular shapes muffled in soft linen swaddling.

Oliver helped Genevieve unpack them, leaning them carefully against the walls, a nascent art gallery.

'Mother must have been planning to send them to Kingsford, before…'

Genevieve trailed off. Before she'd died, she supposed, though she remembered nothing of it. Whatever had happened, whatever illness or accident had struck her mother down, it must have been abrupt. She had not even had time to attach the shipping label, and the crate must have been bundled up with her other effects when the McAveys made the shift from Belgrave Square to Holland Park. Genevieve had missed them, when she'd gathered up and sold all of Antoinette Locke's other works.

She frowned at that. She still could not believe she'd done any such thing. Perhaps they had been desperate for money. That would explain selling the Belgravia house to her cousin, too. But she couldn't quite remember what could have put them into such straitened circumstances, and certainly they had had enough to fund the purchase of a household full of new furniture and furnishings, all to Reuben's tastes.

That recalled her to her purpose here, remaking the house into her own domain.

'The tea?' Oliver said quietly, sounding oddly anxious.

Too eager to see her mother's paintings again to heed him, Genevieve unwrapped the first offering. It might be suitable for the drawing room wall, or her bedroom, or the study. Perhaps it could even suit the nursery, which she was debating if she should reestablish in the empty bedroom beside hers. That was against tradition, but would leave a room upstairs for Mass. Spy or not, he had nowhere else to go, and really was the most undemanding of guests.

Of course, the guestroom would be available again soon. Shaking her head at thoughtful, silly, Fletcher, she held up the exposed painting.

She couldn't place it for a moment. Antoinette Locke had been famed for her colours and layers – she'd been an early user of gumtion – and her confident brushstrokes, and her unusual compositions, which captured the spirit of her subjects with honesty and compassion in equal proportions. She typically used the smallest size of standard canvas, traditionally for head portraits, in any sort of arrangement she saw fit, including by turning the canvas the landscape way and portraying intricate dollhouse type details across crowd scenes, or painting the downcast eyes of a mysterious maiden in such close aspect it felt painfully intimate. Variety was another of her hallmarks.

This painting was relatively simple, depicting a rakish and bare-headed young man in oratory, arms akimbo, frock coat billowing, a storm brewing behind him. Oliver began to absently hum a song that had been immensely popular nearly twenty years before, and Genevieve finally understood what she was seeing.

It was Mrs Keeley in breeches, in full flight as the titular in *Jack Sheppard*, the dramatic scenery of the set writ large behind her, a blue-tinged shadow where the gallows would loom large beyond the last act. A real copycat murder the following summer had taken the gloss off the fictional version somewhat, at least for the more respectable classes, but that autumn and all through the winter, the play had been a runaway hit at the Adelphi.

'And here I am, pals, merry and free,' Oliver sang softly, deep from his chest. It was a silly song, as so many of the most popular were; it sounded ridiculously good in his low growly voice, honey and gravel. *'Nix my dolly, pals, fake away.'*

Her parents and Uncle Reginald had taken Alex and Lulu – though she wasn't Lucinda back then, not yet, or at least, she had not yet begun to let others, not even Alex, meet Lucinda – to see the play, that gory and melodramatic adaptation from Ainsworth's penny dreadful. Genevieve, despite being three years older than the twins, was disallowed. It had been the first inkling that her childish idyll with her cousins was mere illusion and that an unexpected ushering into adult – womanly – respectability was beginning.

She fought it. They waited until the elder Lockes went out for a long evening of engagements. The twins were already tall, though not nearly as tall as they would become, and not yet taller than their statuesque cousin. Genevieve managed to get into a spare pair of Lulu's trousers, cinched at the waist and not too shamefully short at the ankles, and one of Alex's older coats, tucking her pale plait under a borrowed hat and wearing her father's boots over two pairs of thick socks. They'd left the house shortly after the servants retired.

Jack Sheppard was always the first performance of the evening. They'd arrived in time for the last half of it, and left before the second performance, one about a barber, to be sure to be home before their parents. She could, abruptly, taste the roasted chestnuts and hear the raucous cheers of the audience. She was enthralled, watching amid tightly packed bodies in the gallery, her cousins bookending her as bulwark against the noisy, cheerful West End crowd.

They'd had to knock to be let back in, because one of the servants must have come across the unbolted door after their departure. Alex, forthrightly charming even then, had easily talked the junior footman who opened the door to them into holding his tongue about their transgression even as he folded his hand closed around a tip in an impressively confident imitation of his elders.

Smiling at the memory – it felt good, to have such a clear memory to sink into – Genevieve rubbed a hand over her stomach, telling the baby, 'I hope you don't give me half the trouble we junior Lockes gave our elders. Or perhaps, I merely hope I find out about it as infrequently as they did.'

Her smile turned rueful. It struck her suddenly how sad it was that this little one would not have cousins to lead her astray, or to lead astray. Well, not unless Lulu and Miss Knight continued in their mutual and growing regard and decided to come to a convoluted solution vis-à-vis marriage to Sir Kingsford, a legal contract bringing Miss Knight inalienably under the protection of his wealth and title, and the further arrangements vis-à-vis the begetting of the theoretical cousin none of Genevieve's business.

It was not beyond the realms of possibility, she supposed, nor was it entirely impossible that she herself would marry again before her child-bearing years were behind her to give this child younger siblings to torment. Mrs Murphy reassured her that she knew women with a good decade on her who'd successfully birthed children.

That presupposed she'd successfully birth this one, the probability of which she could not bring herself to think on, and then meet a decent man willing to marry an abandoned wife with a child and, apparently, very few assets until she found a reliable nursemaid and got back to Artisan work. *And* that she'd be able to break herself of the hopeless, despairing love she still felt for her lost husband, who, she remembered again, had lost *himself*.

She found herself, in her abstraction, looking at Oliver. He stopped singing, blushing a little.

'Did you sneak out to see that one, too?' she asked.

He smiled. 'I didn't have to sneak out.'

'Of course not.'

'Me and my brothers went en masse, when they were on shore leave that winter.'

Genevieve tsked. 'But Oliver, shouldn't you have been improving your minds with rational amusements and serious contemplation of the moral condition of man?'

To her great pleasure, his smile became an appreciative chuckle, rumbling from his broad chest. 'I think we went back three or four times. This painting evokes the memories, vividly. I can almost taste the ginger beer.' He paused. 'She was a great talent, your mother.'

Startled, she glanced up from her fond admiration of the canvas. 'Do you mean that mundanely, or in relation to Artistry? A talent like Turner or a talent like the twins?'

Oliver looked startled in his turn. 'I meant a great artist. But…' He shrugged. 'I haven't had a memory as true as that for some time. Have you?'

He was a man who chose his words carefully. Another might have said *clear*, but he said *true*, and that felt right.

Thoughtfully, Genevieve revealed the next painting. This one made her outright laugh – it was of Franz Liszt. Her mother had seen him perform during his visit to London in 1840, and, like many others, had fallen victim to the craze, though not to the extent – Genevieve assumed – of pulling other women's hair to try to lay hands on a mere handkerchief touched by the celebrity musician. The painting was a memento, capturing his tempestuous locks and mesmerised and mesmerising gaze as he crouched over his piano. She could almost hear the strains of his music as she touched it, could almost see her father playing the great composer's music for her mother. She was sure that Theodore being one of the few men who'd made a proper effort towards an accomplishment thought of as feminine had been a deciding factor in his successful wooing of his carefree artistic wife.

Glancing at Oliver, she saw from his politely neutral expression that this painting had not had a reminiscent effect on him; he hadn't heard Liszt, or not in any memorable way. He could be working up to prodding her about the tea, so she turned quickly to undo the next wrapping.

The two paintings so far had been examples of the more commercial of her mother's undertakings, tokens of the wild fads that regularly swept through London, popular even before the current and growing trend for collecting *carte de visites*. Genevieve expected more of the same as she pulled the next swaddle free, but it was a personal memento this time.

It was a portrait of her father as a young man, the Monument figuring in the background. Her parents had met there, two groups of friends on an outing with, improbably, a mutual connection between them to effect introductions. They'd shortly both agreed to attain tickets to the next Almack's ball to better their acquaintance, and their courtship had proceeded from there.

Young Theodore Locke had made quite the impression on the rising artist: in the portrait, he was dressed in a fine scarlet redingote, depicted astraddle a velocipede to better show off ridiculously long legs tightly clad in silk pantaloons.

Oliver gave a small, astonished laugh. Her father had been unremarkably staid by the time he met him, and Oliver surely had never imagined him aping Brummel and riding a dandy-horse. He looked to share his smile with Genevieve, but she didn't meet his eye. She was overwhelmed by a layered confection of emotion.

Love and grief, triggered by the simple sight of her father's smiling face, captured so skilfully. Beneath that, a fond familial amusement welling up from her foggy past; she could almost hear Antoinette teasing her husband about his youthful dandified figure as she propped the little portrait on the mantelpiece in the back parlour. There was a muted relief there, too:

though Theodore and Antoinette were careful to keep arguments away from their daughter, she'd known they'd been at odds and that the portrait was a gift, a peace offering.

Deeper, quieter, lay an abiding sadness. She had been despondent when her mother had painted this portrait from memory, perhaps rose-tinted. It had been smothering her like a snowdrift. Her father had taken her withdrawal as serenity, a final dutiful acceptance of his plans for her. Her mother had known it for a snuffing of hope. The portrait wasn't only a gift to her husband, but to her daughter as well, somehow.

She could not remember now what had caused her such dejection, or why her mother had thought the portrait would help. Frowning, Genevieve set it aside to expose the next one, vowing that if it was another family memento, she would leave off until later, so as to not bore Oliver or force Bridget to discard the cooling tea.

'Oh,' she said.

It was a simple portrait of herself with Lulu, and she placed it in time instantly, because her mother had captured them both so honestly, exactly as her renown attested. It must have been swiftly sketched and then properly painted sometime in the spring of fifteen years before, when Genevieve had been facing the earliest engagements of her second Season, and Lulu had made it through the first year after she'd revealed her truth to her family and to the wider world, and settled into herself.

Genevieve recollected, vaguely, that that spring and summer had been a lull in the march of history – the Opium War coming to an end, treaties signed, Chartist agitation calming, an heir to the crown and two royal princesses presented, and the full emancipation desired by the abolitionists finally achieved. The disruption of the Springtime of Nations and the Chartists' third petition, and the Great Famine in Ireland, and the various insults of imperialism and further assassination attempts on Queen Victoria were yet to come and unsuspected by most.

But perhaps she merely thought of it as a relatively peaceful time for the nation because it had been such a personally turbulent time for her, and she'd selfishly buried any events not at the centre of her own world. She traced the caked oil of the painting, emotions and flashes of imagery rising like sharp rocks from a dangerous fog, as if illuminated by a lighthouse beacon.

There, her own youthful beauty under her fingertips. She had not known how beautiful she truly was, back then, or perhaps she had not understood the full extent of the love with which her mother regarded her. But her bloom was tinged ever so subtly with a tension about the corners of her eyes and her mouth.

Her Art had just risen, late and thus utterly unexpected, but she hadn't told her parents yet. She was hiding everything, in the moment this portrait captured: her fear that this season would end as her first, with no offer good enough for her father, and herself an object of scorn among the other girls and their high social circle; her anger at her father, for putting her through it, the scalding emotion a secret even from herself and yet hinted at by the dash of her mother's brush in shaping her lips; her desire for the freedom the twins had; her alarm and her burgeoning pleasure at the metaphysical changes sweeping her body that might yet gift her that freedom.

And there Lulu, her androgynously handsome hawk-nosed face, no longer and never again identical to her twin, with the new way she wore her cosmetics and dressed her hair, and the way she'd learned to carry herself. She sported Genevieve's gift of a cameo at her throat, and rings on her strong fingers, one for each brother. Mother had portrayed the defiant scowl with which Lucinda habitually fronted the world, and, too, the quiet, private, fierce joy, that she allowed only her family to see.

Those two young girls, lost forever to time, smiled at each other in cousinly mischief, and Alex wasn't there because Alex had been suffering his own crisis that spring. He'd lurked in his room while Genevieve and Lulu took to the garden to soak up the first warmth of the year, and Mother worked behind her easel in the shade.

And then that night, that very night, after her parents had gone out—

She remembered.

15

'COULD YOU SET THAT TREE ON fire, Ginnie?'

Genevieve looked up at the frost-covered branches Lulu was pointing at. 'I think so,' she said. 'But it would be quite irresponsible.'

Her cousin snorted at the very idea of responsibility. Genevieve, on the other hand, had to consider the neighbours, muttering about the dangers of a headlong rush for novelty – 'not only to your own family, sir, but to the other residents of our street!' – when Father had made the mistake of openly musing about the practicalities of installing the same gas lighting now widely used to illuminate public spaces. A fireball erupting in the back garden of the suspect house would be almost exactly what Mr Hardy next door both glumly feared and smugly anticipated. Even if Mother didn't immediately notice the charred branches on her young plane tree, the complaints would be legion.

With that thought in mind, she added, 'Besides, it would rather give the game away.'

It was a few weeks since the dreadful, amazing, life-changing ball when Genevieve's Art had bloomed. No one but her had witnessed the fire combusting straight through her silk gloves into sheerest conflagration. She cried out, burning hands flung wide, and the fire vanished, leaving scorch marks on the previously frost-tipped shrubbery in her isolated corner of the Marlough garden. The singed greenery and a lingering smell were the only evidence it had even happened.

Wide-eyed, she stared at her bare and unmarked fingers. Nonsensically, her first thought was that her gloves must have been dramatically, unfathomably, faulty, some new cheaper or more efficient silk-weaving technique proving unequal to the soft friction of human skin. It would be in the papers soon.

Logic reasserted itself. She gathered herself up, returned to the ballroom to find her mother, and pled a sudden and irrecoverable headache, naked hands locked behind her back.

'I'd have one, too,' Mother muttered, eyeing the Honourable Mr Marlough, that eldest son of an eldest son; he'd be a viscount when his grandfather died, an earl once his father did.

Her sympathy was appreciated, but in an erroneous direction. Genevieve was still determined to please her father in this matter, and trusted he would not steer her so very wrong. The abrasive manner of the potential bridegroom had no weight beside his eventual title and sterling reputation.

Safely home, her bedroom door barred, still in her constrictive gown, Genevieve knelt on the floor and slowly, carefully, set the air on fire to create her first deliberate fireball. She'd gasped and dropped it, and, thank God, it extinguished in a puff of hot air.

Her first, immediate instinct was to keep it secret, even from Mother, until she could come to terms with it herself. But she had to share it with someone, and who better than Lulu, who had trusted her with her own difficult, life-changing secret.

The carriage arrived within days. Lulu had brought her twin along, citing his need for time and space away from Sir Kingsford, whose strict, cold guardianship had not lessened in chafing on Alex in the months since their father's sudden death.

'If I left them alone together, they'd kill each other,' she told Genevieve without a single hint she was exaggerating, as they sat in the garden in the late spring sunshine.

It was the mirror image of the year before, Genevieve now poring over the etiquette books, Lulu poking fun at them like Genevieve had poked fun at the ridiculous ladies' journals.

Back then, Father had been slightly, shamefacedly, cautious about taking in Lulu, her potential for causing scandal so very high as Genevieve's first Season loomed nigh. She'd thought he would be, accordingly, outright reluctant to host her cousin now she was grimly confronting her second Season without a fish firmly on her hook, her angling guidebooks singularly lacking.

However, he hadn't even needed Mother to talk him into it, but ordered the guestrooms opened for the twins with something like relief. He knew – both parents knew – something was wrong with his daughter, even beyond the increasingly desperate etiquette manual consultation.

She twinged with guilt for not telling them, and yet, she'd still cried off tonight's engagement without compunction.

'Another headache?' Mother had said, laying the back of her hand on Genevieve's forehead. 'Must be catching.'

At least here Genevieve was truly innocent; she herself didn't know why Alex had been hiding out in his room since arriving, flushed and monosyllabic and unusually querulous, complaining of headaches from the incessant noise of London. Lulu *did* know, Genevieve was sure of that, but Lulu knew how to keep secrets, her own and others, and Genevieve was so grateful on her own behalf that she didn't press for answers about Alex.

Once her parents were safely away and the servants had finished their evening duties and retired to their own suppers and beds, Genevieve and Lulu had come here into the garden, where the evening frost seemed a solid precaution against error.

The night was clear and bitingly cold. Lulu had thick petticoats on, her brother's spare coat, and gloves, and a muffler. A few years before, they'd had such a bitter winter, with snowbanks deep enough to swallow a veritable giant, that she couldn't have lingered long outside even in extra layers, but this winter had been mild, comparatively, and the spring weather icy but manageable.

Genevieve no longer needed any layers at all. She was hatless and gloveless, feeling the touch of night air like a cooling breeze in summer even as her breath frosted the air like Lulu's.

It was thrilling, and diagnostic. Artisans could readily be picked out of a crowd, comfortable in summer layers in the worst of winters, and suffering the heat in summer.

Genevieve's first task this evening was to light the brass brazier for her cousin. She held her hands over the bed of charcoal in the rounded bottom and frowned. She hadn't deliberately tried to set anything on fire yet. It was like using a different muscle, she supposed, a twitch in her head that would ignite a thing rather than the air. Or was it the same; was she merely lighting the air that surrounded the charcoal? Artisans had very narrow abilities in that way, didn't they? She'd been scouring the papers and the circulating library for all the information she could glean, but until she told her parents the truth, her sources were limited. She should—

'Come on, Ginnie, I'm freezing,' Lulu broke in, and Genevieve started and clenched her fists.

The charcoal burst alight with a crackling hiss, before settling into a steady low flame. The ignition had been Art; the fuel was mundane, so it would now burn on without her intervention. She smiled, delighted with herself. Lulu gave her a congratulatory tap before huddling close to the warmth, suggesting new and ever more outlandish ways to test the Art.

But she was shortly distracted from encouraging Genevieve to set the garden afire. Fidgeting with one of the rings hidden under her gloves, she looked back at the house thoughtfully. 'Alex is heading out. Must be feeling better.'

'Are you sure that's not an Art itself?' Genevieve asked. 'Psychometric Art?'

'Am I wearing most of the clothes in my wardrobe and half of Alex's?' Lulu countered brusquely, still glancing restlessly in the direction her brother must be moving.

'Where's he going? Should we follow him?'

Lulu ran her gloved hand over the sleeve of her – Alex's – coat and shook her head. 'He rankles enough under Kingsford's guardianship, I don't need to be his nursemaid too.'

They turned, then, to setting challenges for Genevieve's Art. She was expanding her abilities, and testing her limits, growing, blooming, with each attempt. Soon she'd be able to set fire to the pile of etiquette manuals and burn them to ash without even a smoulder mark left on the starched white tablecloth.

She still wanted to win her father a son-in-law with a title, she reminded herself, and present him a grandson in line to an earldom.

But it became more and more difficult to remember that when Lulu said, in her frank way, 'You do realise how much more freedom being an Artisan gives you, right? You'd be a fool to marry some highborn twat now.'

'I *want* to marry,' Genevieve protested, if weakly.

She did want to marry, and run her own household, and have accomplished children; it was the pinnacle of achievement for a woman of her class, as her father – progressive in many ways, traditional in this – told her. Very many people, books, articles and customs told her that, too, her mother conspicuously not among them.

But now, watching her fireballs drift slowly along, petering out at the end of a trail of melted frost, or soar high before swirling into nothing, she wondered: *did* she want that, or had she convinced herself she wanted it because it had felt like her sole option.

If she stopped to think about it too hard, if she listened to Lulu's wild ideas – 'We could work together, Ginnie. We could be a team, and travel the world. We could catch rogue Artisans, I'll track them, you scare them into surrendering! Well. We can do that bit together.' – she might start to doubt that she had ever wanted anything so stultifyingly small.

It had begun to gall, that the Locke brothers had been such iconoclasts in their youth, and Uncle Reginald had remained so when he'd sired three presumed-male children, he and his second wife giving the twins in particular radical leeway. Meanwhile, Father had contracted about his female child in a defensive impulse, a rictus instinct that trapped her just as much as it protected her.

The message had been clear all her life, if she had opened her eyes enough to read it: the male Locke scions could do as they liked, even the one who had turned out female later. The sole female-from-birth Locke scion could not.

She lost herself into the crisp and surreal night, creating fire from nothing, feeling her Art grow from a stuttering flutter to a steady glow inside her, and adding tentative suggestions to Lulu's enthusiastic daydreams, daydreams that might even turn into plans.

'Where's Alex in all this?' she asked eventually, hoping it would be the dash of cold water they both needed. She hadn't even told her parents she was an Artisan yet, she couldn't start planning beyond that.

Lulu looked surprised. 'With us, of course.'

'But he doesn't even have a talent, let alone an Art. It'd be dangerous for him.' Genevieve paused, reviewing Alex's behaviour this last week. 'Lulu?'

'He can handle danger,' Lulu said pitilessly. 'He went out tonight looking for it, the great dolt.'

She'd turned to look, not at the house, but at the rear of the garden, at the mews house, empty, since Genevieve's parents were still engaged. A crash sounded from inside. Lulu galloped off down the garden path. Genevieve ran after her.

It was dim inside. One of the footmen had left a low lamp burning. The tang of oiled metal was in the air, and the sweet scent of the hay from the stalls next door.

They slowed, Genevieve holding onto Lulu in breathless anticipation. It was as if God had heard their outlandish plans and was giving them a taste of the reality. Genevieve couldn't yet decide if she liked it or not. She could feel Lulu's coiled tension beside her, ready to strike.

Ahead, she saw two shapes by the lamp, one leaning over the other, and heard the deep growl of an unfamiliar voice, northern, with the archetypal softening that came from years in the city.

'Do you think we can make it to your bedroom without waking the house, or do you want a stall?'

'Bed.' That was Alex, though the single word was slurred almost beyond recognition.

Lulu gave an outraged shout and stormed forwards. 'Hoi! My brother is in no shape to suck your cock, you shit!'

Genevieve gasped at the shocking language, and again as the implication sank in. She lit a pocket of air overhead, casting the open interior into illumination as bright as limelight.

The stranger, suddenly caught out, straightened up from bending over Alex, and stared at them, looking as horrified as she felt.

He was somewhere in his mid-twenties, which made him a predatory number of years older than the intoxicated adolescent he'd been trying to sneak into bed, and large – heavyset and broad, and substantially topping the twins' already noteworthy height. Despite the cold night, his head was bare, with hair shaved back to bristles, and he—

He had *tattoos* on his hands, good God, who had Alex gotten mixed up with?

'Step away from him or we'll set you on fire,' Lulu bellowed, not at all intimidated by meeting someone larger than herself for once, and why would she be, when she had a weapons Artisan to call on.

Genevieve felt a little ill. She did not think she was *quite* ready to set a person on fire, even one who had apparently decided it was acceptable to take advantage of her sixteen-year-old cousin, still mourning his father and lashing out against his brother, and so drunk she could smell the cheap booze on him from here.

The man nudged Alex, sprawled on the ground next to him, with one heavy boot. 'Locke. Explain.'

Alex's eyes blinked open. He squinted at Lulu and Genevieve. 'Stand down there, my valiant Miss Lockes,' he said, picking his way through each word. 'Despite my very best efforts, Oliver has no intention of fucking me.'

The man, Oliver, didn't say anything, but he looked sternly down at Alex and nudged him again. Any such rebuke delivered by Sir Kingsford, wordless or – as was more typical – extremely otherwise, would have sent Alex into a fruitless rage.

Now, he tipped his head back further and sighed. 'I do beg your pardon, ladies.'

Oliver was evidently unappeased. He waited. Alex tsked. With far more grace than he'd lately given his family any indication of possessing, he made a courtly flourish and said, 'The Miss Lockes, may I present Mr William Oliver Bennet.'

Mr William Oliver Bennet pronounced this satisfactory with a single brisk nod, and Alex, it had to be said, looked more than a little chuffed at the approbation.

'What do you think you're doing?' Lulu snarled, hauling her brother to his unsteady feet and slinging an arm about his shoulders. It wasn't clear which of the two she was addressing until she turned on Oliver. 'He is *sixteen*, he is *grieving*—'

Oliver lifted a hand, a simple and placatory gesture which nonetheless managed to give Lulu a moment of uncharacteristic second thought. He was not of an age to be either of their fathers, but he was not so very much younger than Kingsford, and was a much more commanding presence.

'He wasn't going to lay a hand on me.' Alex sounded somewhat more alert now he was back on his feet, though he was leaning heavily on Lulu. 'Which is a pity, because *look* at his hands, girls.'

In the face of three interested Locke stares, Oliver rather lost his authoritative poise and became an awkward and blushing young man of a social class not normally noticed by theirs. He put his hands – large, strong-looking, the backs tattooed and scarred, the fingers long and thick – behind his back.

He cleared his throat and said in firm tones, 'He was at the dockside taverns looking for a fight or a…' Alex sniggered at the man's sudden loss for the obvious word he'd realised he couldn't use without being an utter hypocrite. 'I kept him company until I could persuade him home.'

'To his bed,' Lulu said darkly, but with a slightly uncertain note now. 'Or a goddamned horse stall?'

Oliver said, 'To sleep it off, only.'

'His *intentions*,' Alex added, 'are nothing but good, and I should know.'

He slowly and meaningfully tapped the side of his head, blinking at each tap as if it had surprised him.

'Shut up, Alex,' Lulu said, squeezing her arm tighter about his shoulders.

Meanwhile Oliver looked at Genevieve, and at the fire she was holding over their heads. He smiled crookedly.

He was not at all a handsome man, sallow-faced, thick-featured, the very picture of the brutish thug that haunted the more lurid Gothic tales of innocent young girls kidnapped and sold into unsavoury fates. But his smile lit up his dark eyes and turned a rather threatening aspect into something almost sweet, an unexpectedly docile bear to cuddle up with.

'You might lower that,' he suggested, 'before the roof catches.'

Genevieve closed her hands together, and the fire winked out. Oliver adjusted the wick of the lamp to give them all more light.

'You are Miss Genevieve Locke?' he said. 'Pyrokinetic Artisan. Your cousin is very proud of you.'

'How do you—' Genevieve began reflexively, before hearing the absurdity of the prescribed greeting, and then feeling obliged to finish it anyway. '…do.'

At least she hadn't performed the little dip she'd copied from the other girls at the balls.

He glanced at Lulu. 'And Miss Lucinda Locke, I take it. Locke said you knew exactly where he was and would come if he got into trouble.'

Lulu whacked her brother. 'It's just a talent,' she said. 'I can only sense which direction he's in, and I'd only know he was in trouble when it was too late and I stopped sensing him at all.'

Shaking her head, she started to walk her brother across the floor of the mews house. But he was unmanageably wobbly on his feet, and Oliver quickly scooped an arm around his waist to help. Genevieve followed in their wake, turning down the lamp and closing the door firmly behind them.

They made it down the garden path, Genevieve pausing to douse the embers in the brazier, and through the back door. At the foot of the stairs, Alex compounded his evening's debaucheries by copiously vomiting on the hallway rug. Genevieve wrinkled her nose at the mess, and the penetrating acid of the rank smell. It did not look like Alex had had much to eat in his guided tour of the dockside taverns.

'Are you fucking kidding me with this, Alexander,' Lulu hissed in a strangled whisper, shuffling her feet to avoid the noisome puddle. 'What were you thinking tonight?'

'It's so noisy, Lucy,' Alex muttered, clutching his head and slumping into her. 'It won't stop. I need it to stop. An hour of peace, that's all.'

Lulu huffed but she also turned her head into his shoulder in a rough bunt that stood in for a hug. 'And did your jollification attempt help it any?'

'Made it *worse*,' he whispered back, loudly. 'Consider lessons learnt.'

'When were you going to tell me Alex has an Art blooming too?' Genevieve demanded, in a more effective whisper than Alex's.

'It's a *talent*,' the twins said together in adolescent high dudgeon, provoking Genevieve into rolling her eyes at them. By God, the youngest and most stubborn of the Lockes were irritating sometimes.

'Soon,' Alex said. He managed to straighten out of his half-collapse onto his sister. 'Wanted to get used to it first. You understand that, you haven't told Uncle Theo about yours yet either. But I don't want people outside the family knowing. Don't want to make people uncomfortable around me.'

'Or lose the advantage of knowing their intentions,' Lulu interposed, with infinitely more understandable logic.

Alex didn't argue. 'So keep it quiet, Ginnie.' He looked uncertainly at Oliver, as if he'd forgotten who he was, before nodding and saying, 'You, too, Mister Seaman William Oliver Bennet.'

He smiled, more pleased with himself than someone who'd just left a puddle of reeking vomit on the floor had any right to be. Then, outrageously, he started giggling.

'Ginnie and a *lime*-y,' he chortled. 'It's the admiralty's favourite cock *tail*-y.'

'You are such a disgrace,' Lulu said, before breaking into laughter herself. 'Gin and lime, Jesus, Lexi.'

Genevieve tutted, hands on hips. 'The pair of you belong back in leading strings.'

Unable to hold her severe expression, she burst into a smile. Covering her treacherously curving mouth too late, she risked a glance at Oliver. She should think of him as Mr Bennet; it was too late for that. He was looking sombre but when she caught his gaze with hers, his eyes kindled into brightness and he abruptly had to turn away to compose himself.

Turning back, managing a serious frown, he said, 'On to bed now.'

'I'd be happy about that,' Alex said, 'if I couldn't read your intentions. Whether I want to or not.' Oliver shook his head, a flush darkening his cheeks. 'Is it my nose? My nose is too big, isn't it, Oliver?'

'You'll grow into it, lad,' Oliver told him.

He was smiling again, though, if reluctantly, and Genevieve had the sudden thought that Alex, charming, confident, rash Alexander Locke, had been exceptionally lucky to stumble into Oliver tonight, instead of a less scrupulous man far more willing to take merciless advantage of him.

The lucky little devil was drooping now, both of his supporters bracing against his sagging weight.

'Take him up, I'll deal with the, ah, evidence,' Genevieve volunteered, and then was left at a loss for how to deal with the thick, wet mess soaking into the rug as the other two stumbled up the stairs with Alex, head lolling and feet dragging.

She couldn't rouse one of the servants; the junior Lockes were in long-standing accord that the senior Lockes did not need to know about any of their less salubrious adventures, and she did not think anyone would be fooled if she tried to pass off a stinking pool of rancid regurgitated alcohol as her own more innocent illness.

But she, unsurprisingly, had never had to clean up effluence, or anything really, before. Perhaps, she mused, she could set the incriminating rug on fire as a way of introducing her new Artisan powers.

She was down in the scullery off the kitchen hunting up a bucket, a bar of soap, and lots of rags when Oliver found her. 'He's out. Miss Lucinda is going to bunk with him tonight, make sure he doesn't…' He paused.

'You can say it, I'm fairly unshockable,' Genevieve said, thinking back to Lulu's *My brother is in no shape to suck your cock*. That was about the pinnacle of shock, she thought. She would manage anything else, surely.

'Choke to death on his own spew,' Oliver said flatly.

She nodded, relieved to find that she was, indeed, unshocked. No doubt it happened, though she wasn't clear on why one wouldn't wake up. 'Does he need a bowl, in case?'

Oliver concurred with that; she found him a deep pudding basin in one of the kitchen cupboards and made a mental note to find a way to discreetly replace it, if Alex used it. Oliver uncomplainingly headed back up the three flights of stairs between the kitchen and Alex's bedroom.

He returned to the kitchen again, where she was filling the bucket from the pump.

'Thank you,' she said. She searched for something adequate to say, and habit conveniently supplied it. 'Can I offer you tea?'

They both paused as if they were simultaneously contemplating fitting his bulk into one of the spindle-legged chairs in the formal drawing room upstairs. Genevieve had to swallow a nervous laugh as one of the interminable etiquette manuals interjected instructions into her head: seat him at the corner of the fireplace, in a stuffed chair. He must stay at least ten minutes, but no more than twenty; he should retain his hat and cane instead of passing them to the maid, to show he understands the brevity of the visit. No topic of absorbing interest may be admitted to polite conversation, for it might lead to that great besetting sin of the social visit, *discussion*.

He'd do better in Mother's comfortable old chairs in the cosy rear parlour, but the access there was still befouled by Alex's contribution to the evening. Not a single manual had instructions for what to do about the social faux pas of vomit moating a doorway, let alone how to deal with the large man your intoxicated cousin had dragged home for unfulfilled illicit purposes.

'I best be off,' he said awkwardly, as if reading her thoughts. He moved his hand as if doffing an invisible hat, adding a polite nod, and turned towards the door out to the area stairs.

She felt a moment of immense relief, before realising how rude she was being. Oliver had kindly accompanied Alex half the night and all the way home, solely to keep him safe, and now faced a long and hatless walk in the cold for his trouble, and she'd managed a single distracted thanks for it, and she'd bet Lulu hadn't even managed that.

She started to lift the bucket. 'Wait here. I'll be back, and I'll make us tea.'

'I'll do that.' He took the bucket and rags, and when she would have protested delegating such a nasty job to a stranger, said, 'I've swabbed worse off decks than second-hand rum, Miss Locke.'

'Thank you, Mr Bennet,' she said, a little overwhelmed.

By the time he returned and rinsed everything out and set it back in its place, she had a teapot on the kitchen table, and was fetching down the caddy. She'd wasted time trying to heat the banked stove back up enough to boil water, before realising she might be able to boil it directly, if she could work that out.

'The rug will still be damp in the morning,' he said, sitting opposite her at the table. 'You might need to come up with an explanation for that, or apply gentle heat before you go to bed. Maybe a few drops of perfume, too.'

He seemed comfortable here, where the servants would eat. She felt bad about assuming that. She should insist on moving up to the family's little back parlour, or all the way up to the drawing room, to treat him like the valued guest he was. But then he might think that she thought *she* was too good to have tea where the servants ate.

Confounded etiquette manuals.

He watched her as she cupped her hands about the teapot, her fingers spread over the thin porcelain with its pretty flowered pattern. She didn't want to set the air on fire now. She wanted to make it hot instead, so the hot air would heat the pot and the water. It felt like a good challenge for her Art, actually, a serendipitous chance to practise something new.

They were sitting in silence, a cardinal sin.

'I'm trying to heat the water in here,' she explained. 'Then I can add the tea leaves and let it brew as usual.'

He nodded. 'Be careful the heat doesn't—'

The teapot cracked in half, releasing a flood of hot water over the table.

Oliver leapt up for more rags to soak up the spill, while Genevieve put her face in her hands and made a distressed noise out of all keeping with such a minor accident.

'Sorry,' she said after a moment, realising he'd stopped in the middle of mopping up the water. She wiped her eyes, and determinedly calm, explained, 'That was my grandmother's teapot. Mother will be sad I broke it, that's all. I was thoughtless; I should have practised on a teapot of less sentimental value first.'

Oliver hung the wet rags up with the others, and then found, filled, and brought over a plain dark brown teapot, of sturdy and stolid earthenware.

'You practise on Betty here – take it slower – and I'll try to fix that one,' he said. When she bit her lip, unsure how he proposed to go about the repair, he added, 'It's already broken, Miss Locke, I can't make it worse.'

They sat in silence again, this time companionable. She looked up from concentrating on her hands, cupped around the globular belly of the brown teapot, feeling the slow-growing warmth. Oliver was holding the broken teapot in much the same way, clasping the pieces together as he bent his head over them, as absorbed as she had been.

She was beginning to see what Alex liked about his hands. They were ugly, really, by the exacting, petty standards of the drawing room, blunt instruments of hard labour, big and broad, but he held the delicate pieces as if he cradled a fledgling fallen from its nest, gentle and competent.

The fracture line began to knit together. After a few moments, her grandmother's teapot was whole again, with just a line as thin as a hair to show where the break had been.

'Oh, you're an Artisan too!' she exclaimed.

Oliver smiled his crooked, oddly charming smile. 'Did you think I couldn't afford a hat?'

'I think I thought sailors didn't wear them on land,' she said. 'Sorry. And you're not even a sailor at all, if you're an Artisan.'

'I'm a stevedore,' he said. Then, hesitating, 'Dockhand.'

'I did already know what a stevedore does,' Genevieve said, slightly reprovingly. She'd already noticed, in ladylike passing, his scent, cinnamon and cloves, which made her think he'd been lading spices that day. 'But you're a materials Artisan, really. Earthworker, is it?' She nodded at the repaired teapot.

He cleared his throat, rubbing a finger along the surface of the table. 'You've studied.'

'A little,' she said, disloyal to her own steadfast industriousness of the last two weeks, and even the weeks before that, when Lulu's talent had made itself known. She amended, 'I've read everything I can get hold of, actually. I'm a pyrokinetic Artisan, weapons type. Though I'm not sure there's any other type, with pyrokinetics.'

'We always need stokers at Wapping.'

He was so straight-faced that it took her a moment; then she gave a startled peal of laughter, and clapped her hand over her mouth; the housekeeper's quarters were off the kitchen. Oliver looked down at the table, smiling himself.

Pleasingly, the water in her teapot was near boiling now. She spooned tea into it, popped the lid back on, and gave it two clockwise turns. Then she busied herself fetching cups and the little strainer and the bowl of sugar. The spoons were sterling silver; she hunted about for a cheap pewter spoon.

'Why don't you work as an Artisan, if you're an Artisan?' she asked as she set her collection down.

'People like you can be Artisans,' Oliver said mildly. 'People like me are still the shortest step removed from trial by ordeal.'

'The Witchcraft Act 1735 *and* the Vagrancy Act 1824 both make it very clear in law that there are no witches, only innocent people accused through superstition and ignorance, or fakers preying on the vulnerable. Artisans are an entirely different class.'

She stopped, because Oliver was looking at her with wry good humour written across his expressive face. 'I'm being naïve and obnoxious, aren't I?'

Oliver held up his hand, forefinger and thumb held a hair's width apart, saying, 'A little,' in gentle mimicry of her own prior understatement. Then he stiffened. 'I beg your pardon, Miss Locke.'

He sounded both alarmed, and deeply surprised at himself.

'Artisans can talk that way to each other,' she told him firmly, because he was, or had been, comfortable with her, and she was comfortable with him, and she urgently did not want to lose that before they'd even had their tea. He was, to her knowledge, the first real Artisan she'd ever met.

Oliver grimaced. 'I should have said…' He shifted in his chair. 'I'm a motley.'

Genevieve looked at him blankly.

'Mongrel mix of secondary Arts, no primary.'

'You've studied, too,' she said. 'But isn't it properly called medley Art?'

'It's called not very useful. Not much better than a collection of talents too numerous to be called talents. Sorry, Miss Locke. I should have told you straight off.'

He fidgeted again, glancing at the kitchen door as if planning an ignominious retreat. Genevieve raised an imperious eyebrow, the eldest of the junior Lockes quelling the frequently infuriating pair of youngest Lockes.

She fetched the biscuit tin, and set it in the centre of the table.

'You run hot, like I do,' she said. 'I bet you're starving, like I am.' She tapped the tin, pushing it towards him. 'I'll wager you have trouble around the iron in the shipyards, like I've had to put aside my silver jewellery. You just fixed the teapot I broke, both of us using some poorly understood metaphysical, if not out-and-out magical, power that manifests inside our bodies without our volition. You're an Artisan.'

She poured the tea, brooking no argument. Oliver drank his tea black, with no sugar. She forwent her squeeze of lemon and had a little sugar. They sipped, smiling at each other and munching biscuits without restraint.

The cup was tiny in his thick fingers. She wished she'd found some more robust mugs. Then she was glad she hadn't. It was pleasing to watch the delicacy those big hands were capable of.

She wanted to ask more about his Arts, how many he'd identified, if he ever used them in his work at the docks, if he ever would consider using them more directly. That, she supposed, might lead to the *discussion* so dreaded by the etiquette manuals, but also, would likely make him uncomfortable again, which was the true sin, etiquette wise.

'Where did you sail?' she asked instead.

Oliver, sparse with his words when tense, was an excellent storyteller when set at his ease. He'd only been asea a few years – though *a few years*, she gathered, covered a goodly span of what she'd known as carefree childhood years – until his Arts began to manifest, but he'd sailed every merchant navy route, and seen so much more of the world than she could even imagine. She brewed a second pot as she listened in fascination, encouraging him to tell her another story whenever he paused for even a moment, lest he take a cue to make his farewells.

At her behest, he laid his hand flat on the table so she could see his tattoos. They were Artistry-wrought artistry, in colours no mundane tattooist could match, bright floral designs that he said reminded him of southern climes, blooming in vine-like profusion before vanishing under his cuff. The other hand, clasping his teacup with such care, was covered in more flower-like ink, but on closer acquaintance, it inscribed corals like she'd seen in colour plates. The tip of a suckered muscular arm, a tentacle, flicked among them.

She cajoled him, thoughtlessly, to take off his coat and push up his sleeves, but he merely smiled and shook his head.

'And when I was fifteen, I grew…' He waved at himself. 'Twice as large as my brothers, and it became impractical to fit into tight quarters aboard.'

Genevieve glanced up from examining the tattoos. He'd given the curiosity tapping its fingers in her head an opening. 'Is that somatic Art, then?' she asked. 'Your size?'

'Strength. Size came along lockstep.'

'Somatic Art. Materials Art. What others do you have?'

'Wards. Telekinesis. That's my best. Handy dockside, like the strength. Always crates to shift. Saves our backs.'

He'd lost his easy words and had put his cup down to stare at the table. She regretted indulging herself; she'd already seen he didn't like talking about it. She had no right to make him.

'You?' he asked, and that was as good a way of turning the topic as any other, so she told him about the evening her Art had bloomed, how feverish she'd felt, how desperately she'd tried to retain the icy calm she needed to get through the interminable socialising with people who would never like her or respect her father.

How the viscount's braying son, heir apparent of an heir apparent, hadn't done anything so uncouth as try to put his hands on her, but that he and his friends had looked at her, *looked* at her, and she had known what they were thinking because sometimes she was too willing to ask questions and the twins were too willing to answer, and to sneak her the same books they'd got hold of—

'I know it's nothing,' she said. 'I know I'm far more protected than other women. He just looked. *They* just looked.'

'That's not nothing,' Oliver said gravely.

—how she'd stumbled out into the garden with a great pressure growing in her head and her stomach and her *bones*—

Overhead, a carriage came along the street. They had been passing the house with more frequency as the hours grew small and the evening entertainments, the suppers and soirees and theatre shows, came to a close, but this one slowed and stopped.

Without a word, Oliver stood and started to clear the table. Genevieve emptied the teapot of leaves and rinsed it out while he quickly washed up, drying their cups and spoons and restoring them to their places, shipshape.

He pointed at the empty tin of biscuits as she put it back on its shelf. 'Problem?'

She liked that he said it as if he planned to solve it if it was. 'The twins raid it to crumbs all the time, they'll take the blame.'

And indeed *had*, as her Artisan-driven appetite had risen like a raging flood over the last few weeks.

Standing by the kitchen door, waiting for her parents to go inside through the front door and for the family brougham to rattle off around to the mews house, he gave her a stiff nod. 'Delighted to meet you, Miss Locke.'

'A pleasure to make your acquaintance, Mr Bennet.' Impulsively, she added, 'Do come for a proper visit when Alex is feeling better.'

Oliver stilled. Then he gave that firm single shake of the head again.

Some unfamiliar feeling was uncurling in her, a grating sense of loss, a window closing on a room that had been airless until now. 'But you're the first Artisan I've ever met.'

'You'll meet better.'

'But—'

'Impossible.' He unlatched and opened the door a crack, listening. His breath frosted in the cold air seeping into the banked warmth of the kitchen as he said with slow, stern certainty, 'I should never have been here. You know it.'

'You're an Artisan,' she insisted. 'It's allowed.'

'I'm a wharf rat.' He eased out into the area, watching for feet at street level.

Genevieve seized hold of his hand. He flinched, but his fingers clenched tight about hers in an instinctive response. Both their hands were warm, because they were both Artisans. That meant something. It *did.*

But Oliver, with the same gentle care with which he had handled the teapot, eased his fingers free. 'You know it,' he repeated. 'I'm sneaking out the servants' door, because we both know navvies don't take tea with the daughter of the house.'

Clenching her suddenly chilled fingers to her stomach, she said, 'They do if the daughter of the house *invites* them.'

In quiet challenge, he said, 'Then take me upstairs and introduce me to your parents so I can leave by the front door.' He nodded to her telling hesitation. 'Exactly so. Goodbye, Miss Locke.'

'It's the middle of the night,' she snapped. 'Come back tomorrow and I *will*.'

He fought a reluctant smile. 'I'll present my calling card to the footman, shall I?'

'Well. We still have to obey *some* forms, Mr Bennet, so Alex will meet you out and bring you home.' Against her will, a line from one of the etiquette books came out of her mouth. '*It is of no consequence to a* gentleman *in what society he makes his friends and acquaintances.*'

Though she bit it back, the tragic sequel to that advice hectored her: *although it is always a mistake for people to go out of their own set, and when gentlemen do, it is a decided mistake, often leading to life-long misery.*

She *should* set those etiquette books on fire, because not one word applied to Artisans.

'By Duck Island cottage, at two,' she blurted. 'You can admire the birds if he's late.'

Oliver turned his face downwards as if to hide the thoughts betrayed by his open expression. She summoned un-Locke-like patience and waited him out; this would become, over the coming years, a familiar tableau.

At last, he said, 'Mr Oliver.' She tilted her head in silent question. 'Seaman Bennet, but if I'm acting the Artisan, I better be Mr Oliver. My mother's family,' he added. 'We think the Artistry came down that line.'

'Not acting the Artisan, Mr Oliver,' Genevieve said. 'You *are* an Artisan. We can help each other.'

He started up the stairs to the street, his heavy tread echoing around the walls of the small area. He called back, 'Until you meet a better one, Miss Locke.'

She met Reuben McAvey barely two months later.

16

GENEVIEVE SNAPPED FROM A REVERIE. DISCORD was jangling in her head: *she met Reuben McAvey barely two months later.*

She had. She had met Reuben a few months after meeting Oliver. Until now, she'd remembered it as the other way around. And by then, wasn't she – didn't they—

Oliver, gaze averted, was running a hand compulsively over his clean-shaven scalp, the dark bristles of his younger days regularly razored away. She was struck by the impossible impulse to run her hand over the bare skin there, to caress the tender nape of his neck, to feel the glide where prickle used to be. Her fingers were tingling, not with heat but with the echo of sensation.

A soft but rapid knock came on the doorframe behind them. Genevieve turned, as tranquil as an expectant mother should be.

Mass was hovering, looking nervous. His eyes had finally faded from Whitely's green, and were a deep, dark brown, much like Oliver's. 'Miss Delacorte sent me to ask…' He stared at the uncovered paintings, and the array still leaning in their swaddling.

'The tea.' Oliver rose from her side and started for the door.

Genevieve didn't quite see what happened then. Mass tripped, she thought, and stumbled forwards, risking the integrity of the paintings. She yelped in alarm; she could not bear to waste a single one of her mother's lost-and-found artworks, and it seemed for a moment that Mass's bodily flail risked the lot.

But even as Oliver reacted too slowly, putting out one massive arm that would miss catching the boy, Mass wrenched himself away from potential disaster, landing in an awkward crouch well away from the makeshift gallery along the wall. His eyes flashed green again as he hunched, panting.

He looked up at them, agonised, mouth twisted, eyes bright, almost aglow. Then he blurred into his cat form and fled. Oliver shook his head and made to follow.

Genevieve's feet tried to start off after him. She planted them, looking again at the uncovered paintings, and then at the row of shrouded ones. 'Go on without me.'

Oliver hesitated. 'You should eat, and rest.'

'One more,' she said.

In the doorway, Oliver slowly straightened to his full height. Taller than her, taller than the twins. Almost as tall and broad as the doorway itself. 'Come away, Genevieve.'

Genevieve heard Whitely's coolly mocking voice: *did you know Mr Oliver has a stern voice?*

Yes, I did know that, Mr Whitely, she thought. 'Please, Oliver.'

She wasn't asking for his permission. She needed no one's permission to put aside her own bodily needs to look at her own mother's paintings. She was asking for…for his *help*. With what, she could not fathom.

Before she'd touched the painting, she would have struggled to give an autobiographical précis of that phase in her life. The lost memory had played like a magic lantern show of the sort that had been faddish around that same time, in the early '40s. Now it had shimmered back to the forefront of her mind, it didn't feel like it had ever been lost, but rather merely something she hadn't needed, nor wanted, to think about. How many more memories did she have like that, not lost but hiding in plain sight? Hiding, more aptly, in a fog that needed a strong breeze to dissipate it?

Yet even as the desire to charge onwards peaked, she felt capitulation on its heels. Yes. She should go to tea. She shouldn't waste time on old paintings she'd have disposed of long ago, if she'd known about them.

Oliver paced heavily towards her, face blank, and for one horrid moment, she truly believed her friend would seize her and drag her from the storeroom.

He knelt and pulled at the next wrapping, big body angled in such a way that it blocked Genevieve's view. He became still, as if he held his breath. She tucked in beside him, heedless of her shoulder bumping his in her eagerness to see it.

Her own breath rushed out of her. It was another from her mother's private collection, and it couldn't have been painted so very long after the last. This portrait was of Oliver, the younger Oliver, black hair chopped into those unfashionable bristles. Mother had depicted his face illuminated as if from a bright source beyond the purview of the canvas's eye. The broad, stark planes of his face were left unflattered by the play of shadows, but his lips were pursed as if for a kiss, and his dark, warm eyes had the lustre of brushed velvet, the way they crinkled and lit up whenever he was amused or fascinated or when he – when he—

'The matches,' Oliver said, and she felt his fingers wrap around hers, and they remembered.

THE GREAT DIFFICULTY of being an untrained weapons Artisan whose Art manifested purely, and entirely without her volition, as flame was that errors were horrific to contemplate.

This was the salient point that earned Oliver his ticket past the barricade of class. Certainly, both Genevieve's parents raised curious brows when Alex marched a tattooed labourer through the front door the afternoon following his disgrace – terrified of missing the appointment at St James's Park, Genevieve had deployed the merciless Lulu to roust her ailing and not nearly apologetic enough brother from his bed and out the door – but neither openly disputed their nephew's unexpected guest. All that affable brass had its uses.

Indeed, Genevieve suspected her father was quietly thrilled to be seen to be so open-minded, harking back to his own youth spent on the periphery of radicals and bohemians. She was also beginning to suspect, with a cynicism she did not like to turn against her beloved sire, that Father had not spent all that long there – and that his dabbling had ended the moment he'd seen the open path to making his fortune in trade and investment.

Still, he'd been among the fringes wholeheartedly enough to meet and subsequently marry an up-and-coming woman artist despite the opposition of his strictly conventional middle-class parents. And Antoinette, at least, shook Oliver's hand with true pleasure and not a hint of disfavour, not even when Lulu and Genevieve joined the young men in the rear parlour to take tea.

Genevieve was, however, shortly summoned away to her father's study, for a gentle remonstration about the care she must take to maintain a snowy reputation, her greatest treasure, so easily and irreparably lost.

Her cousin – both cousins – could keep company as they wished, or as their guardian allowed, notwithstanding that Sir Kingsford had taken their father's death as permission to absent himself from London permanently. She could *not* keep company as she wished, not if she wanted to remain untarnished.

She bit her tongue and asked him to call in Mother, then set the contents of the wastepaper bin on fire in front of their eyes.

To say her father was astonished and her mother delighted would be an understatement – but all three of them were shortly distressed when they discovered that they could not quench the flames, not by smothering, not by dousing with soapy mop-water from a full bucket snatched from a startled maid, not by ill-advised stomping with slippers. This last, in fact, scattered the flames, and it looked for a terrifying moment like they would lose not only Father's study but the entire house.

The twins burst in, responding to the spreading shouts of alarm, Oliver circumspectly in their wake. Even as Alex and Lulu rushed to try the same techniques that had already done nothing but dispersed the Art-flames wider, Oliver placidly spun his warding Art to contain the incipient inferno.

He turned to Genevieve. 'Do you think you can quell this now? My wards won't slow it for long.'

'If I could,' she half-shouted; even with the worst averted, she was watching the expensive rug burn to ashes and the flames weren't dying, because they weren't the sort of mundane flames that needed mundane fuel to keep burning. 'I would have already!'

He held out his hand. Puzzled, and not without a glance her father's way, she took it. Artisan's hands – both were bare. Their fingers interlocked as if they were about to dance. A wave of calm swept over her.

'Were you annoyed?' he murmured.

She'd barely noticed it, but she had been. She'd been quietly seething about the hypocrisy that saw every Locke but her free of the strictures of high society. She'd been seething because she'd been so looking forward to seeing Oliver again, and treating him properly this time, upstairs, and Father had called her, and only her, away.

The moment she was given to notice her own temper, she found it was under her control. It still took an inordinate amount of time and effort – she had a mental image of groping her fingers through the dark to find a lost key – before the wildfire finally guttered and then went out.

Oliver squeezed her fingers in silent congratulations before letting her go. He put his hands behind his back and turned to face her father, a sailor before his irate captain: he fully expected to be dismissed for touching the bare fingers of the daughter of the house, and he fully intended to accept the dismissal and leave forever without a word of complaint.

'Mr Oliver is a wards Artisan,' Genevieve announced, with more strategy than she'd known herself capable of. 'He can stop me burning the house to the ground.'

In the mingled surprise of their daughter transforming from debutante to Artisan, and the shock of discovering what that actually meant, there was no demurral. Oliver would be allowed to become a regular visitor, to assist Genevieve in gaining control of her flagrant Art.

'As long as Miss Lucinda is with her,' her father rallied enough to dictate to Oliver, who nodded gravely in acknowledgement.

'Of course,' Genevieve said, hating the way he was speaking to Oliver in the civilly brisk tones he used with the servants, and thus obstinately inserting herself into a conversation that had been entirely about her in the first place. 'She's her own talent to cultivate.'

Father turned to her. 'And you will begin accompanying your mother to your engagements again?'

Her stomach gave a sickening swoop. Only in her head and not yet by word or action beyond daydreams with Lulu, she had begun to fulminate against his plan for her, which had been her plan too, a few weeks, if not days, before. She realised now how much lighter she'd felt, the moment she'd embraced her Artisan self; it was possibly why, aside from her irritation with being summoned from the parlour, she had made her demonstration so dramatic, and subsequently so unexpectedly dangerous.

She felt as if she had been in a stuffy drawing room, crammed with useless ornaments destined for nothing grander than daily dusting by maids, and she'd managed to fling open a window to let a gale in. It had tumbled over all those useless, pretty ornaments, but it had cleared her mind and lifted her spirits as well. And now her father was blocking the window and trying to drag a curtain back across.

She could not abide it, but she also could not, yet, openly defy her father's wishes. She could, however, bid for time, enough to find a way to wedge the glorious window open. 'Once I can be sure I will not burn others' houses down.'

He gave a curt nod and turned away. Genevieve lingered in the face of the dismissal. She considered herself the least argumentative of the Lockes – the cousins and her mother might disagree – and the most dutiful of daughters, but she could not cede the advantages Artistry gifted her without at least a murmur of protest, if only she could find the right words.

Mother, apparently recognising what the twins called her dissection look, caught her attention with a shift of posture, giving her the smallest shake of the head.

Satisfied that she had enlisted one parent in a gentle campaign against the other, Genevieve retreated with the twins and their guest.

Oliver returned the very next day; Genevieve did not flatter herself that this was a betrayal of some sign of partiality on his part. Indeed, his manner, quiet, calm and standoffish, bespoke a continued reluctance to remain entangled with the Lockes at all. He was here, she suspected, because he felt a moral duty to prevent her from accidentally murdering herself and her entire family and household staff by misadventure with fire, as readily as any small child discovering the wonders of matches.

Indeed, he'd brought along a large wooden matchbox, carrying it out to meet her in the garden. Mother was there, painting in the dappled shade of the plane tree, and the twins, idling in the chancy sunshine.

Genevieve had overheard a conversation that morning between her parents, about her cousins. It had been not quite unintentional. A convocation of drafts within the house meant that a position on the stairs was conducive to catching the drift of conversation from her father's study, even with the door closed. Knowing her mother had just entered with a tea tray and a determined mien, Genevieve had lingered in the hope of hearing how the campaign to allow full Artisan status was progressing.

But the conversation had been about Alex and Lulu. Antoinette professed her concern as to the complete lack of boundaries their Uncle Theodore was seeing fit to establish. She could administer the care and the cautionary words, but she felt they needed a firmer hand from a father figure.

This finally enlightened Genevieve that the twins' gratuitous licence, that she was so very envious of, was a sword not entirely without its double edge. Her father's response had been cavalier, to say the least.

Oliver turned from politely greeting the other Lockes. 'If you are amenable, Miss Locke, we will begin.'

He opened the matchbox. The matchsticks had lumps of red at their tips, which Genevieve puzzled over; the matches she was accustomed to came from a small tin box and had yellowish heads.

'Lucifers are indeed of the very devil,' Oliver said gravely, noticing her silent curiosity. 'These are new.' He paused, watching her for an understanding that didn't come. 'Safer for the matchmaker girls, Miss Locke. Phossy jaw.'

She flushed. She shouldn't have needed it explained. The newspapers had covered the problem. 'Everyone should be using these, then.' She looked back at the house. 'We should be.'

'Only two factories use the red yet.' Again, he paused.

This time, she did see the issue. 'They must be expensive. Allow us to reimburse you. That is, you do intend to use these, in helping me learn my Art?'

He nodded.

'And for your time, too,' Genevieve said, now entirely inspired.

But here he held up his large, capable hand. 'My time is my own, I offer it freely.'

She hesitated, as uncertain of the etiquette here as she was in the grand ballrooms of the upper class her father wanted her to pave the way into. Oliver was of the labouring classes; his time was all he had to bargain, and it deserved recompense, especially if she was taking him away from paid work. On the other hand, he had said he was offering his time freely, so would it insult him if she—

She caught him smothering his smile and demanded, 'Can you read minds?'

'I read faces well enough,' he said. 'That's not Art, though. Do not do yourself an injury, Miss Locke, I am here because I want to be.'

Oliver took up a match, big fingers delicately plucking the stick free from the rest. He ran it along the sandpaper glued to the side of the box. The friction sparked the chemicals, and the match burst into flame.

He then held it out to her. 'Extinguish it.' As she frowned, he added, 'The usual way. No Art needed.'

'I…I do already know how matches work, Mr Oliver,' Genevieve said, hovering somewhere between asperity and uncertainty.

'Bear with me, Miss Locke.' He lifted the match higher. It would burn his fingers soon.

She leaned towards him, and pursed her lips to puff a sharp breath. The flame guttered and went out. He looked at her over the pungent waft of smoke issuing from the charred end. She couldn't have guessed what he was thinking.

As she straightened self-consciously, he took out from his coat a small tin, holding different matches. 'These are weatherproof,' he said. 'They make them for shipside.'

The heads of these ones, she noted, were the sickly yellow of the matches she was familiar with. He once again drew a stick free with that surprising precision, striking it into life and holding it out to her.

This time her puff made the flame dance and dip to the side, but not extinguish. Oliver nodded, satisfied. Genevieve, without thinking, pinched the flame between her forefinger and thumb, and hissed in surprised pain – she'd been working with her own Art-fire for a few weeks now, and hadn't realised that she could still be singed by mundane flame.

Oliver collected the bucket he'd had Alex fetch, seized her wrist in a gentle but implacable grip, and dunked her whole hand into the cold water. They stood side by side, her shoulder brushing his arm, looking down at their two submerged hands, his fingers still about her wrist.

'I beg your pardon,' he murmured, and let her go. Stepping away and wiping his damp hand absently on his coat, he said, 'Keep your fingers in for a spell longer, Miss Locke.'

'Not immune to other people's fire, then,' she said lightly. She was braced for a lecture about being more careful.

'Now you know,' Oliver said. He made a formless gesture, invitational. 'We'll resume when you're ready.'

He moved further from her, blunt fingers tapping the buttons of his coat. He looked a little flushed now himself, cheeks darkened.

'You can take the coat off, Mr Oliver,' she said. 'Artisans are allowed.'

Again, she earned his mild smile. 'There are ladies present, Miss Locke.'

Genevieve looked over at the others. Her mother was lost in her work, focus absolute as she made one of her rapid sketches, that she would later develop with oils. Lulu had left off muttering over fashion plates – sleeves grew ever tighter, waists ever narrower, and both were proving challenging – to relax back in her chair and watch Genevieve's first lesson.

Alex, beside his sister and equally at ease here in the garden with his closest relatives, waved at her. He had three small jars before him, and a big box of old buttons his aunt had found for him. Oliver had suggested a sorting task might help him practise the focus he needed to control his flailing talent. Alex had enough respect for Oliver to try.

She tsked at her insouciant audience. Withdrawing her hand, she discovered her fingertips had reddened but not blistered. She nodded to Oliver.

'Light the match,' he said, holding up one of the large red-tipped matches from the wooden box. 'Art, yes. But make it like the weatherproof one. I shouldn't be able to put it out.'

Bewildered, Genevieve said, 'Mr Oliver, my problem is that I'm creating unquenchable flame already.'

'Not to contradict you,' he said, 'but to define your problem more precisely: you are creating unquenchable flame when you do not mean to. First, learn to mean it. Then you can learn to *not*.'

It took three full weeks, weather permitting, and twice as many full boxes of safe matches.

Three weeks out in the back garden on the days when the sun shone, never daring to try it inside on the rainy days, or even under the mews roof, which seemed terrifyingly flammable now she had more knowledge under her belt.

Three weeks of making a minuscule dollop of Art flame precisely dance atop the matchstick, a feat in itself.

Three weeks of watching Oliver extinguish the tiny flame with one exhale of air and Art, quick as a stolen kiss. She'd not spent so much time staring at a man's mouth in her life.

The lack of progress might have been frustrating – the youngest Lockes soon gave up being an avid audience to such repetitive theatre, though Mother was always appropriately nearby, in the throes of painterly creation, even when Lulu forgot her chaperone duties – except Genevieve could feel a creeping awareness within herself.

The sensation of groping blindly to find a key, the feeling she'd had in Father's study within the ambit of Oliver's wards, grew stronger and stronger. But it was not as simple as reaching out in the dark. She had to feel out the shape of it, inch by painstaking inch. It was, for those weeks, all she thought about, all she read about, until her very dreams were invaded, though she did not make any practical attempts without Oliver standing patiently by with his safe matches and his bucket of water and his warding Art.

And then came the day he directed his puff of breath at the flame dancing on the head of the matchstick, and it did not go out.

He paused, lips still pursed. His gaze came up to meet hers, both wide-eyed with surprise. His smile bloomed in direct proportion to hers.

They were still smiling at each other in that perfect moment of stillness – her blossoming sense of achievement, a whole *world* unlocked inside her mind, and his wholehearted and genuine respect for it – when the match burned down far enough for the flame to lick his skin.

He grimaced and flicked the match into the bucket by his side. Far from guttering, the flame spread merrily across the surface of the water.

'Greek fire,' Oliver murmured, eyebrows raised.

'Should we… Sand, perhaps?' Genevieve asked, hands twisting together, remembering her father's rug. She didn't know why Oliver wasn't using his own Art like he had then.

'We have a little time before we need concern ourselves,' Oliver said in his thoughtful way, though he was closely watching the wooden sides of the bucket, which were beginning to smoke in preparation for charring. 'You know what to do, Miss Locke.'

He wasn't using his Art, she realised then, because he expected her to competently employ her own. That was all the incentive she needed. Leaning over the bucket – Oliver made no move to hold her back, because these were her flames, and she couldn't be harmed by them – Genevieve once again reached into her own mind and discovered the key to hand. Her Art functioned at *her* discretion, not its own.

The fire went out in a wink, as if it had never existed. The water underneath simmered in a low roil. Genevieve knew how it felt. She held both hands over her mouth, staring down at the bucket, a strange mix of triumph and terror making her breathing unsteady.

How powerful she was, with this Art. How destructive she might be, with this Art.

'Oh, I thank my lucky stars for you, Oliver,' she said, holding out her hand to him.

Oliver made no move to accept the offer of her bare fingers. 'The control is yours, Miss Locke. My wards merely slow real Art down.'

She let her hand drop, embarrassed and chagrined. She had been impetuous and presumptuous, terrible sins in the eyes of her husband-catching handbooks, and in the eyes of the wider circles she was meant to move in, as well.

'I beg your pardon.' She clenched her hand by her side. 'I meant only to express my deep gratitude for your assistance, Mr Oliver.'

'Yes.' Oliver's gaze was abstracted; he was either deep in thought, or refusing to look at her, or both. 'I—'

The brand-new clock tower over in the square began its short hourly chime; it had embedded Art within its workings, and was thus both accurate and automated, much to the disgust of Mr Belville, who made a living selling Greenwich time to subscribers and did not relish Artisans superseding his trusty Arnold.

The tower chimes were not loud, respecting the wealthy and willing-to-complain residents, but Oliver stopped anyway. He and Genevieve waited until the St Paul's bells over by Knightsbridge began to belatedly toll, stridently clamorous.

The London News had described the Artistry-infused clock tower in unflattering terms – *a grotesque erection has lately sprung up*, to the great amusement of the less mature in the household – but since St Paul's itself was also recent, as indeed, the whole Belgravia scheme was recent, there was no call on tradition to have the clock tower silenced. Hence the petulance of the sexton. It was likely to rebound badly: the chime of the clock tower was regular and quiet, while the tolling from the church was vociferous and venturing far from the usual sermonising and funerary habits. The neighbourhood would not tolerate the incessant disturbance for long.

They waited, much, Genevieve reflected, like Artisans as a class patiently waiting out the Church whenever it descended into one of its periodic vituperations regarding Artistry and the historic taint of witchcraft. Like the clock tower, Artisans were far too useful to Crown and country for any real threat to arise from the occasional nostalgia for witch-hunting tyranny.

The church bells, having successfully drowned out the clock tower, fell silent. Oliver cleared his throat. 'I have to go.'

Genevieve, now more wounded than embarrassed, awkwardly said, 'You won't take tea before you depart?'

He had, previously, in the garden, with her and the twins, Mother ever in the background behind her easel. It had given Genevieve the chance to observe that Alex had let go of his tendre for Oliver without evidence of an overly battered heart.

'I— There's a meeting.' The man was practically sidling away from her! 'The Society advocating for the establishment of a protective body specifically for Artisans.'

She had heard of it; or, at least, now she was an Artisan herself, she had begun to peruse the reports in the newspapers, though not nearly as vigorously as she had been researching Artistry itself. There had been a great deal of discussion about the advantages and disadvantages of a formal body, and some fearmongering about what it would mean to mundane people if Artisans, as solitary as cats, began to work together. But Oliver's attendance confused her.

'Isn't that only for—' She bit her tongue. She had been about to say, *Isn't that only for men*?, not forgetting – it would be difficult to do so – that Oliver was a man, but unintentionally applying a certain narrow and ingrained definition of enfranchisement. '...people who may vote?'

Oliver paused in his retreat to indulge her with one of his crooked smiles. 'If we only allow people who may vote to have their say in this proposed agency's formation, then whole rafts of Artisans will continue to not be allowed to vote, to their great detriment.'

This was the first time, and not the last, that it occurred to Genevieve that her embodiment as a woman, Oliver's embodiment as a labourer, others' embodiment as anything other than the trifecta of wealthy and English and male, tarnished the edges of the lauded Artisan status she had been so eager to snatch up and hoard.

It was also the most she'd heard Oliver speak since their first night down in the kitchen; it must, then, be something he felt quite strongly about, enough to override his stiff reticence around her parents.

Her mother, she noted from the corner of her eye, had finally lifted her attention from her sketchbooks and canvas on the other side of the long, narrow garden to look with some approval at Oliver. Theodore Locke had, after all, plucked her from among the sort of people who were likely Chartists now.

With the horrible feeling she was rather letting both her mother's politics and her own sex down, Genevieve said, 'May Artisan women attend these meetings, then?'

'Very many Artisan women already do.'

'I'd best come, then, shouldn't I?' Genevieve said. 'I could be helpful, in my position. I could speak for them.'

She wished she'd had the foresight to bite her tongue again even as the words came treacherously out of her mouth. She didn't dare look over at Mother, who probably had her head in her hands at the sheer ignorance of the daughter she had raised.

Oliver was kind enough to merely say, with a gravity that belied the soft amusement in his eyes, 'You'll find they are speaking for themselves already.'

'I will never not make a fool of myself in front of you, will I?' she lamented.

He offered a shallow bow in lieu of a too-honest answer. 'They will be glad of your support, Miss Locke.'

17

THERE WAS NO MORE STERN TALK of retreating to the tea tray. Both she and Oliver moved quickly to reveal the next painting, their hands stymying each other in their rapt haste to see it, experience it, *remember* it.

Genevieve feared it wouldn't be one of the personal familial paintings, and in a way, it wasn't, for it was of a young woman, small and round, sporting the pleasant smile she wore as habitually as Lulu wore her scowl. She stood at the suggestion of a podium, one hand on her hip.

Antoinette Locke had painted Miss Cecelia Delacorte to the bones, because there was no mistaking the steel in the spine and the glint in the eye in this apparently sweet and mild factory girl.

But it wasn't when they'd first met, which had been at a public meeting Mother had not attended, not being an Artisan – though Genevieve was having increasing doubts about that diagnosis, as memories leapt out of strokes of oil paint on canvas and sank waypoints into the fog in her head. Oliver had been inadvertently right – she had had a talent, at the very least, she *must* have had.

This painting must have been made when Cecelia had begun to visit the Belgravia house; Mother had painted her into the scene she most deserved, representing the working-class faction at those contentious Society meetings.

'Cece,' Oliver said fondly. 'She was such a polite firebrand, wasn't she? She got it done.'

'She did,' Genevieve said. 'Though if she'd known it was going to take so very long…'

'I remember—'

*

THE HALL WAS crowded. Artisans were exceedingly uncommon, but London was the largest city in the world; even the tiniest proportion of near enough to two million people rapidly added up to a fair contingent within the small public hall.

Genevieve was asked to prove her Artisan status before the rather officious man on the door would allow her entry past the antechamber. She looked around nervously at the milling people inside and out, but Oliver's simple nod reassured her. She carefully made fire bloom within her cupped hands, remembering with a shudder how thoughtlessly she had experimented in her room that first night. She'd been lucky the Art had still been blooming into full strength.

Then it was only left to pay her crown for the annual membership and enter the Society for Artisans.

The first thing that struck her was the sea of bare heads: in a public hall, men would usually leave their hats on, given a lack of hooks or a cloakroom, and, of course, women did not take their hats off in public at all lest they be left fussing over the disruption to their hair.

But these were all Artisans, and they needed the relief from the Art-gifted fever permuting their bodies far more than they needed to follow the sartorial customs of their various classes or even the most practical of protections from the vagaries of the weather.

Or they wanted the proclamation of their Artisan status that the lack of such accessories so effectively achieved.

The gentry she'd expected were clustered by the lectern at the front of the hall, opening wide their frock coats and tugging at the silk about their necks but otherwise giving no further quarter to the rising heat in the crowded hall. They were decidedly in the minority; the rest of the Artisans wore, in minimal layers, the staid and respectable dress of the middling classes, or the Sunday best of every stratum of the labouring classes.

Everything Genevieve had read in her fixated research into the nascent Artistry scientific studies hinted that, while Art famously manifested even more rarely in the upper classes than the rest of society, it made no discrimination regarding sex or race. Women were not present in equal numbers to the men, however, approaching parity only among the clusters of the working classes at the back of the hall. They rubbed elbows there, too, with the bulk of the faces that Genevieve's first, shamefacedly corrected, instinct labelled as foreign.

There were only a few women with the wealthy gentlemen at the front. Oliver indicated them with the subtlest of nods. 'You will want to join them.'

Genevieve eyed the group, feeling an echo of the dull dread that had come over her every time she faced an evening engagement, that she hadn't even recognised until it finally spiked into fury and fire. The people she had met at those interminable balls had been smugly self-entitled, even beyond what she could see of herself through Oliver's eyes. No doubt those doubly-privileged with Artistry on top of their wealth and position would be so much worse.

No, she very much did not want to join them.

'May I…' She stopped.

Oliver was here to stand in solidarity with his community, Artisans of the lower classes who wanted to be very sure they were properly represented if and when the proposed agency came into being. He could neither desire nor be expected to tolerate her hanging off his arm.

'You may,' he said, and offered said arm without visible qualm.

'Are you sure your Art doesn't extend to reading minds?' she asked with a touch of asperity as he escorted her to a band of loudly animated men and women in the far corner.

'Quite.' He approached a young woman and waited till she turned towards him with a smile. 'Miss Delacorte, good afternoon. Miss Locke, may I present Miss Delacorte.' And then, surprisingly, 'I've been wanting to introduce you.'

Genevieve took the proffered hand and shook, meeting Miss Delacorte's eyes with open curiosity. She was brown-skinned and dark-haired, and shorter than Genevieve, as most women except Lulu were. Startlingly young, barely older than the twins, but dressed in a sober way no doubt meant to make people overlook that. She wore the heavy gloves that bespoke touch-based Art. It was not that those Artisans could not control their Arts, more a polite convention to indicate they would not use them without permission.

Genevieve didn't think she was allowed to ask after Miss Delacorte's particular specialty; it was documented that Artisans gained access to their power at some cost, and not all of them made such a light sacrifice as a tantrum at a ball.

'The pyrokinetic Artisan!' Miss Delacorte said with disarming frankness. 'I'm telepathy, myself – memories. Have you met Mrs Murphy? She's pain.'

'I take it away, Cece!' the other woman said. She had an Irish accent, and a kind but penetrating gaze. 'And this is my very good friend, Miss Adler. She's healing. We're in midwifery.'

And just like that, Genevieve was folded into the Artisans of Oliver's acquaintance, with scarcely more of a blink than he'd shown on that first night. She could tell some of it was a false conviviality, a certain stubborn determination to presume the truth of the lauded equality of all Artisans. But most of it was genuine. She was eyed with as much curiosity as she felt towards them; she wondered what Oliver had been saying about her. She should have found it unforgivably rude, to be spoken of like that, but merely found herself hoping he'd been as kind as she thought he was.

She found she was, as was typical, taller than all the women, and many of the men as well. That was the crushing effect of starvation-level poverty, she knew from her mother's charity work. She would have normally felt acutely aware of her height, as she had been at the balls with the other girls talking behind their hands, but somehow having Oliver tower over her as much as she towered over the shortest of the others was comforting enough that it did not weigh on her. She felt positively delicate beside his bulk, in fact, and not even the twins and their burgeoning size could evoke that unusual feeling.

A tarnished and battered plate was passing around, the Artisans tossing in coins, coppers with a few glints of silver.

'You've paid your membership?' Miss Delacorte asked cheerfully. 'No vote unless you've paid.' She dropped pennies onto the plate. 'We're taking a collection so more of us can sign on for membership before we start making too many binding decisions about the new agency.'

Genevieve did not have enough experience to know what a crown, five full shillings, might represent to these men and women, if they didn't have the opportunity to earn with their Art. She hadn't even paid enough attention to know the salaries of the Locke domestic servants; that was still her mother's domain.

But once she and Mother had persuaded Father that, to be received as a respectable Artisan, she must attend the meeting neither under chaperonage nor via any conveyance so ostentatious as the Lockes' fashionable brougham, he had given her a purse of half-sovereigns and guineas, muttering about precautions in case she needed to summon a hackney to bring her home.

Mother, eyebrows raised, had said, 'All the way home from the Scottish border, is it?', so he must have pressed a considerable sum upon her.

And, she realised now, it had been unforgivably offensive towards Oliver, to imply he would abandon or lose her, or indeed, abscond with her to Gretna like the worst of villains in a Gothic novel. It wasn't as if she even needed the money to get home, anyway: were Oliver to mystifyingly decline to escort her, she could still hire a cab and have one of the footmen fetch ready money to pay the driver.

She thus tipped the whole lot onto the plate on the strength of her annoyance, with her father, and with herself for not noticing the insult to a colleague. He'd stood right there, politely smiling in the veritable teeth of it.

She knew she'd erred again when the people around her gasped. She looked helplessly at Oliver, face heating. The flash of dismay he couldn't keep from his own face told her she truly had made a precipitous mistake.

He stepped closer and lowered his voice. 'Miss Locke, I did not bring you here to scrounge off you.'

'Sorry,' she whispered. 'I beg your pardon, Mr Oliver, I didn't mean…'

She could feel her hands shaking. This was as bad as the Season engagements: she did not know how to fit *anywhere* except with the twins. She didn't precisely know where her error lay, except in rubbing her wealth into these people's faces in a way she would never have done if she'd thought it through.

Oliver paused, and then she felt his strong fingers close over hers. He spoke clearly. 'Miss Locke, your father's donation is very welcome. We sincerely express our thanks for this most noble of virtues.'

It was well-judged: reassuring for her, but also flowery enough, different enough from Oliver's usual tones, that it made the others relax as if they could hear a sarcasm that she herself could not excavate from Oliver's seeming sincerity. She wished she knew him well enough to know if he truly was sincere, or if he had made her the butt of a secret joke, as she deserved.

Genevieve nodded. 'You can let go,' she told him. 'I'm not going to set the place on fire for a little embarrassment.'

He looked down at their joined hands as if surprised, then released her. Miss Delacorte had already gathered up both the plate and a small group of fellow Artisans, leading them over to the official by the door with the membership book.

She added, 'If you were making sport of me, I deserved it. So did Father.'

'I wasn't,' he said. 'I was making sport of the nobly charitable acts of the well-off, of which we've all been on the receiving end, one way or another, and which was not what you were intending.'

'No,' Genevieve said. 'And it wasn't what my father was intending either, but his actual intention was even worse than, ah, condescending philanthropy.'

Oliver smiled. 'He didn't have an intention, Miss Locke. He had a panic about his wife forcing him to hand his daughter into the care of a navvy and solved it the only way he could think of.' She gazed up at him, speechless, as he further confided, 'I don't think I'm abducting a pyrokinetic Artisan all the way to Gretna Green unless she wants to go, do you?'

'I wouldn't think you'd be abducting anyone at all, Mr Oliver,' Genevieve said softly.

She meant it in reference to his obvious trustworthiness; he gave her such a startled look that she could only think he assumed she was referencing a certain level of charm that would lead a woman to willingly elope with him.

A yet more damning interpretation occurred to her. Perhaps his surprise arose because she thought marriage, via elopement or not, was apt for him at all: she'd met him when he'd come home with Alex, after all. He'd not denied Lulu's strident accusation on any grounds other than decency towards a vulnerable boy.

She was saved from further embarrassment – the temptation to explain and thus twist herself into euphemistic incoherence was overwhelming – by the meeting being called to order.

As she'd expected, one of the gentlemen took charge; she didn't think he was an actual lord, rather someone towards the favoured, in other words, wealthy and respectable, end of the infinitesimally-graduated scale they all perforce lined up along.

The Artisans had gathered today, it appeared, to discuss a contentious issue in the slow process of establishing the agency that would govern their interests. At its heart was that very concept: governance. The question was who would police the Artisans.

Genevieve was not a political creature; she had not closely followed the more esoteric topics even once she'd learned she was an Artisan, let alone before that. She listened to the arguments with great attentiveness, understanding for the first time that the decisions undertaken here would directly affect her life as an Artisan.

'It is unnecessarily shackling ourselves.' A young man, a little older than Oliver, broad-shouldered and handsome, spoke confidently at the lectern now. His red hair gleamed in the low gaslight. 'We already have good English law to keep order. The agency-to-be is intended to protect us, not trammel us. We must fight enough for our rights, should we so willingly bend our necks to a heavy collar of iron and silver?'

He received applause and cries of *hear, hear* across the hall, particular among the tiny upper class contingent and a fair swath of the more prosperous-looking middling members.

The next speaker was Miss Delacorte. She dimpled at the man as he gave over the stage to her. 'A touch dramatic, Mr McAvey.'

She sounded very self-possessed and mildly mocking; Genevieve instantly grasped that the previous speaker must have decried Miss Delacorte for being too womanly, too emotional, too hysterical, too dramatic, in one of her speeches.

Mr McAvey gave her a filthy look. She ignored him, raising her melodious voice to address the hall.

'Who does the rule of law serve?' she asked without preamble.

It might have been a rhetorical question, except her faction, Oliver among them, called back, 'Not us!' in a drumbeat chorus.

'If good English law applied equally to each one of us,' Miss Delacorte declaimed, 'then we would trust the law. But we know that it does not. We will not see wealthy Artisans skirt the law as wealthy men do now, using their power, be that position or Art, without care for others, or to hurt others, knowing no policeman will ever come a-knocking on their doors.'

Amid the cries of support from the Artisans around Genevieve, there came blustering from some of the men in the front row. Miss Delacorte stared them down, continuing, 'If we are to have an agency for Artisans, it must be for *all* Artisans. If it is to protect us, it must protect *all* of us. We must have our own laws, our own rules of conduct, *and* we must have our own enforcers of those rules. If Artisans are to be as equal in truth as we are said to be, then we must police ourselves as a community, not rely on the tools of a corrupted state.'

Miss Adler murmured to Mrs Murphy, 'We'll have to set her on dismantling the Marriage Act next.'

'What good would that do us?' Mrs Murphy said.

They laughed quietly together, while Genevieve jolted in an abrupt comprehension: the usual laws of the land still applied to her. To put it as crudely as the twins might, her sex overrode her Art, in far too many spheres. She had been so complacent, both before and after her Art had bloomed.

'And indeed,' Miss Delacorte went on confidently, 'how could we expect a mere policeman to arrest any of us with the more, shall we say, forceful Arts, hmmm? Can any of you claim to be certain a weapons Artisan could be brought to justice, should he or she decide they do not wish to be?' She pointed into the crowd. 'If an ice Artisan should turn rogue—'

A hissing rose in response, but Genevieve could not make out which particular Artisan Miss Delacorte had decided to make an example of. Miss Delacorte pivoted now and pointed towards Genevieve. '—then shall we not require a fire Artisan to tame him?'

Taken aback to be singled out, and blushing – her height was definitely obvious now – Genevieve gave a little wave, and was rewarded with a ripple of appreciative laughter around her, and a few claps to her shoulder, which startled her no end. She was *actually* being treated like an Artisan, she realised, rather than a rich girl who happened to have an Art. It was delightful.

The speeches swiftly declined from entertainingly novel to dully repetitive, but Genevieve made herself continue to pay attention, listening for the nuances. Afterwards, Artisans mingled in her vicinity to greet her, including the first speaker, Mr Reuben McAvey, who politely, properly and irritatingly asked Oliver for an introduction.

'For it is rare to meet a fellow weapons Artisan, Mr Bennet,' he said, bowing slightly in Genevieve's direction. Despite the name and hair, his accent was entirely middling London; his family must have long since relocated.

Miss Adler shook her head, Mrs Murphy audibly tutted, and Miss Delacorte said, 'Would one truly categorise ice as weapons Art, Mr McAvey? Isn't it really weather Art?'

That was, Genevieve realised, a minor revenge for calling Oliver the wrong name, which the three women plainly believed was on purpose. McAvey's handsome face twisted in something approaching a sneer before he recollected himself and pasted on a bland smile while Oliver made short, flat work of formally presenting him to Genevieve's notice.

McAvey did not waste time beyond the most minimal exchange of social pleasantries. 'And are we to hope you see the good sense in not limiting the freedom of Artisans excessively?'

'It does not seem overly excessive to me, to have our own measures in place to ensure transgressions against people with lesser Arts, or no Art at all, are prevented,' Genevieve said, instinctively adopting the same careful tones she used to tread water at Season events. 'Miss Delacorte is correct, we see all around us the great problems that arise when those with power of any sort are given no reason to use it wisely.'

His smile took on a familiar smirk around its edges. 'I think perhaps you have not fully considered both sides of this argument.'

Genevieve did not need Miss Delacorte's eyeroll to catch the condescension. Standing taller, more like the twins, she said, 'I could burn someone alive on a whim, Mr McAvey. I'm sure my neighbours will sleep more easily if they are assured there are measures in place to discourage such an event.'

'Nonsense!' he cried. 'One such as yourself would never stoop to such a heinous act.'

'Because of my class or my sex, Mr McAvey?'

McAvey must have been utterly deaf to conversational undercurrents; many men were. With a flair of misplaced gallantry, he said, 'Both, my dear Miss Locke.'

She summoned her society smile, icy. 'I see. And I imagine you have opinions regarding those *not* of my class and sex?'

He scoffed. 'Obviously the labouring classes need more oversight and firm restraints in place. We cannot blame them for their lack of opportunity to learn appropriate morality, but nor can we allow the urgent need to police the congenital bad apples among *them* to force shackles upon *ourselves*.'

This sounded very much like *one rule for them, one rule for us* to Genevieve, and she strongly resented being dragged into the *us*. She opened her mouth to deliver a piece of retaliatory snobbery. Much as she doubted Miss Delacorte made a habit of poking fun of other Artisans' Arts, Genevieve would not normally have vaunted her upper-class credentials, partly because that would have been poor manners, and partly because she felt acutely both her father's middling origins and her mother's radical leanings and would know herself too much the hypocrite if she'd tried. But something about McAvey's glib and presumptuous manner was stiffening her hackles.

Safely off to one side, Oliver and Miss Delacorte were staring at each other with very straight faces. Genevieve suspected that all it would take for one to burst out laughing was for the other to lift an eyebrow in a mute mock of the supercilious tone. She did not think she'd show herself off well by falling into playing McAvey's game.

Therefore, she instead said, again speaking with care and with mental reference to the various arguments she'd so cavalierly skimmed, 'Artisans have had enormous freedom, thanks to the protection of the Crown. But we've also been solitary, and secretive, and paradoxically powerless as a group, no matter our Arts as individuals. That will change if this agency comes into being, and Artisans take their place in the bright light of the great national progression, as I believe we have no choice but to do if we wish to keep pace with the ructions of change every new year brings.'

She frowned, seeking her next words quickly, because she suspected the fidgeting McAvey was waiting for her to leave a large enough gap into which to insert his next remarks. 'We cannot claim our rights and privileges without also accepting our responsibilities, not if our en masse emergence into the light is to be received calmly, without fear. We all know there are already fulminations against us, in that regard.

'And I, for one, would much rather voluntarily, and publicly, accept fair and self-directed limits in the expectation of minimising our potential for harm and maximising our potential for good, than tolerate harsher institutional limits on our political and social freedoms because our neighbours become too afraid of us. *Any* of us. *All* of us.'

She finished this little speech with a gesture to encompass the Artisans about her, and was rewarded by Oliver's concurring, 'Small individual sacrifice, for immense collective gain.'

Miss Delacorte added, 'Well said, Miss Locke! You may find yourself paraphrased in my next address, with your permission.'

'Certainly, Miss Delacorte,' Genevieve said, though she considered the sally more a kindness than anything. It was highly likely she was parroting the other woman's own words back to her, filtered through the medium of the newspapers.

'We have a Bluestocking here, I see,' McAvey said.

It wasn't truly McAvey's fault that a phrase from one of the etiquette books immediately hissed in Genevieve's ear: *yield not to the female frailty of displaying more learning than is necessary or graceful.*

Oblivious to her sudden dissection-look glare, he went on, 'I must say you show commendable Artisan-solidarity, but very little loyalty to your own class.'

'Then you would be much mistaken, despite my trappings.' She made an indicative wave at her fashionable and expensive skirts. 'I am the child of the rising middling classes, and thus have more in common with those who materially contribute to our society than the idle rich.'

She winced; she *was* the idle rich now, especially when seen via the mirror of Oliver and Miss Delacorte's lived experiences.

'As am I!' McAvey exclaimed. 'And my father expects more of me. He expects me to parley my Artisan status as far as it will take me up the ladder. I share his ambition, if not seek to outdo it. Surely your own father holds such hopes for you, too.'

Unexpectedly, Genevieve felt a moment of pure connection with the man. His presumption and somewhat awkward mannerisms masked the same pressure and ambitions that dogged her.

With a nod towards the cluster of upper society on the far side of the hall, she said, 'Is that progressing any better for you than for me?'

He followed her gaze, and his face darkened. 'Indeed not,' he conceded. 'Our social betters stand ready to exploit us, do they not, be it for our beauty, our wealth, or our abilities, without allowing us beyond their periphery.'

That an ungenerous interpretation might suggest he ascribed the first two qualities to her, and reserved the third for himself, did not quite prevent Genevieve's fellow-traveller sympathy from an exponential increase. It struck her that, as rude as she had instinctively found his direct plunge into challenging her views, it was something she overtly desired. She had railed against those etiquette books that lauded vapid social niceties over any meaty talk, and McAvey was giving her what she wanted, at least now she had proven herself worthy of his attention, which itself was a paradoxically pleasant feeling.

Her smile thus transformed from frostily polite to truly friendly. 'If the Agency comes to true fruition, their periphery will be somewhat besieged.'

McAvey seemed struck; he was silent for a moment, watching her face. Then he cleared his throat. 'You must see that it will go better for us if we are singular incidences easily absorbed into upper society.'

Genevieve's sympathy diminished somewhat. 'Oh, but you sound like you want to turn about and knock down those who are climbing the ladder behind you. Surely we owe more than that, to our fellow Artisans at the very least.'

'That is admirably idealistic, Miss Locke, but hardly practical. We might perhaps bring some worthy Artisans up the ladder with us, but there is not enough room at the top for all of them. You yourself spoke of worthy sacrifice.'

'You mistake me,' Genevieve said, still smiling. 'I do not wish to offer a helping hand instead of an admonitory boot to those below me on the endless social ladder. I wish us to use all our boots to kick the ladder over.'

'Ah, from idealistic all the way to utterly impossible,' McAvey chided, tone taking on the chuckle of an adult patting a child on the head.

Before she could muster a response, Oliver interjected. 'It's late. I must escort Miss Locke home.'

She was embarrassed; she'd been standing by people much better equipped to argue with McAvey, and too boldly taken it upon herself, and foundered herself in wide-eyed naivety. But then she noticed that the crowd around them had thickened as the last eddies of discussion settled and fellow Artisans clotted towards the exit. Oliver was purely stating a fact, not trying to rescue her from her own folly.

Indeed, he was smiling at her without reservation or condemnation as he added, 'Before your father gives himself a paroxysm, yes?'

She met his smile and returned it with her own, quick and fond. She turned back to McAvey to see him glancing between the two of them with a frown clouding his brow. He seemed distracted as she bid farewell to him and the others about her and made for the door with Oliver and his friends.

The fussy man on the door raised a gloved hand towards them. 'Good oration today, Miss Delacorte. I found it quite convincing.'

'Dare I assume your vote is ours, Mr Fletcher?' Miss Delacorte asked.

'I am still considering all arguments, as is only proper,' he said sternly.

She gave him a merry look. 'I shall have you over to our side in the end, I am sure.'

'Perhaps on this particular issue,' he conceded. 'Coercion Art is not exactly a popular one. It would be useful to point to guidelines to demonstrate my assured good conduct.'

Miss Delacorte beamed at him, but Genevieve heard a scoffing sound and turned to see Mr McAvey contemptuously shaking his head at Mr Fletcher.

Outside, she farewelled her new acquaintances and was shortly seated in a hansom opposite Oliver, rattling back towards Belgrave Square. On the way to the meeting, Oliver had been content to sit quietly, a faux pas for the drawing room, but one Genevieve had appreciated. On the way home, however, she felt restless, and his silence no longer felt comfortable but judgemental. It was, she thought, in her own head, and yet she could not make herself dismiss it.

'I must seem like a child to you,' she said at last.

After a long pause, Oliver said, carefully, 'I can assure you that I do not think of you as a child, Miss Locke.'

'Miss Delacorte is barely out of the nursery, and she's *organising*. I know,' she added in haste, 'that there's no nursery. It was a figure of speech. I am aware of the plight of the working poor.'

Oliver's crooked half-smile made its appearance. He kindly did not take her to task for what she was sure, too late, had come across as the same sort of patronisation as bold and impractical claims to intend to kick the ladder over.

'Miss Delacorte is a factory girl,' he said. 'She's been at the forefront of worker rallies for several years. Wants better for her younger sisters. She speaks well.'

'Yes,' Genevieve said dully, knowing she did not. And Oliver had *told her* the other Artisan women could speak for themselves, and she'd still over-stepped.

Oliver cocked his head. Without a change of expression, he said, 'He wouldn't have heard us out.'

'Pardon me?'

'Mr McAvey. He's never bothered to engage with any of us. Definitely not Miss Delacorte or me, but not even Mrs Murphy or Miss Adler, both perfectly respectable professionals. You got his attention, and you made your points.'

'Very naïve points.'

'Might as well reach high, while we're reaching at all.' She was subjected to a plainly evaluative look, before he said, 'It's not really for him. Not for the ones who've already made up their minds. It's for the Artisans who are still listening, still deciding. They need to hear the arguments. Especially from…' He gave a fatalistic shrug. 'Someone like you.'

'I see.' She bit her lip, entirely uncomforted by this reversal.

'Miss Locke. Do you truly believe I am sitting here silently judging you at all times?'

'At the very least, some part of the time,' she admitted, and Oliver frowned. 'You're a very quiet man, Mr Oliver. I am used to *loud.* I am used to knowing what the people around me are thinking.'

She didn't solely mean the twins, though they were at the forefront of her mind. She was thinking also of her fellow debutantes, who, from the first moment she'd stepped into her first dance, saw her as nothing but upstart competition for the most desirable of the eligibles. They hadn't been loud and forthright like the twins, but they had been as opinionated, and as good at getting their message across, with the sweep of an eye, the turn of a shoulder, the curl of a mouth. The men might have wanted to exploit her beauty and wealth, as McAvey had implied. The women wanted to exploit her inability to swim in their world to show themselves the better bridal options.

She had thus become aware that she very often got things wrong, and that people were hoping, keen as knives, to see her get things wrong. She had been a girl who had stridden across the world, and was becoming a mouse who could only scurry.

Shifting his weight, Oliver spoke with even more deliberation than usual. 'I do not have the sense you are judging me, or any of us, for the accidents of our births.'

'Of course not.' She looked down at her lap. She'd twisted her fingers together.

'Then why should you assume we judge you for the accident of yours?'

Beauty, wealth, ability: all lucky accidents of birth. Genevieve, wrinkling her nose, discovered only Lulu's phrasing to hand. 'Because I'm an upper-class twat?'

Oliver laughed out loud, to Genevieve's inordinate satisfaction. She wasn't sure why it left her with such a warm feeling of gratification. He was a serious man, but she didn't think he was a joyless one.

'Those cousins of yours,' he said. 'They're either a terrible influence, or the best possible.'

She hummed thoughtfully. 'I believe my father has failed to consider that they are an influence on me at all. Because I'm the elder, and then he's the elder of the Locke brothers, and thinks all the influence flows from elder to younger. I have this…' She took a breath, but Oliver didn't speak, so she went on. 'I have this idea in my head, of three mongrel puppies, playing, carefree, tumbling about, heedless of all but their game. And then one day, the kennel master looks them over and sees that one of them has all the markings of a pedigree bitch. So he seizes her up by the scruff of the neck and puts her in a golden collar to show her off, without understanding that everyone else will immediately notice that the markings are mere superficiality, and she has no pedigree at all.'

When Oliver remained quiet, she said stiffly, 'I am aware I am being tremendously unfilial.'

'This may come as a great shock, given the overall thrust of our world,' Oliver said, 'but it's not my experience that fathers always know best.'

This encouraged Genevieve to continue, still carefully picking out words. 'And I've been resenting the freedom of the other two puppies. They're able to do so much more than the pedigree bitch, you see. They may go about the world without a leash. They might—' It would not do to push the metaphor too far. '—marry where they like, or not at all. They may run as far and as fast as they take it into their heads to run.' And they *were* going to run, soon, part of her already knew that. 'They might seize life in their teeth and chew it down to the marrow. And I want it. I want that freedom and that, that—'

She hesitated. She'd been about to say *passion*, and couldn't do it, not to a man who was mostly still a mere acquaintance. It was symptomatic of her whole situation, which truly did not deserve the look of warm sympathy Oliver was bestowing upon her.

She stiffened her spine, and turned from fruitless complaint to her actual worry. 'But I'm beginning to realise my fa— the kennel master would be only briefly saddened should the mongrel puppies be dropped in the river in a weighted sack. Figuratively, of course.'

After a pause – she was beginning to realise these were habitual with him, to be sure she had finished her thought, or in this case, her unforgivably traitorous admission – Oliver said, 'He's washed his hands of any responsibility for his niece and nephew?'

'He says he does not wish to presume upon an ungifted authority.' She recalled the conversation on which she had unrepentantly eavesdropped before their first training session. 'They are Sir Kingsford's wards and since he has yet to administer any instructions as to their disposition, my father could not possibly take any action that might contravene their guardian's wishes. I find it reprehensible.'

'I wonder if Mr Locke has perhaps overlooked the fact that Sir Kingsford himself also unexpectedly lost his father and may be rather at sea himself, forced so suddenly into a paternal role.'

Genevieve privately did not think this excused her father's benign neglect of Alex and Lulu. The whole Locke family knew Sir Kingsford was a little odd, as eccentric as his parents but in an entirely different direction. Kings had been eager to decamp out of crowded, noisy London to gratefully take charge of his new estate; Father should have been able to guess he would struggle with the rudderless human charges that came along with it.

Oliver added, 'I think Alexander might have overlooked that, also.'

'Alex is unreasonable in the extreme,' Genevieve said. 'It baffles me. He's usually so affable.'

'Brothers can be difficult.' That had the ring of true knowledge to it. When she lifted her brows in invitation, he added, 'They disapprove.'

'Of your *Art*? You can hardly help it, Oliver.'

He smiled at her tone of outrage. 'The Art's fine. Being an Artisan, though. No better than I should be.' She must have looked blank. He added, in a thickened accent and plainly quoting someone, 'Too big for 'is britches, that one.'

'Oh. They must think that's very funny.'

'The height of wit.' He shrugged, a ponderous motion. 'Brothers.'

'You've never said how your Arts came on,' she said tentatively. 'Do you… Is it the done thing to ask, or not?'

'Not,' he said, 'but I don't mind telling you. I think you possibly need to hear that I suffered no great single blow, either. I just… I have a lot of brothers, we have a lot of work to do, on and off the ships, not always safe, and I'm the eldest. It was, *is*, will always be my job to keep them safe, and fed, and clothed.' He looked down at his thick hands, lying upturned in his lap. 'I wanted to be able to work longer, faster, harder, that's all. And…not to die doing it. Wanted it very badly.'

He gave a small smile, almost dismissive, but she could feel suddenly the weight of the unspoken words. Hungry mouths to feed, small bodies to keep warm and out of harm's way. All those pitying newspaper articles about the grinding poverty of the underclasses. She'd read them, and tsked over them, and pointed them out to Mother so she could use their wealth to partake in subscriptions and perform charitable works, and she never had really understood, not until she sat opposite a man whose life of relentless drudgery had triggered his mind and body to transform.

'I'm sorry,' she said. 'And they tease you for it!'

He shrugged. He shifted again, and looked at her contemplatively. 'Have you thought, at all, that your feelings on the night your Art bloomed might not have *entirely* been about your host's son?'

'What do you mean?' Genevieve asked, nonplussed by the change of subject and still flushed with her righteous indignation on his behalf.

Very gently, he said, 'Who else were you angry at, Miss Locke?'

And then he waited her out, through her surprise at the question, her confusion, her almost-affront as a slow dawn of understanding came upon her, her guilt, and then, finally, her acceptance.

'My father.'

He nodded like a schoolteacher satisfied with finally winning comprehension from a particularly doltish student, or at least that was Genevieve's narrow-eyed and somewhat uncharitable interpretation. He must have caught her mild dudgeon; he raised a thick brow, prepared to take pushback.

'He is acting always in my best interests,' she said, a little uncertainly; even as she said it, the new thought was rising: *not* my *best interests*.

For could it not be suggested that all his overbearing insistence on keeping her reputation pure and negotiating the best possible match was not on her behalf at all, but solely because he saw that he could make of her a ladder for himself?

It was a shockingly bitter thought. She flinched from it, and saw Oliver's open face wince in deep empathy. She had to shut her eyes.

She'd thought her father's wealth would shield her from the worst meted out to women – and it did, mostly, but not all of it. And she'd thought her

Artistry would elevate her above it completely, and now it was clear to her that she would still be held in her role as woman, wife, mother, a shackle about her ankle tethering her as surely as if it had truly been of iron.

And it *was* a shackle, or perhaps a golden collar a naïve puppy had thought she was wriggling out of. All her father's talk of the opportunities her good marriage would bring – they had been his opportunities, not hers.

She fortified herself enough to open her eyes. 'Sorry to whine,' she said. 'Little pedigree bitch, hmm?'

She won another outright laugh, that low rumble of amusement with its note of pleasurable surprise, and it made her smile in a way that even she could tell was a little soft and silly.

Oliver's hand was warm as he helped her from the carriage and bid her a good evening.

18

GENEVIEVE WAS ASTONISHED BY THE UNDERSTANDING that she had not much liked Reuben McAvey at their first encounter, finding him presumptuous and condescending.

But she could feel, too, the connection, the sympathetic recognition, which must have grown into more over the course of that summer and autumn; they'd married in February, after all, a scant nine months from that initial meeting.

She looked warily up at Oliver, suddenly shy at the thought of allowing the courtship to play out in front of him. With the benefit of experience and familiarity, she could appreciate that his regard for her, even in the earliest months of their friendship, had been subtly different in quality to his brotherly fondness towards Cecelia or the twins. Her younger self had never noticed it, or at least, not until well after her and Reuben's mutual regard had become too great for any alternative outcome. Perhaps if she had…

There was little point to what-ifs. The difference in their social positions had been almost too great for mere association, let alone anything beyond the vaguest of speculations. Their one choice had been the path they'd taken: quietly and sensibly ignoring anything other than friendship.

But it still felt unfair to make Oliver relive memories of watching her fall in love with someone else, especially a man who'd proven unworthy of her love.

Genevieve pulled up short, chiding herself as the fog in her mind eddied. She loved her husband. He had behaved incomprehensibly, even cruelly. It did not, yet, follow that he was unworthy. Perhaps discontent with his barren, difficult wife combined with the obsession the copper knife seemed to provoke had caused some sort of rupture that could yet be healed. He might yet be restored to her.

Oliver brushed her arm as he took up the next painting, shaking her from her reverie. He'd unwrapped it before she could tactfully find a way to suggest he might not want to.

It was a portrait of Genevieve again, and she laughed when she saw it, but Oliver didn't. He touched the edge of the canvas. It depicted Genevieve wreathed in flame, great wings of fire rising up behind her. She remembered practising that, over and over in the garden, with Lulu's caustic commentary helping her make it ever more dramatically terrifying. She remembered what a hash she'd made of her first deployment of the technique in the field.

And she remembered—

She glanced sharply at Oliver, an acute twist in her chest, part alarm and part recognition. She remembered—

WEEKS SLIPPED PAST, deep into summer. Genevieve doggedly practised and practised and practised, until she turned the threat of wildfire that might burst forth without her volition or control into flame that would only ever appear, persist, and disappear under her precise direction.

Eventually, she resumed attending engagements, at some minimum level that appeared to have been negotiated between her parents. She found them easier to bear now she could tell herself that the snubbing was due to jealousy, or even fear, over her Artisan status, and that such pettiness lay far beneath the notice of her newly-acquired elevation. She refused to wear so much as a flower in her hair, discarding any form of headdress with Artisan pride. The ice she had once used to cool her frustration and resentment now became her social weapon of choice.

She considered, albeit briefly, that perhaps her defensively icy persona might have been the chief reason for the rejection of the other girls, and the reluctance of the men to make offers – especially once her father, acting on her behalf or his own, had refused two seemingly fine matches in her first season.

The twins begged off church, another foible Father should not have indulged, yet did. Genevieve continued her regular attendance. Church and Artistry were technically reconciled in this modern era, and she personally found no great crisis, and some gratitude, in her admittedly mild theology, though she knew of other Artisans, more devout than her immediate circle, who struggled.

She had her birthday, turning twenty. The twins had already had theirs, turning seventeen, and spent the summer shooting up another foot between them. They bounced between the Locke townhouse and Northfield, according to Alex's level of tolerance for the invasion of intentions that came with the crowds in the city, versus the unremittingly and apparently offensive good intentions of Sir Kingsford in the country.

Oliver made a try at teaching him to control his talent, but it had been plain since the early days under a private tutor that Alex's natural abilities did not to extend to scholarly pursuits. Alex, though no longer enamoured, remained somewhat in awe of Oliver, which was enough to make him sit through a few lessons before he quite simply, and very rudely, began to absent himself from the house in anticipation of their appointments. He was doing himself no good, and Genevieve despaired to see it.

Lulu's talent, too, remained stubbornly limited despite her own best efforts and Oliver's, in exploring word-of-mouth methods rumoured to have a strengthening effect. It had always been a rare achievement, in Genevieve's understanding of the few articles on the matter, but if anyone possessed the sheer strength of will to make it happen, it would be Lulu.

Then came the bad news she'd been braced for.

'But *why*?' she asked miserably, for the third time.

'We have to get out of London,' Lulu said again. She knew Genevieve was distressed; she was being remarkably patient. 'And we can't go back to Northfield, it's almost as bad for Alex there. Not that he gives Kings an easy time of it either.'

'But you don't have to vanish all the way to the Continent!'

'That's where our new job is taking us,' Lulu said.

They'd hired on as junior members of the security escort for some sort of expedition, using their talents to access an impromptu Grand Tour. It was along the lines of Lulu's daydreams, except Genevieve had been thoroughly left out of it. She greatly resented the note of pride in Lulu's voice at the mention of her first formal employment.

'He doesn't even want to do this sort of work,' she said, unable to hide her sulk.

'He dreams of exploring the world,' Lulu said flatly. 'And since he can't do it as a member of a scientific expedition, he can do it as a fixer for a scientific expedition. It's as close as I could get him, and as far away as I can get him from crowds.' She lowered her voice, leaning closer. 'He needs this, Gin. He needs to get away, and he needs me. Don't tell him I said that, he'll hate it.'

Genevieve knew then that it was a lost cause. In a tug-of-war over the loyalties of a Locke twin, the other twin would inevitably win; it was not a contest. The greatest irony was that this continental work entailed each twin upending their own desires for the other's happiness, sending them both off on some third path it had never occurred to either of them to want for themselves, and yet neither would hear it.

'*I* need you,' she said, but with more despondency than demand.

'You've got Oliver.' Lulu paused for an unseemly space before adding, 'And Miss Delacorte, and your other Artisan friends.'

Genevieve glanced around. They were, as ever, in the garden, and her mother was, as ever, painting under the small plane tree. Oliver was meant to be calling on her shortly. He no longer attended solely to help her contain her Art. Miss Delacorte was a regular visitor now, too, and a few others of what Genevieve recognised had become her faction in the Society.

Lulu said, 'Anyway, it's plain now I'm not going to force my talent to develop into an Art. I'm wasting Oliver's time with that, like fucking Lamarck wasted mine. You two need to focus on what you're going to do next.'

'We two?' Genevieve repeated, eyebrows raised in mild rebuke.

The back door opened then, and Oliver was escorted through to the garden by an expressionless footman. He greeted all three women with his usual polite equanimity. Over the many weeks of their growing acquaintance, he'd become less standoffish, but he maintained a respectable distance that the other Artisans, like Miss Delacorte, did not seem to deem necessary.

He looked twice at Genevieve. Her eyes must be reddened. She said, 'Oh, don't mind my dramatics, Mr Oliver, the younger Miss Locke has merely notified me of her imminent desertion and bodily theft of my actual favourite cousin.'

'Hoi!' Lulu said, swatting her. 'I *better* be your favourite, missy.'

'I've come to invite you for an outing, which may cheer you up,' Oliver informed her. 'We're going to tackle a fellow Artisan up to mischief – proof of the pudding, regarding the question of enforcement.' He turned towards Mother. 'Miss Delacorte will be there.'

Genevieve expected her mother to remind Oliver, as she gently but consistently reminded her husband, that Genevieve was an Artisan, and as such did not require a chaperone, as much as it aided his peace of mind when she invariably had one anyway. But Mother nodded to Oliver, as if, between the two of them, they'd decided it was necessary after all.

She had sharp words lined up about that, but Lulu got in first with her own commentary. 'My talent's more useful than some memory Art! I want to come.'

Genevieve seized the chance for some teasing revenge. 'You go off on your little expedition, Lucinda. This is for Artisans.'

Lulu scoffed. 'I shall tell Alex you said that to me, and you see if *you're* still *his* favourite cousin.'

'I have to be, I'm his only cousin.'

This was not true; the twins had plenty of cousins on their mother's side, and more amid their father's first wife's family, too. But Genevieve was their only Locke cousin, and all the Lockes knew that was the only thing that counted.

Indeed, Lulu sallied with, 'There's…Mildred,' which was a name she'd entirely made up because none of her maternal cousins' names tripped off her tongue.

Genevieve made a rude noise and went in with her mother and Oliver to obtain her father's permission for the proposed outing, a step which remained essential but which was increasingly chafing. He was mollified by the mention of Miss Delacorte's attendance, less subtly than her mother had been.

'Go and ready yourself, Ginnie,' Mother said, when she saw Genevieve's hands go to her hips.

She was still fuming at both parents when she reached her room, though had to concede the new wardrobe her mother had engineered took some of the sting out of the paternalism.

The dresses in current fashion were awfully constricting, both the bodice about the torso and the long sleeves about the arms, so much so that bending from the waist and lifting the arms could both be difficult. The hemlines of the domed-shaped skirts brushed the ground, not sensible for any quarter of society that had to venture into the streets of the city, let alone the active Artisan woman Genevieve stubbornly claimed her right to be.

Miss Delacorte wore trousers under a long frock coat, sometimes, on Artisan business, and was very fetching about it, too. It made Lulu, cursing the current fashion trends, take note, but Genevieve had already stolen pieces of Alex's wardrobe and found the makeshift ensemble too ill-fitting to countenance; her father would not countenance tailoring. The obvious solution, a riding habit, left her looking like she was merely a fool girl who'd lost both hat and horse.

It was truly a fool's game that, having so greatly begrudged the expensive and constraining gowns of her other life, the symbol of her expensive and constrained existence, Genevieve wished dearly to wear an Artisan outfit as opulently pretty. The vanity made for an annoying convergence with her father's firmly conventional opinion that, Artisan or no, she still represented her family's status, wealth and merit whenever she stepped out their door.

Antoinette, the artist, the diplomat, the wife with her devoted husband wrapped around her little finger, the mother with unerring insight to her daughter's desires and needs, as shallow and fickle as they were, proved herself the equal even of this fashion dilemma, especially after some consultation with both her own artistic circle and the other women of Genevieve's new Artisan circle. After all, the matter of Artistry Dress was a perennial issue whenever orthodox sartorial fashions swung back to the impractically constrictive or poorly manoeuvrable.

And so Genevieve wore what amounted to a modified and trimmed version of the loose wrapper, commonly worn by women about the house, with stays to make it acceptable for public outings, and all of unpatterned shot silk that shimmered in the light to make up for the unfashionably soft lines, and loaned her the gravitas of an older woman. She sported a looser corset, too, supportive but not confining – speaking of symbolic clothing items – with ventilation panels, too, as if she were off to play croquet and wore a so-called health corset.

An unexpected benefit of a wrapper-inspired gown was that she could fasten it up the front herself, without assistance. Today she chose a periwinkle gown that brought out a brightness in her eyes. She did still need help with her hair. Since her dress did not meet current style, she didn't try to make her hair do so; ringlets would not do. She asked the maid to braid and pin it in a manner she thought reminiscent of paintings of the shield-maidens of the long-ago northern raiders, the sea-wolves on the shores, these days called Vikings and quite popular in particular novels.

Genevieve paused at the top of the stairs to adjust her matching pelerine, taking a deep breath, refreshingly easy to do. She'd become used to venturing forth without bonnet or gloves, but this was her first excursion outfitted entirely as an Artisan. Aside from the chemise and drawers that protected her skin from the whaleboning of the corset, she wore a single petticoat. She had to remind herself she was perfectly modestly dressed, even as she wondered if anyone had thought to sew closed drawers yet.

After a moment, she took off the pelerine and cast it heedlessly aside. She glided down the stairs as if making a grand entrance at a ball. She was strangely pleased to see the phlegmatic Oliver look up from the hallway, instantly turn his gaze from her, and then return it like it was being dragged by magnets.

Far from taking her as a Viking shield-maiden, however, he said, 'The Greek exhibition.' Then he coughed and said, 'Athena, I mean.'

He looked away again as he said it, though, and it struck her as odd. Perhaps he was embarrassed to have accidentally compared her to a goddess.

The niggling feeling coalesced in the family carriage, which her father had insisted on as a condition of his permission, instead of hiring a growler, or, God forbid, a speedy cabriolet he refused to believe had any safety features at all.

'I attended that exhibition,' she said. 'The parts I was allowed to, anyway.' She had it on good authority from Alex that the nudes had been a cultural experience, but they'd been curtained off from women attendees; she could have set the curtains on fire and her Artisan status still wouldn't have won her entry. 'Athena wasn't there, Mr Oliver.'

It occurred to her the goddess might have been behind the curtains – Alex had been fairly well rapt with the male form, so might have overlooked mentioning female nudes – but Oliver confirmed, 'No, she wasn't.'

'It did feature the Judgement of Paris, but the first panels were missing or defaced. The first clear representation was Paris awarding the golden apple to Aphrodite.'

She was puzzled: Oliver was a careful man; he didn't make errors like that. Possibly that was why she was being so priggishly pedantic about it.

'I know.' He smiled reluctantly. 'And should I have requested Mr Locke geld me before or after I compared his precious only daughter to a goddess of love?'

'Oh!' Both her eyebrows had shot up. She schooled her expression back to coolness. 'I thought his reluctance to allow me full Artisan freedom has been about protecting my reputation in general. Are you telling me he has been worried about *you* in the particular all this time, Mr Oliver?'

'It does make his concern somewhat ridiculous.'

'It casts unforgivable aspersions on your honour and my—'

She stopped in horror. She had been about to reference her moral rectitude, which quite abruptly, to her ear, implied that her moral rectitude was not as…erected?…around Oliver as it should be. Which was—

Which was—

Well, it was unfair, was what it was. Simply referencing his honour would never be taken to imply it was weakened in her presence, would it?

She suddenly found herself looking at Oliver, properly noticing herself look at him, since the first night they'd met. For all he made no pretty oil painting for a parlour, she had become fond of him for his other qualities – his thoughtful calm, his mild good humour, his understated intelligence, his gentle encouragement.

And the way his crooked smile lit his warm, dark eyes.

And the shape his mouth took when he tried to blow out her match.

And the delicate strength implicit in his chapped and calloused hands.

She thought he could put those large hands about her hips and pick her up all the way off the ground.

Genevieve jolted. *And do what?* she asked herself. Good Lord, those naughty books the twins insisted on passing her…and that she insisted on reading. No wonder pulpits and opinion pieces were united in fulminating against them!

Likely puzzled by her sudden silence, Oliver was staring at her, in a way *he* hadn't looked at *her* since the first night they'd met. Flushing, Genevieve turned blindly towards the carriage window, willing the telltale heat from her cheeks.

She was relieved when they arrived. She wasn't entirely sure where they were, having not paid attention to the direction of the carriage, and with the sight of familiar landmarks blocked by the tenements around her.

They left the carriage to await their return and walked around a corner to meet Miss Delacorte and a man Genevieve recognised. The pair were waiting by a dilapidated wooden warehouse, small and rundown even amid the definite signs of a poverty-stricken area.

Miss Delacorte greeted them briskly, effecting rapid introductions. 'Mr Fletcher, Miss Locke. Our illicit Artisan's inside. We had word of this one because his partner rolled over on him. It's a strong teleport Art, he's been using it to open portals into the banks' family vaults and snatch heirloom jewellery.'

The plan, it seemed, was for Oliver to smother the man's Art. He wasn't strong enough to stop him completely from opening a portal, but he should be able to make sure it took too long to grow large enough to fit a full-grown man.

Genevieve's role was to threaten. No one wanted their target actually set on fire, thankfully, merely unbalanced, so that he couldn't concentrate enough to create the Artwork. It rather tickled her that, between her and Oliver, *she* was providing the muscle.

This thought almost made up for the fact that it had only now struck her that Oliver's wards, though adequate for a tiny flame contained at the end of a matchstick, had never been strong enough to quell her Art if she'd lost control. His placid calm in the face of her flames had always made her feel safer than it really should have. It made her want to shake him by his broad shoulders, or perhaps take his hands and squeeze them tight.

'And that will give Mr Fletcher time to get close enough to lay a full compulsion on him,' Miss Delacorte finished. 'This is an excellent chance to demonstrate how real enforcers will work, so we shall try for quick and seamless. Everyone clear?'

They averred that they were. They split into pairs, Oliver and Genevieve making their way down to a side door while the other two went to the front.

Oliver, looking a little tickled himself, gave Genevieve a silent and unnecessary countdown with his fingers before easing the door open. The lock had been broken long ago.

The place was derelict, stripped of any useful equipment, begrimed and dusty, and strewn with the detritus of the destitute taking shelter. None were here right now; the police had moved them on for the absentee owner, or the Artisan might have temporarily scared them off. They were still thought of as witches, among the most superstitious. An official agency would help with that, too.

It was dim, the high windows too narrow and dirty to let in the waning light. Quiet clinks came from the far corner, and a few irate mutters.

They eased their way closer, keeping by the wall. The rogue Artisan was alternating sips from a gin bottle with a stare off into space that Genevieve knew bespoke concentrating on one's Art. From his irritated and intermittent cursing, he was having trouble managing it. If he did, though, at this sensitive juncture, he'd be a whisker from escaping.

'Thompson, is that you?' he called abruptly, straightening and turning to look their way.

He jerked to his feet at the sight of them, bottle still in his hand. Urgency overcame his spluttering Art, or perhaps it was fear, though Genevieve's reading suggested emotion was good for power but dreadful for control. This seemed like an Art that needed copious quantities of both.

Nevertheless, a hazy space like a whirlpool of dust began to spiral into being before him. Oliver spun out an Artwork, and the spiral slowed, fighting the wards.

The portal had already grown big enough for the Artisan to almost get his shoulders through, however, and it seemed he was about to dive into it and shimmy like a man wriggling into a tunnel.

Genevieve had given a great deal of thought as to the best deployment of her deadly Art. She had no wish to immolate people, criminals or no, and did not trust her control to deliver only a warning scald instead – if she even had the stomach for deliberately dealing such an injury. Setting things on fire around her target might work, but she felt she needed more control for that, too: the Great Fire was a historical touchstone she refused to emulate, and this wooden warehouse was ripe for any spark.

Therefore, the one safe place for her literal fire-power was herself.

She burst into flames. The conflagration lit the warehouse from one end to the other. She barely heard Oliver's surprised cry, concentrating hard on the next step: spreading a magnificent pair of wings, all made of flames.

It was meant to scare her victim into frozen compliance. Lulu had assured her, when she'd practised in the garden, that it was incredibly intimidating. Her mother had even painted it, with some glee.

Indeed, both the thief and Oliver stared with open mouths as she mantled her great flaming pinions, geysering small fiery tornados from her palms for good measure. Both their Arts shrivelled to nothing. Only, Oliver kept staring, while the thief shrieked and bolted, hurling his bottle at Genevieve as he went.

Innocent enough to be genuinely startled at the prospect of assault, she ducked with perhaps more enthusiasm than strictly required, thus tripping over a broken crate. She tumbled to the ground, ankle twisting. Her flames flared in brief concert with the pain before extinguishing along with her focus. Oliver moved sharply towards her, but she gestured after the rogue Artisan, who was halfway out the main door already.

Their target ran straight into Mr Fletcher. One touch from bare hands and a murmured command, and he was docile.

'Excellent work!' Miss Delacorte said, beaming from beside Mr Fletcher, her excited pleasure reminding Genevieve, with some surprise, that they were taking orders from a girl at most a year or so older than the twins. 'Magnificent, Miss Locke! Help her up, Will!'

She and Mr Fletcher escorted their catch outside, to make arrangements for a handover to police, iron cuffs in place, while Oliver offered Genevieve a hand. 'That was…dramatic, Miss Locke.'

She was still breathless, heart thundering in her chest. 'I meant to stun him,' she explained. 'It worked on you!'

'Yes, but I don't need to fear divine justice,' Oliver said, smiling. 'He apparently thought the wrath of literal flaming angels was about to fall upon his head, and reacted accordingly.'

Taking his offered hand, she said, more archly than she'd intended, 'And are you so very sure you're sinless, Oliver?'

He said, 'I'm a saint, Gin,' as he pulled her to her feet.

The slight effort meant the words, no doubt *never* intended to be provocative, came out in his lowest growl, and his assistance accidentally set her onto her injured ankle and made her stumble against him. He caught her, hands on her hips, eyes lowered, the rumble of his voice still echoing in her ears, the faint spicy scent he carried after lading filling her nose.

Her heart was still beating fast, so fast it felt like it was trying to take flight out her throat, almost painful. She was standing as close as she ever had to any man outside her family, closer than dancing, and he was a wall of warmth and strength. She felt a rush of response through her body, confusing and yearning and right: every nerve chimed a simple carillon. *Yes. This. Him.*

She didn't know what *this* was, but she abruptly wanted it more than she'd ever wanted anything.

But Oliver wouldn't meet her eyes. He jerked his hands off her as if touching her seared him, before seeing that she couldn't put her weight on her ankle. He instinctively moved to put an arm about her waist, and stopped, eyebrows knit in a ferocious frown.

He felt it too, she realised. He wouldn't hesitate to assist an injured fellow Artisan, if the fact of her womanhood wasn't ringing loud.

'Oliver.' With the serene inevitability of a dream, she leaned closer, lifting her throbbing ankle fully off the ground and letting her full weight tip into his arms. 'Artisans are allowed to touch each other.'

'Not like this, they're not.'

But even as he said it, he wrapped his arms around her, perhaps so she wouldn't fall, perhaps because—

She went up on tiptoe on her good leg, resting against his broad chest, and lifted her face to his. He lowered his to hers in reciprocation: she'd have to remind herself of that later. She instigated the kiss, but he helped her do it.

She'd never kissed anyone on the mouth before, bar childish games with Alex and Lulu, chaste pecks, during pretend weddings and the like, that sent them off into ridiculous fits of giggles. She resolved to not be tentative about it now, and pressed her lips against his firmly enough to surprise him; she felt his lips part under hers.

His soft capitulation sent another rush of that confused longing through her; she slipped her hands about the bare nape of his neck and, shameless, pressed ever harder against his immovable bulk, deepening the kiss to the best of her rapidly-improving ability, squirming to get closer and closer to him, to what end she did not know, except it presumably had something to do with the male member all those risqué novels went on about, and that was when Genevieve encountered a rock-hard obstruction against her hip, the lesser layers of Artisan clothing doing very little to obscure it.

Oliver had tightened his hold, he was kissing her just as much as she was kissing him, but when she made an exclamation, half-puzzled, into his mouth at the feel of him, he thrust her away so violently she nearly fell over, and he had to lunge back and catch her.

And then hold her at the very long extent of his arms.

He was flushed and wild-eyed, more discombobulated even than when Alex had slyly encouraged her and Lulu to admire his hands.

He took a few deep breaths, then asked, 'Can you walk, Miss Locke?'

'No. Oliver, I—'

'I can't send you home with a sprained ankle, your father—'

They stared at each other in mutual comprehension. If her father would be beside himself if she returned from this outing with a mere physical injury, there could be no telling his reaction should he discover the battering of her pristine reputation.

Miss Delacorte returned then, still bustling with exhilarated energy. 'Oh! Are you hurt, Miss Locke?'

'My ankle,' Genevieve managed.

'Goodness! I'll call your carriage around, we'll take you to Miss Adler.' She paused. 'It seems you will have to carry her, Will.'

Oliver scratched his ear. Carefully, very much not looking at Genevieve, he said, 'I'm not allowed to even acknowledge Miss Locke possesses an ankle, let alone pick her up merely because she happens to have injured it.'

But Miss Delacorte was in full organisational flight. 'If I had the somatic Art, I would assist, but since I don't, you must.' She waved a dismissive hand to his further attempt at demurral. 'She's not a woman, William, she's a fellow Artisan, you are being ludicrous. Isn't that right, Genevieve?'

The uninvited use of her given name was in support of the fellow-Artisan argument. Some devilry took hold of Genevieve, possibly sparked by the mischievous gleam in the other woman's eyes. 'Thank you, Cecelia. I would be *most* gratified by your assistance, Oliver.'

It was a great irony, really, that he now had no recourse but to oblige her, in a way he wouldn't have been constrained to do, *and* in a way he wouldn't've at all been bothered by doing, if Artisans truly were as sexless as they were meant to be.

He scooped her up effortlessly, and cradled her to his chest. She looked up at his face, rather breathless. He was stubbornly keeping his expression set at its most neutral, the face he wore when talking to her father. He marched her through the warehouse without a word, Miss Delacorte – Cecelia – darting off ahead to summon the carriage.

Genevieve now knew why her heart lifted whenever he came to visit her. She now knew why she felt so paradoxically calm and yet strangely taut whenever she was with him. Her heart thudded. She would have given a great proportion of the wealth due to come to her to possess the courage it would have taken to press her bare hand against his shirt so she could ascertain if his own heart was so affected. Instead, she tightened her hold about his neck, tucking her head against his shoulder.

The coachman, an old family retainer, raised his eyebrows when he pulled up the Locke brougham to see her in a man's arms, and leapt down to open the door with alacrity. Oliver was gentle as he settled her, Cecelia fussing about to help lift her ankle onto the seat. Mr Fletcher joined them in the carriage, murmuring about escorting them, but Oliver doffed an imaginary hat and took the opportunity to retreat.

He hadn't let himself look at her again.

19

GENEVIEVE STAYED KNEELING, FROZEN IN PLACE. Oliver sat back on his heels, face tilted downwards and away. He was refusing to look at her, exactly as he'd refused to look at her after she'd kissed him.

'That's…' she started, and couldn't finish. A niggle between her eyes bespoke a rare incipient headache.

She'd been about to say *That's unexpected*, but she wasn't entirely sure it was. Her body was thrumming with the feeling of rightness that had enveloped her during that kiss, and it was the same feeling that had shocked her when Reuben had played his cruel game, and the same feeling as when Oliver had so bewilderingly brushed his mouth over the pulse point of her wrist.

She'd been too self-centred, too innocent to notice she had an admirer in Oliver back then, though it was plain to her now that her mother knew and her father suspected. But once she *had* finally recognised the small frisson between them, she'd thought that she – *and* Oliver, both of them – had decided to pretend it did not exist.

She hadn't ever suspected that her immediate reaction had been to fling herself wantonly into her friend's arms and demand to be kissed. She lifted fingers to her lips as if she could still trace the remnants of the long-ago press of his mouth, stomach fluttering.

Quite abruptly, she was again convinced that a resplendently sinuous Art-drawn dragon writhed across Oliver's broad chest, its tongue hunting his nipple. His *pierced* nipple, gold hoop gleaming temptingly.

For all Reuben's lack of prominence in these memories, she must have been deepening her acquaintance with and mutual admiration of him during this period. Thoughts of other men had been beyond her once she met her future husband. Even knowing Reuben had abandoned her, it still made her queasy to contemplate such a dreadful betrayal.

And yet, she'd kissed Oliver. And her knowledge of that dragon suggested she'd persuaded him into far more scandalous activities before she married the love of her life.

She eyed the next wrapped shape with some trepidation, waiting for Oliver to take it up, as he had the last time she'd hesitated. But he didn't move, except to glance at the door as if he'd finally remembered the others at the tea tray.

She stiffened her spine. 'We might as well see what happened next.'

But when she picked up the parcel, the second last, its texture within its swaddle was different to the canvases. Unwrapping revealed that the memory was only for her, a tucked-away piece of her mother's heart, in the form of rough ink sketches on thick artpaper. Mother hadn't turned the sketches into a painting, but page after page of quick black lines had captured the essence of the scene: Genevieve and her cousins, sprawled on the stairs in deep conversation.

'They were about to leave,' Genevieve said softly. 'They'd taken their first commission.'

She traced the lines, touching first Lulu's face, then Alex's.

And she remembered.

THE TWINS HAD their trunks packed and set in the hall. Genevieve sat on the stairs in somewhat of a sulk to watch the preparations for their departure the next day. They'd played this scene out often enough in the endless shuttle between town house and country estate, but this was different: the twins, all grown up, were finally off to fulfil the first commission of their new career.

They weren't *all* grown up. Alex, over six foot tall, newly broad-shouldered, flung himself down beside her like the overgrown pup he surely was. 'All right, Gin?'

Not even out of London yet, the sheer anticipation of adventure had made him much happier. Even dreading their departure, she had to admit that. Brusque as Lulu was, she knew her brother to his core, and he knew her. Each choosing a third path to benefit the other had been exactly what they'd both needed.

Thus, Genevieve found herself able to sling an affectionate arm about his neck and genuinely wish him well on his travels. 'You will keep in touch?'

'You know I won't,' Alex said with blithe ownership of his apathy towards writing. 'Lulu will, though.' He tugged at his coat, disarranged from his outrageously louche lounge. 'I've not known how to ask this, so I've left it late, but I reckon I've still got time to do something about it if the answer's yes…'

It was unlike him to dance about. 'Ask what?'

'That Lord Whatsit, the night your Art bloomed.'

'Lord Marlough?'

'His son.'

'Oh. He's just an Honourable until his grandfather dies,' she said dismissively. 'What about him?'

'I know he's unpleasant as a general run of the mill, but did he *do* something? Something I need to go, you know, take care of before I leave? Punch him on the nose? Not to imply you couldn't take care of it yourself, but – do I?'

Genevieve had to blink at him a few times before she understood. 'Oh! Lord, no, Alex. Why on earth would you think that?'

She'd barely spoken to either cousin about her Art's genesis: she still carried a small shame about how trifling it all seemed, in light of their own loss. Her circumspection had obviously left their imaginations to run wild and presume the worst.

Alex touched the side of his head. 'You know,' he said vaguely. 'It's all a jumble in here, it's impossible, but Oliver's intentions are so loud now, they're cutting through the chaff whether I like it or not. Either that, or my talent is stronger around him.'

'*Mr Oliver* wants to punch Mr Marlough on the nose?'

'Not quite.' Her cousin smiled at the confused expression she must be wearing. 'Every time he comes through the door, he's floating this very strong intention to *not* be like "that knobby pillock who bothered Gin", and since he's well more than halfway in love with you—'

'Alexander! That's—'

'—I assumed he must be resisting the overwhelming urge to push you up against a wall and kiss you.'

'He'd never act so dishonourably,' Genevieve corrected him reflexively, still digesting how casually he'd proclaimed their friend's affections.

'I'd assumed, yes,' Alex said. 'So what is it Marlough did, that Oliver is needing to remind himself not to do?'

'He looked at me. Listen, Lexi, Oliver is most certainly not in love with me.'

'Oh, it doesn't bother me, Gin,' Alex said cheerfully. 'I let go of any hope of seducing him ages ago. The poor man's been trying not to *look* at you since the night we all met.'

'Stop it,' she said, glaring. 'Mr Marlough looked at me like he wanted to… Well, you know.'

'You don't think our Mr Oliver wants to—'

'*Stop.*'

Her sudden flush of embarrassment came, not so much from the abstract idea of Oliver's possible desire, but from her own naïve surprise, a week ago, when she had felt the…concreteness…of it. She'd first believed he'd withdrawn because her innocence had alarmed him, that if she had been able to pretend to be as worldly as the twins pretended to be, he might have let her keep kissing him.

Except. He'd pushed her away. He'd refused to look at her, as if her behaviour had been reprehensible. And it had been, by every single metric she'd been surrounded by her entire life, swimming in rules and judgement and thinking she was safe from it all because the twins were.

Alex drew her hands down – she'd clapped them over her ears like she was five – and spoke to her gently. 'I believe he deeply esteems you, Gin, and wants nothing other than to be tediously respectable towards you. That's *why* he won't let himself look, in case he slips up and proves himself as lecherous as the rest of us despicable weak men.'

'Lucinda,' Genevieve shouted up the stairs. 'Come and shut your brother's mouth for him.'

'So. My next question is, what are you planning to do about this news, cousin?' He looked at her closely. 'If it *is* news to you, that is.'

He was straightening his cuffs with some care, but his gaze was flicking to over her head, where she knew he saw – "saw" – the play of intentions. The overwhelming backwash from everyone in the house and the street outside usually tangled him too much to actually read any individual's intentions, but that didn't mean he wasn't developing some tolerance and approaching competence. Just because he wasn't subjecting himself to lessons with Oliver didn't mean he wasn't practising in his own way.

Gin waved a hand over her head as if she could brush her flickering intentions away from his view.

'Tsk, you know that's metaphorical,' he scolded, grinning.

'When our agency is established, it will be illegal,' she scolded him in turn.

'Illicit Art's only a problem for Artisans,' he told her. 'We talented few will be unpoliced by you self-righteous lot.'

'I shall set Miss Delacorte on that little loophole, then.'

She was pleased to see the threat give him pause, although the reality of the contentious Society was such that every nuance was so fought over, every agreement so hard won, that even the dauntless Cecelia would consider twice before she decided to unpick a decision merely to sew up a hole.

Lulu, dressed for an outing, came thundering down to see what her annoying brother was doing. She flung herself down next to him, unimpressed by Genevieve's recital.

'Yeah, Oliver's been in love with you for months. We thought you'd figured that out. He thinks it's hopeless, of course.'

'Why is it hopeless?' Genevieve demanded, feeling her face set in Lulu's sort of scowl. She started. 'I mean…yes. Of course. In the extreme unlikelihood of your fantastic assumption being true, he would assume it to be unrequited. As he should. But there's no other reason why it should be hopeless.'

The twins stared at her. 'He's a Wapping wharf rat, and you're a Belgravia heiress?' Alex spelled out.

'We're *Artisans*.'

'You're still an heiress and he's still a labourer. You'll be cast beyond the pale, socially.'

'Why would we care to any greater depths than you two do?'

'*And* cast from your respective families. Or do you think Uncle Theo won't threaten disownment?'

'That's not a recommended experience,' Lulu said, with unusual meekness. Alex squeezed her shoulder.

'You brazened it out, why do you assume I don't have the brass to do the same?' Genevieve snapped, before remembering. 'Sorry. Sorry, Lulu, I meant—'

'Father would have come round,' Alex agreed, 'if he'd lived. And you think your parents would, too, in this hypothetical situation in which Oliver's love for you is *not*, in fact, unrequited?'

They were both looking at her with varying degrees of expectation, Alex with a half-smile, Lulu with brows raised. It reminded her of the moment Oliver had waited on her to realise her suppressed anger at her father had contributed to the bloom of her Art, except much more smug.

'Let us say,' she began. 'Stop giggling, you pair of utter *twats*. Let's say I may have some inappropriately tender feelings for Oliver. He doesn't for me.'

'Why so?' Alex asked, eyeing her narrowly again.

So then she had to admit, to a chorus of muted whistles, that she had kissed him, and that he had pushed her away, whether in disapprobation of her innocence or her audacity, she could not know. At least she could be sure the reason had not been lack of desire.

'It's because he's being tediously respectable,' Alex explained once she'd managed to glare them into behaving less like the raucous audience at a melodrama. 'He won't be pushing you away once you're married. Pushing you against those delightful walls, more like it.'

'Hmm, something to look forward to,' Lulu added.

Both twins looked ruminative for a moment: they were, Genevieve guessed, savouring the thought of Oliver, or at least someone larger than themselves, pinning them. And then *she* had that thought, and it was definitely Oliver, and he was definitely holding her very firmly against a wall so he could very firmly have her mouth, which was about as far as her innocent imagination could take her.

It wasn't as innocent as it should have been – she'd been apprised of the existence and…enthusiasm…of the male member by the euphemistic teasing of the twins, and the scandalous yet entirely unhelpfully oblique novels they liked to sneak to her. That didn't mean she had more than an inkling of what went on in regards to said male member. She'd still need a talk from her mother on her wedding eve, and perhaps an instructional manual, preferably illustrated.

Still, her imagination was making the most of what it did have available: Oliver's big hands about her waist, or perhaps even her wrists. Oliver's mouth covering hers. Oliver's big body crushing hers. Oliver's…

Oh, where was her mind going?

'When have *either* of you had *any* sort of chance to know *anything* about being pushed against a wall?' she said crossly, to cover her sudden flush.

This earned a smirk from her male cousin. 'Your little-h-honourable Mr Oliver couldn't gaol-keep me forever.'

Genevieve mused over the revelation that Oliver had apparently been chaperoning Alex until his utter ass of a self-inflicted charge had escaped him.

Alex laughed at her. 'And it got much easier once he was distracted from his nursemaid duties.'

Distracted by…me*?* she wondered. Alex's grin gave a blindingly clear answer to that.

Lulu said, 'Men! So much more freedom, it's incredibly unfair.'

'You had your chance and you threw it away,' Alex said cheerily.

'I…didn't really, Lexi,' Lulu said, suddenly very quiet.

Subdued in his turn, her brother touched her arm. 'Sorry, baby sister. Uncalled for.'

Genevieve stepped into the breach. 'Why are you telling me to look forward to…marital congress with Oliver?' They, on cue, sniggered. 'You're both against this theoretical marriage.'

Lulu scoffed, her abrasive self again. 'We're not.'

'Definitely not,' Alex said. 'He's the reason you're striding about like a queen again, instead of trying to mince about like a *girl*.'

Lulu gave him a flick on the ear for his temerity against her sex, while Genevieve said indignantly, 'You *just* provided me a list of points against it.'

'That's *Oliver's* list, Gin.' Alex was speaking with sudden authority, masculine and self-assured. This was the Alexander Locke who was about to go out into the wider world and do very well for himself. 'That's why he thinks it's hopeless. That's why he pushed you away. He knows he could never marry you. No gentleman courts a woman when he knows her family would disapprove, and the man's a gentleman in his soul, if not his circumstance. He'd not countenance snaring you into marriage, and not so much as dream of kissing you again under lesser licence than marriage.'

'It makes no difference to him whether you love him or not,' Lulu added. 'You could go on your knees and profess undying love, and he still wouldn't touch you unless you're kneeling by him before an altar and a priest.'

'Well.' Alex shrugged and sat up from his loll at last. 'It'd make it worse, if he knew she did, don't you think, Lulu?'

'Agreed,' Lulu said. 'So perhaps you need to think very, very hard about what action to take next, Gin.'

She stood and looked up the stairs, where, to Genevieve's alarm, she saw her mother waiting, face pensively turned down towards them, sketchbook tucked under an arm.

All she said, however, was 'Come along, Alexander, Lucinda. Your uncle wishes to speak to you.'

'What about?' Lulu demanded, with disrespectful yet understandable surprise.

'I believe your imminent departure has awoken him to latent familial responsibilities,' Mother said breezily, notwithstanding that she must be quite pleased about that outcome.

The twins groaned in unison but without heat. As much as they protested, they were probably missing a fatherly bollocking as much as Aunt Nettie apparently suspected they were. Genevieve smiled at her mother, relieved both that her father was finally stepping up to the mark, and that the pensive look her mother had worn had nought to do with anything she might have overheard.

Antoinette Locke smiled back at her daughter, and her eyes were very thoughtful.

Before trailing Lulu into Father's study with suitably sullen mien for the occasion, Alex patted Genevieve on the shoulder. Softly he said, 'We'll be back for the wedding.'

She shook her head at him.

'But if you want us here to stand with you and Oliver against your parents, you better act before we leave. Think hard, Gin, but think quick.' He smiled. 'Not that we won't come back for you, you understand. But you'd have to wait, when you might not want to.' His smile became a grin. 'You really won't want to.'

20

A SINGLE PAINTING REMAINED SWADDLED, LEANING against the wall at the end of the row. Oliver was already moving to unwrap it – those sketches hadn't opened any lost memories for him – and Genevieve put her hand over his.

He stilled at her touch, hunched and tense. 'You don't want to know?'

'There is, perhaps, some poor behaviour from, perhaps, both of us, that we are going to see next.'

Oliver looked doubtful. 'That your mother openly painted?'

'That my mother's painting may impel us to remember.'

He turned his hand so he could hold hers. 'I don't see that either of us could have done so very wrong by the other, Gin.'

'I know you have a dragon inked on your chest,' she blurted. 'And a…ring. On your…'

She made a vague gesture with her free hand, towards her own chest. He flinched and let go of her hand, which was all the confirmation she needed, though she was seething at herself. She was a grown woman, a married matron. She could say the words. She could say it like the twins would. *Oliver, we've fucked and we're about to remember it.*

'I think we've had relations.' She scrunched up her face, despising her mealy mouth.

'No,' Oliver said.

'No?' she said, taken aback. Oliver could be monosyllabic but that was unusually abrupt.

'I did not. I wouldn't have.'

'But I…' *I remember you writhing under me. I remember you staring at me like you've never wanted anyone more in your life. I remember feeling like I was on* fire, *and not in the Art way.* 'I really think you did. We did, I mean.'

'Even if you somehow saw my dragon…'

Genevieve turned her indignation outwards. 'Then why do I remember sucking on your *nipple ring*, Oliver?'

That was better. More Locke-like, though not as much as she could have been. She could very well have been exceedingly more explicit about the parts of each other's bodies she was increasingly sure they'd mutually sucked on.

He blushed, mortification written all over his expressive face. He had to clear his throat before he answered. 'I can't say. But I would never treat you with such disrespect.'

'Or you managed to treat me like an *Artisan* for once instead of this endless priggish—'

'I would not have fucked you and not married you, Genevieve!' he said over her, almost strident.

Despite herself and every last intention, the vulgarity still made her blink. 'Artisans—'

'Still don't get to fuck each other willy-nilly.' Oliver folded his massive arms. 'We're still bound by what's right. And that wouldn't have been right.'

'Perhaps it felt right, at the time,' Genevieve said, quieter now, finally registering that he was truly distressed at the thought he might have engaged in such disreputable behaviour.

'I'd've hoped,' he said, and stopped.

His gaze turned plaintive; in his distress, he was losing his eloquence, but she could read the rest of his thought: *I'd've hoped you knew me well enough by now to not assume I am dishonourable because I was born poor.*

'I am aware it would have been very unlike you, Oliver,' she said. 'For all we know, *I* fucked *you* and then refused the marriage. Perhaps I am the disreputable one here.'

He smiled, then, a little. 'Miss Genevieve Locke,' he said, with a decided effort towards lightness which nonetheless fell heavy. 'Did you attempt to seduce a poor innocent working boy?'

She heard his qualification. He accepted that Miss Locke, the self-centred, headstrong girl she'd been back then, might have tried. He still didn't think he'd have partaken.

Well, then. She held out her hand to him again. 'Shall we find out how far I got, Mr Oliver?'

Their fingers tangled together, like the very night they'd met. And both their hands were warm, because they were Artisans, and they were friends, and that meant something, and she hoped to God it always would.

Still holding hands, they pulled the wrapping free together.

It was nothing but flames, Genevieve the merest suggestion at the centre, a shadow within the heart of a conflagration.

She remembered.

As it happened, Oliver visited that very afternoon, after Mother and the twins had departed on a shopping expedition for last-minute travel necessities and Father had gone to his club. It was Genevieve's turn to host a gathering of the leaders of Cecelia's Society faction. The next vote on some tiny arcana nailing down the structure and governance of the nascent agency would happen very soon. It was like hammering water to a tree, Mrs Murphy always said with a sigh, but each round of votes was another chance to influence its eventual shape when it finally froze into place.

Oliver, Cecelia, Mrs Murphy and Miss Adler took tea in the cosy family parlour. The women delicately enquired after the well-healed injury to her ankle, while Oliver maintained an entirely disinterested expression, giving her not a flicker of either complicity, embarrassment, or distaste. Then they hashed out their strategy for the larger Society meeting taking place in a few days.

When that was done, Genevieve raised her own suggestion. 'I wonder if we could not have a different salutation for women Artisans. Miss or Mrs are limiting.'

'We generally solve that by not marrying, Miss Locke,' Mrs Murphy said, rather bewilderingly.

Genevieve managed to not look at Oliver – *damn* the twins – but said, 'I don't have that option, Mrs Murphy. Could we not propose another term? The historical mistress, perhaps? It obscures marital status.'

'Very witchy in its connotations,' Cecelia mused, though not disapprovingly.

'Not to mention the modern meaning,' added Miss Adler, and all three women looked at Genevieve with varying quantities of curiosity, while Oliver conspicuously aimed his gaze elsewhere.

'I am aware of the modern meaning, thank you,' Genevieve said crossly. 'I'm not *that* innocent.'

They gave her the courtesy of not doing more than smiling, quickly smothered. Miss Adler said, more gently than Genevieve perhaps deserved, 'I suggest that if you're concerned about the loss of status to a woman Artisan when she marries, you might direct your attention to improving the plight of all women, hmm? Married or otherwise.'

Genevieve's shoulders slumped. 'Yes, of course. I see that.'

Cecelia gave her an encouraging pat. 'And, if you really must, marry yourself a sympathetic fellow Artisan in the meantime. That helps. Right, William?'

There came the business of leave-taking then, the easy friendliness of the others smoothing Genevieve's latest blunder. As they made their way out, though, she called, 'Mr Oliver, if I might have a private word before you depart.'

She thought she'd field askance glances from the other three, but they did not seem to find it unusual, or at least did well in their pretence as they said their final farewells. Oliver remained sternly neutral.

Genevieve hesitated over the door of the little parlour before finally choosing to close it.

She turned in time to catch Oliver giving the closed door a look she might have called panic on a less phlegmatic man.

'Artisans are allowed to be alone together,' she said, more sharply than she'd intended.

He nodded, appropriately chastened. She sat on the divan, and gestured for him to do the same. He picked a chair about as far away as he could get.

'I'm not going to *bite*, Oliver.' Lord, she was having trouble controlling her temper, in direct proportion to the trouble controlling her nerves.

Smiling, he moved to a closer seat. 'Miss Locke.'

She fidgeted, searching for words. But there was really only one way to say it. 'Is it your intention to simply ignore what happened?'

'Yes,' Oliver said, dismayingly quickly. Her heart fell within her chest, a stone cast down, until he added, 'Be assured there are no circumstances under which I would besmirch a lady's reputation.' She raised her eyebrows at him, forcing him to go on. 'You don't deserve to be punished for a moment of…ill-advised…'

He trailed off, apparently unsure how to finish his sentence without insulting her. Without insulting her *further*.

'It was *not* ill-advised,' she informed him crisply. 'It was not impulsive. It was not imprudent, or reckless, or anything else of which you might like to accuse me.'

'Not accusing you.'

'Excusing me,' she said. 'Like I have not a thought in my head, nor the capacity to make my own decisions. I kissed you, *on purpose*, and I don't want to ignore it, Oliver. So how do we proceed?'

Oliver looked down at his lap, and Genevieve made herself bite her tongue and let him think. He was a thoughtful man, of few words, and his next words were going to be the most important words she'd ever heard.

'We do not proceed,' he said at last. She gazed at him, unable to hide her hurt. 'No, Miss Locke. I cannot marry a woman of your standing, I will not make a woman of your standing into a mistress, and—' He frowned, heavily, almost scowling as he pushed out the rest. 'And frankly, I will not make of myself an agent of your vengeance against your father.'

She leapt to her feet. 'Is that what you think this is?' she demanded, heedless of her raised voice.

'I need *you* to think about what this is.'

'I know what this is,' she shot back. '*You* are acting as if it's an inconvenience for you, when I am the one making the sacrifice.'

She regretted it the moment the words were out of her mouth. Oliver stared at her unsmilingly. 'Miss Locke, would my family come to our wedding?'

'If you're implying my father is so snobbish as to refuse to allow them—'

'They won't,' he said, 'because they'll be so intimidated by the very thought of ever moving in these circles—'

'Then we will marry at *your* church. The banns are read in both parishes, it's pure tradition that compels us to marry in mine.'

'And the wedding breakfast in my stepmother's parlour amid the coal smut and discarded bottles?'

'If we must,' she said.

'Starting the sacrifice right from the very beginning, are we?'

She looked down, shamed. 'I shouldn't have called it a sacrifice.'

'I don't see why not,' he said. 'It's nothing but the truth. You recognise that.'

'I do not,' she said, unable to wash the sulk from her voice. 'We'll conduct the wedding breakfast however it suits us to conduct it.'

'That appears to be our wedding day planned,' Oliver said. 'And the marriage?'

'We shall conduct that however it suits us, too!'

'My family will not know how to speak to me.' He sounded dreadfully tired. 'We will be estranged.'

'Why do you care?' she snapped. 'They treat you terribly.'

He folded his arms. 'They're my family.'

'Then they will come round to the notion, as I trust mine will, too.'

'Miss Locke—' He stopped. 'Genevieve.'

Again, he stopped, rubbing at his forehead, but the use of her given name had restored a modicum of optimism. Though he occasionally slipped into the nickname with which he constantly heard the twins address her, it was the first time he'd deliberately spoken her given name, a rapid step forward in intimacy that suited the topic.

Eventually he said, 'We are too removed from each other in status.'

'We are both Artisans, equal in status,' Genevieve insisted. 'The sole relevant question is whether or not you wish to marry me.'

'The highborn lady happily marries her salt-of-the-earth gardener in stories only,' he said. 'Her family and his do not go on to coo over the grandchildren together.'

That was the most blatant deflection she had ever encountered. 'Answer the question. If it's no, it's no, but say so, Oliver.'

He opened his mouth and she braced herself for the end of her hopes. Then he closed it again. He stared at her like a starving man stared at a feast. No. Like Dickens's Oliver and his fellow orphans, *staring at the copper, with such eager eyes, as if they could have devoured the very bricks of which it was composed.*

She moved closer to him, a step or two, so she could hold out her hand, her bare fingers open to his. 'We're Artisans, Oliver,' she said again. 'We don't have to abide by any rules but our own.'

He looked at her hand, and the fingers folded in his lap gave a responsive twitch.

The parlour door opened. Mother said, 'Genevieve, I shall *not* return home to find my daughter unchaperoned behind a closed door. Mr Oliver, I *certainly* expected better of you.'

Oliver clenched his hand back to himself on the instant.

Perhaps if it had been her father, Genevieve might have taken the sharp reprimand with some semblance of good grace. But it was her mother, who had until now been on her side when she had claimed Artisan freedoms, keeping that metaphorical window open onto the fresh air, also metaphorical in London, that blew the stultification from her heiress role.

'Artisans. Are. *Allowed*,' she snarled, and her flames erupted out of her, and obliterated all else.

She came to herself a few moments later, collapsed onto folded knees on the rug, Oliver clasping her from behind, his wards in full effect. She twisted her fists into her puddled skirts. Her last memory was of her mother's shocked cry and a slam of the offending door.

'Is anyone hurt?' she gasped.

'No. You controlled it yourself,' he said gently. 'My wards were a precaution. You kept yourself under control, Gin, it's all right, you're all right, love.'

This last was because she had burst into tears as suddenly as she had burst into flame. He tightened his hold, shifting so that he was cradling her properly. He was pressed up against her back in the most intimate of positions, and he must have noticed it as much as she did, but he made no move away, merely held her as she cried.

After a little while, he ventured, a smile in his voice, 'You do not like being thwarted.'

'I am a Locke,' Genevieve pointed out, sniffling. 'I do have the Locke temper.'

Of course, it was perfectly well for the Lockes to indulge their tempers; Cecelia and Miss Adler, and their families, no doubt had their tempers too, and could not ever risk showing it, not to their supposed betters, their employers, their husbands, not even their persecutors.

No wonder Oliver wanted nothing to do with the selfish and self-entitled heiress who expected a marriage proposal to follow on from an indeed ill-advised kiss, and who recognised only the sacrifice on her side, and none on his.

Thus, though her heart pained her, she managed to say, 'Let me go, Mr Oliver, before you find yourself forced to marry me, whether you desire it so or no.'

'We are unlikely to be disturbed. I dare say the floor, if not the house, has been evacuated,' he murmured, but he did disentangle himself, and then helped her up.

Looking up at his sombre face, she tried to accept his reasons for refusal: that she was immature and spoilt was foremost, but the mismatch of their positions loomed insurmountably large. She was as condescending about her willingness to descend as she was presumptuous about his readiness to ascend. His doubt about her motives was the single point she could justifiably refute, and she could barely summon the heart for it.

But she would not allow herself to remain daunted. As much as the flowery speeches of the most popular novels tried to flood into her head, she decided he would respond best, and perhaps only, to a simple and honest declaration.

'I used to judge all men by Alex,' she began, 'and now I judge them all by you, and even Alex comes up lacking. This has nothing to do with my father and my feelings towards him. It is solely about you and my feelings towards you. Oliver, I love you. You are the best man I know. I wish for nothing more than to spend my life with you in a marriage of equals.'

Oliver was mute. She had laid out her heart to him, and he had nothing to say.

Quelling the sick roil of humiliation, Genevieve made herself face it, and him. 'But marriage to me is not what *you* wish.'

He shook his head.

21

GENEVIEVE'S EYES BLINKED OPEN. Oliver was staring back at her. She felt an echo of her younger self's selfish and self-righteous indignation, the shield against the humiliation he'd inflicted on her with his damnable good sense. She let go of him.

Some hint of burgeoning temper must have communicated itself in her suddenly narrowed eyes, for he held up his palms placatingly. 'Fifteen years ago, Gin.'

She had to make herself not stare at his hands, that she now knew were as calloused and strong and sure as they looked. She swallowed and answered calmly. 'I know, Oliver. I plainly managed to set it aside at some point. I trust I was not too unpleasant towards you before I did.'

She knew the sequence of events from this moment of devastating rejection: the twins had indeed come back from their continental jaunt to support her in her chosen mésalliance – to Mr Reuben McAvey, after their initial connection had properly kindled as the various factions melded and worked together to create the Agency.

They'd all four sat in that spot on the stairs where conversations in the study could be overheard, one floor up from where the twins had sprawled like puppies and erroneously informed her that Oliver loved her. This time she'd had Reuben beside her, holding her hand.

A frown had gradually grown onto Oliver's broad forehead, his hand over his coat pocket, running fingers over some object within, its hard rectangular shape deforming the fabric. After a moment, he checked the shipping crate, tipping it on its side, and then began to fossick about the covered furniture stacked by the wall, lifting drop sheets to check underneath.

'What…' She had to force herself back to the present. 'What are you doing?'

He said, 'Looking for more memories, Gin. That can't be— You won't persuade me I said no to you and then let that be the end of it.'

'But it was,' she said. 'I married Reuben.'

He craned awkwardly to peer behind shrouded chairs. 'There must be more. I'd like to hold on to some shred of belief that I'm not an *utter* fool.'

She gave a shaky laugh. 'You are far too honourable to take advantage of a girlish infatuation for the sake of a mere heiress's fortune, Oliver. And too sensible.'

'I was a coward,' he said bluntly.

She raised her eyebrows at this assessment. 'You were rightfully concerned about estrangement from your family. I shouldn't have expected anything else.'

He shook his head. 'They were the excuse I hid behind. My brothers already mocked me for taking up Artisan status; an Artisan wife wouldn't have surprised them.'

'A high-society one would have,' Genevieve said. 'You were simply far more practical than I, and…I do understand.'

She didn't much like what she saw of herself back then, immature and self-entitled and thoughtless; no matter what the older Oliver now thought, knowing and esteeming her own older self, the younger Oliver must have been appalled to be the victim of her juvenile attention. At least Lulu hadn't fallen too, or he would have had to fend off the trifecta of Locke puppy-passions.

'I can see why I erased the whole embarrassing enterprise so effectively from my memory,' she added.

Struck, she wondered if she'd done more than metaphorically erase it. Perhaps she'd asked Cecelia to do it for her. It would explain how completely she, and Oliver too, had forgotten it, except for those occasional moments of frisson. Reuben must have noticed some of those minor ripples, provoking his jealousy, that she had thought so strange and gratuitous. As he had constantly remonstrated, he was right far more often than she was.

Oliver levered himself upright from his precarious lean. 'Where are the rest of your mother's paintings?'

'I sold them,' she said absently. 'And, Oliver, even if we found more of these personal ones, all they will show is my entirely reprehensible behaviour towards you for a time, I'm sure. I trust I did not take much longer than Alex to recover myself.'

It was a blessing that the months between Oliver's rejection and her first clear memory, sitting on the stairs with Reuben and the twins while her mother rode into battle on her behalf, were still hazy. Beyond embarrassed, she would have been icy to poor Oliver, probably for months, and she was grateful their friendship had survived it.

Unless Cecelia really had taken those memories away, and Genevieve had made a terrible mistake seeking them out.

'We're still friends,' she said hastily.

He shook his head.

'Oliver!' She clambered to her feet, using the wall as a support, since Oliver wouldn't come closer to help. 'I know it was infantile and disgraceful on my part, but you said it yourself, it was fifteen years ago. You will allow me to apologise and we will remain friends.'

He shook his head again. 'Gin, we…' He looked like he was fighting his words, and she had to resist a foolish urge to run from the room so she would not have to hear them. But when he got it out, it was utterly unexpected. 'How did you know about the dragon tattooed on my chest?'

She was shocked, and drew herself up, as prim as any maiden aunt despite the incongruity of her pregnant swell. 'I *didn't* know that. You can't tell me things like that, Mr Oliver, it is entirely unacceptable.'

He stared at her. He heaved a breath like he was about to lift something very heavy, and then he said, 'Gin, five minutes ago you thought we'd fucked.'

Her mouth dropped open. 'I thought no such thing. *We* did no such thing!'

Oliver turned away in a swiftly-muted fit of frustration. He went along the line of paintings, touching each one, until he came to one of the first, the memento that depicted her father in the full flight of dandification, right down to straddling the highly fashionable early velocipede.

He held it out to her. 'Touch it again.'

It was the way he'd ordered Whitely to try to explain, so blunt it was rude, some underlying emotion shredding his extensive vocabulary into flat syllables.

She tried to wave it away. 'It merely makes me feel sad.'

'Why?'

'I don't know.' When he kept proffering it, she reluctantly let her eye fall on it, taking in the fine figure of a young Theodore Locke in his scarlet redingote, lovingly painted by his wife twenty years later as a reconciliation gift. 'I miss my parents.'

'When did they die?'

'They—' She licked her lips. 'I don't know.'

'It might tell you.' He pushed it into her hands and her fingers reflexively closed over it before she could protest that she was not sure she wanted to know.

Again, she felt the confusing roil of layered emotions, love and regret and relief, and quiet misery. The fog tried to smother it, and something within her cried out in fury and fought back.

She remembered.

GENEVIEVE WITHDREW INTO herself. She tried not to be melodramatic, but thoughts of figurative lights snuffed out did cross her mind. She lacked the gumption to tell the twins before they departed the next morning, and was somewhat in disgrace with her household regardless. She had to restrain herself from writing a letter to chase their wake, excoriating them for their mistaken encouragement. It would only catch them long after her annoyance had dissipated into missing them like third and fourth arms.

She filled her days with practising her Art, plainly still vitally necessary, and reading all she could find about Artisans and their history and future prospects, knowledge she did her best to meekly contribute to the Society meetings and debates with McAvey's faction without stepping onto the toes of other people's areas of expertise and experience.

She attended the balls and gatherings and respectable public dances in West End assembly rooms that her father expected her to attend, and drifted through them without later being able to account for her evening or call to mind the men she'd danced with. She barely noticed the end of her second Season, except that she now had fewer engagements, the more informal round of theatre shows, suppers, and small parties with family friends who, like the Lockes, chose not to decamp to pastoral or continental climes.

She nursed her broken heart, telling herself fiercely it had been a small attachment not much stronger than Alex's, so that she could manage to be scrupulously polite to Oliver. He was stiffly neutral in return. The awkwardness began to fade, and she did not demur to be partnered with him again on forays with Cecelia's little group.

They confronted a fraudulent medium, a mindreading Artisan in desperate straits, garnering an enormous success for their faction. Not only did they dissuade the Artisan from her illicit exploitation of grieving people, but the offer of immediate community support and chance of eventual legitimate employment via the Agency brought her into their fold.

Their third prototype mission involved tackling an earthworker Artisan with a flair for extortion, threatening to tumble the homes of the wealthy if he wasn't paid out. It wasn't quite an unalloyed success, since they did not engineer his arrest, but they did run him out of London, gaining gushingly positive press in the process.

Her father suggested a potential match, the son of an marquess. Apparently, she'd danced with him twice at the Season's final private ball. It seemed to Genevieve that if she could not marry for love, she could at least show respect for her father's wishes and make the glitteringly high match he so desired for her. All she would ask of a husband was that he not interfere with her pursuit of her Art, so long as she held up her side of the marital bargain and presented a dowry, children, and a calm and well-run household. She thus greeted the news with a nod of acknowledgement, and did not argue.

Her mother did. Genevieve heard them in the study late at night as she passed through the eavesdropping point on the stairs. She didn't linger to listen in; their voices were quiet but sharp, with a disturbing note of bitterness that only grew stronger as the weeks went past. Her mother began to look pinched, her father tired and grey. His late evenings at the club, strengthening connections to aid his marital plot, turned into entire nights there, availing himself of the lodgings rather than facing his hectoring wife.

Antoinette changed tack.

On St Thomas's Day, lacking mere days till Christmas, Genevieve joined her parents at the breakfast table to discover her father scrutinising a new Antoinette Locke portrait over his eggs while the artist herself stood by his chair to await his reaction, ostensibly flicking through the post, always copious at this time of year.

'Mr Cole sent us one of his innovative little Christmas greeting cards,' she was saying as Genevieve came in. 'I suppose that partially atones for choosing young Horsley over me to illustrate it.'

Glancing embarrassedly at his daughter, Father laid the canvas facedown with suspicious haste, which was enough to pique a spark of interest for the first time in weeks.

'I think it's for the drawing room mantle,' Mother informed him, setting her collection of letters down. She smiled at Genevieve, mischief written across every line of her face.

'Nettie!'

'Theo!' she teased. 'And why not? Most people would be proud to display one of my portraits.'

'But I look ridiculous.'

In answer, her mother flipped it back over so Genevieve could see it. There her father was, a youth of perhaps five-and-twenty, sporting a tightly-fitted bright scarlet redingote, long legs clad in custard-yellow silk, bootheels high, moustache luxurious, the dandy atop his dandy-horse with the Monument in the background. Genevieve helplessly lit up in a smile, again her first for some time.

'Wasn't he a fine figure back then, Ginnie?' Mother tickled his ear.

'An illusion achieved with corsetry,' he scoffed, but his face flushed with pleasure at his wife's flirtation.

Mother shot another mischievous look at Genevieve before leaning close to whisper, 'I did so very much enjoy unlacing you out of your corsets. Still do.'

Father started to cough, very red. Genevieve studiously made a production of pouring herself a cup of tea and becoming extremely absorbed by the early edition.

Eventually he muttered, 'I'm more likely to be in a corset for a bad back than a trim waist these days.'

His smiling wife tilted his chin up for a kiss. 'It still has laces, darling.'

When Genevieve ventured a peek, they'd finished kissing, but Mother was petitely perched on her husband's welcoming lap, head resting against his shoulder. Relief swept over Genevieve. Those bitter recriminations in the study were over, surely. The pretty, silly portrait had done its conciliatory work.

It had done more than that. With his wife's head tucked against him, Father was gazing between her and the portrait with a look of fond reminiscence, apparently lost in memories of the days when he had wooed and wed his artist wife despite the opposition of parents far more staid than either of the Locke brothers had turned out to be.

Then he slowly raised his eyes to look at his daughter. 'The match with Lord Hayfield's son.'

She tried hard not to change expression, to let the lightness she felt diminish. 'Yes, Father?'

'It's off. I didn't like the stories about him, at the clubs. Same as those two making offers last year. Not proper husband material.'

Genevieve blinked. She hadn't known Father had refused matches on any grounds other than that the titles weren't high enough for him. She'd never even suspected he would turn any down because the men weren't good enough for *her*.

'Thank you,' she said. 'I appreciate your consideration of my future happiness.'

He frowned at her. Her mother openly snorted.

'I wasn't being sarcastic!' Genevieve protested. 'I am trying to be a filial daughter, you two.'

'By reciting nonsense from a conduct book?' Antoinette Locke tapped her husband firmly, but spoke gently. 'Do you see, Theo, what we've done to our precious only child?'

'What I've done,' he said. He wore an odd expression, both shame and resignation. 'Ginnie, I'm sorry. All these balls and endless dull gatherings… It's not for you, it's not for any of us. Consider yourself relieved of any duty to attend the more tedious of our engagements.'

'Oh!' said Genevieve, clutching her stomach. His announcement had been so unexpected, so sudden, so welcome, that it had set warmth roiling dangerously through her. 'Oh, thank you, Daddy.'

Mother sat up and kissed his cheek.

Mingled with Genevieve's surprise and relief was minor generalised annoyance that took a moment to pin to a source. She could see how Mother had manipulated Father. Even in this, the best of marriages, the wife had to work around her husband, exercising so-called soft influence in the sickening arena of *queen in his heart, yet servant in his home.*

She didn't blame her mother, nor her father. She merely strongly resented the entire marital edifice that made manipulation and soft gloves necessary.

'I do still expect a decent match, among our most respectable contacts,' Father hastened to clarify. 'But it is at your leisure, at your discretion, and entirely your choice. As long as it's decent.'

'There remain differing definitions of decent, of course,' her mother murmured.

This was possibly an inopportune moment for the bell to ring. It had to be Artisan business at this unfashionable hour, and indeed, Miss Delacorte and Mr Oliver were announced.

'Show them in,' Mother said, standing and shaking out her skirts very respectably. 'Any idea what this is about, Ginnie?'

Genevieve turned the paper so they could see the headline of the article that had riveted her attention. 'I imagine you are about to be very politely requested to allow your precious only child to go away overnight to chase down a rogue earthquake Artisan.'

Indeed, that was exactly what it was. The earthworker Artisan had not taken the expected escape route of a border crossing to Scotland or the ferry to Calais, but instead fled via London and South Western, disembarking in Winchester. He'd be making for the coast, Oliver said with some authority, to connect with contacts among the smugglers, traditional income stymied by the sudden governmental embrace of free trade, to take him across the channel. He must have run out of funds, though, because he'd made the paper for plying his extortion trade again, this time threatening Winchester's wealthiest homes.

It took all of Cecelia's forthright charm, and all of Oliver's stoic respectability, to persuade Genevieve's father to allow her to go, but allow it he did.

'For,' Antoinette pointed out, 'it's the same as going to Bath with cousins, is it not?'

'Depends which cousins you're thinking of,' Theodore said, but he gave the nod, and Genevieve rushed upstairs to hurry the packing along.

It was a direct line from Vauxhall to Winchester, and from there the foursome picked up the rogue Artisan's trail down to Selsey via Chichester. They arrived at neighbouring Sidlesham at late afternoon, the sun already low, the air chilling, and the tide at flood across the causeway, obliging them to ferry across for a half-penny apiece.

They made a simple plan as they walked towards the village centre, which comprised Oliver and Genevieve scouting about while Cecelia and Mr Fletcher innocuously chatted to the locals.

'He most likely came here because his people are here,' Oliver cautioned as they made their way along the potted main street. 'They won't give him up easily.'

Mr Fletcher drew off his thick gloves with relish. 'I shall compel them to tell us where he is cowering.'

Cecelia tutted. 'Fletcher, it's the same as at the courts. You can't use your Art against civilians without explicit consent or authorisation to override the lack of it, no matter how good the cause. It's the very definition of the use of illicit Art.'

'There's no such thing as illicit Art. Not until the Agency is actually empowered.'

She led him off down the cobbled street, ardently saying, 'But if we use illicit Art to combat illicit Art, it rather proves Mr McAvey's point about disregarding illicit Art and other people's right to not be subjected to it!'

'So we should waste time finding a magistrate?' Mr Fletcher demanded.

Still amiably bickering, the pair ambled down towards where a glimmer of lamplight fell through the six large windows of the public house on the next corner, bright in the dull grey of the rapidly-encroaching gloaming.

Alone with the man who had spurned her, Genevieve looked around with studied interest. Any village was inevitably going to be small and sleepy to someone from the biggest city in the world, but Selsey was somewhat larger than she'd expected, mostly clustered by the pier, fishing boats bobbing offshore. Her and Oliver's reconnoitre would be complicated by a multitude of side streets and hiding places.

Like last December, this year's start to winter was remarkably mild; Genevieve, her Art having bloomed in the intervening period, found herself completely comfortable in only the lightest of summer shawls. Nonetheless, the shadows were lengthening and the salt-tanged breeze was strengthening. The residents were retreating indoors, not without over-the-shoulder glances, somewhere between curious and suspicious, at the strangers.

The Fisherman's Joy Inn would already be nicely crowded, then, a good hunting ground for the other two. She and Oliver should get along with their half of the task.

Genevieve fortified herself with a quick breath, and then turned to Oliver. 'Where should we begin? Are there any useful Gothic ruins where nefarious smugglers secrete their goods?'

Oliver smiled tersely, and consulted his guide book. A hasty purchase at Vauxhall, it was one of the Ramble's Travels collection, really meant for children, but the best they could do at a pinch. He pointed in the opposite direction to that taken by the others.

'The rectory's a bit of a walk. Rumour suggests it hides an entrance to the smugglers' tunnel network. There's a mound beyond it, maybe ancient fortifications, even a standing stone. And there'll be conveniently secluded coves along the coast near there, too.'

It did sound promising, isolated and with plenty of cover for the clandestine seawards escape their quarry needed, plus the standing stone for an Artistry boost. But Oliver made no move that way. She realised he was waiting for her to make the decision, as he would normally wait for Cecelia, a habitual, and very stubborn, resistance to societal norms.

'So we start there and work our way back to the inn to see if the others garnered any titbits?'

She hadn't quite meant to make it a question. It was a way of batting back the same esteem he was trying to show her, this time across class lines instead of those drawn up by their respective sexes.

He nodded in genial concurrence and they made their way along the street. The last of the brick-and-thatch cottages soon petered out into fields, the road into well-worn clay. They walked in silence, Oliver offering the occasional arm across particularly muddy terrain. Otherwise, Genevieve walked on the other side of the wheel ruts from her quiet companion. The walking itself was not onerous, but tedious, and rather hard on city footwear, even her comfortable Chelsea boots. She had not thought about having to take a rural stroll during the pursuit.

The countryside was quiet in the dusk, mournful cries from a few night birds sounding from nearby coppices and one last cart creaking past, the farmer giving them a judicious nod. Oliver glanced at Genevieve for permission, then jogged along to flag him down. The offer of a penny saw Genevieve invited to perch up by him, Oliver relegated to swinging his long legs at the tailgate.

The driver was about as garrulous as Oliver. By the time he let them down at the crossroads and trundled off, Genevieve not only had no hints as to the possible launch point of their France-bound Artisan, but not even a recommendation of the best Selsey overnight accommodations.

She looked up the lane to the rectory. It was already very dark, overcast by old, tall oaks, while the surrounding fields were still under the last soft glimmer of twilight. Salt was a distant underlay now; the air here smelt earthy.

Oliver looked back along the way they'd come, to a derelict cottage, built in the style of some three hundred years earlier. Its walls were crumbling, but its chimney-stack still stood, though the two chimney-pots atop it had been shattered, perhaps by weather, perhaps by bored boys throwing stones.

'I was teasing about the Gothic ruins,' Genevieve said.

The polite man blessed her with a smile her weak sally absolutely did not deserve. 'I thought I saw a light as the cart took us past.'

They had to squeeze through an overgrown hedgerow and clamber over chunks of stone and flint, Genevieve additionally hampered by holding up a small flame in the palm of one hand, perforce taking Oliver's arm with the other as she lit their awkward path.

She one-handedly plucked leaves from her hair and shook out her skirts as she examined the shadowy ruin, holding her small light high before deciding to experiment and lowering her hand to let it float. It did.

The roof beams had collapsed and rotted away or been taken for firewood long ago, and the front walls were entirely rubble, but the side and back walls were partially intact. Underfoot, soil and weeds had covered whatever flooring might have survived.

The chimney-stack stood proud, its base broad and thick enough to hold two wide fireplaces built back-to-back. The bricks between the fireplaces were gone, making the space under the chimney cavernous.

That was, Genevieve mused, a fairly likely location for a highly unlikely smugglers' tunnel. She brightened the flame at her shoulder, bending to peer in just as Oliver said, 'Wait,' and the scent in the air registered.

It was the familiar whiff, acrid and smoky, of a doused lamp.

She heard a clink and a curse, and then a figure moved half-crouched from the invaded darkness of the great dual fireplace, running for the back of the cottage where gaps in the ruined walls would give him quick egress to the fields and coppice beyond.

Genevieve had never stopped working on her control of her highly dangerous Art. And here, surrounded by old stone and green weeds and damp loamy fields, she felt much safer deploying it than in the crowded, flammable city.

She made a sweep of her arms, and a thin, high, precise line of fire sprang up, circling outwards in a heartbeat to enclose the cottage, trapping the earthworker Artisan within.

He retaliated. Of course he did: she hadn't given Oliver time to deploy his smothering Art.

And of course he aimed for the Artisan who was brazenly thwarting his escape.

His fear made his Art strong but uncontrolled, as emotion tended to do, though Genevieve was not convinced he'd have reacted differently if he had been in control, merely less…violently. The ground tore open underneath her, old flags boiling up, the earth above and below the ancient stone floor dancing and sundering in response to the bolt of earthworking Art. The juddering spread, and the last of the walls tumbled. Cracks shot up the towering chimney-stack, showering grit.

Genevieve staggered as earth and stone roiled beneath her, lost her flames, and fell. Oliver made a grab for her, but was tumbled away by the next volley of shakes. With some difficulty – her skirts were caught, her legs trapped by chunks of debris – she twisted until she could look about. The rogue Artisan had already fled into the evening. She couldn't see Oliver. Her call of his name was drowned by an immense and ominous *snap*.

The chimney-stack toppled towards her.

Genevieve, still pinned, lashed out instinctively with an enormous gout of Art, which naturally had the unhelpful effect of transforming a collapsing tower of bricks into a collapsing conflagration of bricks.

She cried out and cast her arms uselessly over her face. Then Oliver roared, 'Gin!' and she discovered him crouched over her, shielding her with his body as he violently jerked both hands upwards.

The entire edifice flew into the sky as if flung by a catapult, arcing almost gracefully across the earliest glimmer of stars like a reverse meteorite. The flames flared bright, streaming in the wind of the rapid transit, before abruptly extinguishing when Genevieve encountered, for the first time, the limits of her Artistry.

She was shaking as Oliver pulled her loose and dragged her into his arms. He was shaking too, breath coming in harsh pants. He ran big hands over her shoulders and down her sides to her hips, feeling, she understood after a scandalised moment, for the sticky dampness that would bespeak blood. It was too dark for anything but the gleam of their bare faces and hands to be visible in the starlight.

'I'm unharmed,' she said stupidly. 'I'm— Are you?' Their hands tangled as she tried to copy his movements, palms spanning ribs that heaved as he fought to calm his breathing.

'Yes,' he said, 'yes.' He stroked her hair, and pressed his face there. '*Gin.*'

She hadn't stopped shaking, though it had subsided from shudders to a tiny continuous tremor now. She was keeping her palms pressed to Oliver's ribs, under his coat, to anchor herself. Otherwise she might faint. The backwash of extreme fright was exhausting, and her Art was almost entirely drained. She needed to eat, urgently, and rest. Oliver would be in the same straits.

Her thoughts kept scattering. She kept seeing the dark tumble of the stack. She realised Oliver was littering kisses in the wake of the comforting brush of his fingers over her hair, murmuring grateful little sounds. She reached up and caught his hands.

'Pardon,' he choked.

Genevieve took his face in her hands and turned it firmly to hers. This close, she could make out his features, stark with fear, with relief, with more. His eyes were dark, brimming.

'Oliver,' she said, and he kissed her.

It was frenetic, all the spiking emotion of her brush with death surging through her as she responded, her mouth opening to his, tasting his tongue. She grappled at him, pulling him in harder, fingers scrabbling for a hold on the short bristles of hair at his nape, fighting to get her body closer to his. He subsided to the ground, hand cupping the back of her head with tremulous care, mouth never leaving hers. She was fully atop his breadth, heat roiling through her, nothing like her Art, but something narrower, deeper, right at her core. She could feel that same hardness that had startled her last time, and this time she pressed into it, rocked her hips. The heat spiked; she did it again.

'Gin,' he gasped.

'Let me,' she demanded, not even knowing what she was asking for.

'Anything,' Oliver said, though the problem with that blanket permission was that it gave her no further ideas whatsoever.

His big arms wrapped tight about her, holding her locked to him, and they kissed and kissed, Genevieve rocking against him, whimpering into his mouth as that unfamiliar heat slowly coalesced. Her body was afire but her mind was dreamy, lost in sensation, like when she'd been playing too long in the snow and was overwhelmed by the warmth of a hot bath on chilled skin.

Too soon, Oliver turned his face from her, in an alert attitude of listening. 'Horses.'

Not only that: voices, calling their names. Between them, they had practically shot up pyrotechnics of the sort recently begun to be used to signal distress at sea. It had been, damn it all, effective enough to bring the team's other pair searching for them, with, from the sound of it, a few villagers inclined to be helpful.

Oliver scrambled up and searched around the broken-tooth stub of the fireplaces, coming back with a cheap horn-pane lantern, which the earthworker Artisan must have dropped in his flight. He lit it with a match and waved it slowly over his head until the calls became shouts of acknowledgement.

He set the lantern atop a high pile of rubble and retrieved a handkerchief from some inner pocket. 'You should wipe your face.'

Between the earthquake and rolling about on the ground with Oliver, she must be a mess. It still seemed unnecessarily pedantic, to the Mr Fletcher extent, to point it out.

'It won't make a dent,' she said. 'I'm entirely covered in dust.'

'Not…' He cleared his throat. 'Not your mouth.'

'Oh,' she said, and took the handkerchief. It came away streaked with grey after she'd run it over her cheeks and forehead. He took it back, folded it, and wiped his own face.

Since Genevieve was shivering and weak-kneed, she didn't feel capable of the clamber over the rubble to reach the road and walk towards their rescuers. She hoped they'd thought to bring food.

It left her sitting awkwardly in the low light with the man with whom she'd just engaged in a scandal, but who had no wish to marry her.

Eventually, she ventured, 'I didn't know your 'kinesis Art was so powerful.'

'Terror,' Oliver said. 'Good fuel.'

'Yes.' Taking a leaf from his succinct pamphlet, she added the informative, 'Shaky. Light-headed.'

'The same.'

'Yes,' she said, seizing the offering with both hands.

He looked stern in the low cast of light. 'That's no excuse,' he said. 'We'll need to discuss this, once we're rested.'

'It's not necessary to reprise the same conversation regarding our lack of prospects, Oliver.'

'It's a different conversation, Genevieve.'

'Why, because we kissed again?' The horses were close. Genevieve used the excuse to rise, lifting the lamp. 'Over here! Please say you have food.'

'Yes!' Cecelia called back. 'Thank goodness you're all right, Gin! We saw a great flaming ball and figured we better head out this way.'

'Because we—' Oliver stopped short. She didn't need to see his face clearly to know he'd be blushing.

Well. He could hardly say, *because you rubbed yourself on me like an alley-cat*, could he?

He might have started it – she supposed he had leaned in for the kiss the barest moment before she had – but he had not been the one who had taken it far beyond any shade of pale. He should not be forced into marriage because he'd had the misfortune to work with a Locke with even less self-control than Alex.

'There's nothing further to discuss,' Genevieve said, folding her arms.

The cluster of horses had stopped on the road, and two shadows were coming through the hedgerow with the accompaniment of a call-and-response routine of mild curses and mild admonishments.

'We will talk about this,' Oliver said stubbornly, under the surfeit of exclamations as Cecelia and Mr Fletcher burst into the ruin, 'once we're rested.'

Genevieve indulged herself by briefly allowing the spirit of the stroppier Locke twin to inhabit her body: *no, little-h honourable Mr Oliver, we fucking well will not.*

22

THE UNDERRATED BENEFIT OF WOMANHOOD WAS that all Genevieve needed to do, to avoid a discussion, was dive into being chaperoned at all times, which is what she must have done after that shocking, wonderful moment in a ruined cottage on the Sussex coast, so that Oliver could not honour-bind himself into an unwanted marriage.

Seven weeks later, in the middle of February, she'd married Reuben. She truly thought he'd have featured more in some of these memories. A treacherous part of her murmured about a broken heart, precipitous actions. The fog rolled over her mind, insisting she loved Reuben, fading the memories of Oliver, his mouth, his hands, his strength, her palms pressed against his ribs.

It pushed the memories into the recesses of her mind where they couldn't hurt her. She finally brought herself to look at him.

'Really, Oliver!' she said, voice as bright as gaslights at the theatre. 'You're meant to debouche maidens in alpine castles or Italian convents, not Elizabethan cottages at the seaside!'

He'd been running a thumb over his mouth, gaze abstracted – trying to capture the feeling of kissing her, she realised, and her stomach flipped over in mingled alarm and thrill.

Or it was her baby. *Reuben's* baby, turning in horror at the mother it was cursed with.

In the face of her bright artificiality, however, Oliver covered his face with one hand. The other hand ran over his coat pocket, stroking the rectangular shape deforming the cloth there.

'I'm sorry,' Genevieve said, startled. She came to him, touched his arm. 'I'm sorry, my dear, I wasn't trying to cast you as a penny-blood villain. It was…an aberration, that's all.'

The fog thickened. Dully, she added, 'Best forgotten.'

Oliver dropped his hand and stared at her. He yanked the rectangular item from his pocket and held it out to her. 'Do you remember this?'

It was *A Christmas Carol*. She had seen Oliver take this book from the study. She'd been unreasonably indignant to see him stash it away in his own pocket instead of giving it to her, and then she'd immediately forgotten it.

'My parents gave me this,' she said slowly. 'Christmas of '43.'

'No,' he said. Then, 'Yes.' Then, 'The inscription.'

He held it out again, and she took it. She opened to the flyleaf. There was the simple inscription from her parents. She touched the faded ink, a burning behind her eyes, tracing the loops of her own name in Antoinette Locke's familiar handwriting.

It was the wrong inscription, though, in the wrong hand. Almost absently, she checked the next few pages. She knew there was no other inscription. She knew there should be. The sensation was so strong, it was like another ghost, joining Marley and the three spirits of the story.

Finally, she handed the book back to Oliver. 'My parents gave it to me.'

'But—' For a long moment, he looked full into her face, meeting her gaze with a boldness that felt challenging. 'Please, Gin.'

'What is it?'

'Do you remember?' he asked again. 'Please.'

As she started to say that she *didn't remember, she couldn't remember*, he took her hand. The sensation of his lips over her pulse point bolted through her, but he didn't repeat that strange, intimate, shocking gesture. He closed her fingers over the book again.

'Please,' he said again, desperately. 'Remember. At Adler's?'

Speechless with frustration and rising annoyance, she shook her head, trying to turn away. He tightened his grip. The book was locked between them. She thought of the Ghost of Christmas Past, with its jet of light, *burning high and bright*, as it showed Scrooge his terrible past. Like her own flame, burning away the endless, thickening fog. She turned her head aside, sick with the rise of distress, of panic, of…

Oliver cupped her face with his other hand, thumb brushing her cheek. '*Remember.*'

She closed her eyes as he leaned over her immensely swollen belly and brushed his mouth over hers. *Impossible*, her mind shrieked.

But below that rang a refrain like a fog bell sounding out its warning to guide ships to port.

Yes. This. Him.

The memory stole up on her. It wasn't like the memories opened to her by her mother's possibly-Art-laced paintings. Those had riveted her into a trance state and played out like magic lantern shows. This was more natural, like the sudden and vivid recall of childhood Christmases because the bright citrus spray of peeling a ripe orange triggered a long-held association.

Fingers pressed to her mouth, looking up at her friend, she remembered the most important fact of all.

WITH THE TWINS abroad and Sir Kingsford stubbornly at Northfield, the London Lockes had a quiet Christmas. On Christmas Eve, they decorated the house with evergreen boughs and attended the Temperance Hall to hand out fruit and little gifts to the children, and celebrated mass on Christmas morning to the joyful accompaniment of bells. They walked about to exchange well wishes and mince pies and apple dumplings with the neighbours still in residence, everyone cheerfully complaining about the warmth – 'It barely feels like Christmas,' Mr Hardy grumped, glaring at Genevieve like the fire Artisan next door was to blame for the unseasonal weather – and humoured the wassailers. They overindulged on goose and the plum pudding they'd each stirred on Stir-Up Sunday, and sipped port by the barely-needed fire after the servants had been let go for their holiday.

Genevieve read her new book while her parents, a little flown on the port, giggled over silly carol duets on the piano. She was nothing but a bundle of contradictions: relaxed and merry, and greatly enjoying her Dickens. Melancholy, because the twins weren't here, and hadn't even written. Miserable, because she couldn't have Oliver, but resigned over it, and a little self-satisfied about her own noble selflessness, too, if only because it redeemed her behaviour during her ill-fated proposal, when she'd blithely offered sacrifice in aid of getting what she wanted.

And relieved, with a dose of surprise, because she'd half-expected Oliver to front up and request audience with her father, though, upon reflection, that was not something he would do without her permission. If he'd come calling on her instead, she'd have easily thwarted him by insisting her mother sit with them.

But he hadn't done that.

And that was very sensible of him.

In the new year, she attended Adler's Apothecary, windowpanes decorated with ivy and holly, for a meeting of her Society faction. She ensured she was exceedingly well-dressed, right down to sporting fashionable ringlets. It had been some time since she had outfitted herself in anything other than Artistry Dress, and thus she received surprised looks from both her parents as she departed home, and from the other Artisans as she joined them in the small parlour over the apothecary.

She ignored the glances. The important thing was that Oliver take note of the switch from Artistry Dress to Heiress Dress, and be reminded of the gulf between them so he would be dissuaded from doing anything irredeemably foolish.

He was wearing his neutral face when he met her eye. She was sure he had the message.

The meeting was a blur. There were mince pies, and even though they were only halfway through the twelve days, they were all already thoroughly sick of mince pies and ate each other's out of grim mutual obligation to be polite.

Genevieve was complacent as they went back down the stairs and through the apothecary shopfloor afterwards. She knew the requirement for an upper-class unmarried woman to be chaperoned would trump any attempt by Oliver to inveigle her alone to have another dreadful conversation. She was mildly smug about her own crafty twisting of restriction into protection.

She'd quite forgotten she was also an Artisan, and had been fighting to be treated as such for months.

So when Oliver announced, 'I need a private word with Miss Locke,' like a damnable ambush when she'd thought she was safely away, Mrs Murphy's indifferent, 'Use the workroom, it's empty right now,' floored her for long enough for Oliver to whisk her in there and close the door with a firm thump behind them.

Genevieve ran gloved hands down her richly-clad sides, preparing herself to act the cold heiress to the hilt. She'd forgotten how constrictive the current styles were, now she'd become used to a looser fit. She cast a pointedly indignant look at the latched door, before deliberately stepping past him and examining the workroom, spine very stiff.

She hadn't been in here before. But— She glanced up. Yes, there was a kissing ball hung from a nail over the doorway. She had seen Mrs Murphy and Miss Adler kissing under this quintessential Yule decoration, distracted on their way up to host the meeting. Genevieve had had a moment of astonishment, mingled with the exact opposite feeling, an unsurprise. There were, in both her mother's circle and the Lockes' wider circle, not a few female couples who were known to be more than friends, yet never openly recognised as lovers. That oversight was something to do with the societal discourse that insisted women would not feel desire unless excited by undue familiarities. Genevieve hadn't needed her mother's oblique commentary nor Lulu's direct denouncement to know that couldn't be true even before she'd sprawled atop Oliver in a ruined cottage by the coast to take *thorough* familiarities.

The big bench where Miss Adler and her assistants worked was covered with jars and bottles, pestles with green-stained mortars, sharp little knives, bundles of drying herbs. The herbal scent was strong in the air. A smaller worktable in the rear corner held an array of sewing implements and—

Genevieve took a second glance. 'Am I meant to ignore the row of…'

Oliver turned to follow her gaze. 'Ah. Yes. That would be best.'

It was a production line of sorts, with a pile of membrane-thin material, several large bowls arranged to be used in series, and then a large number of distinctly shaped objects, some covered, some bare.

'Are those…' The word was unfamiliar. She'd heard the twins giggling over it. '*Dildos*?' And then, with rising bemusement, tinged with amusement from one direction and horror from the other, 'Why would you need *so many*?'

Oliver had his arms folded, face turning red. In the dire tones of a man who had apparently promised himself he would never lie to the virginal heiress and was now deeply regretting it, he explained, 'They are for French letters. Condoms, Miss Locke. Miss Adler has her girls prepare them. They soak and rinse the gut, check it for holes, and stretch it to dry over the…stands. It's a good money-spinner, if you have a reputation for reliability.'

He then had to explain what condoms were for, though he did end that discussion with a suspicious look and a rather stern, 'Miss Locke, you are reminding me of Alexander when he was weaselling out of lessons on controlling his Art.'

'Talent,' she murmured, judiciously ignoring the apt accusation by staring at the row of proud wooden stands with only a little more fascination than she actually felt. 'And…are there different…sizes?'

Though Oliver had rumbled her strategy, she didn't quite intend the glance she gave him to be quite so distractingly significant. Nonetheless, his face reddened even more, and that finally made her start to blush in tandem.

Oliver ran a hand over his burning face. He mumbled, 'There's a ribbon. To tie it on. So sizing doesn't matter so much. Can we talk about…not-this?'

'It's a toss-up which subject is going to be more awkward, Oliver,' Genevieve said, tearing her attention away from the condom factory with difficulty, and not only because her distraction ploy had failed.

'Really?' Oliver said. 'I'm on the easy downhill now.'

It made her laugh, but she also said, 'Nothing's changed,' before he could gather his words.

'Everything's changed, Gin.'

'So we kissed again,' she said dismissively, adding a gay little gesture to underscore how ready she was to dismiss it.

'We did a little more than that,' he said. 'If we hadn't been interrupted—'

'I was hysterical from overusing my Art,' Genevieve said, showing a distinct lack of solidarity with her own sex. But if she was going to be subject to such preconceptions, she might as well get some use out of them. 'It is of no consequence.'

'It is of consequence,' Oliver said, 'to me.'

'No.' Genevieve paced in a tight circle before drawing herself up and facing him square. 'Stop being a, a, a *pillock* about this, Oliver.'

He smothered a smile. 'I'm very much trying to, Gin.'

'You're not! I will *not* have you nobly accepting consequences that do not apply. No one saw. No one knows. I am not ruined. I do not need my honour salvaged by your sacrifice.'

'My sacrifice.' It was very flat, especially after her increasingly savage tones as she lost control of her voice.

'I will state this clearly, and then we will not discuss it again.' She tugged at her fine gloves. She hadn't had her hands covered for months. Her palms were hot and itchy. 'I will not be responsible for trapping you into a marriage you do not want with a woman you do not love.'

She swept regally around him and made for the door. He was so much taller and longer-limbed than her that it only took him a step and a lean to get a hand on the door and instantly undo the inch she'd yanked it open.

Genevieve glared at the closed door under his spread-fingered, tattooed hand, before turning around with the sort of slow menace that would have had the twins running for cover, though they would have been laughing as they did it.

Oliver met her icy gaze with equanimity. 'Have I made you think I don't love you, Gin?'

'You—' She stopped, temper disrupted. In a small voice, she said, 'I told you you're the best man I know, and in reply, you said… Well. You said nothing.' The memory of that excruciating mortification was enough to rally her; she rapped out, 'So forgive me if I somehow have the idea my affections are not returned.'

'I'm sorry. I don't always find the right words.' He looked down. 'It overwhelmed me. You overwhelm me.'

Tartly, she said, 'Easily impressed, are we?'

Oliver smiled at her, his warm and crooked smile, and she caught her breath. 'No,' he said. 'But I hope *you* are. Turns out words don't come any more rightly written down.'

He drew from his pocket a wrapped rectangle, offering it like a dare. She took it.

It was wrapped with heavy, pretty paper, with lace and ribbon, expensive. Oliver had gone to painstaking lengths there, so she unwrapped it with equal care, though she could see from the way he was smiling that he very well knew she was not normally the type to do so.

It was *A Christmas Carol*. It didn't matter that she already owned it, that she'd already read it. He'd somehow managed to find a copy – the edition had been all sold out by Christmas Eve, her father had had to use his club contacts to get their copy, a far more pleasing use than sourcing her a husband. It must have taken Oliver a great deal of effort, tromping about the bookstores whose proprietors might have lifted their nose to the tattooed navvy each time he lumbered through their doors.

But to her genuine thanks, Oliver merely shook his head. 'The inscription.'

If he was a man who paced, he'd be pacing. Puzzled, she opened the book – its pages were already cut – to the half-title, and saw the crabbed inscription written in black ink.

Oliver had been taught to read and write in the merchant navy. It had been a policy, as she understood it, to impose literacy on the young boys recruited in droves from the lowest classes, an improving initiative. He had, accordingly, the distinctive sailor's hand, legible without elegance.

The inscription read, *I could not abide it if the Ghost of Christmas Past returned to chastise me for failing to take the hand you reached out to me, my love. I will not face the Ghost of Christmas Yet to Come knowing my own cowardice left me by a lonely hearth without you.*

Genevieve looked up at Oliver with her heart in her throat, unable to speak. 'But…'

Stepping back until her spine met the door, she rested her head against the solid surface, closing her eyes. She felt the stir of air as he moved closer, felt his chest brush against her. She reached up blindly, and her fingers touched his cheek. He turned his face into her palm.

She had harped on the sacrifice she would have to make, to marry him, but it hadn't truly struck her. It had not been real, not until he had turned her down for fear of having to sacrifice his own family. She could brazen it out with her parents, because she knew Alex and Lulu would stand with her, one steadfast, one defiant, both bold and true.

Oliver would have to face his father and stepmother, by all reports a bitter and judgemental pair, and not one of his brothers would stand with him because not one of them cheered on his rise out of their ranks.

She found her courage, even as it felt like something was tearing in her chest.

'Nothing's changed,' she repeated, notwithstanding that she was cupping his face and valiantly resisting the impulse to kiss him. 'You fear the reactions of our respective families, and you are correct. I can't do that to you, Oliver, I can't make you give up your family for me.'

'They'll cope, or I will,' Oliver said, and Genevieve's eyes flew open. He grinned at her expression. 'I know what I said before, Gin. I was hiding behind my family's initial reaction, because I was scared.'

'Scared?' she said, aware she was subjecting him to her dissection look and that her palm was so hot he could probably feel the heat on his cheeks through the kidskin.

'Not of you.' He covered her hands with his own. 'You are…you are *magnificent*, my love. I was scared – I am *terrified* – that I cannot give you the life you deserve. If I let you— If we— This will be the most selfish thing I have ever done.'

'Oliver,' Genevieve whispered. 'I grant you full authority to be selfish.'

'I will dedicate my life to making you—'

'No speeches, my dear,' she said. 'You'll use your annual quota of words before the end of January.'

Smiling, he lifted one of her hands, and drew it down to his mouth. He turned it, and inched back the glove, and kissed the pulse point of her bared wrist. 'Miss Locke, would you do me the honour—'

'I have to write to Lulu!' she said. 'The twins have to come back right this instant.'

'Dare I presume the yes?' Oliver asked.

She deliberately looked upwards, drawing his gaze with her to the kissing ball, woven all about with holly and ivy, a good luck charm at its centre. 'Is that mistletoe above us?'

They were still kissing when Mrs Murphy opened the workshop door, tutted, and closed it again with a murmured, 'About time.'

23

GENEVIEVE DROPPED THE BOOK.

It hit the floor on its spine and fell open nearly halfway, to one of Leech's illustrations, one of the smaller grey ones. In it, Scrooge had snatched the extinguisher-cap and pressed it down over the Spirit of Christmas Past. His face showed his intent determination to put out its light, the illumination of unpleasant memories, but his eyes were wide, almost panicked.

The words that accompanied the vignette caught her eye.

The Spirit dropped beneath it, so that the extinguisher covered its whole form; but though Scrooge pressed it down with all his force, he could not hide the light: which streamed from under it, in an unbroken flood upon the ground.

She exclaimed in annoyance at her own clumsiness and bent, with some difficulty and twisting of her body around the salient obstacle of her stomach, to retrieve the book.

She turned to Oliver, who was standing strangely still. 'Shall we go to tea?'

Oliver looked from her face to the book and back again. Then he said, 'Whitely's right. We have to get that necklace off you.'

'What necklace?'

'The necklace.'

He abruptly strode at her. For a big man, Oliver was very good at managing to not loom over people, especially women, but he wasn't bothering with that now. She tensed even before he stretched an ugly hand, large and meaty, blunt-fingered, towards her vulnerable throat.

'Stop it!' She threw the book aside and grabbed his wrist with both hands to wrench it away from her.

He freed himself with the merest shrug of effort. He picked a book up off the floor, and looked at the frontispiece before shaking his head, a heavy frown between his brows. He pocketed it and faced her.

'Gin, I'm taking the necklace.'

'You're not!'

She tried to pull away when he reached for it; he took hold of her shoulders to keep her still, and she lashed out at him, near spitting in outraged fury. He stumbled back, hands held up, immediately contrite.

'I can only beg your pardon,' he said. 'I— I had to get it off you before I forgot.'

'Forgot what?' she half-shouted at him.

'I don't know,' he said, with miserable confusion. 'I've already forgotten. I can't imagine what I was thinking. Sit down, would you, Gin?'

She was running her hands over her stomach, she realised; he was worried his impertinence, or her outsized reaction to it, might have harmed the baby.

She did sit, if only to assuage his concern. They had both been possessed, she decided. No other explanation could exist for her trying to rake her nails down her old friend's face like she wanted to take his eyes out. No other explanation could exist for Oliver *ever* laying even gentle hands on a woman, let alone one in her advanced condition, let alone Genevieve herself.

He crouched beside her, penitent. 'Should I summon Mrs Murphy?'

'No.' The rage with which she had struck at him with clawed hands was such that she felt obliged to ask, 'Did I burn you?'

'I rather think I earned it, if you did,' Oliver said, which was not an answer.

'Let me see your hands.'

She shushed him when he would have protested again, taking his hands in her own and turning them over so she could see his palms. His hands were work-bitten, scarred and marked all over, but there was no telltale fresh scarlet scald.

When she let him go, he dropped one hand to touch the rectangular shape deforming his pocket. He had, she guessed, a book in there, and it snagged at her.

She said, 'I don't know what came over me, either.'

He smiled at her, his dark eyes warm and fond. 'I think I do,' he said, even as she became aware he'd spun up his wards, and then he plucked a chain from about her neck.

A pendant, a large sardonyx cabochon set all about with intricate cogs and wires, hung from the thin gold chain, and it was her most precious possession. Catapulted straight back into cold and clawing fury, she lunged for it, knocking into him.

They were abruptly grappling, him trying to catch her wrists to stop her clawing at his face, held back more by the bulwark of her own swollen stomach than by his restrained efforts. Part of her watched this performance from outside her own body, wondering at both Oliver's appalling perseverance, and her own appalling rage, cold and overpowering.

Not so cold – she might be icy in her rage, but her Art was fire.

Oliver yelped and backed off, one hand curled defensively into his chest, the other still dangling the chain. They both paused for breath, then, Genevieve panting with exertion, eyes fixed on the hypnotic swing of the precious pendant.

Taking advantage of her brief physical incapacity, he flung it to the ground and stamped on it with the same brutal efficiency his colleagues at the docks might have taken towards rats. Her wail drowned out the musical tinkle of tiny cogs scattering across the floor.

She fell to her knees. It was the sort of sharp, uncontrolled movement that could only bring harm on the child in her womb, but she could not have stopped herself, and neither could Oliver, for he had been struck too, dropping down beside her with a muffled groan.

It was maelstrom.

Genevieve clutched at her head, trying to contain the whirl of imagery through her mind. Memories, treasured, precious memories fluttered this way and that, as one man was torn out of them strip by strip, and another took his place. She could hear her own breath panting in and out of her. She could feel the weight of the baby pulling her down. She was going to vomit.

Time was moving away, in the wrong direction. Her husband was sitting by her bedside, holding her hand as silent tears ran down her face after she'd woken from the twilight of the stillbirth.

Her husband was striding beside her as they went off to tackle a rogue Artisan for the Agency, Cecelia and Fletcher there too, making for another breathless article about the Myriad.

Her husband was acting as chief mourner at her father's funeral, standing by her as she and her mother comforted each other.

Her husband was bringing her soup because her incompetent womb had lost another child. And again. And again.

Her husband was lifting her off her feet, holding her close against his neck, murmuring words of adoration for no particular reason except he loved her, blindly and blindingly.

Her husband was holding her hand at the first funeral, their baby girl's, consigned to the cold ground the barest of days after taking her first breath.

Her husband was coming to her bed, wreathed in smiles, as she exhaustedly but triumphantly held their swaddled daughter in her arms after the tribulations of labour, with no inkling of the grief that would soon follow.

Her husband was suggesting that the other weapons Artisan of their acquaintance take over her defensive role in the so-called Myriad until after the happy event. It would be an olive branch to the other major faction, he said.

Her husband was hugging her tight as she tremulously announced the best of all news to him halfway through their first year of marriage.

Her new husband was leaning over her on the first evening of their wedding tour, very slowly sliding his big hand along her thigh. His chest was bare. She was seeing his dragon tattoo for the first time, and it was gleaming in the lamplight, the gold of the nipple hoop winking from between its white teeth.

Her husband-to-be was sitting with her and the twins on the stairs in the new year, the air chill, listening to her parents argue about whether she would be allowed to marry a damned navvy.

The man who would soon be her fiancé was handing her a wrapped book in the apothecary workshop, and she was unwrapping it, and opening it to read the inscription he had painstakingly written for her, and there was mistletoe over their heads, berries shining amid the evergreen.

The spin and shudder of the storm generated by smashing the embedded clockwork Art eased, settled, and stilled.

Genevieve opened her eyes and looked at her husband.

'Oliver,' she said. 'We're *married.*'

24

IT TOOK A GOOD LONG TIME before Oliver found the wherewithal to drop his hands from his own temples to say a simple, 'Yes.'

'He took our memories,' Genevieve said. She was still too stunned for anything more than astonishment: the rage and horror were yet to crash over her. 'Reuben McAvey stole our memories and he stole our marriage.'

'Yes.'

This new, enormous fact sat right at the centre of her being, like a great glowing bonfire, blotting out every other thought with its fierce blaze. But that did not mean there was not a good deal of administration to be done in the far corners of her mind where the bonfire's heat and light could not obliterate the shadows.

Genevieve looked at the man who had very suddenly become her husband. 'And you released us.'

She took the hand Oliver had cupped to his chest when she'd used her Art to try to force him to relinquish the treacherous necklace. She'd left a blistered swath across his palm, as if he'd attempted to pick up a red-hot iron bar, dangerous to an Artisan's bare skin in both the physical and metaphysical realms.

She held the offended hand cradled in her own, but there was nothing she could do for him here: she would have to call for salve and bandages, and perhaps Miss Adler and her healing Art to avoid a scar.

She stood. Her legs were shaking, but when she ran her hand over her belly, she felt the baby's reassuring kick. 'We must tend to your hand.'

'Gin,' he said.

'I could use a stiff drink myself, my dear,' she said absently.

Before she could fetch Bridget, the door flung wide. Cecelia stood there, and her face was sallow, sickly with the same shock that had numbed

Genevieve. She must have come dashing across the garden and up the stairs, for she was out of breath.

'He stole my Art,' she said. She had her hand pressed to her breast. She seemed distraught.

'Fletcher's compulsion Art, also,' Genevieve said. 'And Oliver's wards, I suppose. If you will excuse me, I must send messages to the twins before they feel obligated to return. Please see to Oliver's hand.'

'Wait, we—'

But Genevieve had already gone about her business. She had letters to write.

Carrying the last painting, the one of her father in front of the Monument, that had delivered up the memory of a ruined southern cottage, she returned to the house. She baulked at the threshold of the study. It was decorated in dark, masculine colours, all Reuben's tastes. This was Reuben's room. She went down to the drawing room instead, with its flock wallpaper and parquet tiles and spindly furniture. It had never truly felt like hers, but at least Reuben was less of a presence here.

She propped the painting on the mantle, where her mother had once threatened to position it back in the Locke townhouse, and went to the writing desk.

Her writing paper was bordered in black, as befitted a widow.

After a time, Fletcher entered to offer assistance. His breath smelled of cloves, with a sour tang under that. She suspected he'd been vomiting.

'Send these, would you?' she told him, not looking up from the little writing desk.

She'd dashed a little ink around the surface, she noted, and blotted at it with her sleeve. They sent their laundry out; it would not be Bridget's problem.

They'd had a whole staff, at the Belgravia house. Reuben had dismissed the lot before they'd moved, and hired on young Bridget, and Cook and her daughter. To save money, to pay what he owed for the embedded clockwork Art, and to limit the number of people whose deep memories of *not-him* the clockwork would have to fight. That would have made it last longer.

She handed Fletcher the pile, with instructions: the terse note to Alex – *I am safe, Oliver is with me, do not come home* – would have to be sent so that it arrived before he did, which meant accessing the network of telepath Artisans stationed at ports across the world for this exact fast, but very expensive and not at all private, service. She could only hope that by the time the ship docked and he received the message, he would be calmer, and she would have sent an update with a resolution. Whitely, she thought grimly, would have to keep him in hand in the meantime, and would no doubt manage him admirably.

Lulu was receiving a dispatch posthaste, commanding without subtlety that she stay out of the way. Genevieve would follow it up with a longer letter, but not right now. Sir Kingsford was easier; she'd written the simplest of missives explaining that, despite what he would now be remembering, she was safe and well and not in need of his assistance. He would accept that with some gratitude.

A few others deserved notes, she supposed, but she could not quite think who they might be, at this moment. She was too busy working in the scant shadows around the raging bonfire in the centre of her mind.

Fletcher seemed grateful to be given a task, and went without demur to take care of it. That was what she liked about Fletcher. He tried very hard to do the right thing, even when he wasn't sure what the right thing was.

When he came back, she would set him on sending to consignment every single item of furniture Reuben had chosen for this blighted house.

Oliver and Cecelia were having a murmured conversation in the hall outside the drawing room door. It was beyond irritating. Genevieve frowned and summoned them in.

'Gin, *please* let us—' Cecelia immediately began.

'Fetch the shapeshifter,' Genevieve said. 'Oliver, you need to remove your effects – you will take the bedroom by mine now, of course – and install a bolt on your previous room to contain it.'

'It?' he repeated.

'The shapeshifter. I suppose you might also need to nail shut any crack or other egress, if you think it can transform into anything very small.'

'Mass? He has a name, Gin.'

'Fetch him. I need to interview him.'

'Interview.' That had a very flat note to it.

'This is tedious, Oliver,' she snapped. 'Go fetch him. Move your effects. Put a lock on his bloody door.'

Cecelia shifted, but Oliver didn't. 'What is it you wish to achieve by interviewing him?'

'Do any of you remember my mother's funeral?' she said abruptly. 'I remember my father's, but not hers. Admittedly, my memories are not entirely clear yet. Do any of you remember it?'

Cecelia mutely shook her head. Oliver said, 'No.'

It was nothing she hadn't expected. She found herself jerkily nodding. 'My father was older than her, and in poorer health – all those cigars and desserts and ports – so he was taken from us sooner than we hoped, but not so very surprisingly. But my mother was in perfect health. I don't remember her ever being ill. And I don't remember some sudden accident. And I don't remember her funeral. She just wasn't *there*, after the stillbirth. So she's alive, and Reuben took her, he took her, and that shapeshifter knows something about it, so God help me, I will make him—'

'Genevieve.' Oliver hadn't raised his voice but his use of her full name was enough to give her pause. 'This isn't good for the baby, love.'

She was bewildered by the endearment for a moment. It made her look at him. It made her acknowledge one of the truths she had been running from, with her hectic activity at the desk with ink and black-bordered paper.

Oliver did not feel like her husband. He felt like the interloper. His reinstatement into her memories of their fifteen-years-long marriage felt like the violation.

'Never mind about the baby,' she said. 'If he has my mother, and he has the copper knife – it's obvious she has an undisclosed Art, isn't it? All those memories, locked away into her portraits. She kept them safe for us, and he's going to try to cut the Art out of her, we have to help her before he does it.'

'He would have already done it,' Oliver said, 'if that was his plan. He's had months.'

'No, because—' She could find no reason to hand, except that she wanted it so. 'No.'

Cecelia came cautiously closer. 'Gin, I know you have to be furious at us. But you must know we didn't willingly deliver our Arts over to use against you. I hate that he used mine to do this thing to you. You must know how sorry we are. Will you let us help you?'

'I've told you how you can help me,' Genevieve said. 'I need to question the shapeshifter.'

'He doesn't know anything,' Oliver said.

'He might know some clue as to where my mother is being held. We have to find her, before—'

'Your mother had a talent, that's all. *If* Reuben took her, it wasn't to cut an Art out of her.' He crouched down and tried to take her hand. 'I'm sorry, Gin, but we don't even know if she's alive. We all remember her as passed over.'

'We all remembered me as married to Reuben, too,' she snapped, jerking her hand free.

Cecelia, wringing her hands, said, 'We need to give it a few days more, to let our memories clear entirely. Then we'll know one way or the other.'

Genevieve gestured angrily at the bulk of her stomach. 'Does it appear that I have time for that?'

Oliver straightened; she stared straight ahead as he stood tall beside the desk. 'You already don't have time. You are in imminent condition: she is due any day now. You cannot go gallivanting about on a wild chase.'

'How dare you presume—' she began to shout, before remembering again. 'Ah. And is that your husbandly decree, sir?'

Oliver made an inarticulate noise. He strode from the drawing room, shoulders tense.

Arguments had never been so readily won with her previous husband.

This repulsive thought gave Genevieve a moment of pause, a brief flash of sanity in her terrible, frantic concentration on any action she could take to stave off the inevitable reckoning with the last year of her life.

'I shall go fetch the shapeshifter myself,' she said wearily. 'Stop hovering, Cecelia. I am not angry with any of you. We merely have business to conclude with McAvey, and I would like to have it done before my travail.'

Cecelia said, 'I will bring him down.'

She went away, moving as slowly up the stairs as a woman twice her age, perhaps trying to give Genevieve more time to return to herself, perhaps weighed down by the same enormity that confronted all of them.

Genevieve closed her eyes. Recollections were showing themselves in brief flashes, shy and frustratingly teasing. She tried to still her body, her breathing, the bonfire in her mind, wilfully enticing more memories forth into the light.

And, there. She remembered now the agony of the long days waiting for the twins to come home in response to her urgent summons. She knew now that they must have set overland records to apply for formal leave and make it home within three weeks of the proposal, but back then she knew only impatience and self-regard.

She remembered leaving Oliver in the family parlour with the travel-soiled twins and knocking on the door of her mother's room. Her mother's grave nod to the news. The sudden break in tension as she burst into a smile and hugged her daughter and told her not to fret.

The way Mother had straightened her shoulders and girded herself before striding into Father's study.

Sitting on the stairs, listening to her father shouting with her heart sinking ever lower. Oliver and the twins joining her, crowding close about in mute but unbreakable support.

Her father had been so insulting. He'd called Oliver a damned navvy, and a fortune-hunter, and other things besides. She'd stood up, and Oliver had said, 'Can't fight fire with fire this time, Gin,' and made the twins laugh.

When her father announced he would cut her off without a penny, her mother's words rang clear and strong. 'Theo, she is an Artisan. She does not need your money, and as soon as she turns twenty-one, she will not need your permission. That is if, in the interim, she does not lose the last of the scant patience with which the Lockes are so very blessed and abscond to Gretna, and then perhaps onwards to Canada.'

Genevieve's father's response was inaudible, too low and savage a growl to carry to the stairs. Her mother remained implacable. 'Do you wish to emulate your younger brother to such an extent that you die estranged from your only daughter?'

Genevieve twisted in her perch. Alex had already slung his arm around Lulu, whose face had set like stone. Genevieve let go of Alex's hand and took hers.

Lulu squeezed back. 'Aunt Nettie's landed the killing blow, I think.'

She hadn't, not quite. That came next, when her firm, calm tone wavered for the first time. 'What is this truly about, Theo?' The eavesdroppers had to strain to hear her past Father's bluster as she asked, with true pain, 'Do you fight her mésalliance so hard because you regret your own?'

Silence, as clanging as a tolling bell. And then, brokenly, 'No, no, Nettie, never.'

On the stairs, the twins slapped palms in a wordless acknowledgement of victory. It was, Genevieve reflected even as she tumbled into Oliver's arms, a rather brutal and merciless victory. It did not seem to have been a pyrrhic one, however, for the younger Lockes and Oliver shortly had to depart their eavesdropping nook for fear of overhearing far too much conciliatory marital relations. They were all sitting innocently in the rear parlour when Genevieve's parents came downstairs to face the first hurdle of awkwardness: permission granted in short and overformal tones. Genevieve's father was rigid as she embraced him, but he patted her back.

She remembered the enforced delay of the reading of the banns. Oliver visiting at proper intervals. Stilted conversations in the family parlour, barely made tolerable by Alex's heroic effort in making himself dull with travel tales. Genevieve's father caught Oliver staring at the inlaid walnut chessboard table in the corner, salving his discomfit by mentally playing out the half-completed game – the game Father had been waging by correspondence with his brother when Uncle Reggie had taken his fatal fall. It had stayed exactly so, mid-gambit, ever since, the barest glimpse into Father's stoic grief.

Theodore Locke harrumphed when he saw the direction of his inevitable son-in-law's gaze. 'Do you play?'

Oliver nodded.

'It's White's turn,' Father said, and gestured for Oliver to move his piece. That was the first drops of a thaw that took years to complete.

Genevieve remembered – her throat constricted – she remembered Reuben McAvey taking her aside after a Society meeting as news of the engagement spread.

'You don't have to marry him just because he has wards,' he had said, voice urgent.

She'd raised her eyebrows, adopting her frosty high-society mask. 'Excuse me?'

'You're worried your fire will get out of control,' he informed her. 'You don't need to marry Mr Bennet for that.'

'You overstep yourself, Mr McAvey,' she said. 'Do not presume you know my reasoning for the bestowal of my affections.'

His face had begun to mottle as red as his hair. 'With your beauty, you could marry the highest and greatest in the land. Do you need your power yoked so badly you'll throw that opportunity away and let yourself be ground under by a lumbering oaf?'

He tried to take her hand, as a fellow Artisan was allowed to do; she yanked free. It had always felt natural, when it was Oliver. She found him too presumptuous for words, her turned shoulder answer enough.

McAvey was not finished committing his outrage. 'He is above himself, and you lower yourself. I cannot tell which is the worse sin.'

That was finally too far to be answered with mere cutting silence. 'Perhaps you believe the besetting sin is not so much that I lower myself to Mr Oliver, but that I do not lower myself to *you*.'

She strode away, leaving him red-faced and spluttering.

She wondered if he'd held onto the snub for fifteen years.

It wasn't all awkwardness and difficulty. She remembered her wedding, walking the aisle in white satin, not at all feeling the cold in the draughty little church. Sir Kingsford had sent flowers from his greenhouse in lieu of himself, so that she carried a lilac bouquet throughout the unfashionably wintery ceremony. It was far from the grand affair her father had wished for, but she felt herself glowing.

On the other hand, the wedding breakfast in the small parlour of a carefully selected middling hotel had been as graceless as Oliver had predicted. His brothers with scrubbed faces, stuffed into their Sunday best, the twins loud to compensate. Both fathers stiff, their opposing class-based resentments meeting in the middle. Oliver's stepmother's head crammed full of what must have been a marathon perusal of every etiquette book she could get her hands on, Genevieve's mother's natural grace barely a match for it.

She and Oliver had exchanged gifts afterwards, privately. She'd given him a paper-knife, its ivory handle shaped into the likeness of coils of an octopus's tentacle, a mimic of his arm tattoo, which he'd deigned to roll up his sleeve and display to her curious, admiring eyes, and fingers, once the engagement was official.

He'd given her a bejewelled gold ring. The twins, predictably, scoffed. 'Sentimental tosh,' Lulu had said, and Alex had said, 'Who knew Oliver had it in him to be so middling *soppy*.'

Genevieve had held her hand at arm's length to admire her rings. Her wedding band was relatively plain, gold ornated with an inset band of copper, a coy reference to Artistry, and their wedding date etched on the inside.

Oliver's more personal gift was set with seven little gems, nearly palindromic in colour, but not in type: beryl, emerald, and lazuli gently arched over a central opal, with vermeil, emerald, and diamond curving below.

'You two,' she'd informed the twins, 'are simply jealous because no one has given either of you a ring that spells out a secret message.'

'If we had gemstones to represent F and K, I'd be spelling out a secret message for you right now,' Lulu said.

They were still giggling when Oliver, smiling fondly, had found them on the stairs, entirely too willing to let the twins make fun of him as he swept his new bride into a kiss.

Genevieve sucked in a shocked breath. Her eyes flew wide open. She stared down at her hand, and then in an instant, she wrenched McAvey's gold band from her finger and flung it with a hard, convulsive jerk across the long length of the drawing room. It spun and bounced over the rug and clinked onto the polished parquetry at the far edge of the room.

It was not far enough away from her, from her skin. Without her conscious intervention, her Art flexed. The ring burst into flames. The gold melted into the wood tile, which itself began to smoulder and char. The wallpaper above began to blacken.

Genevieve came to her senses. This was too alarmingly reminiscent of the recently recovered memory of setting her father's rug alight, that dangerously uncontrolled wildfire from her earliest days with her Art. She clenched her fist, quelling the Art flames, with more of a wrench of volition than it really should have taken.

'Here's Mass, Gin,' Cecelia said from the doorway.

Probably following both the smell and the clue of Genevieve's guilty face, she glanced over at the mess, a small puddle of gold setting into a gleaming organic pattern in the middle of copious scorch marks. Saying nothing, she walked Mass over to sit by the desk and wait on the pleasure of the lady of the house.

Already abashed by her momentary lack of control, Genevieve felt her implacable determination shiver away at the sight of the young shapeshifter. Whether he knew more of McAvey's plans than he'd let on, he was still a child, whom she had copiously fed and inevitably grown fond of. She gave Cecelia, who was hovering, a meaningful nod, and the other woman retreated, looking relieved, leaving Genevieve alone with Mass.

He perched on the edge of his chair as if wishing to flee. He might have done so, effecting that effortless transformation into the little black cat and darting away. That he stayed, and raised an anxious but resolute gaze to meet hers, spoke well of his good intentions.

'You were sent to us by McAvey,' she began, far more gently than she'd been planning. 'Do you know where he is?'

He shook his head. They'd asked this, and other questions, when he'd first come out of the box, but he'd been confused and exhausted then. Genevieve didn't know if any of the others had persisted since. She hadn't, too taken by his air of timid innocence. She suspected they'd all forgotten his dubious origins, the twisted combination of her friends' three Arts working to protect the shapeshifter spy in their midst.

'But he must have given you a task here,' she pressed. 'I know it's not your fault, Mass. We know about the compulsion now.'

An inarticulate noise from the doorway made her look up. Fletcher must have returned from his postal errand; he was retreating into the hall with his hand over his mouth. Part of her regretted inadvertently reminding him of his Art's part in her victimhood. Part of her thought, savagely, *Good.*

'I was meant to take Whitely's place,' Mass said earnestly. 'Kill him, and take his place.'

Genevieve was not convinced this had been the true scheme. She would firmly avow that McAvey was overconfident, but not even he could have believed this sweet boy could keep up such a deception for long, and, once discovered, none of them would have been quite so kindly inclined towards a catspaw who had managed a fatal blow at Alex's cherished door Artisan, meltingly innocent brown eyes or no.

However, the immediate failure of the supposed plan had gained him access to her household. 'To do what?' she asked aloud.

'Help.'

'Help McAvey.' She drummed her fingers. 'But how?'

Mass fidgeted uncomfortably. His eyes had shifted from the deep brown that reminded her of Oliver's familiar gaze back to Whitely's cool green-eyed regard. Frowning fiercely, he appeared to be fighting his own mouth, but he was able to spit out a single word.

'Chaos.'

He had played with the discarded cogs from the clockwork lock in front of them; the sight of them had almost tricked her into calling Lulu to London despite Alex's firm injunction. Only Whitely's timely, if accidental, epistolary intervention had distracted her. The shapeshifter had given out a birthdate the same as Rose's, the poor lost mite, and that certainly seemed pure malice intended to create dissonance and gloom. And he'd found her and Oliver looking at the paintings and had almost managed to destroy them through what had seemed like natural clumsiness, the growing, addle-limbed adolescent tripping over his own feet.

There was no real pattern there, apart from sowing discord and impeding any scant progress they might have made in the fog McAvey had stranded them all in.

Chaos, indeed.

But Reuben McAvey surely had a plan, no doubt both cogent and cruel. He might have held a grudge against both her and Oliver for not keeping to their rightful places, but surely this whole nasty, expensive farce had more to it than mere revenge and robbing an heiress.

She appraised Mass, the shapeshifter squirming under her dissecting stare. 'Where are you from? Do you remember now?'

There was no particular reason he should; it was mostly memories involving her marriage that had been stolen or twisted. Mass's haziness about his past had a different source than the pendant's wicked influence. The fact that he was fighting to speak suggested he was still under a compulsion of his own.

Indeed, he shook his head, saying again, confused and confusing, 'Magdalen?'

She matched the shake of his head. She rose and spoke as gently as she could, though it still came out cool and stern. 'May I touch you, Mass? In case you're wearing embedded Art like I was.'

He nodded, and she stepped to his side, gently turning back his cuffs and collar, looking for rings, bracelets, a necklace like her own. His wrists were reddened, and she wondered briefly if he had been wearing a pair of too-tight bracelets, unfastened before he presented himself to her. But he wouldn't have been able to voluntarily remove them, not even in self-preservation. She made him pull up his trouser legs; his ankles were bare too. For any further investigation, one of the men would have to strip him bare, which was an uncomfortable thought but might yet prove necessary.

'Did your master give you a message to pass along to me?'

'No,' he said, and then, 'I don't remember.'

'That is one thing that did not go entirely his way, then.'

Again, a noise by the door drew Genevieve's attention. This time, it was Oliver, quietly watching. Here to protect the child from her temper, she supposed. Her palms were hot. She glanced down, and saw the bare skin where her wedding ring had been.

There was nothing to be gained here. Mass could or would not remember more, could or would not admit more. She rose. Oliver moved aside, gaze lowered. She passed him in silence and went slowly up the stairs, to the study, which McAvey had left locked. She closed the door behind her.

She emptied the drawers one by one, depositing papers and the usual bureau scree onto the floor, but couldn't find her rings, or Oliver's. She melted the lock on the safe, but when she swung the heavy door open, it lay empty except for a few bits of official-looking paperwork. The open bookshelves were unlikely. A safebox at the bank was possible. That he'd destroyed the rings, like he must have destroyed the telltale inscribed copy of *A Christmas Tale*, was more so.

Still. He did like to gloat. Genevieve could very well imagine him smirking himself to sleep over stolen tokens of her and Oliver's usurped marriage.

She stepped out of the office, and over to his bedroom. It took a moment to make herself push his door open.

The room was stuffy, hot from the heat of the waning day and from too many days closed up. Oliver had not obeyed the instruction to claim the chamber as his own.

Genevieve began a methodical search. The drawers by the bed were obvious, but perhaps too risky even for McAvey; indeed, they did not hold the rings. The dresser drawers afforded no luck. She was checking the pockets of the umpteenth trousers, acres of clothes thrown to the ground behind her, when Bridget diffidently knocked on the door to ask if she was home to visitors.

'I am not,' Genevieve said. She looked about at the strewn contents of McAvey's wardrobe. 'I apologise, Bridget. It wasn't fair of me to make this mess.'

Bridget gave a nervous little dip. Genevieve studied her. 'I suppose you are aware of developments within the household?'

'Yes, ma'am.' Bridget twisted her hands together and said in a rush, 'I made Mr Oliver help me with the coal scuttle so many times.'

She sounded desperately guilty and anxious about a request Oliver had always cheerfully pitched in on. She feared, Genevieve realised, she would be dismissed for setting the master of the house to chores.

'And you may continue to do so, until we hire on,' Genevieve said. 'He's done worse, shipside *and* dockside. Actually, your assistance would be appreciated, Bridget. Might you request your registry office trace the servants dismissed from the Belgravia house?'

'Yes, ma'am,' the girl said again, stilted.

'Not to replace you,' Genevieve said, again making herself speak gently despite her distracted, seething state. 'Your service has been more than satisfactory this past year. I wish only to ensure the Lockes' retainers were not summarily turned off without severance or reference and reassure myself they have found new positions to their taste. If some wish to return to the household, I will welcome them, but not at your expense.'

She would have to assure herself, via Fletcher, that their household could afford more servants, but she now rather suspected McAvey had kept a single live-in maid-of-all-work as a cost-saving on the embedded Art his misappropriated wife wore, not as a cost-saving on the household budget. The price for the clockwork had been extravagant, but McAvey himself had not been. She must have some inherited wealth remaining to her, under Oliver's careful, respectful control. Fletcher and Mr Hartley would need to conduct an audit and discover where McAvey had applied falsified paperwork atop falsified memories to shift funds, and reverse that if they could.

If not, so be it. Both she and Oliver were well-paid for their Artistry work, and their early years together had been ones of careful economising.

She didn't fear frugality.

'Thank you, ma'am,' Bridget said. 'I will go by the registry tomorrow morning.' She hesitated. 'And you are not at home to Mrs Murphy and Miss Adler?'

Florence and Rachel. They'd been on that basis, before this past year. Another tally mark to chalk to McAvey's account.

'I am not at home to visitors,' Genevieve confirmed. 'Thank you, Bridget. Close the door behind you.'

She really did not have time for the competent compassion of her female friends right now.

Shapeshifter

IN THE DISTRESS ENGULFING THE HOUSEHOLD, they had all forgotten to watch Mass.

He wished he could take advantage of their inattention, and depart. He wasn't allowed to do that. His job here wasn't finished. He had nowhere to go, regardless.

They had been so kind to him.

He hid in his room, Oliver's room. The toy train was overturned on the rug, where it had run into bits of the broken lock he'd stolen and fallen over, wheels turning until the dash of Art powering the clockwork ran out. He couldn't look at it for the guilt.

He rubbed fretfully at his wrists, which were hot and itchy, like a rash was coming up. He had felt so light when they'd first let him live in this house, and took him to the Agency to register like a real person, and were kind to him, and made him feel welcome, and made him feel safe, even though he wasn't.

It had helped him maintain the last echoes of Kit Whitely's imprint much longer than he'd thought he could. The discipline of the man had met the desperate need in the child, and Mass had held on with every ounce of strength that discipline and kindness had loaned him.

But the bulwark was almost entirely dissipated. He was fighting mostly on his own now. The voice was getting stronger.

I made you. Without me, you'd be nothing. You'd be mud, dirt underfoot.

Mass guessed he'd be alone a little while longer. He tried to shift back into Kit Whitely's shape, reaching again for the feeling of *this one, you are this one, you are this one who can scoff at horrid voices and make decisions for yourself and resist compulsions*, but it had been too long since he'd touched the man, too long since he'd violently slammed his head into the cupboard wall, acting under the grip of the same compulsion he was now barely holding at bay. Artistry roiled over and through him, leaving flickers in its wake but unable to effect a full transformation.

His head throbbed. It was the sort of headache that felt like the sharp hammer of spikes through his skull. He couldn't remember ever having any sort of headache. Artisans didn't have headaches. It would get worse, the longer he resisted.

The headache had lessened when he'd gone into the storeroom where Mr Oliver and Mrs McAvey were looking at the paintings. He was supposed to find out things like that. He still didn't know if he'd been meant to destroy the memories or not. He'd been fighting so hard that, when he'd tripped and flung himself aside, he couldn't even tell which action had been at the service of his master and which had been defiance of it.

He pressed itchy wrists to each temple, bringing his two physical sources of discomfit together as if they could annihilate each other.

They're being kind, he thought. *They're being so kind.*

Miss Delacorte read to him and told him she would listen any time he needed to talk, and Mr Oliver had given him the little Art dribbler and taught him to play chess. Mr Fletcher had undertaken to show him proper manners in a fussy and awkward sort of way which amounted to how to choose the right fork in situations Mass was not convinced he would ever find himself in, but at least reassured him that the man didn't still think he should be turned out into the street.

Mrs McAvey-no-longer pushed plates of cake his way whenever she noticed him and sometimes absently patted his head, and he much preferred her distracted fondness than the lancing nature of her full attention.

He was still alone. He couldn't hear anyone coming. He took the opportunity to relax out of his current shape. Mr Oliver and Kit Whitely had been right: it took substantial Art to change shape, but only a little to maintain a shape.

He was careful, though, to not relax all the way. He thought he wore the form of his original self now, as strange and unfamiliar as it felt, its own shape altered without his intervention or volition whenever he returned to it, but he could not be as entirely sure as he wished to be. The grown-ups had their memories back, but he didn't. He had the vaguest impressions of steamy heat, of lugging weight, of other children.

The voice whispered in the back of his mind, *you are made of mud, you are made of mud*, and though Kit Whitely had been quite certain he wasn't, he still could not bring himself to entirely release the constant trickle of Art.

He was exhausted, and scared, and his head hurt, and his wrists itched, and he might be made of mud, and they had been so kind, and he was going to betray them.

25

ALL WAS QUIET BEYOND THE FIRMLY closed door as the afternoon crept into early evening; Bridget, as diffident as she was, had loyally held everyone at bay.

Despite Genevieve's fatigue, her mind would not settle, circling and circling around the central truth that now consumed her. Having torn apart McAvey's room to no avail, she passed through the paired dressing rooms into her own chamber.

Bridget had been in to turn down the sheets but had left the room dim, pale walls grey in the gloom. Genevieve uncurled her hand from the fist it persisted in making and flared up a small flame to light her way through a space that this morning had felt familiar and cosy, and now felt invaded.

She could feel the heat of her Art fire, adding to the stuffy warmth of the room. Knowledge arrived fully formed in her mind. She took the heat away from the flame, leaving only the light. Despite her state, she felt an echo of pleasure. All those years of discipline and practice were coming back to her with her memories, skills of Artistry merely forgotten, not lost.

She went to her dressing table. Her last and flickering hope was that McAvey had never laid hands on her rings at all, that they had stayed, unrecognised, as part of her own possessions after he'd usurped Oliver's place. She might not have resumed wearing them yet, after the stillbirth, if she'd still been tender and swollen. She might have been wearing them on a chain about her neck instead. She might have been able to save them, before the embedded Art took her.

She set her light to float by her shoulder – another trick it distantly satisfied her to remember she could do – and opened her jewellery box, running fingertips over the rings there. Gold and gems gleamed at her, but she found no copper-inlaid wedding ring, no faddish acrostic ring.

A single thought and a concentrated burst of flame consigned her false wedding ring to the same fate as McAvey's. She threw the little gold nugget into the fireplace; if Bridget raked it from the ashes, she could keep it.

Her gaze stubbornly skated over the neatly-made bed where a thief and worse, far worse, had conceived an illicit child upon her. She stared at the great ballast of her stomach with a murky, dismal regard.

Perhaps some part of her had known. Perhaps that was why she'd refused to give thought to the child growing within her. Reuben McAvey's child, treacherously planted within her incompetent womb during the cold months of a stolen marriage.

She firmly reminded herself that other women, less privileged than her, suffered through far worse than finding out the man they had consented to lie with had tricked them. At least her affront lay only in a change of circumstances, transforming a few unpleasant occasions that she already avoided dwelling on into something she need not think of at all. The consequence was the important thing, not…not…

She felt his limp weight on her, his panting breath in her ear, her own passive, dutiful acquiescence. A sound came out between her teeth. 'No,' she said, and the bonfire flared high in her mind.

There came a tap-tap, jolting her. She exhaled, willing herself to calm. She supposed Cecelia had noticed her light, leaking out onto the hallway runner through the crack under the door, and was coming to fuss over her again.

The softly insistent tap-tap came again. Her throat filled with bile.

But when she opened the door to politely dissuade her friend, Oliver stood there in his shirt sleeves, filling the entire doorway with his breadth and yet ducking his head, shamefaced. In the light floating by her shoulder, he looked at her in deep silence.

Oh. She was beyond startled. It seemed unlike him.

They had made love during her previous pregnancies, of course, except her last one, when she had been so determined to follow every stricture laid down by the authorial experts. Prior to that, Oliver had known, among his kinfolk, too many perfectly easy births and healthy babies to put any credence in doctors' warnings to better classes than his, and Mrs Murphy was happy to reassure Genevieve on that front too. Which was all to the good: she had felt insatiable at times during the natural progression. But they'd left well enough alone as confinement approached.

She supposed, grimly, that this was to be expected. He needed to reclaim her as his wife. She was abruptly aware of how exhausted she was, how heavy in her body. Her lower back and legs ached. Her throat burned with acid. She was wearing the gloomy garb of a widow.

She said, 'Come in.'

'I don't wish to disturb you,' Oliver started, before his ears caught up to her soft words. He looked surprised. 'Into your bedroom?'

Coldly, she said, 'Shall we go to yours, then?' as she turned towards the closed door further along the hallway.

'That's not my room,' he said flatly, before taking a slow breath, spinning up calm in exactly the same way he might have spun up a ward. 'I thought, the drawing room? If you don't mind the stairs one more time today.'

Genevieve raised her eyebrows in a frostily arch riposte. 'It's the *stairs* that concern you about this situation?'

'Everything concerns me about this situation, Gin,' he said. 'But you're entirely right, we don't have to talk about it now. I'll wait until you're ready.'

He smiled at her as he turned away, his oh-so-familiar crooked little smile, and her icy anger shattered under the gently implacable force of it. She'd been judging Oliver by the rules of a man who was a villain and the habits of a marriage that had been illusory.

He still felt like not-her-husband, but she remembered now he was her friend, and an honourable man.

She gave a shaky laugh. 'Sorry. Let's…let's go talk downstairs.'

She held out her arm, and he took it. Her tiny fireball bobbed behind them as he escorted her along the hallway, casting long shadows before them. It was not at all a late hour, but the house was still and quiet, lights extinguished and shutters closed. Fletcher must have gone home, Cecelia upstairs with Mass.

Oliver's face was sombre; she knew he'd worked out her misunderstanding. It still took him the entire flight of stairs before he said, 'He claimed the marital prerogative quite often, then.'

If he wasn't going to shy from it, neither was she. 'Often enough to train me to it, plainly.'

No wonder the familiar tap-tap, soft and insistent, had made her want to vomit. Her body had known before her conscious mind did.

Oliver didn't say anything, but her fingers were resting on his thinly-clad arm. She felt the tension in his forearm like the taut lines of a rigged ship under storm wind.

The steady tick of the ornate clock on the drawing room mantle greeted them. Oliver lit the lamp so she could release her nightlight, and then guided her to sit on the sofa. He took the armchair. He was so far away. She had enough recovered memories of her true marriage to know he would once have sat right beside her, his thigh touching hers.

As she sat, the baby gave a hard kick, just in case she could have forgotten its presence. She huffed and pressed her hand over her rounded stomach, cupping the unsettling bulge. If she'd not been dressed, she might have seen the clear outline of a tiny foot.

'Is she kicking?' Oliver asked, smiling a little. He moved to sit by her, hand hovering over hers where she cradled herself. 'May I?'

For a moment she was shocked; then she remembered he was her husband, and he had liked to do this during the two other times her womb had managed to cling on to a quickened life.

She said, 'You may do as you like.'

It came out more bitterly than she had truly meant it to, though she could not deny she had intended some acerbity in the barb. The nascent pleasure in his face died, and he sat back.

Abashed, she took his hand and pressed it over her belly where the baby made itself known. It seemed to respond, kicking a drumbeat against his hand rapidly enough to leave her breathless.

'It can't be yours,' she said with the last of her air. 'There is *no chance* this child is yours.'

'I know, Gin.'

'I have been turning it over and over in my head and it could not have been conceived until some weeks into the false marriage.' Her eyes were filling with tears; he was a bulky blur beside her. 'I'm so sorry.'

'Never apologise to me,' he said, almost before she had the words out. 'Never.'

McAvey had tricked her into doing the worst possible thing she could do to her husband, taking her sense of duty and twisting it into betrayal.

She began to cry in earnest. Oliver's weight creaked the sofa and his arms came around her. Though it still felt strange to be held by him, she turned her face into his shoulder and managed to gasp out something of her distress.

'Oh, love. You're finally crying, and it's over the wrong thing,' Oliver said. 'That's the one part of this confounded mess that doesn't bother me.' He spread one large hand over her stomach, again surprising her with the intimacy before she again recalled she had been naked in front of this man hundreds of times. 'So she's my child in name, not nature. She's still my child to raise.'

She wiped at her eyes. She felt pathetic. She fidgeted enough that he unslung his arm from around her, leaving her bereft and unable to admit it.

'I do not yet know what I wish to do with this child,' she said. 'Conceived in such a horrid way. I do not know if I can love it. I don't even know if I can bear to *look* at it when it comes into the world.'

He was silent, one of his slow, thoughtful pauses. At last, he said, 'Oh well. A child of two Artisan parents will be in great demand at a baby farm.'

She started up in high dudgeon, both arms wrapping possessively around the baby nestled within. 'Don't you dare—' she started and then caught his tiny smile. 'That was unfair, Oliver!'

'Sorry,' he said, reaching to lay a hand over her knee before clenching it back to himself. 'And please, allow me to apologise for being cavalier. I don't care about her natural father, because I care only for her mother, but of course her paternity looms large for you. I won't tell you that it shouldn't. I won't deny the circumstances are awful.'

She baulked. 'Not nearly as awful as for other women. Cecelia…'

Cecelia, with her own experience. Cecelia, at the courts, braving other women's experiences, to ensure they had their chance at justice.

'Please don't do that, Gin. Cecelia would be the first to commiserate with you, if you would allow it.'

Genevieve wiped her face again, stiffening her spine. 'We were speaking of the baby?'

Oliver regarded her. They had, she thought as she met the weight of that sombre, sympathetic gaze, been married for fifteen years. He knew her. He knew her coping techniques. He knew when she could be pushed – and when she shouldn't be.

After a moment, he nodded slowly. 'I need you to know I intend to be father to this child, come what may. That's my choice. Whether that care is within your household, or somewhere safely fostered out of your sight so you never need think of this—' He paused, delicately, before sighing and deciding on the innocuous. '—matter again, that is *your* choice. I will support your choice, and your child, and you.' Now he hesitated. 'If that is what you want.'

She looked up at him questioningly.

'It's not escaped my notice that you are angry with me,' he went on.

'I'm not,' she insisted. 'None of you chose to give up your Art to McAvey to wield as he did.'

'Not that,' he said. 'Yes, that, but no. Me. I failed you, Gin.' He paused, gathering his thoughts, which were no doubt racing despite his usual placid demeanour. Every inch of her was taut to make the rebuttal, but she gave him the courtesy of waiting for his full argument, as he so often did for her. 'After we lost our son, last summer. You turned to those books, reading them over and over while you were lying in. I didn't… I thought you were finding comfort, but you weren't, were you? You were letting them blame you. And I turned away and I let you let them.'

'You were grieving as much as I was, Oliver.'

'I let a distance grow between us. Did you think I blamed you, too?'

'No,' she said immediately, but then she paused, biting her lip.

'You did.' He hunched over, touching his fingers to his forehead briefly. 'I cannot tell you how bitterly I regret ever allowing my behaviour to convince you of that.'

Genevieve shook her head. 'I didn't believe it, then. But—' Her hands found the tassels on her wrapper and began to knot into them. 'I think I learned to think that, during…when…'

'When you believed yourself married to him.'

'Because he was so different to the way I remembered him being before.' Because he *had* been different, a completely different man, ripping bright patches from a perfectly well-made quilt and replacing them with raggedy scraps made of deception and fakery and spite. 'I thought it was grief. And I thought, he treated me with such disdain sometimes, that he must hate me, for failing, for failing…'

She'd begun to cry again. She had her hands clasped tightly together, not daring to touch Oliver or the sofa – she thought it would *scorch*. Oliver gathered her unhesitatingly into his arms, tucking her against him so that he cradled her and her rounded stomach. She could no longer fight it off; sobs tore from her throat, wracking her whole body. She was helpless to stop. Oliver rocked her, stroking her hair, murmuring soothing words. Again, the oddness of his touch and the rightness of it warred within her.

She couldn't touch him, for fear of scolding him. But as the storm began to recede, leaving her limp, calmer in a wrung-out sort of way, he gently wriggled his fingers between her clenched-together hands.

His fingertips ran over her palms. 'Not burning, my love.'

'I never know, these days,' she said wearily. 'Whether it's my situation—' She indicated her stomach. '—or *our* situation, I feel somewhat out of control.'

'To be expected,' he said. 'Note, however, that I don't think you are truly out of control. I think you merely feel that way. I'm not tempted to put up wards against you.'

'On your head if I burn our home down, then.'

She won his fond and crooked smile. 'You can burn this house to the ground for all I care,' he told her. 'I'll be sorting an arrangement with Kingsford about the Belgravia house. *That's* our home, if anywhere is.'

She squeezed his fingers, finding herself able to smile too – the thought of going back to the Locke townhouse, its small, dark rooms and old-fashioned layout, had lifted her spirits. Oliver was right: she had never stopped thinking of it as home. She found herself longing for it, an instinct for safety and familiarity that near overpowered her rationality. She knew this feeling, too, an animal desire for a nest. She just hadn't experienced it yet with this child, their cuckoo.

No wonder she'd kept wanting to make excursions from home so close to confinement. This wasn't her home.

Oliver gained her attention back with a quiet clearing of his throat. 'Gin, I wanted to talk to you now because we need a private and uninterrupted conversation.'

It was true that they were unlikely to have that opportunity again in the next few days. He seemed lost, however, when she lifted her gaze to his and waited. He eventually managed a smile, reaching a hand as if he would touch her cheek.

Genevieve didn't flinch, she was sure she didn't. But he pulled his hand away and rubbed his face tiredly.

'This is a nightmare,' he said. 'You're looking at me like you used to look at him when you knew he was about to say something you didn't like, and you were going to sit there and put up with it because he was your husband and you had to.'

'Oh,' she said. 'Was it particularly obvious when I was doing that?'

Oliver grimaced. 'Possibly only to me,' he said. 'I spent so many years in love with you—'

Her lips parted; she must have made a small sound, for Oliver paused, and eyed her. Dryly, he said, 'I can say that now—'

'Because we're married,' she finished for him, almost smiling.

'Because we're married,' he agreed. 'Unless you find it overfond?'

'Not at all,' she said. 'Might I say, in return, that I have always found your voice unfairly attractive, and have for a solid decade and a half.'

His answering smile did not last long. 'It's like a cursed wish from a fairy tale.' He set his fingers to his temples again, that brief telling gesture of distress. 'I still remember quietly loving my married friend, who I had no right to pine over like a lovesick fool. And wanting so much for her to, I don't know, see me. Not forsake her vows. Just to *see* me.' He dropped his hands into his lap, and turned to face her, expression sombre. 'I felt so guilty when he deserted you. I felt like I'd wished it on you, with the force of my longing. And even though I knew anything between us would be impossible, I still wanted more. That perhaps one day you might turn to me as more than a friend. One day you might love me, as I'd loved you for all those years. And to have such an ignoble wish come true like *this*.'

'But none of that happened,' she said. 'You were never pining over me at all. Reu— McAvey put a *memory* of pining in your head. Probably solely to torment you.'

'I don't think he could change feelings,' Oliver said. 'I imagine he'd've enjoyed leaving my feelings for you intact, either way. But I don't think our combined Arts let him manipulate them, otherwise he would have absolutely revelled in making Cecelia and the twins adore him. Given our respective Arts at his disposal, he could only change our memories. My feeling of pining arose naturally from the intact memory of loving you, without being allowed to show it.'

Genevieve had slowly stiffened all over as he spoke. She felt like she had a fever in all of her joints. 'Don't say that.' To his querying look, she whispered, 'I remember genuinely loving him as my husband, Oliver. Don't tell me that feeling was real.'

'I would rather it was,' he said. 'I would so much rather you truly loved him, Gin. Even if that means you still do.'

She shook her head. Tears were threatening again, but she'd had enough of crying. She forced herself to take on her defensive coldness. 'Explain that, please.'

'If he'd used the embedded Art to outright steal your love and every moment you spent with him was forced and some part of you was in there screaming and unable to escape… I don't want that to be something you have to bear. But it didn't have that power. It confused our memories, and coerced us into not ever wondering why. The closer to you, to the clockwork Art, physically, the stronger the effect. And you were wearing it. It must have been outstandingly strong for you. He stole your memories away, so that you could make your choice over again, and this time you chose him. At least it was a choice.'

She felt a sudden sense of disquiet, inflamed by this notion of choice. She wanted to shove the idea away with both hands.

'It wouldn't have been a choice,' she insisted sharply, 'because I wouldn't truly be choosing him, merely the false self he presented to me. And… God in heaven, I would rather believe he compelled me than to think I willingly chose an evil man. What kind of a woman would that make me?'

'A woman who mistakenly trusted the man she loved.' Oliver sounded very bleak.

She shuddered. 'It's not what happened, Oliver. Yes, he stole my memories, and he kept the ones that he couldn't twist into his narrative. But for the rest, all the rest, from the moment we told my father we wanted to marry, he fed those ones back to me. With *him* in them, instead of you. He pretended he was you. And that's what I loved. The memory of who he used to be, before we lost our son. I thought his grief had changed him. You. But I still loved him, because he was my husband. I love my husband, so I loved him. It was circular.'

Oliver took a heaving breath. She could feel the tension ratcheting through his body where he pressed against her, where they sat together as closely as they always had since the first days of their marriage.

'I'm sorry,' she said. 'I know you didn't want to have to know that. It's better to be honest, I think.'

'Please don't apologise, Gin.'

'I have to. Because I'd rather pretend *you* are the most injured party in this horrid mess, than have to accept it's me.'

He was silent, his face turned down. 'Fair, for now,' he said at last. 'But no more apologies. And now, I have to say what I actually brought you down here to say.' He took her hand, a gentle, familiar gesture which brought her close to tears again. 'Know that I am here for you in whatever capacity you need. I will be father to your child, nothing will change that, but…' He closed his eyes briefly. 'But I do not have to be your husband, if that is no longer what you wish.'

She could barely breathe. 'What are you saying?'

'Divorce is a little easier now,' he said. 'I'll have to take the adultery charge, of course, but if you can avoid an accusation of cruelty, I'd appreciate it. Not that the other grounds are much better…though Alex might barely need pressing to testify for—'

She tried to stand up, but found herself too tangled in his arms. 'Stop. No, I do not want a divorce, Oliver, what are you thinking?'

'That's your sense of propriety speaking.' When she started to protest again, he said, 'You don't love me.'

She froze. 'I—'

'You don't, Gin. I remember what being loved by you feels like. It feels like…' He half-laughed. 'Not to act the terrible cliché, but it damn well feels like being on fire. You don't love me.'

His gaze was steady, but she heard the thread of pain in his voice. 'I love my husband,' she repeated, sounding almost angry about it.

'I'm not him to you.'

'Neither's McAvey.' She made herself sit up straight, despite the ache in her back, the ache in her chest.

'No, I didn't think that,' he said. 'But… Confound it, this is hard.' He hunched over again, almost but not quite dropping his head into his hands. To himself, he murmured, 'I just have to say it.'

'Say it, then.'

'Gin, you didn't love me even before McAvey did this to us.'

'That's not true,' she said despairingly, her stomach roiling.

'After we lost our boy, we turned from each other, and I knew it then, that you no longer loved me. *That's* why you felt me withdraw. That's how I failed you.'

It struck her full then, the cause of her disquiet when Oliver had hoped she'd had a choice: Reuben McAvey had been able to get that cursed necklace onto her.

He had somehow put a necklace around the neck of a married woman. Had he presented her with it, an utterly inappropriate gift? Had she *accepted* it? Had she willingly worn jewellery given to her by another man, flattered by the attention, assuming Oliver, in his withdrawal, wouldn't notice?

Had she bowed her head and let him fasten the clasp, let him touch her bare nape with his bare fingers, let them brush her decolletage as he adjusted the sit of the dark gemstone against her skin?

By God, had she taken off the chain holding her rings to let him do it?

Was Oliver right? Had the loss of their son finally been too bitter a blow for their marriage to survive? Had she been so disillusioned by her quiet husband whose strength had not been enough to save their son, or to drag her from her own morass, that she had responded to the flirtations of another man, opening herself to his trap?

She closed her eyes and desperately tried to locate a real memory from those dismal days, trying to pin down the exact moment McAvey had displaced Oliver, trying to discover if she'd accepted that necklace from his hand.

She knew – she shuddered to know – the night her husband had tapped on her door for the first time since the stillbirth. That had been McAvey.

Because if Oliver had thought she didn't love him anymore, he *never* would have come to her. He'd have, eventually, done exactly what he was doing now, brought her down to the drawing room – to the family parlour, back at Belgravia – and offered her both unconditional support and unconditional freedom, no matter the cost to his reputation or wellbeing.

She put her hand over her mouth, fighting nausea. She'd *enjoyed* that night, or at least, she'd enjoyed her husband's passion, which had dwindled over the many years of their marriage, amid their losses. She'd appreciated being wanted in a way she hadn't felt wanted for quite some time. She wanted to scrub until her skin came off.

Was Oliver right?

'I love my husband,' she said, to herself, reminding herself: those feelings of enjoyment and pleasure, appreciation and gratitude, had been for her *husband*. She'd felt those feelings precisely because she loved her *husband* and had been so glad he had broken their ice to come to her.

'You've convinced yourself you *should* love your husband,' Oliver said. 'That's different. And it no longer has to follow, one from the other, with the new divorce laws.'

'I don't want a divorce, Oliver.'

'Why not?' he said, with such sudden vehemence that she recoiled as if from the sudden, slow but certain, eruption of a volcano. 'Holy *God*, Gin, *I failed you*. I saw your pain and I turned away from it out of selfish fear that you'd reject me. I was a worse coward even than when you first told me you loved me and I turned you down.'

'And I almost conflagrated over it,' she said, not sure if the lump in her throat was laughter or terror, clinging to the clear, painting-induced memory. 'Spoilt brat that I was.'

'And I made you wait months to prove you really loved me,' he said. 'Coward that I was. And when I saw I'd lost that love, as I always knew—'

'Don't you *dare*,' Genevieve snapped. 'You were always worthy of my love, Oliver, our respective fortunes never had anything to do with that. You haven't failed me, and our marriage won't fail either.'

'The marriage was blighted from the start,' he said. 'Mésalliance. I couldn't give you a healthy child.'

Genevieve spat in blind outrage, 'Good Lord, Oliver, pray you are correct that I have more control than I feel like I do.'

She looked down at her hands, set white-knuckled on the sofa's smooth upholstery. The material, to her surprise, was not smouldering. He thought the marriage was a mistake. It was simple. It was devastating. She took a few moments to breathe, carefully lifting her palms. There weren't even scorch marks to mar the pretty cream stripes.

Her pause gave space to Oliver too, to regain his own calm, so very rarely sundered. 'Didn't it ever cross your mind?' he asked after a time.

'Never. I only ever looked to myself for the explanation. I didn't blame our very union.' Her voice almost broke on the last words.

'You never blamed me?'

At this, her injury lessened. She understood what he was really saying, snatching all the blame onto his own side, as she had done on hers.

She caught his hand, insistent. 'As you never blamed me!'

Despite herself, despite how raggedly broken she felt, raw edges rubbing together inside her, Genevieve began to laugh. Slowly, clumsily, she quoted Oliver back another painting-gifted memory. 'I do not have the sense you are judging me. Why, then, should you assume I judge you?'

It took him a little time to recognise it; then his crooked smile appeared.

It gave her the courage to say, 'If you want the divorce for your own sake—'

'*No*. I merely don't want the woman I love locked into a marriage that cannot give her what she needs.'

She wiped her eyes, dashing away more infuriating tears. 'This is ridiculous,' she announced. 'We're in a merry little footrace to martyr ourselves for each other.'

'Seems that way.' He'd put his arm around her again, and at last it began to feel natural. He wasn't her husband, not yet, but he was, had always been, her friend.

'That little shit Whitely can manage a marriage of a sort, why can't we two perfectly sensible people?'

Oliver gave his growly chuckle, low and warm. 'Whitely is not the type to let go. And Alex is not the type to give up. So that pair can manage it, and not even notice for the bickering. Not everyone can.' He turned to look at her fully, and spoke with deep sincerity. 'It's all right, to not love me anymore. We were married for a long, long time. Sometimes that happens, that love doesn't last. We'll always be friends. I'll always be here for you and for our child. But I'm strong enough to let you go. And you're brave enough to accept when you should give up. And that's all right, Gin. It's all right.'

This final, urgent, reassurance was because the tears were coming fast again. Turning her face into his shoulder, she stopped them by force of will; if the heat boiling within her was good for anything, it was drying pointless tears.

'I will not accept it,' she said. 'I love my husband, and always have. You must simply give me more time to remember properly who that is. I know that's not wonderful for you.'

'It's fine,' Oliver said gravely. 'I'm sure it wasn't wonderful for you when I made you give me more time because I didn't trust you truly wanted to marry me.'

Genevieve snorted. This was her friend, even before he'd been her husband: she knew him. 'You still can't quite believe you did that, can you?'

'I cannot,' he agreed, smiling at her. 'In retrospect. In fact, I want to shake my younger self till his teeth rattle.'

'I'd quite like to slap *my* younger self,' Genevieve said.

He tightened the arm around her shoulders, snuggling her closer into his safe, strong embrace. 'My love. You were always wonderful. I turned down a beautiful, accomplished Artisan I was already in love with, like a complete and utter pillock, from stupid, cowardly, fear. You accepted it with more good grace than anyone would have any right to expect. I can only do the same.'

'Oliver,' Genevieve said. 'If the situations are truly analogous…you're implying I'm the one being the pillock now.'

It took a heartbeat of dead silence before he said, 'Shit!' and she laughed aloud, because it was so very rare for him to trip over himself like that.

She cupped a hand over his cheekbone, pressing her thumb against the crease at the edge of his lips. The affectionate touch should have felt familiar; it felt daring, though not in a bad way.

'I promise not to make you wait all the way till Christmas, Oliver.' She paused. 'Did I call you Oliver? Or William? Cecelia calls you Will when she's teasing you, but I don't think I ever did.'

'Always Oliver, to you,' he said.

For a moment she was puzzled by his dotingly fond tone; everyone called him Oliver, it hardly made for a special pet name from his wife. Then she understood. She had been the *first* to call him Mr Oliver. She'd been the first to insist he was an Artisan, and not let him brush his own strengths away as if they were nothing. She had been the first to give him permission.

She still rested against his broad strength, without enough strength of her own to abandon the warm support of the man who had always been her loyal friend and admirer.

She felt his hand gliding over her hair, tender. 'Oh, love, you're exhausted. I shouldn't have insisted on talking all this out tonight. Time enough after the baby comes. And after we've dealt with McAvey.'

She smiled, but it felt precarious. 'How are we dealing with him?'

So softly that she could barely hear him, Oliver said, 'I'm going to kill him, Gin.'

26

IT WAS, REMARKABLY, EARLY ENOUGH THAT the mail receiving house was still open. Before she retreated upstairs to face her bed, Genevieve sent a second note to Lulu, even shorter than the first missive on whose veritable heels it followed.

Four simple words flying across the miles between them by the night train.

Was it worth it?

Lulu would know what she meant.

27

In the morning, Genevieve, calmer, wrote yet another note to Lulu, this time to accompany two clearly labelled packets.

One held clockwork bits from the lock on the box Mass had been delivered in, the other the tiny wires and cogs that had spilled from the pendant when Oliver had stomped on it, which Fletcher had carefully collected from the floor of the storage room. She slipped the pendant itself off the thin gold chain she'd worn for all those months, and put it in, too. The bent clasps still held the central sardonyx securely, though its smooth faceting was cracked now.

She was sending the packets onto Lulu solely because her cousin had to be made useful to guarantee her ongoing safe absence from London, out of McAvey's pettily vengeful reach. Even if the broken necklace somehow held a solid enough connection for her talent to engage, it would likely lead back to an anonymous jeweller's, or to the clockwork shop, exactly as the broken bits from the box lock would.

That clockwork shop, the jolly proprietor with his secret ledger below the counter, was their one link to McAvey now, and they did not need a tracking talent to tell them so, because their burgeoning memories supplied that information readily enough.

'Reuben took me there,' Cecelia said slowly. 'McAvey.'

She was perched uneasily on one of the uncomfortable chairs in the drawing room. They'd gathered there without Mass, their probable spy. He'd remained upstairs, Bridget watching over him as she went about her morning chores in the bedrooms.

The enterprising girl had gone up to the attic and managed to unearth a trunk of Genevieve's dresses from the previous summer, still enlarged with extra panels to accommodate a growing figure. With no time for adjustments, the cut and colour were not quite the thing anymore. They were still a far sight better than continuing to sport the colours of an empty graveside when not only was her husband not dead, he wasn't even her husband.

Bridget had also apologetically delivered her mistress a milky posset she'd prepared herself, because Cook, upon discovering the news, had declined to step foot into the house of a fallen woman who'd openly cavorted. Genevieve had poked at the bland pudding with her spoon until it was time to emerge downstairs.

Now she took a sip of thankfully decent tea and nodded to Cecelia in mute encouragement.

Cecelia continued, 'Last July. I encountered him at the apothecary's when I was visiting the Missus Murphys. It seemed a chance meeting. We had been on friendly terms.'

'Didn't we… Is my memory correct that we brought him in…' Genevieve carefully set down her teacup before she spilt hot tea into her lap. She balled her fists, willing away an incipient tremor. 'In advance of my first confinement and lying-in. Because we needed a temporary weapons Artisan to manage the sort of enforcement contracts the Society was already sending our way.'

'And because…' Cecelia's mouth twisted; an unfamiliar bitterness made her gentle face harshly stark. 'We wanted to build bridges with his faction. For unity as we moved ever closer to forming the Agency.'

'We asked him to step in every now and again after that,' Oliver said.

Whenever Genevieve had caught pregnant, he meant. Whenever she'd withdrawn from Myriad work in a futile attempt to cajole her womb into competence.

He'd given her a long look when she'd walked into the drawing room this morning wearing striped skirts of cream and royal blue. She'd assumed he'd be pleased to see her put aside mourning worn in remembrance of another man, but instead his expression had remained studiously neutral.

Here was another husband she was failing to please, she supposed. Her fingernails dug into her palms as her fists balled tighter. She made herself unroll her fingers, and stroked the smooth silk cladding her belly. She knew she was not being fair, that she was still veering into the glassy state of yesterday afternoon, cold and hard but so fragile as to shatter at a tap.

She made herself focus, frowning as she tried to force the shape of the previous year to shimmer into clarity. 'And so, last year. I was trying to protect the baby from the very moment I suspected his presence. I didn't want to use Art at all. So McAvey must have been working with you on all our contracts by the new year at least.'

'He was always very respectful,' Fletcher said. 'He never argued, not even with Cecelia.'

Cecelia winced. 'That was our first clue.'

'He was playing a very long game,' Genevieve said, managing a more diplomatic response than the snarl she'd had to bite down on.

'He waited for a rift to form between us,' Oliver said frankly. He met her eye. *Gin, you didn't love me even before McAvey did this to us.* The echo of his calm diagnosis the night before would have been painful enough, but Oliver didn't shy from his next pronouncement either. 'And for your mother to pass.'

Genevieve closed her eyes. She now understood his stubbornly blank expression when he saw she'd put aside mourning clothes. He thought it meant she was still trapped in the delusion that Mother was still alive, held captive but somehow miraculously unharmed.

And some small part of her did cling to it, because she so very desperately wanted and needed her mother.

But she could feel, as Cecelia had said she would, more memories emerging from the murk. Her mother had been there before she went into the chloroform twilight. She was sure of that, and the colours of last summer's dresses implied her confidence was warranted, because they weren't mourning colours.

She could not yet remember properly if Mother had been there to comfort her on the other side of the twilight, when she'd woken to the news, when she and Oliver had turned from each other in their silent, separate sorrow. She did now know, in the detached way she knew family stories that had happened when she was too young to truly remember the events for herself, that Antoinette had been struck down very suddenly by a hectic fever.

Genevieve knew she had not a chance to say goodbye, nor attend the funeral. Perhaps because she had still been lying in, weak and drained from the stillbirth. Perhaps because, despite Oliver's notion that he'd waited for Genevieve's most stalwart protector to fall before acting, McAvey had taken his place by then, and had forbidden her out of sheer cruelty.

Either way, it had made it easier for her to pretend it had not happened. It made it harder now, as grief struck her a violent blow, the vital loss piling onto the loss of her child, her father, her first child.

She clung to a single small comfort. Her mother, in her hectic state, must have been full of hallucinations and strange fears, as was common in that sort of sickness. McAvey was already circling, sniffing out the crisis in the Locke household, acting oddly enough to niggle at the ever-observant artist and trigger an apt paranoia in her dying days. Or he'd already invaded, and the sudden fever had begun to burn away the necklace's fog, allowing suspicion to bubble.

Either way, Antoinette must have stolen from her sickbed to hide her personal paintings, tucking them away into that nondescript old crate. It was enough to ensure they were overlooked when McAvey got rid of the rest, the later ones that must have openly depicted Genevieve's engagement and marriage, and the course of her first maternal progression, all those quick sketches her mother would have made to celebrate her growing family.

Genevieve had known, even deep within the manipulation he'd subjected her to, that she would never sell paintings of the Locke family, never. McAvey might have, because genuine newly-discovered Antoinette Locke portraiture would have been worth more than a few pennies and he'd had prohibitively expensive embedded Art to fund. The risk, though, of her or a family friend coming across them, hung in a private home or a public gallery, would have been immensely high. She would have seen her love for another man glowing in the famously vibrant colours her mother was renowned for.

He would surely have destroyed them, ripped the canvases, cracked the frames, making very sure the remnants were worth only burning as waste. Her heart ached for the loss, even as she bowed her head and said a quiet prayer that her brave and determined mother had preserved the precious handful that had rescued them all.

Genevieve lifted her gaze and gave the room a vague nod, indicating she was strong enough to continue. Oliver had been reaching for her, she saw, and desisted at whatever he read in her expression. She wanted to reach for him in turn, recapture the comfort she had found in his presence the night before. She couldn't. He wasn't her husband yet.

'He was friendly,' Cecelia repeated. 'When I met him at Adler's. He asked after you, you and Oliver both, amid the expectation of happy news. He understood the implication when I said you were unwell. He was full of such sympathy.' She swallowed hard. 'He asked me to accompany him, to help him select an appropriate bouquet to send.'

Genevieve was helpless to stop her frustrated grimace. The very idea of McAvey requesting assistance of Cecelia, of all people, should have hoisted flags of warning in every direction. But she could not blame her friend. It would have been flattering to be asked to apply feminine expertise, especially by someone as generally supercilious as that man. She would have been taken in, too.

Face tight, Cecelia finished, 'He walked me into the clockwork shop on the excuse of running an errand first. The pendant was already on the counter. And that's the last memory I have inside that shop.'

'He caught me fairly well the same way,' Fletcher said. 'Except he said it was a new American custom to bring by a proper condolence gift, and took me into the shop to help me select an appropriate item. Probably after you, Cecelia, because I don't remember what happened once I was inside either.'

'I was first,' Cecelia said, voice low.

'No,' Oliver said. They all three turned to him. 'He had the news before he met you at Adler's, Cecelia. He approached me. Said he'd found an exceptional jeweller's, where I could find the perfect little token. I picked out the necklace. Dark striped sardonyx, less common than Whitby jet. A birthday gift, for my grieving wife.' He sat slumped, head lowered, broad shoulders bent. 'I picked out that fucking necklace for him.'

Genevieve truly did want to put her arm around Oliver in comfort. But the part of her flickering with outrage and overwhelming grief felt the urge to slap him for needing it. *She* didn't. She was going to stiffen her lip and march on through this until it was done, and collapse into needy emotion afterwards.

'How, then,' she said coolly, 'did it come to the clockwork shop?'

'Engraving,' he said flatly, nodding to her as if he'd read her thoughts. He'd soldier on too, then. 'He had me leave it there for engraving. More reliable than the jeweller's. Some fancy new modern technique. Whatever that clockwork Artisan is, he built a trap for embedded Art around the pendant.'

Cecelia counted on a finger. 'First, my memory Art, caught within the necklace and turned back on me on the instant.'

Fletcher held up two fingers. 'Second, my compulsion Art, embedded over the top to force our attention away from the lost and changed memories that we'd soon all be experiencing. Used on me before I departed the shop.'

Solemnly, Oliver, left-handed, raised his three middle fingers. Bare. He hadn't found his own wedding ring either. It had probably been melted down with her two. 'And used on me when I returned to collect the necklace. My warding Art, stolen, embedded. Twisted backwards to make the other two Arts radiate outwards, to any mind that came too close, that knew us too well.'

No wonder the clockwork had been so expensive. If it had not been used for such evil purposes, the intricate engineering skill involved would have been Great-Exhibition levels of impressive. The clockwork Artisan surely earned his outrageous fees.

And no wonder they'd struggled with their Arts. The silent, invisible drain into the necklace's embedded Artwork would have been exhausting for all three of them. They'd found even their everyday lives and usual routines a trial, the uncharacteristic decline in their spirits creeping over them more and more over the course of the year.

Her own troubles had arisen from grief, and the stinking heatwave, and her condition – and struggling to control a powerful, dangerous Art while holding no memory of the years of training and practice she'd put in, therefore holding no faith in herself.

McAvey must have been musing on such a trick for months, if not years, jealously judging and weighing his fellow Artisans' Arts, at the very least plotting how they could be best manipulated for his own advantage. Genevieve remembered, now, his occasional pointed jape towards upright Fletcher, of the if-I-had-your-Art variety. He had always kept a covetous eye on other Artistry. He must eventually have got wind of the illicit activities of the clockwork Artisan, and begun putting coin aside.

Then rumours of the copper knife began to circulate, a knife that might very well steal Art in an instant, a knife that the Agency would absolutely want safely under its own control, and would surely send the trustworthy and competent Myriad in pursuit of.

Perhaps this whole awful affair was not even as personal as it felt. Cecelia and Fletcher happened to have their useful, usable teamwork, Genevieve and Oliver happened to have an opposing useful, usable rift, her inherited wealth a decided boon to advance the plot most efficaciously.

Perhaps Reuben McAvey had gone to the time and effort and expense the clockwork required solely for his chance to steal a knife which would require none of that…if he could work out how to properly use it, which Varley had not.

His scheme might therefore have had nothing to do with his hatred towards her for daring to lower herself to marry Oliver, towards Cecelia for daring to be young and female and opinionated, towards Lulu merely for her own transgressive, defiant existence.

Even so, his hatred had certainly informed the way he'd treated all of them once he'd usurped control of the little foursome, the Agency's Myriad.

It had informed the way he'd used his marital rights.

The way he'd applied them, with such casual contempt. Putting her firmly in the constrained and lessened place he'd marked out for her in his sick little head.

Genevieve clapped her palms together, folding her fingers tight, feeling the pulse of heat run through her. The others flinched.

'Sorry,' she said. 'I'm in control. I also apologise for how I behaved yesterday. I am not angry with any of you.' She raised her brows imperiously to their sceptical expressions. 'We were all tricked, my friends.'

'I suppose he…' Fletcher suddenly looked very doubtful. '…gave you the necklace, Genevieve? As a…as a gift?' The implications had dawned on him mid-sentence; he both reddened and spluttered. 'Not to say, I do not mean, I would never—'

'I don't know how I came to wear the necklace,' Genevieve said.

After a silence, Oliver said, 'As you say, we were all tricked, one way or the other.'

Gin, you didn't love me even before McAvey did this to us. He suspected, as she suspected, as they all now suspected, that she'd accepted the necklace from McAvey's hands.

Genevieve bit her lip, deeply shamed. 'We were all tricked,' she made herself continue. 'But it took more than one bastard Artisan to do it. McAvey is currently out of our reach. Gatwick, the clockwork Artisan, is not.'

'You want to go back to the clockwork shop.' Oliver was looking sterner by the moment.

'We have egregious and habitual use of illicit Art to bring to the attention of the Agency.' She smiled. 'If we happen to winkle from him the location of one of his clients while we're about it…'

Oliver did not return her smile. 'Cecelia and Fletcher, then.'

'And me.'

He shook his head.

'I am your weapons Artisan, Oliver.'

'You are also imminently expectant, Genevieve.'

He was braced, stiff in his chair. He was waiting for her to toss the same flash-bomb as yesterday afternoon: *is that your husbandly decree, Oliver?* She paused, detachedly curious as to whether it would work again.

She didn't think it would. He withdrew from conflict, if he could. He wouldn't count this matter suitable for withdrawal. The way he'd braved the conversation in the drawing room the night before, faced his own failure to brave similar difficult conversations before the sundering in their marriage, told her to her face, very politely, that she was delusional if she thought her mother yet lived, suggested he might never consider a matter suitable for withdrawal again.

Regardless, last night's conversation had drawn her claws. Oliver might not feel like her husband, but he had always been her friend; McAvey hadn't been able to wipe every trace of those memories at least, as much as the fog had obfuscated them. He didn't deserve a repeat of the dirty trick.

Moderating her voice to be painstakingly gentle, she said, 'I know it makes you uncomfortable to think of me leaving the house so close to my time. But *I* am uncomfortable at the thought of you all going without me. We don't know what tricks Gatwick has up his sleeve, but we do know he has a shopfloor full of mechanical devices. My fire may be your only deterrent.'

'His box was impervious to your fire.'

'That may have been McAvey's precaution, not his.'

'Between my wards and Fletcher's compulsion…' Oliver began, shooting a look at Cecelia freighted with strong encouragement to volunteer to stay home with his wayward wife.

Cecelia said, 'Gin, perhaps you and I can keep an eye on Mass—'

'Will your wards stop an ice spear?' Genevieve demanded over the top of her. She tried to keep her tone calm, but the roil of bitterness inside her was simmering higher.

She swallowed: her friend, her friends, they were all her friends, none of them had betrayed her on purpose, none wished to thwart her now out of malice.

Oliver didn't answer the overly-sharp question. They all already knew his warding Art was thin and only weakly protective. He could, to use the old-fashioned phrase that the more scientific *embed* had replaced, lay charms to detect Artistry in the immediate vicinity. It was this effect that had been mutated by the clockwork Artistry. And he could spin a version of the warding out to slow down or weaken another's Artworks, without fully suppressing them. Like Fletcher's compulsion Art, it worked far better if he was able to touch his target.

It couldn't have stopped the earthworker Artisan. It couldn't stop an ice spear.

'Do you think McAvey might still be in London?' Fletcher asked. 'Watching us?'

Genevieve stroked her stomach, trying to make a very pointed gesture appear as absent-minded as it usually was.

Cecelia, unknowingly or obligingly, took her cue. 'Mr Whitely thought he might be interested in the baby.'

'No Art in babies,' Fletcher reminded them, in the aggrieved mutter the mention of Whitely tended to provoke.

Copious Art in me, Genevieve thought.

And if McAvey's whole plot had been centred on gaining a knife that could steal Art for his own ambitious aspirations, with revenge for a nursed multitude of perceived slights merely a substantial side-benefit, then which Art would he most covet? Not Oliver's medley collection. Not Cecelia's harmless memory Art, as horrendously useful as it had proven Not Mrs Murphy's Art, if she even had one; McAvey wouldn't want to *take* pain. Not Miss Adler's healing Art. Not even Fletcher's compulsion Art, not when he had to touch to bring its full force to bear, its verbal effects amounting to not much more than the temporarily persuasiveness of any decent orator.

There weren't even that many other weapons Artisans about. Art was rare, Art like Genevieve's rarer yet. The Agency enforcers, and the Myriad, and the Locke twins, had seen to it already that any Artisans both too powerful and too inclined to use that power were well-regulated. Their network would have warned them if McAvey had gone for one already.

No. If McAvey had come back to London, the mysterious box and his innocent young spy his opening salvo, the timing had less to do with Genevieve's imminent travail and more to do with what her imminent travail implied – vulnerability. He thought her condition made her weak. He might even believe her still ensnared in their false marriage, held fast by duty and coerced love, and thus unable to act against him.

She looked down at her hands, feeling the burn in her palms. He was in for somewhat of a surprise, in either case.

'I think we should stay together as much as possible,' she said at last. 'Your wards can give us warning, Oliver, and slow his Art down. But only I can give us true defence.'

In the end, they left Cecelia at home with Mass and Bridget, securely bolted and warded doors, and a judicious word to the neighbourhood constable on patrol. Genevieve, Oliver and Fletcher took a cab, quicker and more anonymous than summoning the carriage, over to the Artisan district.

Stiggins was there again, declaiming to the people prepared to venture out into the reeking air, as Oliver helped Genevieve disembark. Even he sounded low today, his words coming slow and heavy. Deuteronomy's fulminations against sorcery deserved to be thundered with old-testament fervour but not even the most enthusiastic of preachers could remain impervious to the endless days of heat and stink forever.

They ignored his desultory oration, hurrying straight into the clockwork shop, both men rather ridiculously trying to shelter Genevieve and her ballooning stomach. For herself, she carefully raised her Art in the opposite way to her little light the night before: solely heat now, the air shimmering with it, so any ice McAvey saw fit to toss their way from ambush would melt before it could touch them.

Their entry was again unmarked by any merry little tinkle of a bell on the door, but the jolly-looking clockwork Artisan was behind the counter and looked up with a pleasant expression as they filed into the aisle formed between the clockwork mechanisms displayed across the polished shopfront floor.

Gatwick took the merest glance at their faces – and at Genevieve's colourful dress – before raising some sort of contrivance from underneath the counter and saying, 'Turn about and leave.'

The compulsion-laced Art hit them fully and unexpectedly. All three of them had obediently turned before Oliver recovered a modicum of free will and spun out his warding Art. That gave Fletcher enough space to wrench off his gloves and raise his hands towards the clockwork Artisan.

He commanded, 'Put it down. Put your hands on the counter.'

He was definitely stronger than he had been, now his Art wasn't being secretly diverted into the pendant. But without touch, he could not compel, only *very strongly suggest*; it worked best with suggestible crowds who would follow each other, not a single strong-minded Artisan. Still, Gatwick dropped the device immediately, and his fingers and arms twitched and spasmed all the way to his shoulders as his hands tried to obey the command.

Then he snatched a second, much more recognisable item from underneath the countertop. A pistol.

He pointed it at them. If they'd not been accompanying a ponderously pregnant woman, the two men might have sought cover in the array of large clockworks on either side of the shop. As it was, they both tried to step in front of her at once.

'Don't move!' Gatwick snapped. 'And keep your mouth shut, puppet-master.'

Fletcher looked offended and put his hands on his hips, but, though Genevieve was sure it cost him dearly in willpower, he did obey. The pistol had proven more effective than more hijacked coercion Art, and was that not a potent signifier of the modern times they lived in.

Oliver raised his hands soothingly, palms out. 'We're here for information, no more.'

'I've nothing to say.' He gestured with the pistol, jerking the barrel at the door behind them. 'Out, before I set my Artworks on you.'

Genevieve stared at him past the shoulders of the men trying to shield her, hating his jolly round grandfatherly face. She should have kept to her mourning clothes. Perhaps then he would not have been so quick to realise his secret enterprise had finally been rumbled. Fletcher might have been able to approach the counter and get a hand on him.

Well. They were the Myriad, here to arrest an Artisan for the use of illicit Art. She had a certain role to fulfil there, element of surprise or no.

Genevieve swept her arms out, and flame rippled from her to blaze among the clockwork Artworks. But her fire danced over the wood and metal, refusing to catch. After a moment, she released her Art, and the flames went out immediately, leaving not so much as a scorch mark.

Gatwick laughed. 'Do you truly think I couldn't anticipate this? They're entirely proofed against your fire, pyro.'

Most of the clockworks on display were harmless enough, akin to the toy train he'd so mockingly sent them away with last time, differing only in purpose and scale. But in the corner, one of the largest began to creak and stir as it responded to its master's Art. It rolled menacingly towards them, a broad swath of metal with prongs and sharp spinning cogs.

Gatwick stepped backwards, steadily aiming the pistol their way. He was going to escape through the rear door while they fought off some sort of cog-endowed distraction. He shot them a last smirk.

This amoral piece of shit with his harmless aspect and jolly smile and twinkling eyes had sold McAvey the means to steal her memories and her life and her marriage and her autonomy and her very body, and he thought he was going to merrily walk away into a happy retirement, on wealth partly stolen from her own coffers, and never once have cause to regret it.

The bonfire in Genevieve's mind ignited.

'Are *you* proofed against fire?' she snarled. Shoving past Oliver and Fletcher by means of main force and belly, she raised burning palms and threw flame right at him.

She'd never deliberately directed her Art at a living being before.

The polished wood floor between her and the counter caught alight as the fireball roared bodily out from her. The clockwork Artisan screamed and dived behind the counter, which burst into flames. If he'd had the nerve to try to fire the pistol, the shot would have melted.

Genevieve marched forwards, impervious, her Art burning high and bright on the fuel of her fury. Oliver shouted from behind her, but he was no match for the flames.

The clockwork Artisan scuttled back as Genevieve came around the blistering inferno that had been the counter, but he had nowhere to go. The counter was ablaze. The floor to either side of them was a wall of flame to the ceiling. The doorway he'd been backing towards roared like the mouth of a furnace. The air itself was blistering his skin.

He raised the pistol in shaking hands, and Genevieve turned the metal white-hot on the instant. He threw it away a moment before its powder ignited, and raised trembling palms striped scarlet where he'd been touching it. She loomed over him, flames leaping from her fingers like gaslights turned far too high, making the air hiss and pop.

'Stop,' he begged, barely audible above the crackle of the flames. 'I don't know anything.'

Part of Genevieve knew she was behaving reprehensibly, and well beyond that, into the sort of Artistry that the government called the twins in against.

And part of her knew she would not be able to behave so for much longer. All Art was finite, no matter how strong an emotion might be lending it additional power, and Art poured out with such extravagance could not last.

Best get the job done, then.

She wrapped a hand around his throat. 'Where is he?'

'I don't know, I don't know,' he sobbed, clawing helplessly at the grip she had on him.

His skin was blackening under her hand. She could smell the sweet char of flesh. She would, she thought, shortly burn all the way through his skin to his oesophagus. He'd have to answer before she scalded the voice box right out of him.

He thrashed, and then let go of her wrist to punch at her belly. She screamed in rage, twisting her body away even as she tightened her grip and shot even more heat into her palm. He screamed back, voice curdling.

And then Oliver was pulling her away, shouting her name. In the same moment, her Art gave out and the fire roaring all about them went out in a blink. There came a last wave of superheated air before the stuffy but normal heat of summer pressed down.

Genevieve came back to herself.

The air was full of smoke and the reek of hot metal and burnt paint and oils. She'd been lucky, though, or more in control than she'd thought she was, because there were no ordinary flames catching and spreading, as could sometimes happen in the wake of an excess of her pyrokinesis. Perhaps her Art fire had burned so intensely, it had starved its mundane cousin of fuel.

Gatwick sobbed in wild and hysterical gulps on the floor, her handprint scorched in black and red onto his throat.

Oliver was panting beside the clockwork Gatwick had set on them. It had a spill of cogs and wires from a hatch in its chest. He'd ripped open its guts to deactivate it and then used it as a fireproof shield, in concert with his wards, to push his way through immense flames to her side. She could see burns and blisters on his face and hands.

'I'm sorry,' she said helplessly.

Her husband stared at her in bleak silence, before kneeling by the injured man. 'Where is he?' he asked.

Gatwick's voice was hoarse, a ruined whisper in the ruined workshop. 'I don't know, please. He never gave me a real name. He never told me an address. I don't ask – I never ask!'

Oliver stood. Fletcher was easing his head in through the door, looking very cowed. Oliver would have shoved him outside before risking his own life to reach his wife.

'Miss Adler, please,' Oliver told him. He looked at Genevieve's stomach, where she'd have bruises because a fellow human had lashed out in a desperate attempt to save his own life. 'Mrs Murphy. And Agency enforcers.'

Fletcher bustled to obey, no doubt relieved to have been set tasks to complete.

The counter – the secret ledger – was in ashes. In her uncontrolled rage, she'd destroyed the proof.

Oliver took that in before bending over the sobbing, choking Gatwick. 'You'll sign a confession.'

Upon a fervent gasp of agreement, Oliver stepped back and gave Genevieve a nod, exactly as he would have done at the successful conclusion of any of their Myriad contracts. She had to fight not to burst into tears.

It was almost an hour before they'd cleaned up enough of Genevieve's mess to be able to respectably retreat. Gatwick healed and arrested; Oliver healed; Genevieve checked over and thoroughly chastised and embraced by Mrs Murphy but not arrested. This last blessing was either because she was far too pregnant for the enforcers to stomach it, or Gatwick was far too terrified to manage a complaint.

Trouble might come later, in that regard, but Genevieve was too shaky and exhausted to worry just now.

Stiggins approached them as Fletcher went to flag a hansom.

'Not now,' Oliver growled.

The street preacher ignored him, leaning past his bulk to point a trembling hand at Genevieve. Even in her state, she started at the sight of his swollen fingers. They'd turned blue-black and sported glistening blisters.

Like leprosy, she thought, and found the energy to recoil.

He hissed, 'Five sixteen,' before Oliver gave him a most uncharacteristic shove and shouted for Fletcher.

Fletcher came to chivvy him away with a careful touch to the unmarked skin of his nape and a murmured command to march himself to the apothecary to beg help from Miss Adler.

Once in the cab and on the way home, Fletcher said, musingly, possibly only to break the heavy silence, 'The fifth commandment? Why did Stiggins feel it so urgent to remind you of honouring your parents? I doubt he wishes our days long and all to go well with us.'

And Genevieve realised Stiggins's fingers hadn't been black from leprosy, which did not manifest like that.

They'd been black from frostbite.

28

Lulu's answer was waiting when they got home. Though her head was pounding, her body heavy, Genevieve opened it and read it in the hallway.

It was one word, to her four.

Yes.

She wasn't going to let Oliver kill McAvey.

She knew what she was capable of now.

She was going to kill him herself.

29

SIR KINGSFORD HAD ALSO REPLIED. With his simple, awkward generosity, he gave Genevieve back the Locke townhouse.

It was always yours, he wrote.

Genevieve passed this silently to Oliver and took herself to bed for the afternoon before she broke down into tears of gratitude and relief in front of the others. She felt drained – *was*, in fact, drained – and aching all over, pain radiating from her lower back down both legs and from the back of her skull into both temples and neck.

She was, typical of the Artisan constitution, much improved when she awoke, and came downstairs to find none of the others about but a hearty meal of thick stew on offer in recompense. Bridget had done what Genevieve so desperately wanted to do, and called in her mother. This august personage had taken over the kitchen with ruthless efficiency, and emerged from her domain, iron grey hair tucked neatly under her mop cap, to meet the lady of the house and be sure she ate.

This proved slightly difficult, since the other occupants of the household had also been busy that afternoon. Fletcher had found definitive records in the opened safe, and so could aver that the house and carriage were on lease contracts, but the furniture was owned. And so he and Cecelia had sent every piece they reasonably could to consignment while Oliver and Mass brought all of Genevieve's mother's furniture out of storage and helped Bridget beat the dust out of every cushion and drape before bringing it inside.

Genevieve looked about at the miracle they'd wrought and had to fight not to cry for the third time in one day.

Their thoughtful industry meant the dining room was entirely empty, and she had to perch on her mother's sofa to eat her stew in the drawing room in a most unconventional manner. The old pieces did look shabby in this modern room, and couldn't begin to fill it. Most of the polished parquet floor was empty now. She saw that Fletcher had even had a workman in to remove the melted gold and scorches from the far end.

Genevieve scraped her bowl clean and then lay on the sofa like she'd done as a child and revelled in the shabbiness with furious pleasure.

She began to feel sleepy again, in a more natural way than the drained exhaustion that came with depleting her Art to its dregs. She might have dozed off, if Fletcher and Cecelia had not returned from the consignment office.

Fletcher made embarrassed ahems from the doorway. Genevieve sat up. 'I apologise for my lack of decorum,' she said dryly.

Fletcher grimaced as he followed Cecelia to settle in the old stuffed armchairs across from Genevieve. 'I know you think me a fusspot,' he began.

'Not at all,' Genevieve hastened to assure him. 'This—' She gestured about. 'Only you could have managed all this in a single afternoon, Fletcher. You have my gratitude.'

'It was Cecelia's idea,' he said, looking deeply mortified and deeply gratified.

'Oh, Oliver's,' Cecelia said, 'to be fair. I merely pointed out that Belgravia is somewhat more convenient for Mrs Murphy than Holland Park.' She gave a confidential nod towards Genevieve's mound of a belly, as if her meaning might have been unclear. 'If we can make shift within the next few days, that is.'

'Oliver's gone to see about opening the Locke townhouse, with Massimo,' Fletcher added. His face was still telegraphing discomfit. He harrumphed, mostly at himself. 'Might I beg permission to add myself to your lodgers, Genevieve? It seems safer than risking the journey to and fro from my own apartment, since we cannot know how wide McAvey will cast his stones.' His mouth twitched. 'Hailstones.'

'Of course, Fletcher, you are always welcome,' Genevieve said sincerely.

Cecelia, on the other hand, took the opportunity to twit him. 'Goodness, Fletcher, if you already had an eligible bride turning up her nose because you visited us, how ever will you find yourself a suitable helpmeet if it gets about that you cohabited with us?'

'As to that,' Fletcher said. 'I…' He wore a strange expression as he fidgeted in his chair. 'I have not been my best self this past year.'

Genevieve smiled at his prissy tone. 'I do not think any of us can venture to lay claim to that.'

'No. But, despite all, I feel a lifting of my spirits, now that the drain on my Art is gone.'

'I, also,' Cecelia said, nodding along. 'We have all been low, have we not?' Genevieve was silent. Cecelia winced. 'I do not mean to say that we do not feel the very great injury—'

'I know,' Genevieve said quickly. 'Go on, Fletcher. You have had some sort of revelation, it seems?'

'I no longer think I can quite go along with this notion that I should marry a near-stranger simply so I have what amounts to a live-in servant for less cost than hiring a staff, when I am perfectly well capable of shifting for myself.'

Cecelia clapped her hands, her delight burbling up as she recognised her own argument. 'Mr John Fletcher, you iconoclast.'

He smiled thinly to her teasing, but was painfully earnest as he went on, 'And I am troubled, also, by the notion of marrying a woman with no Art. What if something like this happens again?' He waved a hand about to denote the spectre of McAvey lurking about the street. 'She would have no means to defend herself. Worse…' Swallowing heavily, he muttered, 'She would have no means to defend herself against me.'

Genevieve felt her brows rise, and exchanged a surprised glance with Cecelia.

'This past year, I have become dreadfully complacent about using my compulsion Art. What if she thought I was doing it to her? What if…what if I *did* do it to her?' He turned to Genevieve. 'Did you see how quick I was to make Mr Stiggins march off to Miss Adler?'

Yes, she thought. *And* you *saw how quick* I *was to turn my Art on another living being.*

She should have been heavy with guilt; part of her was. But she couldn't let that part of her win out until she'd taken vengeance on McAvey.

Fletcher at least had the excuse of aiding the frostbitten street preacher, and Genevieve said as much. Cecelia added, 'And I believe you are too upstanding to use your Art in such a disreputable manner, my old friend. Do not give up on a happy home quite yet.'

'I am not declaring I will *never* marry,' he said, blushing a little. 'I shall…leave myself open to the vagaries of love. Cecelia—'

'I am flattered, but I must decline,' Cecelia said promptly, and then burst into laughter as Fletcher immediately descended into a flurry of disavowal, until she was moved to say, 'I'm beginning to be insulted, dear!', exponentially increasing his fluster.

Genevieve chuckled along too, much soothed by the beginnings of a return to normality between her and her friends. A great deal of bitter bile had been sapped from her along with the outrush of Art at the clockwork shop. The cold determination left in its wake was a relief, for it could abide while she waited for their next step to make itself apparent. It did not infect her like the bitter anger had.

It made her thoughts clearer, her resolve steadier.

She found herself thinking about Gallentry, where they'd taken the knife from Varley, and McAvey had in turn taken it from them. Fletcher had had no qualms about misusing his Art then, but he, like all of them, had been under the influence of his own compulsion Art pulsing out from the pendant, corrupted into a blanket injunction against questioning McAvey and the strange gaps in their memories. The control had not been total, as Fletcher's control was not total when he wasn't touching his victim. Cecelia had at least *tried* to resist, when told to raid Whitely's memories without permission. Genevieve had been worse than both of them, because she'd been prepared to use deadly fire on Whitely, if McAvey – her *beloved husband*, and it made her want to throw up – had ordered it. She wouldn't have done the same to her cousins; small comfort for her, none for Whitely.

Whitely hadn't had to dodge her fire in the end, but he did have to dodge McAvey's ice spears, which he'd managed with his own twisty teleporting Art. That nimble facility didn't prevent Alex from wanting the man all the way out of the country rather than tangle with McAvey's Art again.

Genevieve looked at her two friends, a long-time team that mostly worked the courts, always well protected by mundane policemen when they had to lay fingers on a criminal. They had useful, strong Art, but they had even less defence against ice spears than Whitely did.

When she went after McAvey, they would be at best a distraction, and at worst a pair of liabilities.

Oliver and Mass came in then, both damp from a fresh scrubbing. She hadn't heard the door: they'd come in the servants' way, to wash up in the scullery. They must have been coated in both the dust and sweat from shifting furniture about all afternoon and the additional grime of the miasma of heat and clinging stink of the summer streets.

Oliver, coatless, had his shirtsleeves folded back, tattoos on display. She looked at his strong, decorated forearms, looked away, remembered he was her husband and she was allowed to look, so did, and then remembered he'd barely spoken a word to her since she had almost incinerated a man right in front of him, and looked away again. By this time, he'd rolled down his sleeves over damp skin.

Bridget brought in dinner trays with more bowls of stew, including more for Genevieve. Afterwards, she began to unstoppably yawn. Despite the long nap that afternoon and the hearty food, she was not fully restored from the excesses of Art overuse, nor from the strain on her body from her advanced condition. Cecelia's voice, as she read aloud to Mass, became hazy.

Oliver returned again, this time from accompanying Fletcher while he fetched a small trunk of necessities from his lodging. Her husband held out his arm to her, silently offering to escort her early to bed.

On the threshold of her room, he finally spoke. 'May we talk?'

This time he didn't demur when she drew back in a wordless invitation to enter her chamber. They'd cleared so much of the elegant, modern furniture that there was nowhere else private to sit, unless they wanted to take to the floor.

She sat on the bed, he, awkwardly, at her dressing table. He lit the small lamp there, and touched the charred marks, tracing the shape of Genevieve's fingers.

'You're feeling better?' he asked.

'Recovering.' She held up her hand, showed him a play of flame limning her fingers. 'Full force in the morning.'

'Good,' he said, distractedly. He shifted, and the chair creaked. It was a delicate thing, too small for his bulk. She'd been cautious on it herself, as her condition had progressed.

Oliver rose and paced a few steps. 'I always admired how you used your Art.'

'Oh?'

'You were born with privilege but no power. And then you were handed great power, and it would have been a simple, easy thing to abuse the status it gave you. But from the very start, you questioned your right to it, you looked for ways to make it useful, you worked incredibly hard to be sure you would never accidentally hurt anyone, and you undertook to never, ever, *purposefully* hurt anyone. And then today…'

Genevieve, having begun flattered, grew indignant as she saw the direction of his thoughts. She felt ambushed. 'My other husband has sullied the moral purity of your wife, is that it?'

'That's not what I'm saying,' he said, sharply, and then sharper still, the words slicing out of him and into her, 'And stop calling him your husband, he never was.'

She took a breath and bit down on an escalating answer. Oliver, too, turned away, rubbing his face. 'I didn't mean to snap,' he said wearily. 'I'll go.'

'But you've been doing so well,' she said, drier than she'd meant to. He shook his head with a small, frustrated grimace. 'No, wait. You have been. We were good at being happy together, weren't we, but we always did have a tendency to ignore our bad days. Let our small tensions simmer and boil over instead of facing them before a crisis point. I see you making a concerted effort to break that habit. It's a little alarming, that's all.'

'If we'd been better able to talk about our troubles as well as our joys,' he said, 'he might not have found such an easy wedge.'

A pattern, culminating in last summer. Her grief, and his, and each of them keeping it to themselves. She could pretend she was trying to protect him from her frailties, but she'd been scared he blamed her. He could pretend he was giving her space to mourn, but he'd been scared she didn't love him anymore. They'd mutually made a crack into a gap and Reuben McAvey had stepped on in.

With a great deal of irony, Genevieve realised that she and Oliver had been better at listening to each other this past year as dearest friends, the single sentiment the necklace's influence had left to them, than as an old married couple accumulating bad habits and laden baggage.

'Fair,' she said. 'Ignoring our conflicts while you're doing a half-arsed wooing job—'

He huffed, crooked smile growing. 'Oh, come now!'

'Oliver,' she said, very severely. 'You proposed to me against the highly unromantic background of a row of dildos. I grant you no grounds for appeal.'

Oliver said, 'Condom drying stands, Gin,' only just managing to suppress his smile to match her mock-seriousness.

Genevieve laughed, and then she sighed. With true gravity now, she said, 'It's all fun and games during a courtship, but it doesn't work in a marriage, does it?'

'No, it doesn't.'

'So you have something to say?'

Oliver nodded slowly. 'I hear you, Gin, that you'd rather not think too closely about what he did to you.'

'I am very much trying not to dwell on that, for now.' Genevieve took a slow breath. 'I'm aware it came out somewhat inappropriately at Gatwick's.'

'Somewhat inappropriately.' She thought for a moment he was fighting disapproval, but then realised he was struggling not to laugh.

'I'm being a twat,' she said frankly. 'All right. It was awful behaviour. I cannot feel bad about it at the moment.'

'Yes,' he said. 'You won't feel bad about it until you've murdered McAvey.'

Genevieve paused, but knew better than to deny it. 'How did you know?'

'My love. I know you. And I know you will feel *terribly*, afterwards.'

'Afterwards is far enough ahead to not yet concern me.'

'Fine,' he said. 'Cram those feelings down if you must. And make me the most injured party if you must. But if you also will not allow me to express my *own* distress, or even my distress on your behalf…'

He'd seen it then, her flare of irritation when he mourned his part in creating the necklace. 'Yes, I see. You end up carrying it all. I am sorry for that. You may speak as you need to, and I'll do better in that regard.' Making an abrupt decision, she patted the quilt beside her. 'Come lie with me now, Oliver.'

He paused, gazing at her.

'We'll keep talking,' she assured him. 'We'll talk in the dark.'

They'd shared their bed, before the necklace. It would only become more awkward the longer they left it, particularly once the baby came to give the readymade excuse to put it off for weeks more. And it was a little easier to contemplate now, when there was no possibility of congress, given her imminent condition and their current state of unresolved tension.

Her stomach was still fluttering with nerves, or perhaps that was the baby, as she stood and opened her arms, inviting him to help her undress.

He'd done this during the first year of their marriage too, when their work for the Society had earned the merest stipend and they'd been getting by mostly on his piecemeal work at the docks, much of his wages still funnelled to his stepmother for the sake of his youngest half-brothers, who his whole family acted as if he'd abandoned with his high-society marriage. They'd had a charwoman come into their little lodging, but otherwise made do without.

Of course, back then, his hands across her skin as he unbuttoned and unlaced her, laying her bare, almost invariably led to a tumble into the sheets, his mouth tracing the paths his fingers had taken, over her throat, down her back, across her thighs.

Genevieve closed her eyes, the memory of then interweaving with the feel of him now, big hands deft and gentle but very, very careful about where they touched. The air, so warm, still felt cool on her bare body as she stood nude before her husband, breasts swollen and veined with blue, nipples darkened and stippled with bumps, hips and thighs dimpled and silvered with stretchmarks, belly grotesquely taut, great with another man's child.

Oliver tugged her nightdress over her head, following its hem down over her thighs, the barest brush of his hands across her hips to smooth the clean, soft fabric into place.

As she undid her hair and brushed it out, Oliver began to strip his outerwear. He hesitated with his hands at his shirt buttons. 'I'm older than I was when we first did this.'

Genevieve gestured down at her own body in the cool linen nightdress, the distended swell of her stomach beneath loose pleats, the sagging heaviness of her breasts straining the bodice. 'Oliver, I'm a whale.'

'You're beautiful,' he said, so matter-of-factly it made her breath catch.

He bared his broad chest, and she put down her hairbrush to touch the gleaming tattooed dragon, as wonderingly as she'd touched it on their wedding night. Index finger circling the golden hoop she remembered sucking on, she raised her gaze to meet his. His body responded to her, nipples stiffening under the touch of her fingertips.

'Sorry,' he said. 'My mind is trying to tell me this is the first time you've touched me after I've wanted it for fifteen years.'

'Don't be sorry,' Genevieve said. 'I wish I could…' She hesitated. 'I could…' If they'd failed to address their troubles head-on, they'd at least always managed to be open about sex, so she looked at him with a feeling like defiance and said, 'I could kneel for you.'

When she'd offered it to McAvey during their false marriage, trying to rekindle the lost pleasure of lovemaking with her husband, he'd turned her down with such disgust that she'd felt sordid. As transgressive as such acts were held to be, it was cleansing to be able to offer her real husband something no other man would ever have from her.

Oliver cupped her face and kissed her. 'Just lie with me for now, love.'

She crawled without grace under the sheets, and he put out the lamp and joined her in the dark, stripped to his drawers – he'd cheated, there, by dousing the light before showing her his magnificent thighs. He lay on his side behind her, cuddling around her, arm looped over her waist so he could rest a big hand on her bulge.

For a moment, the shock took her again. She lay rigid, mind roiling with the surging strangeness of it, cozened in a bed wearing a thin nightgown with a man not her husband. The confusion of it, the shameful sense of betraying her husband, and then the flood of anger of what McAvey had done to them, was overwhelming.

Oliver's big body settled closer to hers, he murmured her name, and all at once, familiarity, rightness, swept over her. Her tense muscles relaxed and she melted into him, interlocking her fingers with his and closing her eyes.

She nestled further, and felt familiarity there too. 'Sorry,' he said again, shifting. 'My mind thinks it's been fifteen years, my body knows it's been at least eighteen months.'

She'd abstained as soon as she'd sensed she was quick with life, for both this pregnancy and the last. This one, because she hadn't wanted her husband touching her. The last one, because she most assuredly had, but she'd been too fixated on following the useless advice books to heed Mrs Murphy's calm and consistent counterindication. It meant she and Oliver hadn't made love since perhaps the Christmas before last, months before McAvey had usurped their marriage.

She was not particularly aroused herself, the fatigue and bodily discomfit at this late stage overwhelming any better reaction at having her true husband wrapped around her. On the other hand, she wouldn't refuse it, even at this scandalously late stage, if it would definitively erase the crawly echo of McAvey's touch. Transgression as cleansing, again, because it was with Oliver.

She pushed back against the hard ridge. 'You could…' she began, and then stopped as she properly parsed his words. 'I thought we'd decided to be merciless in our honesty. You don't have to spare my feelings.'

'I do want you,' he reassured her, squeezing his fingers about hers. 'So much.'

'No, I mean… You've thought yourself unattached for a year, with false memories for years prior. You must have been lonely.'

His silence was entirely baffled.

'It has *not* been eighteen months for you, Oliver. I accept that.'

He still made no response. She could feel him tilting his head on the pillow beside her.

'Your previous landlady was fond of you, I believe?' she tried.

'Oh!' Oliver said. 'No. Not so much as looked at another woman since the night we met, Gin.' He misinterpreted the blank silence she now returned him. 'Or man. The twins made you think seafaring buggery's much more prevalent than it actually is. I wasn't in the *royal* navy, after all.'

She clarified her confusion. 'Since the night we *met*?'

'Alex made that stupid joke about Ginnie and a limey, and you tried not to laugh,' he said. 'And then you did.'

She was utterly asea. 'But…'

His rumbling voice growled deep and slow into her ear. 'I'm not sure you entirely comprehend what it's like to be smiled at by you, Gin. Damn well flattened me. Every moment with you since then set me on fire. How could anyone else compare?'

'But you were so—' She lifted their joined hands off her stomach so she could give them an indicative wave. 'Calm and self-assured. Always.'

'You were a Belgravia heiress. I was hardly going to profess undying devotion that instant. Or ever, really, outside the confines of my own head. You did have to prod me into it, remember.'

She breathed a laugh. 'That's right, I did. You pillock.'

She earned his low chuckle. Then he said. 'In the interests of honesty, I want to say this. I felt, and do still feel, that I took too much from you. You said, in that carriage ride home from the first Society meeting, that you wanted so much more than what I gave you. You wanted what your cousins have, travel, and freedom, and opportunity. They've explored half the world – Alex is off to explore the other half – and we married and barely left London. You told me what you wanted that day, and I didn't give it to you.'

'Oh, Oliver,' she said. 'All my verbiage that day was because I was too naïve to realise what I *really* wanted was for you to fuck me right there in the carriage.'

Oliver coughed in something between alarm and surprise.

She wriggled against him, as much as her condition allowed a wriggle. 'I can say that now…'

'Because we're married,' they chorused together. Genevieve gently shifted their joined hands so he was cupping her heavy breast, and felt him sigh against her neck.

He said, stubborn in the face of provocation, 'But I was wrong to offer you a divorce last night. It's symptomatic of running away. We're not doing that.' He paused, then, meaningfully.

'We're not doing that,' she agreed. 'We're worth more than that.'

'Yes, my love, we are.'

He nuzzled into her hair, lightly laying kisses over her head, as he had done in the ruined cottage all those years ago. His thumb moved restlessly, stroking her nipple through the thin fabric. It tightened under his touch.

Genevieve rubbed her fingers over his, encouraging this train of thought. 'He managed to get your wedding ring off, too,' she said, since her unobstructed touch had reminded her she'd noted his bare fingers earlier.

'Yes. I see how he could've got your rings off. Not sure how he got mine.'

She tensed, letting go of his hand. 'Apt metaphor.'

He stroked over her shoulder and down her side, trying to soothe her sudden stiffness. 'How so?'

'You see how he could have…' She hissed through her teeth, then said, fiercely, 'How did he get that fucking necklace around my neck, Oliver? You were wondering it yourself, earlier. Did he… Did I…'

Oliver suddenly moved away; it chilled her all the way to her core. He sat up and spoke into the dark. 'That was guilt, Gin, not suspicion. *I* gave you the necklace, after your lying-in. It was a birthday gift, remember? It was delivered to the house, as expected, and I left it by your bedside on the morning of your birthday, in the hope that if you wore it…if you wore it, it would mean you still loved me. Stupid, *cowardly*. Pretty tokens instead of honest words! Never again.'

'Come back here,' Genevieve commanded.

He obeyed. He put his arm tight about her, pulling her close against him. 'I didn't realise you didn't remember that yet.'

'None of my memories around the crisis point are clear yet,' she admitted.

'Ah. Well. You came downstairs, wearing the necklace, and kissed me. I took you out to the Clarendon. And then when we came home, my trunk was packed and waiting in the hall. You graciously thanked me for the lunch, and I thanked you for letting me stay with you and McAvey while my lodging house underwent essential repairs, and I took my trunk, and I left. And I knew where my lodging house was, *had been for years*, and I went there, and never had so much as a second thought about it. I don't recall seeing my wedding ring again. It would have puzzled me no end if I had. I probably slipped it off sometime during the lunch without even noticing myself do it, and absently discarded it.'

His was probably gone, then. Hers were most likely gone, too. They could be replaced, she knew. She still panged over the loss of those silly, pretty tokens, that Oliver now so strongly decried.

She cleared her throat, and said steadily, 'It wouldn't have been different if you'd handed the necklace to me in person, you know. It would merely have increased your guilt exponentially. The trick was already done, either way. But I am immensely relieved I took it from your hand, not his.'

'In the interests of honesty…'

'That will get old fast, my dear,' she said severely. 'Go ahead and say it.'

'Not pleased to hear you think it was a possibility.'

'I didn't! I was very confused about it, thank you.'

He chuckled, face pressed to her hair. 'Quantities of that going around. One last thing, and I'll let you sleep. This notion you've taken, of killing McAvey before I can.'

'Better me than you,' she said stubbornly. 'Better the rich woman from the sort of background society will feel sympathy for when she accidentally kills a fellow Artisan with her dangerous Art, than the tattooed navvy who murders his wife's lover, yes?'

He made a demurring noise deep in his throat.

'I have unwarranted privilege,' Genevieve told him. 'Let me use it.'

'I would not stoop to gainsay you,' he said, 'but it appears we are in a race to see which of us will get to him first, and…' He stroked the side of her belly. '…you're also in a different race. I shall win by default, I think.'

'That would be cheating, Oliver.'

'I am,' he said warmly, 'completely willing to be dishonourable in this case, Gin.'

'Oh, and do we think upper-class twats play fair, do we?' She hesitated. 'You will think less of me?'

'Never,' he said. 'I despise the man with every fibre of my being. He deserves everything he's got coming to him. I simply want it to come from me.'

'You don't want me to take *your* vengeance away from you?'

'Vengeance rightly belongs to you. But I don't think vengeance is good for you, for anyone.'

'You sound like Alex.'

'Good for Alex,' Oliver said. She could feel him smiling into her hair. 'Standing firm against the Locke women, quite a feat.'

'But *you* plan to take vengeance… Ah. You are protecting me from myself.'

He nuzzled in closer, murmuring, 'Yes.'

'Pillock.'

'I love you, too, Miss Locke,' Oliver said, very gravely, and her laughter burbled out of her.

She felt asleep wrapped in her husband's arms, and slept like the proverbial baby she was due to meet any day now.

30

GENEVIEVE AWOKE THE NEXT MORNING WITH a dull ache in her lower back and an idea.

She'd had intense dreams before waking, of the sort she recognised from her previous pregnancies, vivid and full of anxiety and a looming sense of import, of rushing towards something, of carriages overturning, of empty cots, of being caught unprepared.

The day's newspapers did not help her slightly fretful mood. She was frowning over an account of a dreadful train derailment when Oliver casually derailed her nascent plans just as abruptly.

They were sipping tea after a breakfast of simple porridge, again taken on trays on the small cluster of parlour furniture at one end of the drawing room. Mass was with them, as quiet as ever. Genevieve made sure he had an extra helping of porridge, and pushed the cream and sugar bowls towards him.

Oliver leaned back and said, 'I've been thinking about what Stiggins said. Five sixteen.'

'Deuteronomy 5:16. Honour thy father and thy mother,' Fletcher said with a nod.

Oliver said, watching Genevieve, 'And frostbite on his fingers.'

Cecelia looked up from her tea. Both she and Genevieve were still in their wrappers, close enough, these days, to Artistry Dress that Fletcher had only been moderately flustered by the shocking informality of it. 'You think it was a message from McAvey.'

'It must be.'

'But what?' Cecelia said. 'Are we playing into his hands by returning Gin to her marital home, her parents' home?'

'I think he means us to find him at Kensal.' He glanced at her. 'Sorry, love.'

He was mistaking her silence for dismay, which it was, but not at the thought of her parents in their graves at the General Cemetery of All Souls at Kensal Green. Her stomach gave a lurch. She looked up at the painting on the mantle, her mother's depiction of her father in his dandy outfit. She was being very unfilial, to dismiss their loss so cavalierly, but she had to put it aside for now.

'Somewhere by the Lockes' tombstones.' Fletcher looked pinched at having to be so crass as to mention it, notwithstanding that death was a constant presence in the overcrowded city.

This was the exact idea Genevieve had awoken with. But her intention had been to hold her tongue until after the birth, which had to be within the next week; by the end of June, certainly. Then she and Oliver would go to McAvey's macabre hideout together, *without* involving the two more vulnerable members of their team, who did not need to be made party *to* murder, and who would not be needed *for* murder. But Oliver had solved the puzzle in front of them, which put paid to that notion.

'Plenty of hiding places,' Cecelia said, trying to barrel past Fletcher's awkwardness. 'Tombs.'

'You can't go, Gin,' Oliver said, tone wary.

She raised her brows. 'I must. It takes a weapons Artisan to stop another weapons Artisan.'

'You are too close to your time.'

'I am only one day closer to my time than I was yesterday, when you acknowledged you needed me for defence.' When Oliver showed no sign of being moved by this cogent argument, Genevieve twigged to what was happening. She couldn't help a smile. 'This is you cheating.'

Oliver gave a nod, slightly pleased with himself, and a good deal more than slightly repentant already…but not enough to renege.

Genevieve wanted to take him aside and point out that murder did not need witnesses. He was smart enough to know the dangers of taking Fletcher and Cecelia, both to their persons and his plans, but she supposed he would accept that risk over the risk of his very pregnant wife facing McAvey.

She'd concede that deliberately seeking out a rogue Artisan was of an order of magnitude riskier than waiting behind their metaphorical ramparts. Still, it was, in fact, her actual job. 'I'm with child, not without Art.'

'Yes, but the…but the child will soon be without you,' Fletcher said. He almost went cross-eyed in alarm. 'I didn't mean *without* you. I don't think you're going to— I meant, with-out. Outside you.'

Cecelia scrunched up her face, fighting laughter.

'Yes,' Genevieve said evenly. 'I understood.'

'You must rest,' he said earnestly. Then he apparently decided he was already embarrassed and it couldn't get worse, because he threw caution to the wind. 'Did you know the baby is some six per cent of the maternal body mass, which is twice that of a chimpanzee mother's burden? You *must* rest!'

Now even Oliver was struggling to keep his expression neutral.

'Thank you, Fletcher,' she said, hand on one hip. 'You are ever enlightening.'

'Do stay home and rest,' Cecelia said, leaning to pat Genevieve's hand. 'Oliver will do a fine job of warding us, and all we have to do is get Fletcher close enough. We've done that plenty of times before.'

'With my help,' Genevieve said stubbornly. 'It is the same argument as yesterday, when we went to the clockwork shop. I am best placed…'

She trailed off, because all three of her friends were looking very sombre. None of them liked what she had done yesterday. She flushed and changed tack. 'Besides, who is to say it is not McAvey's plan to have Fletcher within arm's length? Mine is not the only Art a power-hungry Artisan would covet.'

'That man never did think Fletcher applied his compulsion Art with enough abandon,' Cecelia said thoughtfully. 'I'm sure he thinks he can make better use of it.'

Fletcher paled. But he said stiffly, 'If we need bait, then I shall be very good bait. We three together will be enough to overpower him before he manages to…harvest…me.'

'And then we will hand him over to the Agency.' Cecelia's voice had taken on an unusually uncertain note. She looked from Genevieve to Oliver.

'Yes,' Oliver said, blandly.

Cecelia had known Oliver for even longer than Genevieve. She stared at him for a very long time before she said, slowly, 'Yes. That is what will happen. As per our usual procedure.'

'Yes.'

Ever slower, ever firmer, she said, 'It is no different, regardless of our personal feelings on the matter.'

'Yes,' Oliver said. 'I know.'

An expression crossed Cecelia's face which suggested if she and Fletcher could have tackled the ice Artisan alone, she absolutely would have chosen that path.

'Perhaps we are too close to this,' she said. 'Perhaps we should call in the Agency enforcers now.'

Oblivious to the undercurrents Cecelia was too adept at sensing, Fletcher scoffed. 'But it's the exact sort of rogue Artistry the enforcers contract out to us.'

'I'll have them standing by.' Oliver rose. 'We should make a start.'

He strode out into the hall and up the stairs, effectively cutting off both women's arguments in one inadvertently fell swoop. Cecelia was still frowning as she, Oliver, and Fletcher departed, Oliver conspicuously not having sent a communication to the Agency to put the enforcers on notice.

Genevieve had no way to know how the expedition had gone until they returned safely, or not.

Mass was normally quietly cheerful about helping Bridget with her chores – he liked both ironing and folding – but today he retreated to Oliver's old room, rubbing his forehead like he had a headache. Genevieve sent Bridget up with a *Boy's Own*, a glass of milk, and diluted vinegar for bathing his temples.

She herself stayed in the drawing room, feeling heavy and slow and fretful. Her legs hurt. The relentless heat began to invade the house, though thankfully the smell was mostly kept at bay with the bowls of chloride of lime. She was unable to settle, eyes glazing over when she tried to keep reading the papers.

The post had not come, not the early call with last night's letters, and not the midmorning call. One was possible, but not both. There had to be a delay. Perhaps the derailment had involved a mail train. She couldn't focus long enough to finish the article about it. The tick of the clock seemed to be slowing down.

Bridget put her head around the door. 'Ma'am, are you at home for a visitor?'

Stirring, Genevieve sat up. She hadn't heard the door; she'd been more than half-dozing, having fretted herself into exhaustion. She nodded, and quickly patted her face and hair to be sure she was in order before Bridget showed in the unexpected visitor, who turned out to be *extremely* unexpected: Miss Edith Knight, Lulu's companion, all the way here from Lovelly.

Genevieve politely, if bemusedly, welcomed her in. She was a regular little doll, shorter even than Cecelia, with big blue-grey eyes and deep dimples, and an enviably healthy complexion that owed nothing to cold cream. She was dressed entirely practically, from her golden hair in its simple rolled bandeau, to her striped cotton skirts, to her Balmoral boots.

Her bonnet, on the other hand, was an absolute confection. Lulu loved Miss Knight's bonnets.

Since Miss Knight seemed nervous, Genevieve tried to put her at ease – the etiquette books still whispered in her head, even after all these years – by offering a compliment towards the very same bonnet.

'Why do none of the Lockes like my hats?' Miss Knight said, quite plaintively.

'I just said I did!'

'Oh,' Miss Knight said. 'You're somewhat less sarcastic than your cousins, then.'

Genevieve smiled at that, which prompted Miss Knight to dimple and say, 'But you smile exactly like them.'

'Lulu adores your hats, Miss Knight,' Genevieve informed her.

Miss Knight looked enchantingly delighted by this, but only briefly. She turned the offending bonnet in both hands, still wearing her gloves. 'I must say I am very sorry to barge in on you at such an inopportune time, Mrs Locke.'

'Oh, I'm not—' Genevieve began, and then had the startling realisation that she did not know if she was Mrs Oliver or Mrs Bennet. The former seemed truer, but the latter was, as far as she knew, the legal choice.

Her professional name, then, would have to do until she had a chance to ask Oliver, or perhaps they'd have to check the marriage registry, if he also couldn't remember and if McAvey had destroyed all their marital papers, which, if Fletcher's second, more thorough, search of the study was any indication, he had.

Her abrupt stop didn't matter; she was met with a veritable wall of words.

'I will try not to disturb you for long but I truly did feel I should come by and let you know that Miss Locke is perfectly well, she is recuperating at the Locke townhouse. It is merely a broken arm, you see, I say *merely,* because she says it hardly compares to the time a telekinesis Artisan snapped her ribs for her, and it really sounds like Mr Locke dropped the ball on that one, doesn't it, reading intentions and all, well might Sir Kingsford be cross with him sometimes, but it is still a weeks-long healing even if it is merely an arm, and of course all the bruises and scratches, and I *know* she said not to bother you with it, but she did write to you to tell you she was coming, and if you're expecting her here and she doesn't arrive for no reason you're aware of because she sent a message to *me* but not a word to *you*, you're going to be worrying about her *anyway* and so I thought I better pop over and reassure you she is absolutely fine, aside from the broken arm. And a nasty sprain in her ankle, but apparently that will heal quickly enough and I'm not to bother over it.'

Genevieve had been saying 'What?' repeatedly and with increasing volume throughout this surfeit of alarming information. Finally, she set her hand on Miss Knight's forearm, and she could only pray her palm wasn't burning with the suppressed heat running in shudders through her.

'Start at the beginning,' she said through gritted teeth. 'What's happened to Lulu?'

Miss Knight went very still, turning the sickly colour of old milk, pale enough that her scatter of delicate freckles stood out. Her dimples were no longer in evidence. 'You didn't know she was coming up to London at all, did you?'

'No, because I told her to stay away!'

Here Miss Knight recovered enough to give her a rather pointed look, which Genevieve had to return via a rueful shrug to acknowledge her own hopeful naivety. Of course Lulu wouldn't stay away.

'She sent a reply to a message of yours, and then she immediately regretted it and got on a train to come and tell you so herself,' Miss Knight explained. 'She was on the Bristol train that derailed on the outskirts of London yesterday evening.'

'Forty-five people died,' Genevieve said, appalled.

'Forty-eight, now,' Miss Knight said mutedly. 'I wanted you to know Lulu wasn't one of them. But I see now I should have listened to her. She said you knew nothing about it, or you would, firstly, have sent an urgent telegram ordering her not to come, which you didn't, and secondly, badgered the railway office and searched the hospitals for her, which you didn't, so you were either in the middle of giving birth, and not to be disturbed, or her note telling you she was coming had gone astray, and therefore you didn't *need* to be disturbed. I should have known she wouldn't leave you to worry if she knew you thought she could be on that train. That was really rather foolish of me. But she's so *stubborn* sometimes.'

'I know,' Genevieve said. 'And I'm glad you came and told me.' At Miss Knight's concerned look – she was running her hand over her stomach, where the baby was performing acrobatics – she added, 'I'm with child, not made of glass.'

She began to page through the papers, looking for more news of the derailment. Over her shoulder, she asked of the nervously hovering Miss Knight, 'Do they yet know what caused it, have you heard?'

Miss Knight squeezed the bonnet, crumpling the brim. For a woman of very many words, she seemed oddly reluctant to answer. Eventually, she said, 'Ice on the tracks.'

'In high summer,' Genevieve said flatly.

'Indeed.'

Reuben McAvey had intercepted their mail and guessed Lulu's train via extrapolation from the Bradford guide. Or perhaps he had people watching the house and her friends and her family. He was well-funded, after all. Either way, he'd known Lulu was on her way to London, and known or guessed her train, and he'd derailed it.

He might have lurked at the station and put an ice spear through her – she was indisputably more vulnerable without her brother by her side to read intentions – but he hadn't done that. He hadn't wanted to simply devastate Genevieve. He'd wanted to send her a message, writ large across the entire city. He so admired his own cleverness.

The derailment was the message, not some bible verse they thought they'd decoded. McAvey was not hiding out in cold tombs at the cemetery, that had nowhere near the flair he'd desire. She should have known that.

She thought of the others, perhaps still systemically quartering the expanse of the cemetery, or perhaps on their way back by now, unsuccessful. Kensal Green was not so far from Holland Park, close enough that a funeral procession might go entirely on foot, the mourners walking in stately procession behind the dark hearse drawn by black-plumed horses. From Belgravia, for her father's funeral, they had left the house on foot, and approached the cemetery on foot, but in between, they'd ridden in carriages. Processions had become simpler since then; her mother's funeral wouldn't have been like that. *Honour thy father and thy mother.*

Her thoughts were scattering into flashes of the vivid dreams of the night before, the slowly turning wheel of an overturned carriage. Genevieve shook her head, hands flat on the newspaper, ink smudging across her fingertips. She made herself focus.

The others would be coming back. But they would not come on foot, because they would want the protection of a hired carriage, which Oliver could ward for them.

'Is this your cat?' Miss Knight said, breaking into her thoughts. She stooped and made encouraging squeaks at the little black cat with the huge green-gold eyes. 'Aren't you a pretty kitty?'

This made her inexplicably giggle to herself before she continued making a fuss over Mass, tickling him under the chin. Genevieve widened her eyes dramatically at him in lieu of literally shooing him away; like most cats, he elected to ignore her. She hadn't seen him come down the stairs, and wasn't sure why he'd come down in his favoured alternative form. Nervous about the stranger, she supposed. She thought they'd all underestimated how tense their quiet young fosterling had been.

Miss Knight was rubbing him behind the ears when he finally felt safe enough to turn back to human, and gave an inordinate yelp of alarm as he transformed under her hand, recoiling hard enough to almost trip over her own sensible heels.

It occurred to Genevieve to be grateful Mass shapeshifted into a clothing-wearing human. She started to wonder at that; didn't it suggest—

'I'm sorry,' Mass whispered.

He scurried over to the mantle and came back with the portrait of her father. He held it up to her, his bony wrists sticking out from his cuffs. They were rubbed red, raw and tender. He looked at her with big dark eyes, waiting.

'What is it?' Miss Knight asked. 'Who is that? I like his pantaloons! Is that the Monument to the Great Fire behind him? I should like to climb it, on one of these visits. Perhaps not *this* visit, since Miss Locke's ankle is sore and her arm will be useless on the railings, but another time. Three hundred and eleven steps, and quite the view!'

Genevieve let the words wash over her as she stared down at the little painting, her father's smiling face. How often had McAvey seen this on the mantle at the Belgravia house, her mother's tribute to her father?

Often enough.

Stiggins's bible verse had been a message after all, one they had understood, yet solved incorrectly. The derailment was a warning and a command: *Don't delay. Come find me now, or see what happens.*

McAvey would do to her friends' carriage what he had done to that train. Oliver was warding against a direct attack, because McAvey relied so heavily on ice spears. He wanted too much to be classed as a weapons Artisan to dally with anything that might be classified as weather.

But he could. He could put ice under the hooves of the horses, or freeze the iron wheels to shattering point, and overturn their carriage as easily as he'd derailed an entire train.

Absently, she said, 'No, not this visit,' answering a comment from Miss Knight from several minutes before. 'You must—'

She'd been about to tell her to summon Sir Kingsford's carriage from the estate, so Oliver could ward it and it could carry the two women safely out of London, but carriages weren't safe anymore, and neither was any public conveyance, and she couldn't *think* with this backache and this headache and this slow, strange claustrophobic anxiety enveloping her.

She pressed her palms together, feeling the heat.

Feeling her power, which had always been more than the equal of McAvey's, and perhaps there, above all, was where the worst of her sins lay, in his envious eyes.

If an ice Artisan should turn rogue, then shall we not require a fire Artisan to tame him?

She, weapons Artisan of the Myriad, was exactly who the Agency would call in to deal with a dangerous rogue Artisan. She only needed the other three if she wanted to bring him in alive.

Immediately calmer, Genevieve said, 'Miss Knight, I will escort you back to the townhouse.'

Miss Knight chewed her lower lip and then said, 'I don't think you should venture far from your bed, Mrs Locke. My sister had a baby, you see, and—'

'I must. And you must latch every door and window and answer the door to *no one*, and stay that way until you hear from one of us.'

Summoning Bridget, she repeated more-or-less the same injunctions as she dashed out a note to Oliver, telling him in simple terms McAvey's threat to him and all their friends, why she felt she could not wait lest she give McAvey too much time and incentive to act on the threat, and her destination. She folded it over and made to hand it to the maid, before pausing.

It was a brief factual message. The derailment, the implicit threat, the new solution to the biblical riddle, her choice.

Genevieve took up her pen and wrote one last fact. *I love you, Oliver.*

Leaving her mother to deliver Miss Knight and Mass cake and tea, Bridget helped Genevieve dress. After deliberating, Genevieve decided on widow's weeds, as if she still mourned a lost husband, and hung a gold chain about her neck. If they were being watched closely enough, McAvey might know she had shed her mourning clothes yesterday. If Mass was enough under his thrall, he would know she'd shed the necklace, too. But it might give him a moment of pause, her a moment of advantage.

Bridget flagged them a cab and then bolted back into the house and slammed the door definitively behind her. Miss Knight quickly came down the steps and scrambled into the cab, Genevieve's grim manner enough to make her glance about nervously at the pedestrians and the passing carriages. Mass stood demurely by Genevieve as she made herself count to ten on the doorstep, making sure she would be seen.

She wouldn't spot a clever spy; her street was quiet, but any street in London provided plenty of cover. She didn't think she'd even spot McAvey, despite his distinctive red hair. But he or his agent would see *her*, would see that she was emerging from her haven. Her move would surely trigger his next gambit in this ridiculous chess game, diverting him from targeting her friends' returning carriage to preparing for her arrival into what he would consider his trap. She had to pray that it was so.

The driver was looking dubious about her prominent situation. Genevieve thrust a solid handful of large denomination into his hand and hauled her body into his cab.

At the Locke townhouse, she went in long enough to check on Lulu. Her cousin was out cold, probably on some laudanum-type concoction. Her face was pale and smooth, arm bound in plaster.

She'd regretted the answer she'd sent, and rushed to London to tell Genevieve so in person.

Genevieve kissed her forehead, murmuring, 'Stay safe.'

She bid farewell to Miss Knight, with one last instruction to call in Miss Adler as soon as the current crisis was over. Miss Knight lingered at the door with a grim set to her smiley face, looking like she dearly wished she had her friend's Artistry with locks as she watched Genevieve clamber back into the cab.

Then she and Mass were on their way to the Monument.

31

It was long into the afternoon, but the sun was still high: it was the summer solstice tomorrow. Genevieve stood in the shade on the south side of the little square and looked up along the fluted length of the Monument's Doric shaft thrusting proudly into the sky, thinking extremely uncharitable thoughts about the male ego.

Hands on hips, she announced to the stifling air, 'If you make me climb up three hundred and eleven steps, McAvey, so help me God, I won't be the only one in an *interesting fucking condition.*'

If she remembered correctly, the spiral staircase and the railings and the platform's safety cage, installed long after her parents had met here, were all of wrought iron, which made it an odd choice for staging a showdown between two weapons Artisans. Perhaps McAvey assumed she, laden with both incipient baby and fresh grief about parents whose love story had begun here, would be more affected by the iron. Perhaps the memorial was meant to make her nervous about being overly flagrant with her Art; the Great Fire had begun here too, on Pudding Lane.

It would not work on either of those counts. She turned to Mass, quiet as ever beside her. 'Are you still beholden to him, Mass?'

His eyes flashed, deep brown, then cool green, catching the diffused sunlight. 'Yes. No. I don't know.'

She had brought him with her because there would have been no way for Bridget to keep him in the house. He could have become the quick little cat under the maid's very nose, and a mouse to dart through the smallest gaps and out, and a bird to outrace Genevieve. If he did not know where his loyalties lay, then she could not know either, but at least she could ensure she knew where he was when McAvey put him into play.

Besides, he could still be useful. The Monument, open to the public for sixpence, had a rope across the entranceway today, and a closure sign. The square around it teemed, as everywhere in London teemed, even in the stench, with carriages and carts, and barrowmen and flower sellers and matchgirls, and people hurrying to and fro on foot. She was already catching attention, the well-dressed widow in an advanced situation.

If she tried to push past the barrier, well-meaning or interfering passersby would try to stop her, or perhaps call for the constable. There hadn't been a successful suicide at the Monument since the cage over the viewing platform had been installed. Its reputation in the popular imagination lingered.

'Mass,' she said, 'will you be my distraction?'

In answer, he stepped out and became a rather convincing tiger, orange pelt shining in the unrelenting sunshine. She felt the urge to run a hand down its side, stroking the bright length like silk. Mass padded across the square with regal head held high. Ignored in the wake of consternation and amazement, Genevieve crossed through standstill traffic and to the Monument entrance. The door was ever so slightly ajar. It was the work of a moment to unloop the rope and slip in, closing the door almost completely behind her.

The counter was unmanned. She went past, to the spiral stairs corkscrewing up the inner wall. She touched her bare palm to the ironwork, feeling the sting.

A mouse slipped through the minuscule gap she'd left between door and jamb, and then Mass was back, emerging from a glittery cloud. He, too, looked at the evenly-spaced steps of the spiral rising up and up over their heads. He frowned.

'He's not up there?'

'He's…' Mass circled the tiny chamber, going behind the counter. 'Oh.'

She followed. There were iron hinges set into the oak planks. A trapdoor. 'Down?'

'Yes.' He faltered. 'I think so.'

Some sort of basement chamber. She did know that; it was one of the pieces of lore a Londoner picked up: Robert Hooke's laboratory. He'd designed the Monument to be a giant telescope, but the constant vibration of wheels and feet had put paid to the grand notion of a gigantic scientific instrument, leaving a neglected room below.

Fire flowed in the palm of one hand, eager to flare bright and high. She had come here fully intending to kill McAvey, for what he had done to her, and tried to do to Lulu, and for the harm he had dealt her friends and the harm he would yet do, if not stopped.

She could lift the trapdoor and rain hellfire down on Reuben McAvey's head without taking so much as a single descending step. So much for all his clever plans.

Except – he *was* clever, or perhaps *crafty* was the more apt characterisation. She had to consider that he might not be alone. He probably wouldn't deign to have accomplices, his tolerance for incompetence too low, but he might have hostages. He might even have – she knew it was ridiculous, and hopeless, and pandering to his cruel game, but she couldn't help wondering if he could have – her mother down in that basement.

And...perhaps it was foolish, but she didn't want to kill him from a distance. She had to face him. She had to demand answers, a reckoning. She had to see him lose. She had to see him *know* he'd lost.

Genevieve awkwardly bent over her distended stomach, and found the small hoop to lift the hatch. She paused again.

She could be sensible, and wait. She'd left a note, telling Oliver where she'd be. She could put a single foot on the trapdoor and hold McAvey captive until she had her true husband by her side, and then perhaps they could stop arguing and engage in the marital bliss of a mutually desired endeavour. If Oliver planned ahead, he'd leave the other two at home.

Unless there was a second way out, a door into a neighbouring basement. That wasn't uncommon. McAvey could slip out and come around to surprise her, or make good on his threat against her friends. Perhaps he wouldn't try to target one hired carriage among hundreds. Perhaps he'd go to Adler's Apothecary. Perhaps he wouldn't even need to, if he already had one or two hostages with him.

He'd enjoy punishing her for refraining from descent into his trap.

Mass abruptly made the point moot, linking a finger into the hoop and tossing the door open. It hinged back with a muffled thump, raising dust. A waft of air came out of the square hole, cooler than the stuffy air of the little antechamber but musty, a scent as familiar as that emitted from any subterranean space in the city. Swirling through it came a disconcerting blast of icy air, as strange as a frigid current when swimming in tepid seas. She didn't need the dim glow of a lamp to tell her McAvey was waiting for her.

She could make out the shallow treads of a set of stairs, made of the same Portland stone as the Monument itself. She could just about manage them. She wasn't sure if she should go first, to protect Mass from an ambush of ice, or if he was likely to finally give in to the compulsion ruling him and push her down the steps.

Again, the boy acted first, either trying to be braver for her, or responding to silent, irresistible impulse. He slipped down, and she went after him, far more awkwardly and having to combine a clamber with a twist of her whole body that her bones and joints protested as one. Her already aching back gave a twinge of extra protest. The narrow way had not been designed for a woman in her condition, and for a moment she thought she might stick like a cork in a bottle, which would quite ruin McAvey's dramatics. But then the stairs opened out a little more, and she was able to follow the shallow spiral downwards.

She emerged with Mass into a stone chamber, round and with a domed ceiling. McAvey stood on the far side, waiting with far more patience than he'd ever shown in their faux marriage. She could feel his gaze on her, making her itch, but she wouldn't look at him directly, not yet. As Mass stepped back behind her, cringing, she took a leisurely perusal of her new surroundings, braced to fling up fire as a shield against ice.

Overhead, a square grate let in a faint light from the dim room above. If the iron doors concealed in the decorative urn atop the Monument had been opened, the grate would have allowed afternoon sunlight to fall all the way down upon them as Hooke had once intended for starlight. As it stood, however, McAvey's lamp was the main illumination, showing a bare room, spacious only because it was utterly devoid of furniture or any other trappings. There were also no hostages, and no escape hatches.

It very much had the feel of a tiny private arena for an Artistry feud. She could imagine eager spectators buying tickets to crowd about and peer down through the grate like they were watching a cockfight.

'Vivi,' McAvey said.

Speaking of cocks. Before he could launch into what was no doubt a prepared speech, Genevieve, eyes still averted, set a hand to her black-edged, necklace-decorated decolletage and said, breathily, 'Reuben, darling! I can't believe you're alive. I've been so…bereft.'

As she playacted a starry-eyed joy he'd only believe if he was underestimating his supposed wife – not, she knew, a bad bet on her part – she began to subtly heat the air. In the contained space, it was a small expense of Art for her that would make his own icy Art harder to maintain. Their Arts were equal opposites. If this came down to the simplest of calculations – whose Art would run out first – she wanted to weight the scales her way.

It was why she couldn't let herself look at him yet, lest the sight of his smirking, smug face provoke her: if she didn't outright win with a first strike, the waste of Art would be telling in the ensuing battle.

He cleared his throat, trying for her attention. The hand she'd laid on her chest clenched without her volition. All those times he'd waited for her to be deeply concentrating and then interrupted her with that little harrumph: asserting authority over his devoted wife's time and attention, and keeping her off-balance and foggy and less in control of her temper and her Art.

When she still wouldn't look at him, he said coolly, 'I know the embedded Artwork has failed.'

Even the sound of his voice made her palms burn. 'Good,' she said, dropping her dulcet tones. 'How about you have a go at killing me now so I can get this done and Mass and I can go home. Our *real* home.'

McAvey made a softly amused sound. It did not do to underestimate him as he underestimated her – he knew as well as she did that if he launched his own assault, to incapacitate, or indeed, kill her, he would have to win immediately or risk the fatal expenditure of Art.

'I see widowhood has done you no favours,' he said. 'The bloom quite off the rose.'

Now she did look, making herself catalogue him as the bonfire of rage tried to flare high at the merest sight of the curve of his thin lips, his sneering gaze. He was thinner than he had been, almost gaunt. Tidy, but worn. Face aged beyond the months since she'd last seen him. She couldn't see the copper knife about his person; he did not, at least, have it to hand.

Genevieve indulged herself with a Locke level of blunt honesty. 'You are such a small man, McAvey,' she said. 'All this, merely to feel important to someone without bothering to earn it.'

'Earn it?' he echoed, righteously pompous. 'I've toiled towards this for years.' When she snorted at his melodrama, he snapped, 'You had everything handed to you, and tried hard to throw it away. I've clawed for every advantage and the Agency still refused to recognise me to the extent I deserved. Still licked the boots of privileged Artisans like you, still elevated an uppity little bitch like Miss Delacorte over me.'

'We worked for it,' Genevieve rejoined, fury snapping through every word. 'We took their piddling little contracts till we proved ourselves worthy of their trust. I never used my birth or even my Art to demand extra consideration. We worked, and we earned it. *You* wanted the same old stodgy class divisions within the Agency in the hope the upper-class Artisans would proffer you a hand for any reason other than for you to bend and kiss it. It didn't happen: we're all equals. Don't come whinging to me now that you didn't distinguish yourself among equals when you didn't put any effort into it at all.'

The air she'd been steadily heating abruptly chilled. She felt an icy gust come through her snug cocoon of warmth like the last gasp of a winter wind intruding into balmy spring weather. The air tried to burst into flame in the vicinity of her palms, but she quelled it. He hadn't formed an ice spear yet.

'Forget wanting respect from Daddy,' she said. He'd often spoken of his father's ambitions for him. Tellingly, he'd never mentioned the other member of his household. 'I think it's Mummy who didn't love you enough.'

The taunt almost worked; he raised his hands and frost coalesced before him. But when she flung up her own hands, ready to melt his efforts, he calmed himself with a visible wrench of effort. The ice particles melted back into the air.

'Come here,' he said, as cool and firm as Fletcher issuing a compulsion, and she laughed in his face.

But he wasn't talking to her. Mass slipped from where he'd been silently cowering by the stairs and took a few trudging steps towards McAvey. Genevieve caught the shapeshifter's arm. With an apologetic glance her way, he melted into a different form. Her restraining hand sprang open, instinctively recoiling from the liquid strangeness writhing under her fingers. The little black cat slunk across the room, twinkling back into Mass at McAvey's side.

McAvey slung an arm around the boy's shoulder, companionable. Genevieve's skin crawled. Mass's face was utterly miserable.

'I had this one stashed with the nuns till earlier this year. I suppose it was no surprise the shape his Art took, but it was a boon when it came on early and strong. I'd have expected it, given his mother, though she did insist on breeding with inferiority.'

His tone was insinuating, crawlingly eager. He was waiting for her to grasp some point. 'Don't you recognise him, Vivi?' he prompted. 'Or should I say *her*?'

Genevieve looked at Mass. Master of disguise that he was, he had slowly shifted into a subtly different form, more feminine, slighter body now swamped by shirt and trousers that hadn't shifted along with the change, hair now longer and wavy, ashy blond like the twins', face symmetrically elegant like her own, eyes the same dark brown as usual, like Oliver's. He'd reminded her of Oliver's nephews or even nieces before, she remembered. She cocked her head, frowning.

McAvey crowed with self-satisfied delight. 'Doesn't even recognise her own daughter. What kind of mother *are* you?'

Her breath hitched. 'My daughter died.'

'That's what I paid the clockwork Artisan to make you think happened,' he said. 'Proof of concept.'

Genevieve looked between his triumphant face and Mass's dismal one. Mass? Or…

'Rose?' she said, faltering.

'We only had to persuade you and Oliver,' he said. 'Once you both believed you remembered finding her lying dead in her cot, that's the sad news that everyone else received and never questioned.'

Genevieve straightened, recovering her poise. 'You're lying. It would have worn off.'

'Not once it was a story you'd told yourself too often. Didn't you dream of finding an empty cot? Didn't you dream of meeting a little girl you *knew* belonged to you? Didn't you tell yourself it was your mind playing tricks on you?'

'No.' Her hands had folded over her rounded stomach as if his words could hurt the new baby. 'This isn't Rose. Mass, you're being cruel.'

'I'm sorry,' he said, voice strained high and tight, his hands worrying around the opposite wrists. 'I can't help it.'

His eyes flashed green, brown, green. He was trying to fight, at least.

'This isn't Rose,' she repeated. 'You aren't Rose. You're *nothing*.'

She hadn't meant it. She wasn't trying to hurt Mass. She just wanted him to stop impersonating the ghost of her dead baby girl. But his face crumpled and he sagged, knees giving way, to curl on the bare and dusty floor.

'Poor child,' McAvey said, without inflection. He turned back to Genevieve and resumed his genially superior tones. 'Of course, it took many, many years to develop the technique to make it strong enough to corrupt a story known by so many more people. You accuse me of not making any effort? All my efforts went into funding attempts at a cutting-edge Artisan endeavour. Gatwick was never cheap.'

Genevieve, still wrapping warmth around her as an invisible shield, moved carefully closer. She wanted to reach Mass, who was curled into a ball, whispering something to himself.

'How very typical,' she said, razing him with her dissection look. 'Claiming it as your own achievement because you bankrolled it. And to what end? Revenge on me for slighting you?'

'Don't be ridiculous,' McAvey scoffed. 'No woman is worth the trouble. Especially not *you*. My God, what a waste. Throwing yourself away on a navvy so you had yourself an uxorious husband instead of accepting the strong guiding hand all women need. Why would I dirty myself with a spoilt little bitch like you after you showed yourself capable of lowering yourself to him?' His face twisted with bourgeois disgust. 'And didn't you let him degrade you, drag you ever lower.'

'You were willing enough to slither into my bed.' She was meant, she assumed, to be shocked, even hurt, that he claimed his plot wasn't to do with desire for her unattainable beauty. She curled her lips with thin disdain, because she knew that would injure him far more than the righteous rage he would dismiss as offended feminine pride. 'Suffering through your marital duty as I was? I suppose I must take some solace that it was unpleasant for both of us, then.'

The gibe never had a chance of penetrating his arrogance. He smirked and, outrageously, quoted Patmore's horrid *The Angel in the House* at her. '*Man must be pleased; but him to please is woman's pleasure.* It was always your place to submit to a man, Vivi. I made sure it was to a better class of man.'

She wouldn't let him see he was affecting her. Tucking shaking hands against the pleats of her full skirt, she said, 'Everybody in their place, and your place at the top. Except you never were.'

That simple truth, or hearing it from her, made his face go rigid. 'I wanted what was due to me. Recognition. The same respect accorded you and the rest. The wealth and status I deserved. Power to match what I knew I was capable of.' He gestured around him. 'Just like Hooke, I—'

'The knife,' she cut in with less than microscopic patience.

He smiled, a dog about to bite. 'Ironically, it was when I was finding a wetnurse to raise Rose—'

'*No.*'

'It's a sad thing, for a mother to reject her own child.'

'Is that the secret fear of all small men, or just you?'

A flash of pure rage crossed his face. He grunted and forced himself back into his superciliously paternal tones. 'You were always dreadful for interrupting, Vivi. As I was saying, I came across Orphanage people at that time, and that's when I first heard about Varley and his obsession with the knife. I just had to wait till he finally found it, and find a way to take it from him. I'll admit, I targeted your mongrel daughter for Gatwick's experiment out of disgust at your sordid little mésalliance, but I went after your marriage and your inheritance last year for no other reason than it was a convenient stepping stone to what I really wanted. By then you were so far beneath me, you were barely worth bothering with, otherwise.'

Genevieve listened to this litany in his sneering tones and discovered an astonishing thing: she didn't care. The helpless fury she'd been battling the last few days had crescendoed, and now it dissipated, washed away by sheer contempt.

'So far beneath me, you're not worth bothering with,' she repeated with an enlightened air. 'Oh, indeed.'

He was such a little, *little* man. She felt only weary scorn for his laughable ambitions and his melodramatic plotting and his pettiness, and a shamed worry for Mass, who deserved far more of her attention and concern than McAvey did, and was still uncomforted on the bare floor between them.

'I came here intending to kill you,' she said in wonder at her own foolishness. McAvey took it as a threat, and started to jeer some blustering retort, and she went on over him, 'What a waste of time and effort and Art that would be.'

Raising the temperature of the air about herself and Mass to scalding to ward McAvey off, whether he tried to strike out with Artistry or physically, Genevieve awkwardly knelt beside the boy, putting a hand on his shaking shoulder and leaning down close.

'I am made of mud,' he was muttering. 'I am made of mud.'

'I'm sorry, Mass,' she whispered. 'Stop now, darling. You're not nothing, and you're not made of mud.'

She kept part of her attention on McAvey, though she was sure he couldn't get through the wall of heat she was directing outwards. She could see beads of sweat on his forehead through the summery heat shimmer, his face turning shiny and red.

'You do care for the shapeshifter,' he said. 'I can be generous, if you can manage to rise to the advantages afforded you. We'll put all this behind us. A clean slate. We can be a proper family. You and me, Rose, and our new baby, too.'

Hand still on Mass's shoulder, Genevieve raised her gaze and stared at him wordlessly. As was usual, McAvey failed to read her expression, seeing acceptance in her silence instead of scathing contempt as he heedlessly, hypocritically, demanded what he had so derided.

He went on, a touch more eagerly. 'You must want it, the easy life you were meant to have. Your children will have a father befitting their status as Locke scions, and we'll make sure they rise to the very top of society, where people like us truly belong.'

'Oliver is this baby's father,' she said matter-of-factly, ignoring the rest of his nonsense.

He clenched his fists, ice crystals whitening his knuckles and falling like snow to the floor. 'What? He can't be.'

Genevieve had been speaking the letter of the law: a husband had absolute rights over the union's issue, even children conceived out of the marriage bed. She needn't fear McAvey could seize custody of this baby through the courts now that his marital right was exposed as false.

But she saw he'd mistaken her meaning, and – for all he had been dismissive of her and of the theft of her marriage, treating it as the side-effect of his real plan – her flat statement outraged him.

His outrage pleased her, so she said again, 'Oliver is the baby's father.'

Face mottling, he spat, 'You *whore*,' acting for all the world like a genuinely cuckolded husband.

Genevieve raised a cool eyebrow. 'Aphrodite, remember?' she lied indifferently. 'Chained without her choice to an ugly-souled man, she had to seek gratification elsewhere.'

It was only satisfying for the scantest of seconds. She'd committed the same sins as him, pettiness, overconfidence and underestimation, but she realised it too late, when he howled, 'Hold her!' with the whiplash of compulsion in it.

Mass sprang up out of his ball of despair and seized her wrists, pushing her hands to the ground exactly as the twins did when they were bringing in a rogue Artisan. Unable to produce fire, she sent out instead a directional wall of immense heat, herself and Mass safely behind it.

McAvey fell back, shielding his face, but his fury was such that he rallied, ice forming and melting, forming and melting as he lunged through the kiln-level temperature and got his hands to her skin.

Pain lanced through Genevieve, lighting up every inch of her body from her toes to her scalp. She shrieked.

She instinctively tried to lash out with fire, but Mass pressed her hands down with all of his slight weight and advantageous position. Peter Llewellyn's tales of the bwbach loomed large, how spiteful and slow to forget an insult the little creatures were.

That wasn't right. Mass was holding her down, but he was sobbing despairing apologies all the while.

She pushed out heat, warding McAvey off. 'Mass, fight it,' she gasped, and his gaze came to hers. His eyes flashed green. 'Yes, that's it!'

McAvey iced through the heat and wracked her with his new pain Art again.

Crying out, she collapsed to the ground, body twisting to the side to protect her stomach. She curled around the baby and into the pain, barely able to breathe, let alone reach for Artistry. Mass still didn't let her go.

When the pain ebbed enough for her to lift her head, she found McAvey looming over them both.

He had the copper knife in his hand.

'Good, isn't it?' he said conversationally. 'I experimented on a weather Artisan, but she died before I worked her Art free. No big loss. Almost managed a lightning Art harvest, really wanted that one, but never mind. I did harvest this pain Art, though. Practice makes perfect.'

He bent over her and his voice was almost tender as he said, 'Don't worry, Vivi. This won't take long.'

Genevieve tried to crawl away from him, as blindly as a wounded animal, any ability to muster Art scattered to dust by the throbbing echoes of agony. Mass was still clinging on. She couldn't escape, she couldn't produce fire, she couldn't even manage more heat to tax the ice Art.

'Mass,' she begged. 'Please. Let go.'

'I can't,' he sobbed, 'I can't, I can't.'

'Mass, you have to let me go.' She tried to catch his eye, hoping to see cool green. '*Fight it.*'

All she heard was his despairing mutter. 'I am made of mud. I am made of mud.'

McAvey reached for her. Genevieve felt wetness down her legs and thought her overstrained bladder had let go with the surfeit of shock and pain and terror.

Then the wicked clench of the first contraction hit her and Mass dissolved into thick, sticky mud.

Shapeshifter

I AM MADE OF MUD.
I am made of mud.
I am made of—

32

MASS WAS GONE.

Her hands were free.

Genevieve rode the contraction. It was pain, dreadful pain, but it sat opposite the pain Art that McAvey had inflicted on her. That had sparked like flame through her body, making it feel like layers and layers of her own skin were on fire. This was a cleaner pain, a pain her body recognised, a pain that concentrated itself at her core, wiping her mind clean of all else.

She would never remember her last labour, when she'd been in the chloroform twilight, but she now clearly remembered her first, Mrs Murphy's calm instructions, Oliver holding her hand.

He'd been there in case her dangerous Art had spiralled out of control under duress, but it hadn't been like that, and it wasn't like that now. The contraction took every last scrap of her attention, flaying every last thought from her mind. Her Art had no channel in which to rise, because the channel was full of pain.

She rode it, and she used it, and she let it give her what she needed: pure and unadulterated focus.

The moment it eased, she lifted her hands and flame erupted from her in a great wave, driving McAvey back just as he tried to seize her by her hair.

Flame rippled across the floor and licked the walls. She and the viscous puddle of mud that had been Mass were safe within the burning flame. McAvey, flinging himself to the other side of the small room, managed to create a safe space with a continuously renewed sheet of ice, curved wall at his back. She watched as, over and over again, his ice turned into water at his feet and evaporated instantly in the boiling heat of the enclosed space.

He wouldn't be able to keep it up, she thought detachedly.

She knew from her first travail that she had a good long time before the next contraction came. He did not have nearly enough Art to keep that wall of ice in place.

Directing her focussed fire at the ice, ignoring McAvey's foul abuse, she patted at the mud. It was like cold custard under her palms. Wincing as her fingers sank into it, she discovered two hard lumps and pulled them free. She wiped them clean on her skirt, leaving lighter smudges on the dark material, and held them up, one on each mud-coated palm.

Two gold-and-copper circles, one larger than the other, both filled with tiny cogs, much like the larger ones that had surrounded the sardonyx pendant.

This, then, was the embedded coercion that had been afflicting the poor child, her and Oliver's wedding rings, filled with Gatwick's clockwork Art, a minor working McAvey had seen fit to literally embed into Mass's wrists, probably by forcing him to use his own shapeshifting Art against himself.

Her fire intensified, flames leaping all the way up the walls on each side of McAvey to the ceiling. Heat and steam were shimmering up through the grate. She poked the bits and pieces of nasty clockwork out of her and her husband's rings, making sure the metallic debris did not fall back into the mud. She felt dizzy.

'Vivi, you have to stop,' McAvey shouted at her from behind his wall. 'You're taking all the air out of the room. It'll kill both of us, and Rose, too. And the baby! Think about the baby.'

He'd been calling her all sorts of awful names a moment ago. She felt a mild amusement that he thought deploying his pet name for her would have any effect whatsoever.

Genevieve slid her wedding ring on. She made a fist, looking at the gold band with its copper inlay. 'You're not worth the effort of killing,' she told McAvey remotely. 'But you're certainly not worth the effort of saving.'

Mass was, however, and McAvey's words had paradoxically given her hope. If he thought she could kill the shapeshifter, that meant he was still alive to be killed. He could turn into any living thing, any *organic* thing, Whitely had said. Perhaps this was, then, a sort of mud creature, still able to hear her.

She patted the viscosity again, looking at the smudges and streaks on her palms and skirts with nascent horror. 'Mass? Please come back. I'm sorry for what I said. You're not nothing. You're a sweet boy who's fought so hard and deserves so much more. I want you to come home. Please. I—'

Another contraction took her, startling in its intense suddenness. She rode through it, groaning through her teeth, left fist locked around Oliver's ring, the metal of both rings biting into her skin as she squeezed tighter and tighter against the convulsive, expulsive grip of her womb.

It persisted longer than the first one, which, in retrospect, had been mercifully short. Genevieve watched helplessly as her flames, deprived of Art, flickered out. By the time the throes ebbed again, McAvey had dared to lower his ice wall and was creeping towards her.

The moment she could corral her Art, Genevieve opened her palms, Oliver's ring falling to the ground, and sent fire roaring outwards, once again forcing him to expend his own Art to defend himself against incineration.

She watched him as he crouched behind an ever-replenished layer of ice, water running in sheets off it before turning to vapour. The air was hot and wet. She could barely see him through the steam. She could barely breathe, and she needed to breathe.

She was where she had not wanted to be, in an Art duel that ended the moment one of them ran out of Art. Her power was boosted by pain and fear, replenished with every contraction, but she presumed he wasn't so foolish as to not be experiencing a healthy dose of fear by now for fuel on his own side.

But he had the advantage. Her contractions were coming closer together, and lasting longer, than she had expected at this early stage; she knew that meant the baby was coming very quickly. Every time her body seized its prerogative over her Art, it gave McAvey space to rest, and eventually, he would be able to stroll over to her in the midst of her throes and use the knife.

Genevieve needed a different tactic.

She did not have long before she lost access to her Art again. She could continue to try to talk Mass back into a human shape, beg him to defend her with his tiger shape. But, even pretending she had enough time to persuade him of her true fondness for him, it was not a fair thing to ask of a child.

She patted the mud one last time. 'It's all right, Mass,' she whispered. 'I'll take care of you and the baby both.'

She had iron control of her Art. But once upon a time, she hadn't.

Once upon a time, she had had a wild form of her Art, which burst from her without her control, which persisted no matter her state of mind, which could only be quelled if she worked very hard to will it so.

She picked up Oliver's ring again, closing it within her left hand so it lay by hers. She stopped trying to stay calm and in control so that her Artistry would be strong in between the labour pangs. She needed more than strength now.

Squeezing the wedding ring tight, she thought about McAvey. Not the pointless little man cowering in his ice cage, but the petty ogre of her false marriage, who had been granted absolute power over her and her life and her child by every legal and financial and social structure of their world.

Except he'd been granted *nothing*, he'd usurped the power she'd willingly placed into a far better man's hands, trusting absolutely that he'd never wield it against her.

She thought about what he had done to her, stealing her marriage and her memories. What he had taken, that he had known she would never consent to give him. That was the worst of it, but it wasn't all of it.

The abuse of her trust. The constant niggling undermining of her abilities, her intelligence, her power. The presumption that his time and his attention were always worth more than hers. The dismissal of anything that pertained to her concerns as beneath his notice. The hypocritical accounting of minor grievances that were somehow never any of his doing. The ever-present, almost unconscious, desire to *grind her down* so she fit into his narrow notion of what a woman should be.

She thought about what he had done to her husband, and to her friends. What he had done to her grief for her parents, taking away memories of mourning for her father, taking away, likely forever, any memories of her last days with her mother.

And she thought about a rug, burning with unquenchable flame. A bucket of water, rippling with what Oliver called Greek fire. A cosy parlour, erupting into conflagration. A false wedding ring, dissolving into molten metal. None of that had needed her volition to get started. It had needed her volition to *stop*.

As the next contraction took her, Genevieve released wildfire.

It was more accurate to say that the wildfire escaped her. It swept the room, blazing hot and high, burning clean lines through the steam with a roar that drowned out McAvey's yell. For all the light and heat and noise, Genevieve, lost in trying to breathe deep through the pangs in the steamy, muggy room, barely noticed it.

When the contraction eased, she took stock. The fire was raging uncontained about the room, except in the sacrosanct circle that kept her and Mass safe. McAvey was tucked right into his prison now, his ice wall a thin barrier between instant fiery death.

She would have liked to concentrate the flames directly onto that thin sheet, but any touch of her volition on the firestorm might cause it to remember her reins and thus wink out at the next contraction.

She leaned over the mud puddle, not touching it this time; she had enough mud – Mass? – drying on her hands already. 'Mass?' she whispered. 'I hope you can hear me. Please try to change back. I want you as part of our home. I want you to be safe. I want to take care of you. Listen. If you can change, change to something fast, and get out of this room.'

Her womb gripped and twisted. She lost count of the contractions for a time, rocking back and forth on all fours, making a sound akin to the distressed bellow of a cow, eyes and fists squeezed shut. When she could pay attention again, the flames were still leaping high about the room, McAvey was shouting, and the mud puddle was gone.

Her arms and legs were trembling. She took advantage of the brief respite to ease down to lie on her side. After a moment, cursing Fletcher to the skies, she rolled with agonising slowness onto her left side, curling her legs up.

Her hands were clean now, she noted, before the pangs swallowed her again.

When they spat her out the other side, Oliver was there, holding her hand. 'Hello, Gin.'

She made a soft exhalation she'd meant to be his name. She raised her clenched left fist and forced her fingers open, dropping his wedding ring into his free hand.

He slipped it onto his finger and resumed holding her hand. 'You're doing marvellously, my amazing, strong, brave wife,' he said.

Genevieve lifted her head. Her hair was plastered to her skull and face with sweat. She peered through the haze in the room. The wildfire she'd loosed was still rippling over the floor and up the walls. But a clear path led to her from the stairs. She could feel an ever so slightly fresher breeze flowing in now, too.

'I…' she said, and squeezed his hand tight. 'I didn't know your warding Art was so powerful.'

'Terror,' Oliver said, and he smiled. '*Excellent* fuel.'

She managed a smile, too, but she had tears in her eyes. 'How…'

'We were looking for you above. The whole tower's boiling with heat, we didn't realise where it was coming from. Mass came up through the trapdoor as a lizard. A little singed, entirely beside himself, but otherwise safe.'

'Good boy,' she whispered. 'Keep him safe.'

'All right, my love. Here's the problem. You're nearing the crisis point. Soon—'

'Control your fucking wife, Bennet!' McAvey suddenly shouted from the tiny circle left to him behind his thinning wall. Genevieve took that to mean he could not possibly have long now.

'—you'll need to help the baby come out,' Oliver went on without even a blink. 'And if you keep letting this conflagration go on like this, you're going to be too exhausted to help her. You'll both die. You have to tell the fire to stop.'

She had to ride out another contraction, then. They were so close together now. When she emerged, she looked longingly around at her flames, so valiantly defending her. She knew Oliver was right. But—

'But McAvey,' she whispered.

'You take care of the baby, I'll take care of him.'

She nodded. With Oliver holding her hand – their bare Artisan hands, fingers interlocked, as if they were about to dance – and murmuring calm encouragement, she reached for the key in her mind that let her take control of her wildfire Art. The flames flickered, growing smaller and quieter. As their light died down, the steam in the room grew thicker, shadows dancing within.

'Watch out,' she tried to say.

Oliver batted aside the tiny ice spear that arrowed from the steam with his telekinesis Art, and then he gestured and the copper knife shot out. He unerringly caught it, as he'd caught his own paper-knife, called to his own hands with Artistry.

He lifted both hands, and the hazy air lifted with the gesture, making a thick fog below the ceiling, an eddy forming where it began to push its way out through the grate.

McAvey was revealed, still grimacing over empty hands, where his depleted Art was refusing to form an Artwork, where Oliver had ripped his only physical weapon from him.

Oliver walked towards the defenceless McAvey, a slow, deliberate, relentless tread, the tread of a farmer carrying an axe in one hand and a surplus rooster in the other.

McAvey cringed away from his approaching execution, palms held up in supplication.

'Pain Art,' Genevieve gasped, just in case.

Oliver acknowledged the warning with a nod. But McAvey's begging sounded pitifully real; he really had not a single scrap of Artistry left to him. 'Bennet, no, stop. Please— I didn't— Bennet— *Oliver.*'

Oliver never had been a man who bothered with words when none were necessary. He took both of McAvey's wrists in one big hand and twisted, forcing him to his knees. Then it was one hand in his hair, the hand with the knife to his throat, and Genevieve was grateful she could see neither man's expression, just Oliver's broad back as he bent down, McAvey's last words nothing but abject pleas—

'*Stop.*'

The coercion in the single word was so strong that McAvey's implorations cut off, Oliver froze, and even Genevieve's body, about to wring her womb again, seemed to pause, too.

And then Cecelia dashed past Fletcher, flew across the room, and smacked her hand into McAvey's forehead. With the same intense, slightly panicked, force as Fletcher, she shouted her own single word.

'*Forget.*'

33

McAVEY'S FACE WENT BLANK AND WHITE and he collapsed bonelessly on the instant.

Cecelia turned on Oliver. 'You—'

Genevieve's contraction took her, stronger for being temporarily forced into hiatus, and now accompanied by the inexorable need to push. Her cry brought Oliver and Cecelia to her side, Fletcher hovering awkwardly at the stairs with Mass peeking out from behind him.

'I don't suppose,' Genevieve said to Oliver when she could speak again, 'you could apply your telekinesis Art at all?'

Oliver squeezed her fingers. 'Sorry, love, you're going to have to get her out the usual way.'

'Fuck,' she said succinctly, and rolled on through the next swell of pain, her body telling her in no uncertain terms that it was time to bear down and push.

Fletcher and Mass were dispatched to fetch Mrs Murphy. Cecelia, meanwhile, took charge of what she had wrought. McAvey's eyes were open, but he wasn't moving other than to blink and breathe. It was entirely possible her fear-powered Art had wiped out his memory of all else. She prodded him up the cramped stairs, returning a little time later with a miraculous jug of cool water.

She helped Genevieve take a sip and wiped her heated forehead while Oliver used the copper knife to cut her skirts. 'Baby's crowning,' he said. 'You're almost there, love.'

'Shut up, Oliver,' Genevieve wailed, because she damned well knew she wasn't.

'Shutting up, Gin,' he said, letting her crush the bones in his hand as the urge to push surged and receded, surged and receded.

By the time the Missus Murphys arrived, coats thrown over nightgowns and hair still in bedtime plaits, the urgent need for their services had passed. Oliver was holding a bloodied baby girl as Cecelia helped Genevieve sit up to loosen her bodice, feeling wrung out but accomplished.

Despite the rush to reach Genevieve's side, Mrs Murphy was calm and soothing as she murmured encouragement while Genevieve's womb expelled the afterbirth, and then fixed her a cool drink, sweet and tasting mostly of peppermint. If she wasn't really an Artisan possessing Artistry in the exact opposite direction as that which McAvey had inflicted, she gave a very good impression of one, especially once Miss Adler applied her healing Art in tandem.

Those two competent and stalwart women then helped clean her and the little one up, Oliver and Cecelia delegated to fetch and carry more fresh water from the pump and whatever else was demanded, and then they'd left her to rest before the attempt to climb out of the cellar.

Genevieve sat with her back against the wall of the little round room, the stone still warm from her surfeit of Art, her legs splayed out, and the baby in her arms, wrapped in a clean shawl doing duty as a swaddling cloth. Her daughter had nursed well, and now slept the sleep of the innocent.

Genevieve wished she could join her. Mrs Murphy and Miss Adler between them had made her more comfortable, but she could still feel, whenever she shifted, the ache in her stomach and legs, of muscles not accustomed to the level of exertion they'd been put through.

She leaned against her husband's broad shoulder, both of them gazing down at the sleeping baby.

'Beautiful,' Oliver whispered, gently brushing the very tip of one finger over the tiny nose.

'Well,' Genevieve said judiciously. 'A little squashed-looking.'

'Won't hear a word,' Oliver said. He kissed the top of her head. 'Close your eyes? The others are keeping watch above. Fletcher's sent for Agency enforcers to take custody of McAvey.'

'In a minute. Come over here, Mass.'

She'd heard the whisper of movement on the stairs, the boy peering around the curve of the awkward flight of stairs. He approached diffidently, stopping a little way away but then craning to see the, yes, squashed, face of the baby.

Genevieve beckoned him closer. 'Thank you for going for help. Oliver wouldn't have found his way down here in time if it wasn't for you.'

'I helped him set his trap,' Mass whispered. 'I couldn't stop myself.'

Oliver scooped him in onto his other side, as kind and firm as with his own nephews and nieces. 'We know how hard you fought,' he said gravely, curling his arm around the boy.

Mass's whole body slumped against Oliver, and his head lowered to his chest. Oliver held him close, as close as he'd cradled his baby girl as she'd come naked and squalling into the world. Eventually the boy's eyes, reddened and damp, slipped fully closed.

Genevieve watched for a time, her own eyes half-slitted, until she decided he was probably truly asleep. He'd used his Art extensively today, not even counting pulling himself back from an amorphous mud creature, and had been fighting a compulsion, much harder than that compulsion had allowed them to suspect, for his entire sojourn in their home. His was the sleep of the righteous. But he still kept the form of the young boy he'd worn in his days with them.

If he opened his eyes, they'd be Oliver's deep brown.

Genevieve haltingly told Oliver the trick McAvey had tried to pull. She said, 'Do you think it's true? Do you think he's Rose?'

Oliver turned his head and looked thoughtfully down at him. 'I always thought twelve was awfully young for Art to have come on. Not impossible. But at the extreme lower bounds.'

'Thirteen, now,' Genevieve said. She'd been surprised to discover it was past midnight, and thus the day of the summer solstice, Mass's supposed birthday. 'If he really is. He looks like your nieces, when he's being Rose.'

'You understand that might very well be another guise? That we might not have seen his true self yet? We might never see his true self. He's so wedded to hiding, he can hold it in his sleep.'

She sighed heavily. 'Yes, I think it was probably part of McAvey's game, to make Mass wear your eyes and my hair and the rest. Discounting that, there's no proof he is.'

'And no proof he's not.' Oliver carefully shifted so he could touch her hair, her cheek, and then, lightly, the baby's nose again.

'You seem to be arguing both sides,' Genevieve said.

'I'm making sure you know all the arguments against him, before you decide.'

'*We* decide.' The baby stirred, and Genevieve absently rocked her, as she had rocked Rose in the three days she'd been privileged to know her. 'Whether McAvey really took him from us to test some proto-clockwork, or whether he happened to come across a rare and unusually strong Artisan while he was scouring the charitable institutions for orphans to try the knife on, and was saving his harvest till he could guarantee success…'

She shuddered, feeling her arms tighten around the baby. She spared a thought for the three Artisans, weather, lightning, pain, that McAvey had mentioned honing his skills on. He'd had months. They couldn't have been his only test subjects, merely his last.

'…either way, he's had a rough time of it, and he'll start remembering that properly soon. I don't… I don't think it matters if he's Rose or not.'

'McAvey set him to do harm to us,' Oliver said, 'and he tried so hard not to. That's very brave, for one so young.'

'And he *is* young, whether that's thirteen or sixteen or what-have-you.' She nodded. 'We're not sending him away. He deserves to be safe, and loved, and healed. So…I think he's ours now, isn't he?'

'Yes,' Oliver said.

'Good.' She settled back against the wall, a wave of physical exhaustion washing over her, a certain languid satisfaction following in its wake. This was how athletes felt, she assumed, after they'd won their event after arduous effort. 'At least he's old enough to choose his own name. What shall we do about this one?'

'Your mother's name?'

Rose had been Rose Antoinette. It wasn't uncommon to honour a lost baby by naming the next one the same, but Genevieve shook her head. 'Yours?'

'Catherine?' he said dubiously. 'A little conventional, for a Locke?'

'I am…quite conventional, Oliver.' She watched the baby's eyelashes flutter against delicate skin.

'Beatrice,' he said, 'like the princess.'

'There will be hundreds of little Beatrices her age!'

'Alexandria?'

'And make Lucinda jealous? Catherine. I like Catherine, Oliver.'

He kissed the top of her head in silent agreement. She leaned against him harder, mirroring Mass's slump. Between her massive expenditure of Art and her labour, she needed both plentiful rest and plentiful food. She could not at all countenance the latter at the moment, but she could at least close her eyes.

She stirred a moment later, as Oliver, squished between her and Mass, gingerly eased the copper knife from his coat and let it float before them.

'I don't want to hand it over to the Agency,' he said. 'I don't trust them to secure it.'

It was somewhat lowering to have to admit the organisation they had all put such effort into was not perfect, but she'd be hard-pressed to name an institution that was.

She half-raised one of the hands previously clasped around Catherine. 'Shall I melt it?' She'd have done that in a heartbeat if McAvey had ever let it lie vulnerable to her flame.

'Save your strength,' he told her. 'Not convinced it'd work. My telekinesis didn't work on it, back in Gallentry. It's like it doesn't like the touch of Art. I wanted to be sure it'd work this time, so I….' He frowned as he struggled with his words. '…wove my warding Art into the telekinesis Artwork. Took a leaf from Gatwick's book, I suppose. Stopped it from stopping me.'

He gave her a wry smile, knowing the inadequacy of the explanation; she was reminded of Whitely and his maddeningly vague *I went around it.* 'I'm going to try it with my materials Art now.'

He normally used that to effect minor repairs to household items. Now he raised his hands and the copper knife began to show hairline cracks, amber light spilling from them as they spread and widened.

The knife didn't melt; it crumbled. Oliver diligently swept the crumbs into a pile.

The baby murmured in her sleep, and Genevieve looked down at her with swift attention; love and worry, all intermingled, and perhaps it would always be like that.

'Catherine,' she said, more to herself than the baby. 'Oh. Oliver, I keep forgetting to ask. Am I Mrs William Bennet, or Mrs William Oliver? I'd presume the latter, but officially, I suppose, we had to use your legal name. Or do we have little Catherine Oliver Bennet here?'

He smiled his small and crooked smile. 'You are Mrs Oliver Locke,' he said. When she communicated her puzzlement with a frowning tilt of her head, he said her married name in full, and with a significant pause and then a rush, to make the hyphenation very clear. 'Mrs William…Oliver-Locke. Mother of one Miss Catherine Oliver-Locke.'

'Good Lord, was my father so damnably snobbish he insisted on a royal licence to keep his name shoehorned in there?' she said in belated, guilty, annoyance at her departed father.

'I asked for it,' Oliver said, 'because I knew how much you like being a Locke.'

Genevieve, somewhere between smiling and crying, carefully leaned over, making sure she wasn't jostling Catherine, and kissed his mouth softly. 'I love you, Oliver.'

'I love you too, my dear,' he murmured against her mouth. 'I am very glad I married you.'

'I am entirely pleased with that rather surprising turn of events myself.'

Cecelia squeezed down the steps then, kneeling and giving the sleeping baby a gooey smile, followed by another for the sleeping Mass. 'All right?' she whispered.

'Yes,' Genevieve said quietly. 'Presenting Miss Catherine Oliver-Locke.'

She paused and looked past Oliver at Mass, but she had to ask him first, before she presented him as Master Massimo Oliver-Locke; he might have another name in mind.

'Congratulations.' Cecelia touched each of their shoulders, beaming. 'Very pretty.'

'Squashed face.'

'Very pretty squashed face.'

Fletcher cleared his throat from the stairs. He was being even more circumspect than Mass had been, crouching to peer into the new mother's birthing chamber. 'May I?'

'Come on, Fletch,' Cecelia said, upon receiving Genevieve's nod. 'Come meet Catherine.'

'Enforcers have collected McAvey,' Fletcher informed them. He stood, stiffly proper, before very slightly leaning forward to take an approving peek at the baby. Then he straightened to say, 'Good riddance. I suppose he'll have to go to an asylum. Hard to put him on trial for crimes he doesn't even remember.'

'Clean slate,' Genevieve muttered into Oliver's shoulder. 'He wished for it.'

'Oh, I'll be working with the Agency to bring his memories back,' Cecelia said. Then she added, 'If he doesn't get them back in their entirety…' She shrugged. 'He might turn out a perfectly pleasant individual, when not weighted down with memories of a domineering father constantly badgering him to be better than he was.'

'He'll be very confused when he's executed for murder, then,' Fletcher said, a rather steely coldness entering his tone. 'Not even to mention all the rest of the damage he left in his wake.'

'But if he isn't the same person—'

'Interesting debate,' Oliver rumbled. He glanced down at his daughter, who was making a burble in her sleep. 'Another time.'

Genevieve was inclined to side with Fletcher's view, but it wasn't her who would be directly tangled into the moral quagmire, it would be Cecelia, if she could not restore McAvey enough for him to knowingly face his crimes. She freed a hand to touch Cecelia's arm.

'I'm sorry you had to get involved, Cecelia,' she said. 'I know you don't like to use your Art like that.'

Cecelia raised her brows and looked exactly as she did when she was giving a speech and about to add the rhetorical flourish that devastated the opponents who'd dismissed her as a mere woman. 'Far better an accident born of sheer fright, than what you two were planning.'

Genevieve and Oliver exchanged looks, reflecting each other's guilt.

'Precisely,' Cecelia said direly.

'No lectures, I just underwent a terrible travail,' Genevieve said, affecting somewhat more feebleness than she felt.

'And I'm glad I've chosen never to do that, I can tell you,' Cecelia said, letting the topic rest – for now – with one of her winning smiles.

Genevieve smiled back wryly in acknowledgement. It was the usual thing, though, of which Mrs Murphy had assured her, mind and body already working together to make the intense pain a distant memory.

All of it, a distant memory, and here and now, her husband, her baby, her child, and her friends: her family.

And a bloody onerous climb out of a cellar to look forward to, too.

Epilogue

THEY DID NOT ATTEMPT PROXIMITY TO the clock tower, spreading out a blanket for a picnic under the plane trees in St James's Park. It was much more pleasant to be outside this summer, compared to last, with no new heatwave but plenty of new sewage construction.

Alex, returned in time for Catherine's first birthday a few weeks before, was talking enthusiastically to Oliver about his and Whitely's travels. Oliver had a thoughtful glint in his eye.

Miss Knight and Cecelia were deep in discussion over Miss Knight's latest bonnet, in the poke style and incorporating the new fad for coral, and her new Boudoir sewing machine. Cecelia had a thoughtful glint in *her* eye.

'You don't even wear hats, Cecelia,' Fletcher said. He had his pocket watch in his hand and was switching his gaze between monitoring its tick and peering hopefully in the direction of the river. 'Shush, I'm trying to listen for it.'

'You won't miss it,' Lulu told him. 'Bet it'll crack again?'

'I will not partake in such a mean-spirited wager!' Poor Fletcher. Still so easy for the twins to tease.

That left Genevieve and Kit Whitely in a somewhat strained silence at their end of the rug. Catherine, confident and robust, and showing the same unerring ability as a cat to sense who was least comfortable with her, held out her chubby arms, demanding Whitely take her.

'I won't drop her,' Whitely eventually said, after she'd started to grizzle and make plaintive grabby hands at him.

'I know,' Genevieve said, and ceded her daughter onto his lap.

Catherine immediately pulled to standing on sturdy legs and grabbed for his curls, which he accepted with good grace. Genevieve knelt up and helped him untangle the stubby fingers from their death grip. She was stupidly proud of how strong her healthy little girl was.

Big Ben began to chime for the first time, a great boom ringing out over the rooftops of London.

'Magnificent!' cried Fletcher, who looked like he might rise and salute. He was all-unknowing of the indulgently fond smiles the others exchanged around him.

Catherine looked up with wide eyes and a gummy smile. 'Bong, bong?' she lilted, letting go of Whitely's hair to play pat-a-cake with her own ears, then pointing with modest inaccuracy over the trees.

'Astutely observed, little one,' Whitely informed her, taking the opportunity to brush his hair back so she couldn't grab for it again so easily. 'You'll hear that big bell all the days of your life from now on.'

'Not *all* the days. She'll torment Sir Kingsford every summer,' Alex said, joining them.

He watched with open fondness as Whitely began to play a decidedly serious game of peekaboo with the child in his lap, with whom Genevieve had been mildly disturbed to discover he shared a nickname.

'Wipe that mawkish look off your face,' Whitely told him, without transferring his attention away from playing the game. 'Where's the baby?' he enquired of the palms covering his face.

Alex snorted and nudged his shoulder into Whitely's, murmuring, 'I don't think I will, no.'

'There's the baby,' Whitely solemnly informed Catherine, hinging his hands open.

But as he did so, he suddenly gave way, not to one of his small and controlled smiles from last year, but a truly lovely grin. Alex looked struck to his very soul, the besotted fool, and Catherine pealed with laughter, attracting the notice of the rest of their little family.

'Does Kitty want a cuddle?' Miss Knight cooed as they gathered around.

'Yes, yes, all very funny.' Whitely tried to deposit Catherine – Kitty – into her arms, but the baby squawked and grabbed fistfuls of his shirt. 'It's not…entirely funny. Go to Auntie Lulu, then, sweetie? Auntie Cece? Ah. Uncle Fletcher? *Why*?'

'It's the curls,' Lulu advised. 'I'll shave your head for you.'

She beamed triumphantly at Whitely's mock-indignant grimace. She was freer now, less shadowed, partly thanks to time, partly thanks to the sunshiny Miss Knight, and partly thanks to her beloved brother's return.

Notwithstanding, she'd taken Genevieve aside to remind her that, since

Whitely could open any lock, the secured doors at the asylum would give him no trouble at all.

'And I don't think it's right for you,' she'd said, 'but *I* don't mind doing the necessary.'

Genevieve had had to take a moment to work out what she was referring to. She didn't think much about that man these days. If he did cross her mind, Oliver and Cecelia and the others were always about to comfort or reassure her. She'd made a polite demurral.

'Here, I'll hold her upside down by her ankles, she loves it,' Alex said. His baby cousin squealed in delight, reaching for him.

'Stop that!' Genevieve retrieved her child. Catherine wailed briefly, before discovering the beaded ribbon pinned on the neckline of her mother's bodice. She started to suck on it solemnly.

'Here comes the Missus Murphys and Mass and Oliver's crew,' Cecelia said. She waved. 'Did you hear it?'

'The whole city heard it,' Mrs Murphy grumbled. 'Tongue too big for its mouth.'

She patted Mass fondly on the head as they joined everyone on the rug. 'He did very well.'

Fourteen now, Mass had started an apprenticeship at the apothecary, joining Frederick, one of Oliver's nephews, in grinding and chopping and steaming. Eliza, a niece, was shadowing Mrs Murphy, but might yet turn out as a governess instead: steadier hours and wages. Both young Bennets politely greeted their uncle, while Mass smiled at his parents, before the three adolescents sat on the grass some distance from their adults.

Mass's eyes were bright as he listened to some jape from Freddy. He was still a quiet boy, but it was a restful sort of quiet. He wasn't habitually tense anymore, though sometimes it wasn't the baby who woke them with crying, who needed to be held because of some half-remembered nightmare. Such episodes were becoming rare.

He looked more and more like a Bennet these days, deep brown eyes and expressive face, but with ashy hair like the Lockes. Perhaps that was his habitual echo of those around him. Perhaps it was real. It didn't matter which. He was officially an Oliver-Locke now, whether or not his name had once been Rose.

Mrs Murphy and Miss Adler – Florence and Rachel again these days – settled on the rug, close by Cecelia. Rachel squeezed her arm in greeting as they discussed their next committee meeting, which Genevieve would also attend. Fletcher sat on Cecelia's other side, comfortably solitary, helping himself to an eggy tart from the picnic selection. Lulu tangled an arm with Miss Knight's as they sat by them, perhaps overly friendly but not otherwise worth a second glance by passersby.

Alex and Whitely had to be even more circumspect, for all Whitely's Artisan status. They merely brushed fingers as they sat side by side. After a moment, though, Whitely hooked his surviving little finger about Alex's in a decidedly sentimental sort of gesture. Whitely was much sweeter to Alex when he thought no one was watching.

Oliver took Catherine, eliciting another squeal, this time of happiness. She pulled on his earlobes as he made a silly face at her. He tucked her onto his lap and used his free arm to tug Genevieve close. Even a married couple had to be careful how much affection they showed in public, of course, but she could at least lean on his broad shoulder.

Genevieve kissed his cheek and joined him in smiling down at her daughter, who was too intent on squirming free so she could crawl over to her adored, and very entertaining, older brother to acknowledge her parents' beaming pride. Having relinquished his daughter, Oliver held his wife's hand, running a thumb over her wedding ring, and the new ring replacing her lost wedding day gift, which they never had rediscovered. He'd decried pretty tokens, but only as a poor substitute for communication, not in their entirety, and he was such a soft touch for the ongoing acrostic fad.

The new ring was a thin gold band with small gemstones set in a single line: Topaz, opal, garnet, emerald, topaz, heliodor, emerald, and ruby. It was not so complexly symmetrical as her first one, but its mismatched simplicity was pleasing in its own way.

Genevieve looked over at Mass, tickling his giggling sister as he listened carefully to his cousins. She looked about at her own cousins, and her dearest friends. She squeezed her husband's hand. Fifteen years ago, she'd loftily informed him they'd conduct their marriage however it suited them.

It seemed to her they'd managed it, with some notable bumps. And now their entire big family would go forth under the regular tolling of Big Ben and conduct their whole lives however it suited them through countless more years.

Oliver raised their interlinked hands and kissed her fingers, carefully modulated, entirely appropriate public affection. 'My love.'

'Middling soppy,' she scoffed, and kissed him properly.

By the Author

THANKS FOR READING. If you enjoyed this book, find more titles and bonus material at wendypalmer.au.

The Domain trilogy
Wild Imperative
Cursed Girls
Lost Child

Mosaic Virus duology
Bastard's Grace
Six Feet of Ridiculous
Mosaic Garden: Stories from Aspermonde

Artisans
The Uses of Illicit Art
The Use of Myriad Arts

Standalones
Fair Haven
Domesticated Magic
Little Wolf and the Witch (forthcoming)

'Your ridiculous Art. It's as twisty as you are, and that's saying something.'

Kit Whitely has been exploited his entire life for his unique magical specialty, opening doors and locks. He's finally safe…until bounty hunter Alexander Locke arrests him for the use of illicit Art.

But Alex is a man of divided loyalties and he intends to use Kit for illicit purposes of his own.

How much trouble could one pissant little thief give him, anyway?

Milton Keynes UK
Ingram Content Group UK Ltd.
UKHW030003051224
452010UK00011B/619